THE MISSING BOATMAN

ALSO BY KEITH C. BLACKMORE

Mountain Man
Mountain Man
Safari
Hellifax
Well Fed
Make Me King
Mindless
Mountain Man Prequel
Mountain Man 2nd Prequel: Them Early Days
The Hospital: A Mountain Man Story
Mountain Man Omnibus: Books 1–3

131 Days
131 Days
House of Pain
Spikes and Edges
About the Blood
To Thunderous Applause
131 Days Omnibus: Books 1–3

Breeds
Breeds
Breeds 2
Breeds 3
Breeds: The Complete Trilogy

Isosceles Moon
Isosceles Moon
Isosceles Moon 2

The Bear That Fell from the Stars
Bones and Needles
Cauldron Gristle
Flight of the Cookie Dough Mansion
The Majestic 311
The Missing Boatman
Private Property
The Troll Hunter
White Sands, Red Steel

THE MISSING BOATMAN

KEITH C. BLACKMORE

Podium

For Kate Anne Jack (I owe you several),
Rod Redden (for reading it first),
and Cathy Ryan (for pointing things out).

All rights reserved. No part of this publication may be reproduced, stored in a retrieval system, or transmitted in any form or by any means electronic, mechanical, photocopying, recording, or otherwise without prior written permission from Podium Publishing.

This is a work of fiction. Names, characters, places, and incidents are either products of the author's imagination or used fictitiously. Any resemblance to actual events, locales, or persons, living, dead, or undead, is entirely coincidental.

Copyright © 2010 by Keith C. Blackmore

Cover design by Elderlemon Design

ISBN: 978-1-0394-2691-7

Published in 2022 by Podium Publishing, ULC
www.podiumaudio.com

THE MISSING BOATMAN

CHAPTER 1

Combing his thinning but still black hair with his fingers, Samuel Tobbler drove his well-preserved 1995 Colony Park station wagon on the Trans-Canada highway, heading northeast on a wintry Saturday night. He wanted to be home in his native New Brunswick before dawn, and, having no family or wife, the decision to drive out into the night was an easy one. The office would call him a fool for not waiting until morning, but he didn't care. Sam had stopped at a Tim Hortons before setting out that evening and had, to this point, devoured half a box of Timbits. The bite-sized doughnuts were made for driving and snacking, and Sam's fingers kept finding their take-out box.

Peering ahead at the black velvet strip of highway illuminated by his headlights, Sam saw the road had only been partially cleared and salted. His eyes never left the gum-diseased blackness of the asphalt, and twice he caught himself drifting off, into the dangerous blur between consciousness and hypnosis. Drifting snow snaked across his path and attacked his headlights. It was only 10:42 and Sam figured on being in his own bed with a good five to six hours of sleep behind him at this time in the morning. He had burned some music onto a CD, all the noisiest industrial metal he could get his hands on, but he wasn't really listening to the mix. The noise was there to keep him awake.

Sam was a robust forty-two and, at one time, had had his own radio show during his university days in Nova Scotia. His taste for a wide spread of music had never lessened, and while he thought there was plenty of garbage put out during the mid-nineties, the new century had grown a modest crop of interesting contemporary music. He didn't want anything soft on his night drive. It would be too relaxing, too lulling, even though the war drums of the metal music had almost failed him twice this night. The noise was also there to help keep him from feeling lonely. It was a long, cold, black tongue of highway, even longer at night, and deep into the scream of winter. Very seldom did he see the red eyes of another car ahead of him, or the blinding whites of oncoming traffic. When he did, they were only there for a few minutes before arching off onto a ramp and disappearing into the night, swallowed and gone.

His thoughts were currently on the month of February and how he could raise his sales just a few margins more. He knew of a youth counselor, perhaps twenty-seven or so; a young buck in his sexual prime. Pressed softly enough—Sam never thought of it as a hard sell, but rather steady convincing—he could make the youngster aware of his own mortality. Especially if he could lock the counselor into a permanent policy guaranteed to stick with him even in the advent of something worse than HIV or any other god-awful sexual disease. Sam believed that if he called the policy a lifelong license to fuck, he'd have no trouble at all selling the plans.

Wayne. The guy's name was Wayne. Sam would have to pay Wayne a visit tomorrow, or at least give the man a call, and try to set up a first meeting. He would never discuss money during that first consultation. That was too coarse and the mark of a newbie. Sam was smooth. He would plant the seeds of need in his prospect's mind. On the second meeting, however, he would talk policies and money. He had an eighty-five percent success rate when it came to signing clients up if he met them a second time. And so they should. Making potential clients aware of their own mortality and what could become of their families if, for some dreadful reason, they were suddenly taken by death was a noble cause in Sam's opinion.

Stowing away that name for tomorrow, Sam reached into the box of Timbits with his right hand. He felt the remainder of the holeless mouth-sized dough balls. The chocolate glazed ones had disappeared about twenty minutes ago. Those were his favorite. He fumbled around in the box. There might be one or two left on the bottom that he might have missed. Little bastards had a way of doing that to him sometimes. In his eagerness to find something no longer there, he flipped the box and its remaining contents onto the floor of his wagon.

"Shit," Sam muttered, eyes flicking back and forth, from the night road ahead to the shadows below the car's red and green glowing instrument panel. There were Timbits down there. God forbid any land on the seat. Oh no, the little sugar shits had to drop to the floor. Murphy's Law, he supposed, and stretched his arm to reach beneath the gas pedal. His eyes peeped over the dash. Sam briefly imagined he would be this close to the steering wheel when he was eighty.

His fingers nudged a gathering of Timbits, pushing them away.

"Shit again," he swore, his nose practically on the rim of the steering wheel, his dim reflection in the speedometer and the windshield above. The needle held steady at one hundred kilometres an hour.

And again he pushed the elusive dough bits away.

"Gawddammit," he said, exasperated, and chanced a look downwards to spot the snacks. He took his eyes off the road, and his car began to drift to the side. The tires out of alignment just enough to take the vehicle off its straight course.

A second later, his right front tire struck a patch of thick slush. The car slipped further to the right, the tire cutting though a stiff drift of snow. The snow gripped the tire, twisting it enough to jerk the steering column and wheel.

Then it was all ice.

"JESUS!"

Sam's Colony Park whirled across the highway and shot off into a snow-gorged trench. The car flipped over, crash-landing on its roof. Snow exploded against the windshield with a dull *Whump!* and a dark spider-web of cracks appeared across its entire length. The seatbelt held him, and, as he was leaning forward, it did what it could to save him. Sam cracked his nose violently into the flashing dash, releasing a gout of blood like a broken faucet. His face was thrown into the steering column a split second after his nose was broken, crushing a cheek and sending bone fragments into his sinus cavity with the force of an industrial nail gun. Sam's teeth clamped shut on part of his tongue, scissoring through the muscle as clean as sheet metal cutters and causing a jet of blood to spray out forcefully on impact. A stereo knob broke the orbital bone protecting his left eye, puncturing the white of his eye a microsecond later. His body jerked, stopped from going any further by his seatbelt, but his upper body snapped forward like a frayed steel cable. His knees went into the lower dashboard and split skin underneath. His shoulder popped out of its socket. The seatbelt went tight across his abdominal area, purpling his waistline in an instant. For a brief second, Sam's world rained Timbits, but he could have cared less for any of them, even if they were chocolate. He felt as if he had let go enough homemade chocolate in the seat of his trousers to forever cure him of the affliction.

In the quiet stillness of the aftermath, Sam hung against his seatbelt, upside down, breathing as if he were in a natural birth class. Everything above his dash was black. Snow pushed against his windshield. Blood dripped to his roof. His shoulder did not respond but screamed at his brain. His entire face buzzed. He was fortunate. Shock dampened much of his agony.

"Sweet gawd," Sam breathed, his words coming out strange and his mouth stinging as if he were chewing on broken glass. "Sweet Jaysus. I'm alive."

Sam's breath slowed a bit as he began to get a grasp of the situation. His breath chilled in the air, and he felt something very wrong in his mouth. He weakly spat and drooled a long dark length of something out of his mouth, and wiped it with one hand. He didn't want to look at it. Crashing had been sudden and terrifying enough for him. It was like something had grabbed the tire and steering wheel at the same time. But if he was going to pick a season, thank the Lord for winter. The snow had cushioned the impact and damage considerably. Probably damned well saved his life. He would call the offices of the Department of Transportation in the morning and chew them out a new asshole for their ineffective highway clearing. And what happened to his airbag?

Unbuckling his belt, he eased himself onto his roof. He slowly got a hold of his predicament. He was alive with most limbs working. He gingerly touched his mouth and winced. His eye stung like fuck, as did his shoulder. Perhaps he had a mild concussion. Whiplash even.

Then there was the rest of him, as he became aware of his hurts.

Sam groaned in growing pain as he reached, slowly, for the dash on the passenger's side. He searched for the cell phone in the glove compartment and the roadside assistance number. A thirty minute wait tops and someone would—

There was a sharp rapping on his door.

Sam's head slowly came about. All he could see was snow and blackness.

"You okay in there?" a muffled voice called out anxiously.

"Yeah, fine. Just fine!" Sam shouted back, and grimaced. "I think I shit myself, but I'm fine!"

"Really?" the voice was amused. "How about getting you out of there?"

"Yeah, love to! How?"

"Well, you're in the snow just deep enough to cover—" hands scooped away a section of snow on Sam's door, and he could see a dark face looking in, "—your windows. Hey. How you doing?"

The face smiled, glad Sam was all right, but it glanced anxiously this way and that, almost as if looking for others.

"It's just . . . just me in here. Just me. Got a little busted up, but . . . I think . . . nothing serious . . . considering everything."

"Yeah," the smiling face agreed. "Nothing at all . . ." the voice trailed off. "Lucky for me you're not dead. I don't think I could handle that."

Sam chuckled at that and grimaced at the pain. He couldn't handle dying either.

"Can you open the door?"

"I think so," Sam moved around and tried the latch. The door opened with a cranky groan. Cold winter wind stung Sam's face, and he was grateful for it.

"Let's get you out of there." The man reached in with two large hands and gripped Sam's winter parka. Effortlessly, the stranger pulled Sam from the car and tossed him like a sack of sand onto the snow. The salesman landed on his back with a yelp. His neck and body flared with pain, bright and unmistakable.

"*Christ!* Why'd you do that for?" Sam grated. "I didn't live through the crash to be killed by you! Could've broken my damn neck."

His savior turned out to be a big man with a shaven head. He laughed unexpectedly at the remarks, as if he had just hoarked into the teacher's water glass without getting caught. It was a high pitched sound that reached over the cold singing of the wind.

Sam's eyes slowly narrowed in disbelief.

"Relax," the man finally got out. "I ain't here to kill you. The last thing on my mind, really."

Sam saw, but he had trouble wrestling his mind around the image of his rescuer producing a tire iron at arm's length. As out of place as it seemed, Sam also realized that the guy before him was only wearing a thin denim jacket, open to the waist and exposing a red checked shirt underneath. A smile split the man's dark features, and Sam thought briefly of the human skeleton standing at attention in his old high school's laboratory. There was nothing friendly in that grin, just an unspoken confidence that, though things were fine now, they would be changing shortly.

And then the expression morphed into one of sympathy.

"I *am* gonna make things a mite bit more . . . uncomfortable."

The dark figure reared up the tire iron as if it were a baseball bat. He gave it a test swing, once, twice, and then stepped up to the plate.

Except there was no plate.

There was only a paralyzed Sam.

"Now, don't you worry. I'm an old hand at this kinda thing. A professional. You'll hurt there, but I promise you, you *will* live to see tomorrow."

Sam watched in disbelief as the head of the iron tapped his right knee. It kicked out in reflex. Then the iron rose up.

Sam staggered to his feet, ignoring the pain in his knees and shoulder. He meant to run, but the tire iron flew into his face instead. It crunched into the wreckage of his nose and drove him back to the snow. Sam cupped his buzzing nose with both hands. Blood flowed freely, refusing to be turned off.

"How's that feel?" came a nearby voice.

"Waid," Sam said through his red palms. "Waid," he repeated breathlessly, "I hab money . . . I can pay . . . I hab money."

"Not interested in coin, son. Sorry."

The tire iron wound up again. Sam didn't have the strength in his legs to run and didn't know where to run even if he *had* had the strength. Insurance. He had plenty of different policies on himself but realized with a start he didn't have any on personal injury.

"Wa—" he began to say.

But the tire iron was already flying at his head. It hit his jaw and shards of teeth sprayed across and lost themselves in the gathering snow. Sam fell over like a tree, landing heavily on his chest. The pain of his nose was a whisper in the roar of his mouth and jaw. It was broken. Never had he experienced a broken jaw—or a broken nose for that matter—but the sensation of his bones being actually *broken* made him gasp for air. Whirling stars filled his vision, and, for a moment, the night never looked clearer.

And somewhere, while he was in space, his right leg blossomed in agony. The unexpected jolt of pain brought him crashing back to reality.

"WAID!" Sam spat out, not seeing but sensing his attacker closing in yet again.

His scream brought his vision into focus. He was on his back now, framed in ivory white and staring up into blackness.

"Pluh . . . pluh . . ." his jaw worked as muscles tried to obey and only made the pain that much more intense. But he had to talk this lunatic down before he got killed.

"Shhh . . . shhh . . . relax . . ." came the mellow voice. But there was something terrifying in the tone. There was a breathless eagerness to it. Like a hunter watching and praying for the deer to take that final clarifying step into his line of fire. Then Sam saw the man's eyes above the skeleton grin. He saw the eager gleam in them.

Sam hitched in his breath.

The man stood directly over him. He tapped Sam's shoulder with the iron, drawing his attention to it. The smile disappeared, and the anger replacing it was frightening enough for Sam's bowels to spurt again.

"I said I wasn't going to kill you. What's wrong with you? Think I'm lying?" the man scoffed into the gathering wind. "I'll prove it."

Sam watched the iron rise up.

There was plenty of time to scream, and, as the iron came humming down, he gave it his best shot.

CHAPTER 2

On a Saturday night, freezing wet snow fell out of the black heavens and frosted everything in ceramic white. In the silence of this relentless coating, New York's nightlife slowed. Thick slush, despised for soaking through pricy footwear, coated the streets and sidewalks, causing most to shuffle along like ancients feeling out every careful step. A bout of snow was nothing to the people living in that great city. They'd had their share of snow in the past, enduring and digging out from some of the worse snowstorms along the eastern snowboard. And some of those were ball-breakers. They just had to take their time and hope to get to where they were going before the damp touched their socks.

Barbara watched the 57th Street zombies shuffle by with their wet feet, heedless of smacking into each other and making little effort to get out of each other's way. The sidewalks were filled with the holiday dead foraging for last minute deals and bargain sales. Or at least she thought it was the holidays. She had doubts then. Maybe the holidays were over. She warily watched the hordes. They were an unending parade moving through each other, like two currents sharing the same river. Their faces stared off without truly seeing; their bodies pushing through each other and ankle-deep snow. She hated the snow with a passion, even more than the zombies that shunned her.

The same as rain it was, but colder. Wet snow had a deep, bone-chilling misery to it that clung to a person. The warmth of a fire was the only real thing to shake the chill off, or the coils of an electric blanket. Barbara gazed into her shopping cart of possessions and remembered she had lost hers long ago. Years ago. And where was she now, anyway? She certainly wasn't in her neighborhood anymore. None of the streets looked familiar and there were no holes leading below ground to the abandoned subway tunnels. She needed to get back there.

It was drier there, though not warmer. But she had friends there who knew how to start fires. They would let her stay near one if she showed up. And there were no zombies, no zombies that stared at her and no drunken zombies that tried to beat her. But she had no idea where she was. She had wandered out with her shopping cart of possessions and memories a little too far, and now it was dark and snowing this wet shit. The flask of whiskey she downed earlier had taken her quite a ways from her home, and she was quickly sobering up to the snow on the ground. And the zombies.

"Can't believe I went so far from home," she muttered. "Can't believe, can't believe. I left the kids like that, too. What'll they do? Perry isn't around to fix 'em dinner . . . like he can cook anyways. What'll they do? Ta, do, do, do . . . Ta, da, da, da . . ."

With that thought, she adjusted the worn-looking winter coat she ferreted out of a dumpster a year ago. It was marked with stains she couldn't quite seem to get out, and she eventually gave up trying. Barbara hunched over the shopping cart's push bar like an upside-down L. She was a tall woman, standing at an even six foot when she stood up straight. These days, however, she got dizzy when she straightened up that far. Keeping low to the ground was much better for her senses, and she didn't get the urge to throw up when she was hunched over. Nowadays, as she approached her sixties, she figured it wasn't such a bad thing to have four wheels and two feet under her.

She leaned way over the bar, and tugged down on the peppermint-green and white toque covering her fuzzy mat of grey hair. She didn't want to get frostbite—couldn't get frostbite. Frostbitten ears would have to be thawed out with gasoline and salt, and would sting like a bitch. She slowly turned her cart around, retreating back into the alley, away from the main drag and the slow, arterial pump of traffic. She would retrace her steps back and find the way home, entrusting all to her inner navigator. She had to get back to her kids. The two kittens she found weeks ago had both been beside the body of their crushed mother. It was a good thing Barb had happened along when she did. Had they stayed with their mother in that narrow side street, they would've been squooshed by some other Chevy. Just like their dear old momma. Or the zombies would have taken them. Lord only knew how long they would have survived before the zombies trashed them. Or devoured them. Or worse.

"Da, da, da," she went on, and then started giggling for no particular reason. She did that a lot in her current days on earth. She would be walking along pushing her cart and just start giggling her ass off. There really wasn't anything to be laughing at. Nothing in her life had proven to be so goddamn funny, yet at times like these, hunched over as she was, she would just get to giggling. And giggle. She wasn't crazy. That thought made her giggle again. Then she thought of her kids again. What would they eat? It was terrible to have someone depending on you all the while. It was terrible to wonder what they would do if you didn't come home in time.

She emerged from the alleyway, peering this way and that for the zombies. There was none. In New York, that was a rare thing indeed. She was between two large slop piles of garbage bags. Snow covered the bags and made them look like black boulders. Or snowballs, huge lumpy snowballs just begging to be rolled over and into a child's snowman. Barb could remember when she was a child with her sisters and her only brother, laughing and teasing, and how they would make snow folks. Back then, she was the youngest, and her sisters would fret over her, making certain her tartan scarf was always tied around her neck and face just right. They always took care of her. Not like her shit of a brother. Her sisters even helped wipe her nose when it ran. Who could ask for better than that? Brad was always hoisting her up and using her as extra weight to bulldoze into their sisters, Sam and Bethany. Yelling and charging into them ...

Yelling ...

Barbara looked up into the headlights of a metro bus just as the front bumper connected with her left side. Bone was smashed in an instant. Barbara flew for the first time in her life, but it was backwards, through the night, across the street she had wandered out into during her memories. Her flight was cancelled by a 58th Street lamppost, and it shook in fury as she bounced off its iron girth.

Barbara did not know much. She was in the hurt over her head and her brain was numb from the incoming damage reports. All of them were bad—terribly bad. She wanted to die. She wanted death in all its blackness. She never knew the bus had slowed to a stop some fifty feet from her. She did not know that while the post had stopped her, it had dropped her back into the street on her stomach, with hooked fingers trying to get a grip on asphalt.

The metro bus's engine roared, high from a shot of diesel. If she could have heard the roar, it would have reminded her of her Brad's voice—deep as it could go, trying to growl as fiercely as possible.

The engine cleared its throat again. A double warning that the zombie driver felt more than generous, given the situation. Any other time, the driver would have simply gone and wrecked whatever was available before *he* came. But the driver, a man in a frayed jean jacket and red checked shirt, allowed the engine to idle a moment more. His head was shaven. The grin reflected in the lit gauges of the bus was distorted and toothy. There was no one around. The meat was not moving, and *he* would *not* be coming anytime soon. The driver in the frayed jean jacket sensed this as one sniffing the air for rain. There was no need to rush this time. There was no need to rush at all. He could take his time here. Nobody was coming.

No one at all.

A black leather boot—he loved how they shined—pumped the accelerator once again. It was such a *marvelous* machine! To think people actually rode around inside of them when they were obviously built for a far better purpose. A purpose he was about to teach this one lying on the road before his wheels. He cranked the machine into gear, and the bus moved forward, a silver torpedo building up speed.

Something perverse levitates Barbara up from the depths of her blackness. A part of her senses the street thrumming but can't identify just what it is or why she should be concerned. Her bed is so cold and hard and wet. And where are her sisters?

The metro's gear shifted into high.

The grin behind the windshield shrieked laughter as chrome crashed over Barbara's barely conscious form. It was a howl of release, one for the ages. The front tires went over her, then the rear. The bus ran over Barbara and it slowed to a stop almost immediately. The gears shifted into reverse, and the metro backed up over her again. Rear wheels first, crushing more bones on pavement slick with blood. There was a muted *thump, thump,* as if someone had just driven over a curb or a low speed bump. Winter's snow continued to fall.

The driver pulled the bus around to drink in the sight. Her mashed form was death white in the angry headlights.

The grin became vampiric as he cranked the gear-stick into first and lined up the right wheel with her lower back.

He would take his time with this one.

The second before chrome and rubber crashed over Barbara again, the gear shifted into high and a maniacal laugh split the air; a millennium howl, a scream of mirth heard only at the rave of the century, where the background music thundered and sounded like the brazen smack of rubber against flesh.

Again.

And again.

And again.

CHAPTER 3

Badger Thomas moved through one of the many shortcuts he knew in Halifax's entertainment quarter. He kept to the alleyways and lesser populated streets skirting the areas of Hollis Street and Barrington. It was early Saturday night, and already, traffic gushed through the roadways in an uneven pulse. The red lights would tourniquet the rush for seconds before releasing the gathered pressure of engines, fiberglass, and bad spoilers. Ahead, Badger could see the traffic surge forth and quickly ebb as the lights bloodied from yellow into red. He didn't have a car, and in a sense, he really didn't want one.

A car was only a hole to throw money into in his opinion. He had better holes to keep his cash in. Besides, Badger was pro-environment. He refused to buy a car when the technology to breed cleaner engines was just seeping into the market place. He could wait a little longer. He had gone for so long without actually owning a machine that he really didn't miss it. Or so he told himself. But when one of the new electric models became affordable enough, he would be right there to place an order for a custom job. He might even do away with his mountain bike if the notion took him. Until then, the best hole he had for his money was his girlfriend Alicia. Now, there was a *beeyotch* in heels. She could suck him off in the span of a green light ripening to red.

Alicia. She might be a slut, but she was the best slut he had ridden in a long while. Her name played about in his head and percolated memories of extreme sexual deeds. Badger got the hankering to call her later. Maybe after checking out the Liquor Dome, he would give her a shout. See if she was up for a little driving from behind. She loved doggy style, and Badger loved giving it to her just that way. They were a perfect couple in a sense.

The drug trade in Halifax was nothing compared to Toronto or anything west of the Rockies, but it was quietly lucrative. Transactions were well channeled, screened, and safe. The Mounties rarely bothered Badger, and as long as no one turned up dead or complained to the authorities, they were loath to bother with a small-timer like him. Badger had an established clientele, from the business types down on Purdy's Wharf to the bar freaks and Dal students up on Barrington. Hollis was his major stream of revenue, and though he had friendly competition from a few other independents, he had enough regulars to keep pumping money into his mutual funds. Nobody would move in on Badger, not after the little war he had won.

He and the Stickman had never killed anyone before, but Halifax was a modern city and quickly moving on in years. In 2008, however, there were two bodies floating in Halifax Harbor, and they didn't jump from the bridge spanning the bay to Dartmouth. Badger hated doing shit like that, and he hated having to bring the Stickman in on it. Neither he nor his muscle was the same after those two over-ambitious pushers. Badger had even taken up smoking because of it and became a stout believer in atheism. He had to; else he might go and do something altogether not cool. He wasn't sure of just *what* he might do, but he believed it would involve freaking out, and that would not be kosher. He remembered seeing an episode of *The Shield* where the one detective interrogated a killer. The conversation, though Badger could not recall its entirety, was interesting in that the same detective later felt compelled to strangle a stray cat that was bothering him night after night. The killer did that. Or at least something in the words of the man compelled the detective to strangle a cat and gaze into its eyes as the animal died. Badger came away from that episode thinking if someone killed another person and, worse still, got away with it, maybe they *would* just start to like it. Like a junkie wondering what H would be like after successfully sneaking a few joints in at school or work. Badger didn't feel the need to go on a spree after offing two shitheads who wanted the entire city instead of just a street, so he believed he was safe.

Now, the Stickman, on the other hand.

Badger sighed. He was weightlifting with the Stickman when the first sign occurred that the Stick's wiring just might be a little crossed after the hit. The Stick would just space out for long seconds. That was okay, but one day he did it while he was spotting Badger. Badger was in the bench press position with a total weight of eighty kilograms over his chest, and at the end of a series of reps, when his muscles were about to quit, instead of helping him lift the weight, Stickman simply stood over him and stared. He watched Badger's face turn blood red under the pressure. He watched the weight slowly descend upon his companion's chest and did nothing, even when Badger grunted for help. Even when the help had come from someone else, the Stickman still stood and stared at the empty bench. Badger was certain that the Stickman's consciousness had left him at that time. Badger wondered if there were other times. Perhaps there were prison flashbacks or something from his youth that were bugging him. He wondered if he should even broach the subject with the Stickman. They shared a good buddy-buddy relationship, and Badger had even looked after the lad when he went to Saskatchewan's prison ward, but since the hit, he had never gone up to the guy and asked, "*Are you okay?*"

Frankly, Badger was concerned about the answer the Stickman might give him.

He glanced at his cellphone and pushed a button. The glow illuminated 10:30. He slowed for a moment, big fingers fumbling with the little touchpad, when a figure rose out of the gloom from behind a garbage bin and grabbed him with hands of iron. Something cracked across Badger's jaw, and he saw black stars. His world became soupy then, but his pain-overloaded mind still registered the four rapid punches to his midsection. His breath burst past his lips like a ruptured gas tank, and a couple of ribs snapped in bright flashes of pain.

"Hold on there," the harbinger spoke, now straining with the dead weight of the drug dealer. "Hold. Jeez, you're heavy. They said you'd been working out."

A hand gripped Badger's jaw. A heavy forearm pressed against his upper chest, and something thin, cold, and edged pressed against his throat.

"Don't go makin' this harder for you, okay? Okay?" the voice said, and shook Badger hard enough for him to bite his own tongue and make it bleed. The pain of his tongue brought him back to semi-consciousness.

"You hear me? You better, else I start twisting things," the voice said, close enough now that Badger glimpsed the whitest teeth he had ever seen through the alley darkness.

Badger's vision slowly cleared. He willed it to clear as if it were controlled by a brightness knob on a TV. Darkness still ruled, however, and whatever pressed against his throat kept him from turning his head to get a better look at his attacker. Black eyes flashed into view for a moment, flecks of silver in their depths.

Badger swallowed blood. He spat more.

The fucking terminator had come for him.

"Ah, tougher than you look. That's good," the face nodded. "But don't get stupid, okay? Use the brains tonight man, and leave the fight behind. Use the muscle, so much as fucking flex it, and I'll put my pig sticker up through your roof just like some goddamn buggy antennae."

Badger felt the pressure against his throat increase enough to make his eyes water.

"Okay," he squeaked out. He had never had a knife to his throat before, and now that he did, it was all he could do not to freak out. He'd never been so close to dying. Never.

"I didn't kill 'em," he panted, wanting to say anything to get this monster off of him. "It was Stick. Stickman. He did 'em both. Not me." *Sorry bro*, Badge thought as he said the words, but he also swore he would make it up to his associate as soon as his ass was out of harm's way and in cleaner clothes.

"Who are you?"

The knife at his throat pressed. "I don't think you got time for the answer, Badge." The forearm pressed harder against him. "So, just listen. You remember Mr. Tigh? Your superior?"

"Yeah."

"Yeah, well, Mr. Tigh believes that a little of his merchandise has gone missing on a regular basis. Just a little here and there, not a big lot, but a little nonetheless. And, as coincidence has it, it always seems to be missing on your watch. You don't have any side orders going on do you, Badge?"

If it wasn't for the night, Badger would have been made right there. His cheeks flushed hot while his guts froze and sunk earthwards. He blinked for a second or two.

Mr. Tigh.

He *knew*. Oh, *shit!*

"Cuz if you do . . . *if* you do, I have instructions. The first one involves the blade at your throat. You ever have a knife this close to your throat before that you weren't holding? That wasn't under your control? Scary, ain't it?"

Badger realized he was expected to answer. "Yeah," he managed to get out.

"How does it feel then?"

"Not good."

"Not good, eh?"

"Yeah."

"Yeah," the terminator agreed in a very soft, very sorry voice. "Yeah, well, that's good. Mr. Tigh said you were the honest kind. The sort of guy he knew he really shouldn't have to worry about. That's why I'm really only supposed to dish out punishment on how you answer the next question. Got it?"

"Yeah."

"You never stole shit from Mr. Tigh, now did you?"

Badger blinked again and looked into the eyes of his captor. He swallowed and felt the knife's edge roll with his Adam's apple.

"No. Never," he lied.

Those eyes searched Badger's face for a moment like cat's claws pawing at a balloon.

"No," the voice finally agreed. "I guess you wouldn't. Good thing, too. Apparently Mr. Tigh would hate to lose you, y'know. You do good work up around here."

"Thanks," Badger rasped.

The dark face tilted apologetically. "Sorry about the face, but you'll get better. You get yourself looked at tonight, eh? Get stitched up. Hear me?"

Badger nodded. He would do just that. A bottle of Jack Daniels sure as hell would help the healing too.

"Sorry about your clothes, too. You put some shortening on that, and it'll wash right out."

The pressure disappeared from Badger's chest, and the knife came away from his throat. Badger slumped, feeling his back grate against the alley's brick wall all the way down until he was sitting.

"Anyway, remember what I said, and you'll never see me again. Fuck up, and I'll get a call to pick up where I'm leaving off."

Badger nodded. He was being given a second chance, and dammit if he wasn't going to make good on it. He thought of himself as being relatively smart, and he knew just how close he had come to getting killed. Mr. Tigh knew and wanted to let *him* know that he knew. If Badger persisted in his skimming, he would disappear one evening, and that would be that. Badger was even thinking about how he could put some of the shit *back* and claim it was an accounting error or something. But that was for tomorrow. Right now, he kept on nodding, closing his eyes and drawing in great lungfuls of precious air. He heard his attacker leave.

Mr. Tigh knew and decided only to have his boy kick a little shit out of him as a warning. A good job, too, really. Badger's face ached terribly. Perhaps the right cheekbone was broken and swelling. He could just barely see out of his right eye. A couple of his ribs hurt as well. He wanted but didn't want to see his reflection. It would probably be best if he didn't. He scanned the nearby pavement. There was a length of heavy pipe on the ground, and for a moment, he had to think if it had been used on him. Badger didn't think his attacker had, but it sure as hell felt as if he had. Alicia would be on her own tonight and might even be on her own for the rest of the week. Nothing like a good shit kicking to take the urge out of a guy.

Then Badger sobered up.

Mr. Tigh.

What to do about Mr. Tigh?

Around Barrington, Badger was prince, but Mr. Tigh was under the eastern seaboard crime syndicate. He had only sent one butcher after him when he could have sent a small army. In a way, Badger considered it both a compliment and an insult. He thought he was small enough to avoid detection, and he earned only one visitor. Yet, the fact that he was still breathing informed him of Mr. Tigh's opinion that he was valuable to their operations in Halifax. Maybe he just didn't want to bring in someone new that he'd have to train. Whatever the thinking, Badger was glad that Mr. Tigh gave him a second chance. He could've been dead.

A sigh left him, and his ribs rattled with pain. Badger suppressed a painful, little smile. Whoever the bastard was that put the beating on him, he certainly did the job by the numbers. Lord, he hurt. He decided to sit just a little longer before getting up. The hospital wasn't going anywhere.

"You ain't in a hurry, are ya?"

A guy's voice. Badger looked up into the eyes of the second shadowy figure of his evening. This one wore a denim suit, complete with a lumberjack's checked shirt. The face was hard to see, but Badger could see it was middle-aged, haggard and mean looking. A bald or shaved head. The man smiled at him, exposing well-cared-for teeth. Black eyes gleamed.

"Are you?" The man repeated.

"Do I look like I'm in a hurry?" Badger answered him in a voice he would have to try and duplicate in a round of poker sometime. He didn't bother getting up. He didn't have the energy to bother.

"No," the grin deepened. "Probably not. Shit, man! That guy really danced a number on you. You must be in *agony*."

"Had worse," Badger lied.

"Really?" The voice fell away to a dangerous sounding whisper. "You sure about that?"

That question was as clear as a knife slipping across a wrist, and Badger did *not* appreciate it, given his present condition. It sounded to him like the guy here now was on the brink of freaking out, the kind of freak-out that might occur if he found out his son had sucked off the entire football team, and pictures of the deed had appeared on the net. He liked it even less when the figure bent, picked up the metal pipe and brought it in under Badger's nose.

"Hey," Badger whispered despite the fright building in his heart. "I got the point the first time. I'll be good from now on. You can tell that to Mr. Tigh. No more trouble with me. I'll be good. I promise."

"Ah, yes . . . Mr. Tigh," the voice soothed, cool as a stud dressed in black. "His boy started some good work here." The man paused and studied the alley, ensuring that the two of them were indeed alone and that the shadows were only shadows. A moment passed. They were alone and, feeling secure in that knowledge, the figure moved in closer. Without warning, he brought the pipe down with bone breaking force and smashed Badger's knee. The Prince of Barrington screamed once, a high pitched sound that quickly became a hoarse expulsion of air. His hands hooked into claws as he reached for his ruined knee.

The figure crushed Badger's other kneecap, barely giving him the chance to console his first.

"But I'll finish it," the man promised him with eagerness in his voice. The pipe came up again, tapped Badger's left cheek and drew back a distance. Badger's breath floundered in his chest as he tried to suck in enough of it to plead for his life. It would not have made a difference.

Badger screamed once more before the pipe landed home and a flurry of teeth bounced like angry sleet on the alley floor.

CHAPTER 4

Tony Levin opened his eyes and stared up at the ceiling of his bedroom. Lines ran across the white paint marking the spent thunder of children overhead. The neighbours were being quiet this morning, and it was a rare instance where he woke because of the presence of morning instead of heavy feet thumping across his ceiling. He rolled his eyes over and glanced at his baseball clock. It was exactly 10:43. Maybe the neighbours weren't being quiet at all. Maybe they were already gone, and he had slept through their leaving. Jesus. Did he sleep that deeply last night?

He blinked, and it was 10:44. He believed it was Sunday but would have to check later. As if he were coming out of a cosy thaw, his eyes slid back to the whiteness of the ceiling. He closed them, but it was only a ritual. He could never fall back to sleep after waking up. Once he was awake, that was it, especially if it had been a deep sleep. He felt as if he had sunk into a mire of it from the night before. Running off the energy of a job usually did that to him. He was thankful again he didn't have to kill Badger. His orders were to scare the man, enlighten him that Mr. Tigh was on to him and straighten him out. Tony felt he accomplished that with little problem. It went off without a hitch, and that was reason enough to be happy this morning. A touch of a sleepy scowl appeared on his rough face. He hoped the man didn't recognize him. He didn't need that. He should've used a ski mask, but he was too lazy-assed to go buy one. If there was a limit to the work you were in, if there was a point when you felt that enough was enough, Tony believed he was getting there. He was getting too careless about things, and careless in his work would put him in a cremator. He had to smarten up.

Work. Work meant pay. A deep sigh left him. That would be one of the stops today. Stop at the Beacon and collect his pay from Tigh. There were other things he had to do today as well, but what were they? Jesus, if his mind was like this now, what would he be like when he was fifty? Or even sixty? Another sigh left him. He opened and closed his eyes as if he had just been knocked out, lying on a canvass somewhere and wondering which world he was in. What else did he have to do? Things sauntered across the foggy caverns of his mind. Groceries. He needed to pick up some groceries right after he got paid as his pantry and fridge were running a couple of days low. He also needed to check his mailbox, though it was Sunday. He saw a bunch of letters and flyers shoved into the mouth of his mailbox last night, but he was too tired at the time to wrestle them out. There would be mostly bills if anything. They were the only ones that actually sent him mail. If he ever got a direct deposit line from his bank account, he wouldn't get any mail at all.

Only his mother ever made the effort.

Tony's eyes cracked open. He remembered the thing he had to do today. He had to see his mother. It had been two days since he had last spoken to her, and that was an unforgivable crime for him. Here he was, staring at the ceiling and wondering about what food he would later pick up, while his Mom . . . he didn't finish the thought. Didn't want to, because if he did, chances were he would feel bad enough that he would not eat any breakfast. He would see her today, this afternoon, in fact, at the earliest.

The thought of her made him rise from his sleep-warm bed and swing his legs out over the edge. Went to the bathroom. A few moments later he finished urinating and splashed water over his face. He didn't want to look in the mirror. He only used the thing to check his shaving, and even then, that was enough. He hated the damn thing for the simple fact that it showed him his face. Tony Levin was not an unattractive man, yet he could not stand to gaze upon himself. Like a vampire of legend, he avoided gazing into the mirror's depths. He firmly believed that if there were no mirrors, there would be one less temptation in the world. One less sin. Nobody would care about how they looked if they didn't have mirrors. No one would fuss over their appearance at all. He moved from the bathroom to the nest that was his one bedroom apartment on Windmill Road. He plopped down on his grey second hand sofa and flicked a button on a remote. His small CD stereo flared to life, and he caught the end of some energetic pop tune. The fading chords of music made him snarl in distaste. He hated the pop music of today. The sound was like the lyrics. Just a bunch of bad rhymes stuck together with a digitally adhesive chorus. He thought of digital tar then, and the thought amused him enough to smile. More and more, he found himself wallowing in the music of the past, and he noted that a lot of the popular artists of the day were as well. Drum machines were men back then, and songs were tiny tales of good love, bad love, good love gone bad, bad love getting better, or just plain old-fashioned fucking.

He liked those the best.

Breakfast was a skimpy affair of three boiled eggs minus the yolks. On the side of the eggs were two dry slabs of buttered toast. No jam. He thought he still had some, but he'd scraped out the jar the other day. Dull plumes of green were appearing on the last pieces of bread, but Tony surgically pinched them off and deposited them in the garbage under the sink. He made his coffee and filled a nearby glass with water as the chaser. There was no juice or milk in the house. He might get some after visiting his mother, but he doubted it.

He moved back to his grey sofa and placed his food on the old coffee table a neighbour had placed out on the curb for disposal. It was just fine for Tony. He heard the news but didn't really listen. He consumed his meal slowly, chewing on a cud of toast and staring off at nothing in particular. The stereo said something about Richard Rhodes' birthday, his one hundred and first. A centenarian. Tony snarled again as he shifted the toast from one side of his mouth to the other. One hundred and one. That'll be one helluva party at the home. Bingo all round and maybe even two chocolate bars for prizes. The old bugger would probably cack right there if he won. An image of the old centenarian breathing out "bingo" from behind a respirator before collapsing went through Tony's mind.

He sipped his coffee. Bitter. He put no sugar in it. He kept right on sipping and thinking, and every now and then, his lower face would coil up as if ready to spit poison. He stared at his fists, seeing the fresh bruises on his knuckles for the first time. New additions to the old scars. In his work, his hands were all-important, and his hands were getting old.

Tony left his dishes in the sink while he went about the rest of his morning routine. He showered, decided to shave to impress his mom, ignored the black eyes in the mirror and focused on the lather he scraped away from left to right. He finished the rest of his time in the bathroom quickly. He dressed in denim. A thick black sweater under his jean jacket was his only winter protection, and he topped himself off with a frayed ball cap telling the world to "Bite Me."

Tony paused at the door, the peak of his cap shading his eyes. It was a little after noon now. Would Tigh be at the Beacon this early? He would check anyhow. Was there anything else?

A quick check of his apartment informed him that the radio was still on. The noon DJ was droning on with some news about a small engine plane crashing, managing to sound almost disappointed that the pilot and the three passengers had survived.

Tony grabbed the car keys hanging off the fridge door and crossed the floor to kill the radio. Sounds of motorcycles and children shrieking while playing replaced the news. Tony barely heard any of it as he locked his door. His apathy could be numbing at times. He moved outside, ignored the people cluttered around the apartment building's entrance and forgot to check his mail. Thoughts of his mother drifted back into his mind like the thick smoke from an unseen fire. She would be happy to see him this day. She would be upset it had been a while since his last visit, but she would be happy still.

A blue '85 Ford Mustang waited for him. His chariot and a more faithful car he had never owned. He knew of some folks who swore to never ever own a Ford in their lifetime, but he had nothing but praise for the beast. It was a fearsome creature, and absolutely retro looking with its squared edges and bumpers, but the machine had proved itself to him time and time again by staying out of the machine shop. The body was still in fair shape with nary a rust patch or hole. There were scratches and dents aplenty, but Tony didn't mind those. Like his hands, each scratch or dent in the beast bore a story. Some tales he knew of, others he hadn't a clue about, but there were stories with each one. They gave the machine character in a surly, chained up, pit bull kind of way. No one had stolen the beast just yet. Perhaps the fact that it was an '85 Ford made thieves wary of the thing. Or maybe, the carjackers in the neighbourhood knew who the car belonged to.

That thought hadn't occurred to him.

He didn't have insurance, and he didn't care. He never locked his doors. He got in and paid attention so as to not crack his skull on the door frame. He inserted the key and the engine barfed into life. The beast had never been seriously sick yet, but Tony suspected he had only twenty or so good starts left in the monster. He thought for a moment about spark plugs and quickly dumped the idea. If spark plugs were the only thing he would need, then there was no need to worry about anything else. If only his mother's problem was as simple.

A backfire caused an old man walking nearby to clutch his chest, his jaw dropping in fright. Without apology, Tony threw the car into reverse and eased out of his parking space. The elderly gentleman, wearing Sunday grey slacks and matching winter overcoat, stood paralyzed as the Mustang's rear bumper swung wide to his left. Grumbling with the cold, the Mustang moved towards Windmill road, paused at an intersection and indicated right. A second later, it slipped into traffic and left the parking lot behind.

Tony Levin's day had begun.

He turned on the radio.

"Caller number two, what's the sound?"

Tony had heard the quiz show before. Hear a fragment of noise and identify it. He didn't want the talk right now, however. He wanted music.

"Ah, ah . . . it's a saw?" A nervous voice muttered.

"A saw? No, sorry, man. Let's play that again." The sound that issued from the radio sounded like an old dog coughing unbearably hard, almost as if the thing had just taken its first draw on a butt when no one was looking.

"Whaddaya think?" The DJ blared, sounding like he was perpetually happy seven days a week. "Gimme a call on this gorgeous morning, and you could be seeing these guys in concert on Saturday night! Caller number 3! What's your name?"

"Chisel!"

"Your name is *Chisel?*"

"No, my name's Bruce."

"Oh," the DJ picked up the pace. "You want me to play it again?"

"God, no, you've played it enough already. It's a chisel. Any carpenter would know that sound."

A symphony of horns and strings boomed over the speakers. "You're right!" DJ Jeff. The name came to Tony as he navigated his way through traffic. "You've won man, how's that?"

"Jeff," Bruce asked in a snarky voice. "What are the tickets for?"

"You don't know?"

"Naw man, only just tuned in."

"Oh," the admission caught DJ Jeff off guard. "Well, it's a concert in the Palace on Saturday night with—"

"Bayside Legs?"

Tony didn't know the name.

"Yeah," DJ Jeff said in a perky voice. "You like those guys?"

"Aww, can't go. Too busy. Can I get a t-shirt instead?" Bruce informed DJ Jeff in a bored voice.

"A t-shirt?" this stupefied DJ Jeff, but only for a moment. "*No,* you can't have a t-shirt. I don't even have any t-shirts."

"Whaddaya mean? You guys *always* have t-shirts to give away."

"I don't have any now. We're out, and it's the wrong promotion, and why am I talking to you about this, anyway? It's concert tickets, Bruce!"

Tony had to agree. Bruce could scalp them if he really wanted to.

"Well, I can't go to the concert," Bruce announced over the airwaves in a stand-offish tone.

"Who am I, your counselor? I got Melissa on the other line here who's begging to get these tickets. Melissa, you hearing this?"

"Sure am!" a giggly voice answered promptly. Someone who took in way too much sugar in the morning.

"Whoops, sorry, Bruce. I just hung up on Bruce," DJ Jeff reported in a not-too-upset voice. "It was an accident, man. I was going to arrange a deal between you and Melissa... but you know what I'm going to do now, Melissa?"

"No," Melissa said with hope in her voice.

"I'm going to hang up on you too!"

DJ Jeff did just that and then switched to commercial, promising to give the concert tickets away in the next hour. Tony smiled when DJ Jeff did as he said he would do. The man was a smart ass. He would've hung up, too. Some callers were just too damn ungrateful. His thoughts then turned to wondering just how many weird calls DJs like Jeff got in the run of a shift. Probably a lot. It wouldn't be the job of choice for Tony. He'd be too abrasive with the weird ones. Still, it would be cool to just sit back and play tunes all day long.

That pleasant image hung with him until he pulled into the Beacon's parking lot. Tigh was in. His "pussy bait", as he called it, was parked in plain view, a '08 blue Camaro with a fresh coat of snow on its hood and roof. Tony thought the man was a strange one to venture out to the Beacon just hours after the place shut down. The Beacon was a glowering touch of men's entertainment in Dartmouth. Women's groups, religious associations, and even block parents had successfully closed down all other bars opened up by Tigh in the past. It was a hard town to keep a strip bar alive in, and why he would even keep trying for one was beyond Tony. The Beacon had lasted the longest, however, but it was a month to month thing. Tony really didn't care for the strip shows. He never even rented the hard core stuff from the adjoining DVD shop next door. He wasn't an angel as he had rented something a while back from the corner-store, back-room collection. The porno was a group of amateurs performing "the best amateur ride" or something to that tune. There were pictures of all of the twenty-something young women on the back of the jacket, and Tony remembered the DVD promising a bonus episode. It was either a Saturday or Friday night. He rented it.

The bonus was a rape.

It wasn't a set-up. It seemed too natural for that. Too damn terrifying. A van had pulled up to a mini-skirted young lady of nineteen or so, and the driver asked for directions while two others snuck out the back. They had her in the van in a blink, kicking and screaming a little too wildly for Tony's liking.

Then one of the men brought out the pliers.

Tony didn't watch the rest. He turned off the player and just sat quietly, watching the blackness of the television screen and thinking. He felt sick and *ashamed* about a little voice wanting him to turn the machine back on. He didn't, however. He just sat there and thought and thought, the knowledge poisoning him that by renting the piece-of-shit video, he was funding *more* of the same. The wondering never stopped: what had she done? What could she have done? Hadn't there been papers or something for her to sign her consent to distribute the DVD? Or had someone forced her to sign with the pliers? Perhaps it had been an act after all.

And had she finally got home that night?

Maybe they hadn't even allowed her that. Maybe they had just killed her afterwards. Tony hoped to hell they hadn't. He would have liked to get his hands on the producers of such filth. He had his own set of pliers, and he could be inventive when inspired.

Since then Tony had no use for any medium of pornography.

The Beacon was a concrete bunker of a building, ready for any bomb blast. A dull white sign announced "The Beacon" as if viewed through a fog. The sign was supposed to be ditched for something with a little more flash and bang. Neon was mentioned in certain circles, and then there were the newer digital signs where you could program in your own little slogan underneath. Nothing had been done yet, however, and Tony felt perhaps Tigh preferred the low profile. Ask anyone where to go for exotic dancers in Dartmouth and Halifax, and they would give directions to the Beacon. Word of mouth was the best advertising, and Tigh got plenty of that with the talent he employed. Apparently, he didn't feel the need to slap the protest groups across the balls any more than he had to.

The door leading into the den of gyrating flesh and pouting lips was made of stylish oak, and a single diamond shaped window was set in the upper centre of its surface. Tony knew that the hinges and frame were reinforced with iron, and two more iron bars braced the portal from within when needed. Tigh fondly called it a holy door as most new employees would mutter "*Jesus Christ*" upon seeing the fortification. Nothing short of an armoured vehicle was coming through there. Going through the concrete wall would be easier. No other entrance could be seen from the front. No windows were visible. A passer-by would not really discern the place as a strip bar on the edge of the city. It looked more like a windowless storage building with an adult movie shop next door.

Tony parked the Mustang by Tigh's Camaro, smiling as he did so. It was like throwing dog shit onto someone's immaculate front lawn. The beast coughed and died as Tony withdrew his keys from the ignition. He would've parked somewhere else if it wasn't business, somewhere like a block or two away. But this was only going to be a short visit, and his mother was waiting. He would keep it short. He really didn't want to associate too much with Mr. Tigh. Word was around that he was a high-ranking lieutenant for some European based mob on the Eastern Seaboard.

He slammed his door as hard as he could and regretted it instantly. Something metallic yawned painfully, and splinters of rust sprinkled the snow covered pavement underneath the beast. Tony exhaled, willing his annoyance away until later. With his luck, the door would probably remind him of its trouble by falling off. He forced that thought away as well. He didn't need the jinx.

He marched within three feet of the door when it opened up for him and was replaced by a wall.

"Morning Tony," the monster called Danny greeted him. The big black man's eyes looked as if they ached for sleep, as dark as the boots and jeans that he wore. An off-white shirt stretched over his massive frame, untucked and covering up the leather belt that he usually wore. Danny was the kind of man who tried to clean himself up as best as he could, considering the hours he kept. Tony thought the man looked like he had just gotten in from some far off war, and figured maybe he had done just that.

Danny nodded at the ball cap. "Where you get that?"

"Present. From the Things Shop maybe."

"Mmmmn," Danny nodded again. He still blocked the entrance, watching Tony with a very sleepy set of eyes.

"Mr. Tigh in?"

"MmmHmm," Danny acknowledged. "But he's a little pissed off at you, I think."

This was news. "Pissed at me? Why's he pissed at me?"

"The job you did on Badger."

Tony shifted his weight onto his right leg. "What about the job I did on Badger? I took care of him last night like he wanted."

"A little rough weren't ya?" Danny said, those sleepy eyes unblinking now and boring into Tony's own, seeking a flicker of a lie.

"Rough?"

"You put him in the hospital," Danny reported calmly, stating the facts.

"The job wanted him in a hospital."

"I think the job wanted him to *check out* a hospital, not be a permanent resident," Danny clarified for the man. Levin looked surprised for a moment, but it wasn't the guilty kind. Danny had been around long enough to discern a deceptive face and as far as he could see, Tony was honestly surprised at the news.

"He's in the hospital?" Tony blinked at the big man. Tony himself was roughly five foot ten. Danny Boy outgunned him at half a head taller and so much more muscle.

"Paralyzed," Danny said, stretching the word out. He frowned with the dire news. "His ass won't be moving anytime soon, and from what we hear, he'll be eating through a tube for a while."

Tony's hand came up. "Now, wait. I only bloodied the man's nose—"

"Word is you broke everything else."

"I didn't *do* anything else," Tony immediately insisted, holding the big man's Father Time stare. "Somebody fucked up something somewhere, but it wasn't me. I did what I was told to do. The worst I might have done was broken a couple of ribs at best."

He suddenly straightened. "Why am I talking to you?"

Danny had no answer, their stares still wrestling for the yielding blink and break. Tony could feel his ducts drying out. Danny's obviously dried out years ago.

"Just givin' you the word, is all," Danny finally said to him.

"I came to see Mr. Tigh."

Danny made no move for a long, considering moment, but then, when Tony thought he was going to be told where to go, the monster of a man moved like some granite door of legend having heard the magic word. He stepped aside, his eyes narrowing at the day over Tony's head.

"Going to clear up later," Danny mentioned, but this was pillow talk compared to what might now be waiting for Tony within. Danny waited for the soldier to go on inside, and for a brief moment, the picture of a hunter waiting for his prey to step into the snare came to Tony's mind. He was suddenly uncertain if he should enter or not, but then again, he needed the cash. He needed to see his mom. And he suddenly felt the urge to clear the air of any stink surrounding his name. Whatever the trouble was, he sure as hell hoped it didn't get physical. Not with the twin hammers around. Danny was half of a pair that had far too many urban legends connected to their names, Danny Boy and "Tonight we Boom, Boom" Boomer. He didn't know how many god-awful brawls were whispered when their shadows passed over. How many fist fights did they enter and rule? How many men had limbs broken because they crossed one of the two behemoths? To have half of them upset with you was reason to leave town, go west and be remembered as a very wise man.

Tony did not want to go west. And yet now he was entering the lair of the Ice Dragon with two of its bloody guardians nearby.

Fuck it. Exhaling heavily, Tony stepped past the big man.

As the day was still early in bar hours, and it being Sunday, the Beacon was officially open for unofficial business. Tigh declared it to be a day off for his girls and supporting staff, but he almost always had Danny and Boomer nearby or at least one of the pair. They were hulking mastiffs at their master's heels. They had to be getting a decent salary from the man, Tony thought. There wasn't any day in hell that he would want to ever work on Sunday. Especially in the winter.

Sturdy tables were arranged in a horseshoe around a stage fashioned in the shape of lips and a tongue. Whenever Tony saw the stages he always thought of "The Rocky Horror Picture Show", except in this case, the mouth was all the way open and the lips, made of some soft, red leather and stuffed with God only knew what, were as big as the meat of his thigh. It was a weird effect, and he was getting unwanted vibes. He really didn't care about seeing women strip in the least, and the thought of them slithering around up there on a stage fashioned like a huge tongue made him wonder if Tigh was really okay in the head. At least the lights were off. When they were on, the stage was illuminated with black, glowing, designer teeth. Disturbing, but there were enough guys coming to the Beacon to sit in pervert's row—directly in front of the stage—for Tigh to feel that nothing needed to be changed. Maybe it was a joke, and a sick one at that. A smell of bacon came from the kitchen area, and it was strong enough to make Tony turn his head. Across some tables set further back from the stage was the open wicket for the kitchen. Boomer's shape moved past the window like some great, dark shape on the prowl.

"Over there," spoke Danny Boy.

Tony looked towards the stage. Tigh sat in pervert's row with his back to them, just straightening up in his chair as if he dropped something on the floor. The table he sat at was prepared for a meal. The rumours had Tigh coming up from lower New York as a heroin dealer, and somewhere along in his career, he came to Nova Scotia and decided he liked it. His employers offered him the post, and he took it. Some said he dealt in illegal weapons as well, but Tony never asked, and Tigh never offered. Boomer once told him to never ask questions that might lead to an early-morning meeting and a late-afternoon shit kicking. They hated doing that to good people.

"What the hell you waiting for?" Tigh called out gruffly, gesturing for him to approach. "You need a special invite or something?"

"Bacon smells good," Tony said as he drew closer, remembering the scant meal he had at home.

"Well, fuck, if it smells that good, we'll put some on for ya," Tigh said with a lazy wave of his hand. Tigh was like that. He talked with his hands. Great flourishes as if he were being constantly attacked by an imaginary swarm of black flies or mosquitoes. "Christ, you look like you're starving anyway."

Tony became aware of Danny standing behind him. He thought of his mom. What would she be eating this morning? He knew the answer.

"No thanks. I'm just here on business, Mr. Tigh. Then I'll be going. If you don't mind, that is," Tony said as he moved closer and to one side. He didn't like anyone the size of Danny standing behind him. More specifically, anyone bigger than him and able to lay him out unconscious with one punch.

Tigh regarded him for a second, nodding, "Well, have a seat, anyway. I want to talk with ya."

Tony did so, sitting on the one side where there wasn't any silverware set out. The table was set for three. All three bears sitting down to feast. Tigh himself was a big man but not on the scale of his bodyguards. He looked physical enough to send tingles of danger down a spine if the occasion called for it. He wore his hair short and spiked, and the slashes of grey around his temples made Tony wonder how much of his dark hair was dyed. Black eyes twinkled at him with all the mirth of needle pricks. A second unwanted chin had inflated itself under his first, but it did nothing to his brick jawline. Tigh wore a black sweater this morning, and he sat with his elbows on the table. At least he didn't wear any jewellery. He was the first dealer Tony had ever heard of that never drew any more attention to himself beyond the flash of his car, though rumour had it that he regularly travelled to the Philippines during the darkest, coldest period of January.

All that and he was supposed to be good to his employees.

But if you pissed him off...

"Sure about the food? BOOMER! Put on extra for Tony here. He looks like he's been chewing on his belt or something."

"Really, Mr. Tigh," Tony folded his hands over his stomach as he sat. "I have to get going. No offence meant. I just came to settle up."

Tigh studied him for a moment with a stoic eye. He slowly nodded. "I should do the same I guess. Not eat anything that is. But Boom is just too good in the kitchen. I'd go out and kill a pig if he was going to do it up." He paused then as if he were about to blow a bubble. "Do it like you, too. Like you did Badger. You use a bat or something?"

Danny hauled out the chair and sat down across from Tony. He flipped a napkin onto his lap. A lazy *"told you so"* expression came over his face and disappeared.

Tony didn't like the way his stomach was knotting up. He told himself it was breakfast. "I don't know what you're talking about, Mr. Tigh."

"I'm talking about Badger. The Badger I sent you out to kick the shit out of to remind him who he works for. The same Badger that is now in the hospital being put back together again with everything 'cept Scotch tape and Velcro. That jar your memory any? You do remember old Badge, don't cha? He'll be lucky if he remembers you. Hell, he'll be lucky if he's ever able to chew his own food again from what I understand. A job a little too well done, methinks."

There was a glint in his eyes that was neither humorous nor threatening. Curious perhaps. He wanted an answer as to why this one job had been completed with such enthusiasm. The fingers of his right hand tickled the handle of his table knife. Tony noticed the table knife was a much sharper variety than the regular silverware. He kept quiet, trying not to bite on the corners of his mouth or do anything that might be interpreted as being nervous.

"Look, Mr. Tigh, I did what you wanted me to do and nothing extra. I tapped Badger a few times and that was all. When I left him, he was more than able to walk home or to a hospital, which I told him to do. I didn't do anything else. You told me not to do anything heavy. I had a knife at his throat, but that was it. It was only there until he understood what I had to tell him. On your behalf, that is," he finished, a little too exasperated. He couldn't help himself.

Tigh continued watching him. He watched him hard, and Tony became distinctly aware that this was a man he did not want to have words with. Across from him, Danny leaned back in his chair, making the joints creak. Beyond that, bacon grease snapped and crackled from the kitchen.

And Tigh continued to stare, unblinking. When a barely audible grunt emitted from his throat, Tony wasn't sure if it was one of understanding or damnation. The man's fingers were still on the knife's handle, and Tony was trying hard to appear unconcerned. He had no reason to be concerned, dammit! He had only *terrorized* the pusher! He had only scared him into thinking he might kill him. Tony had built up a quiet reputation around town that he would off someone if he *had* to, but in reality, he didn't kill people, and he certainly didn't *almost* kill people. He could only fake it. The real deal just wasn't in him.

Tigh leaned back in his own chair and sighed heavily. "How many jobs have you done for me, Tony?"

He couldn't remember off hand. He shrugged. "More than a dozen. Maybe two."

"And you've always done me right, too. That's why I keep you on. There aren't too many soldiers out there I can rely on beyond these two bastards." He tossed his head in Danny Boy's direction. "That's why I'm going to give you a reminder here and now and not a warning. I *think* I believe you." Tigh's finger came up like a schoolmaster's when Tony hitched his breath to protest. He kept quiet, and Tigh went on, his finger drawing kanji characters in the air. "The truth will come out anyway when Badger regains consciousness. Then I'll ask him. But I'm sure what you tell me is what happened, and Christ knows Badger's pissed off enough folks for some of them to take a shot at him eventually. Be a coincidence if it just happened the same night you talked to him. And maybe someone came by, saw him down and decided to clean up. But I'll tell you anyway, don't get to liking your license to kick ass too much. That understood? If you do, I hafta revoke it. I don't want anyone in my organization going fucking Old Yeller on me. Puzzles the shit outta me when someone does."

"I didn't do any—"

"Hey," Tigh suddenly cut in, "you give me a chance to preach here, okay? What's this shit you said about a knife? Did I say use a knife? Huh? I listened to your fucking fable, and now you listen to my law. Corporate law. This covers anyone working under me, and I don't care if it's fucking Paul Bunyan over here," he said, his hand finally off the knife and waving at Danny Boy, "so you just be quiet for a second, alright? I don't think a second is too goddamn much of your precious time. Am I right?"

Tony averted his eyes, took in the black lights of the stage, noting the timber-frame ceiling for the first time. He felt the heat rush into his cheeks and neck. "Yes, Mr. Tigh."

"That's better," Tigh told him. "Now, Tony," he started in again but his tone a degree cooler. "You are a valued employee. And as far as I can tell, you are telling me the straight facts, and that's good. And you came here this morning. That's another point in your favour. In my experience, guys that know they've done wrong do not walk into my place with a smile on their face. Not that you were smiling when you came in, but you get my point. That kinda shit happens in the movies, but I haven't seen it yet. But next time you do a job for me, you keep what I said in mind okay? Else I hafta put you through law school. More specifically, a *window* of the law school. Okay?"

"Okay Mr. Tigh," Tony said in a low voice. He was being chewed out for someone else's handiwork. He knew what he did to Badger. Didn't he?

"Good, then," Tigh leaned in. His fingers did a violent rap on the surface of the table. "All I needed to hear. And on top of that . . ."

Tigh reached inside his jacket and pulled out a wad of bills that made Tony's balls draw themselves up. Five brown hundreds were peeled off and snapped to him. There was plenty more left.

"Last night's fee. Thank you."

Tony nodded and took the money. It made Tigh glad. He needed people like Tony around, and he appreciated the service the man provided. He hoped there would not be a repeat of last night's incident. Tigh needed pushers as well. Good ones. Badger was good, but he just got confused and needed to be straightened out. But not demolished.

Tony could see that the man was putting on a face. He could smell Tigh's uncertainty, and he wanted him to swear that it wasn't him that put Badger in the hospital. But the discussion was over, and you did not reopen old discussions with Mr. Tigh. Tony knew this morning's episode was going to bother him for the rest of the day. The only outside hope he had of clearing his name was Badger's talking. Tony rested his thoughts on that one probability and held on.

Breakfast landed in the middle of the table.

"Served," Boomer exclaimed mightily, removing his hands from the platter of food. Fresh bacon and hash browns interested Tony's senses and woke his stomach.

"Goddammit man, you took your time this morning," Danny said smiling, reaching for a fork and a plate. "Smells good, though."

"Looks good, too," Tigh added, shovelling scrambled eggs onto his plate from a yellow hill.

"Never fucking believe what happened this morning," Boomer said. "In Saint John. Guy was a driving a little Le Car, eh? You know those little dinkies with the lawnmower engine?"

"They still make those?" Tigh asked.

Boomer grunted. "Apparently so. So, anyway, the thing was run over by some bus last night. Head on collision. Twenty people involved on the damn TCH."

Danny looked up from his food, chewing contentedly on a mouth full of bacon, and wondered where his partner was going with the story.

"They all die?" Tigh said, licking bacon grease off his fingers.

"Nobody. That's the freaky part. Both drivers were crushed, but they were hauled off to the hospital. I mean *crushed*, man. Even the bus driver got it when he went over the car. I guess he lost it, flipped, went over into the other lane where the oncoming traffic started slamming into him. Cars were flipping and flying in Saint John, man! Twenty people in the pile up, litres of blood all over the place, arms and legs pinched off! Can you believe it? Phenomenal!" Boomer was obviously in heaven.

"Enuff of that. I'm eating here," Tigh warned him. "I can take the movie shit but not the real stuff. And not this early in the morning and *not* over breakfast."

Tony held on, feeling the money in his fist and very much aware of it. He was very much aware of the food on the table. His stomach whined.

"But isn't that the shit?" Boomer went on, muscular shoulders heaving. "Not one of them fuckers cacked. Odds of that happening must be next to nothing! I mean, Jesus! One bastard was mashed into his car, and his shit came out like he was a tube of Colgate! And there were a fuckload of others that'll be wearing plaster for the next couple of months! I mean—*whoa!!*"

Tigh did not share his employee's enthusiasm. His features did light up after having a mouthful of bacon. He nodded at the chef.

"You like?" Boomer asked him. "I did them in flour, eh. Makes the bacon crispier."

"You can never leave here, Boom," Tigh answered and reached for his coffee.

"I'll be leaving now, Mr. Tigh." Tony saw his chance.

"You going *now*?" Tigh asked. A fragment of bacon shot forth and landed on the table.

"Yeah," Tony said, ignoring the faux pas, "I think so." He pushed back his chair.

"Sure you don't want any?" Boomer gestured at the pile of food. Tony shook his head and mouthed a silent 'No'.

"Where's the toast Boom?" Danny asked between rotations of his jaw.

"Fuck. Forgot," Boomer said and got up, streaking for the kitchen.

"Bring some of your mom's jam, too, eh!" Tigh called out after him. He then settled back on Tony. "You got any plans for today?"

Tony froze. "No. Well I hafta do a few things . . ." His mother appeared in his mind, hanging on to that last bit of life she had, measured out in IV drips and morphine. A visit to the chemo ward every now again. A stocking cap to hide her baldness. Tony never thought of going bald before, but seeing a woman go bald, the pity he felt cut him to his core.

Tigh grunted. "Check in with me a little later, okay? A day or two. I may have some work for you to do. Some straight bouncing work. Danny's got a date it seems."

Danny's face smacked and chomped and shaped into a tight smile. His eyes brightened for a moment and became dreamy again.

"It'll keep you outta trouble anyway," Tigh finished.

"I can't find the jam!" Boomer bawled out from the kitchen. Something rattled and plastic crashed to the floor. "Shit!"

"Look in the fridge," Tigh told him.

"Did. It ain't—Oh. I got it."

Tigh grunted and worked at some bacon in his molars with his tongue. He regarded Tony. "And watch yourself, too, eh."

"Watch myself?" Tony asked, wary puzzlement on his face.

"Badger has people," Tigh's voice rattled from his breakfast, and he coughed into a fist. "Close people, okay? People that don't work for me and I have no control over. That's all I'm saying. Just watch yourself for the next couple of days. If they find out you were the one that put the beating on Badger, well . . ."

Tony rolled his eyes and took a deep steadying breath. He wanted to scream his innocence at the man. Instead, he focused on the bare concrete floor. Tigh took the time to speak again.

"Yeah, well, you were the last one in contact with him, okay, so they may want to talk to you. They might not wait for Badger to come out of his coma. Hell, I'll be watching out for myself. I was the one that put you onto the man in the first place."

"Mr. Tigh," Tony could no longer contain himself, "I didn't hurt him that bad. I didn't put him in the hospital."

Boomer could be heard swearing again in the kitchen.

"Well," Tigh said, "if and when Badger wakes up, we'll know the truth, won't we? I'm sure he'll ID whoever it was that did him. And I'm positive he'll want payback. That boy can be bloody when he wants to. My only concern is if his clan decides to start something before he wakes. It's very . . . what's the word I want Danny?"

"Volatile," the man supplied in between scooping up eggs.

"Volatile," Tigh sighed. He paused for a moment and then realized that his bacon was cooling. He shovelled a forkful into his mouth and chewed thoughtfully for a bit. "Blood demands blood. Just sayin', 'Be careful'. That's all."

Tony got up from the table as if it were a poker game gone bad. Believe him or not, Tigh did have a point. He would indeed be careful from here on in. For the next few days at least. He didn't know Badger had a crew, should have expected it. He fought back the urge to swear. He was positive no one had seen him that night, but sometimes events and people could be stitched together if the right questions were asked. Badger was in a coma? The information did nothing for Tony's conscience, but a dull throb of hope began in his gut. It would be a good thing if the pusher woke up soon.

Boomer came back with a plate stacked high with toast.

"Where's the whole wheat?" Danny asked him.

"Out. This'll have to do," the plate was put on the table.

"I don't know why you are so gawddamn particular about bread. I can't taste a difference. Bread's bread if you ask me," Tigh muttered.

"Wheat's better for you," Boomer informed him. "Cleans you out. Like a deep scrub for your colon. Gets out all the red meat. You know red meat can stay in your colon for up to six months?"

"You don't be thinking about my colon," Tigh warned him, scooping what looked to be blueberry jam out of an unlabelled mason jar. "One thought I don't need is that. And I don't give a shit about red meat. Even if it stays in my ass for a fuckin' year. Wait, that didn't sound right. Well, anyway, you call me, Tony. Wednesday is when I'll be needing you."

Tony nodded and left the master and his Dobermans to their breakfast. He had forgotten about his own stomach momentarily. Tigh's reprimand had shrunk it. Then the thing growled loud and long like the rigging of some ancient galley adrift on a very big sea. Tony paid it no mind. He was going to visit his mother.

CHAPTER 5

Outside the hospital, Tony jammed his Mustang into a parking spot on the first try. Getting out of the car, he closed and locked his door, looking this way and that, remembering Tigh's warning. He had a fistful of paper-wrapped flowers, which one of Tigh's hundreds paid for, white and yellow mostly. No red. Tony didn't care for red. He remembered his 'Bite Me' ball cap and cursed. His mom wouldn't care for that. He went back to the car, unlocked the door, tossed the cap inside and locked the door again. Once upon a time, such sensitivities would not have bothered him. Things were different now.

St. Mary's was one of the older hospitals in Halifax, and it showed. The outer concrete blocks were a brownish yellow and begged for new paint. Cracks showed in the surface, and the windows were coated in a late winter frost. Steam issued from the roof from unseen vents and Tony momentarily thought of hot coal in the middle of a snow drift. Pigeons fluttered in and about the eight stories, disappearing into hidden nests. That was great. With Tony's luck, one of the little flying rats would probably shit on his car. He walked across the lot, projecting dirty glares at the pigeons' roost and vowing unholy revenge on the little bastards if any took a shit on the beast. He made his way to the visitors' entrance, not noticing the other people passing through the doors. He hated the hospital. Supposed most people did. He hated seeing the hurt. It was always the hurt you saw, always waiting. He never saw anyone leaving with a smile on their face, and he had visited this place on many occasions in the last year.

One year?

It had been three years since his mother had discovered the lump in her breast. They removed the breast quickly enough. But it took one week for the doctors to discover the rest. It was a shocking case of cancer, they said. The disease had started in her breast and eventually dug into both her lungs. They slowed down the advance with chemotherapy, but the disease was in both lungs and stubborn. It was supposed to be two years for Miss Levin at the most, and an unpleasant two years. That was three years ago. Elizabeth Levin, widow for four years after her husband's car accident, entered the hospital's cancer ward and stayed there, her body playing out the endgame with the disease. Then, the cancer got impatient, probably pissed at being slowed down by modern medicine, and went for her stomach. It wasn't satisfied with robbing her of her ability to breathe without assistance. It wanted more.

The doctors' latest prognosis was weeks. Lung cancer victims are fortunate to last a year. Stomach cancer victims are even more so. Yet Elizabeth Levin defied the odds. She hung on a year after the attack on her stomach. And Tony counted the long days, thinking thoughts he couldn't help thinking. Helpless to only watch the losing battle waged within his mother's body. He wanted to remember his mother as the young woman that reared him up in Dartmouth. He didn't want the image that resided in his mind these days. All he could picture now was a woman, so pitifully small, tied to her bed in a mesh of sterile plastic and handmade quilts of the brightest Christmas red and green. She used to be a hundred and fifty pounds packed onto a five foot four frame.

Now she was seventy five.

He did not want to think of her flesh stretched out like tight plastic on a stick frame. He didn't want to see the bruises in her skin where the nurses stuck their needles, often missing her shriveled veins and having to try again and again. Of how her eyes would sometimes squeeze shut with a machine aided breath. Of how she would ask him what he ate for breakfast, and how that simple question would make his eyes red with tears. How he dearly wanted her to be able to eat . . . anything.

Tony only wanted . . .

Only . . .

A horn blared at him, jerking him back to reality.

"Watch yerself!" the man roared at him from a car. Tony realized that he had just walked in front of some dude's old Impala. He quickly got out of the path of the moving car and went up to the automated doors. A minute later he was in an elevator and thankful for it. He hated the hospital sounds. The cacophony of coughs, the baby cries, and the dead voices calling out missing names. He hated the impatient looks the nurses gave him, no doubt hoping their shifts would pass quickly without any real emergency. Tony would hate to work in a hospital. He only put people there.

A pneumonectomy. That's what the doctors thought would do the trick. But the removal of her left lung did not save her right one from the cancer metastasizing—that lung looked like a scorched battlefield—and, gawd, were the doctors surprised to find the little bastards honeycombing her colon, and talking to her son about the blood in her stool was not something Elizabeth would have at the supper table.

The pain was something else that Tony did not want to think about. It was hard for him to see his mother in agony. He thought of his childhood, and of her reading books to him at night just before sleep, helping him clean his ears, or hearing that wind chime laugh when she was watching something funny on TV while folding freshly dried clothes. Those memories were now under a web of surgical tape and plastic. The cherished laugh replaced by the steady beeping of machines. She had had enough biopsies for someone to construct their own goddamn Frankenstein.

A year. No more.

Three years later.

His mom could be spiteful at times, Tony knew. Part of him was proud of her fight. She was like a big-league wrestler, beaten down, knocked out on her feet, and yet, when she felt her shoulders pinned to the mat, and heard the referee's distant count, somewhere found the guts to flip out from under the cancer. She found the strength to fight back and to hang on for another count of three. She wasn't going down easy. Not Elizabeth Levin.

The doors opened and his thoughts vanished. He ignored the other people in the cancer ward. He ignored the sounds of pain around him. Tony made his way down a corridor to his mother's private room. It was expensive, but her insurance covered it. And then she was before him. The TV hanging above her, glaring. She wasn't watching its snowy reception. Her eyes were shut, and there was a full drip dangling above her head. Tony went to her side and sat there, simply watching her, his face scowling, concerned. He dealt with the anger of finding out about her non-resuscitation request. He obviously wasn't consulted in that decision. It hurt, but he knew, and God knew, it was for the unhappy best. It could be any day now. Any moment.

That made Tony smile just a little. His mom had made it through a thirty man Battle Royale. She was a bullfighter. A tiny bullfighter. Gazing at her cocooned in her bed, he again found it impossible that she lasted this long with so much weight gone. There was a stocking cap on her bald head. A guy could lose his hair, and that was fine by Tony, but he abhorred seeing women lose their hair. It was bad enough that they bled every month. His mom had nothing left on her own crown now, and he felt his throat tighten. She always had a lustrous, jet mane which bounced when she walked. And she had been proud of it.

Now, Tony knew that all that remained of that hair were a few scant ribbons.

All the while he watched her, she did not register his presence.

Her face was mottled and haggard. Her cheeks were nonexistent, mere cavities draped in the barest skin. The room smelled of some alien disinfectant, and pictures of rugged coastlines and sweeping forests covered each wall. A vase of flowers, bright and fresh, stood on the bedside table. He wished he could move her back to her own bed, in her own home. Put the magical healing powers of home to the most trying of tests. When he was a boy and was frightened in the night, he slept between his parents. He was just fine nudged in between the protective hearts of his mother and father, knowing he was safe. He wished he could do something like that now.

He wished she would just get up.

"Tony."

His mother spoke.

"What are you looking at?" she said in a soft voice, the voice of one just waking up.

Her son smiled and felt his throat constrict tighter. He clutched at her hand. She gave the barest of squeezes back and, with whatever strength she still possessed, smiled at her son.

CHAPTER 6

One floor up, and a dozen doors to the right of Tony's mother's room, the Stickman sat beside his still friend of ten years. Badger was in bad shape, the doctors had said so, but the Stickman didn't need to hear a professional doctor to tell him that. His own eyes could plainly see that his friend was seriously fucked up. A broken jaw needed time to heal, but a crushed jaw needed ages. As did crushed shins, kneecaps, femurs, forearms, fingers, toes, and shoulders. The things not broken merely looked like shit. The fact that the man was still alive was a thing of awe and pity. Apparently, when they brought him in, his body was a horrific black with the amount of internal bleeding.

The Stickman looked at the casting job done by the hospital. It looked like a good one. He was told that the steel and the wires were in there to help the healing. They would replace what refused to do so. Stickman did not want to be around when Badger had to eat, however. The absence of teeth was one thing, but imagining him trying to slurp up blender-shredded soup through *that* mess of a mouth turned the Stickman's guts. Badger was just fucking lucky he was in a coma. If he ever did regain consciousness, it would only be for a second to realize that he had been fucked up, and then he would probably pass out again. The pain would pull him under like a harbor riptide on a moonless night.

If it were anyone else, the Stickman would've laughed at the thought. But this was the Badge.

This was blood.

Not by actual blood but by deed. Badger had helped the Stickman back when he was still Crawford Ryan, a delinquent youth from the isle of Newfoundland trying to get away from the rugged hopelessness of that place. He had left his father in the tiny town of Heart's Delight. He did not care what happened to the abusive drunk. He never looked back once he left the hole of his youth. Hitchhiking his way across the island with a pocketful of money he scabbed from his father and his ancient blue piggy bank, he got his short and skinny ass to Halifax. Once there, he became a haunt of the back streets between Hollis and Barrington, asking for loonies or quarters or even a fucking nickel—who needs a nickel, right? Begging was set in his mind as a career, but he made a short living of it. The soup truck that appeared on Hollis Street every day gave him at least one meal a day, and there were a few shelters around that supplied a bed for a night. No, life wasn't so bad, and if there was something he really needed, there was always money to be made doing an assortment of jobs—hand and blow included when he really needed the money. It wasn't something that he liked doing, but he was *surviving*. He was on his *own*.

Then Badger appeared. Brother Badger in his brown leather jacket, grinning from ear to ear in that scalding, shit-eating grin that he had. The kind that could make a person feel stupid even if they were only asking for the time. Badger had got him working as a courier. Got him out of the odd job business and gave him enough money to actually rent a small hole in the slums of Quinnpool. To a seventeen year old runaway, it was a free kick to the mouth of the world. It was the chance that the Stickman was waiting for. He didn't care what he was delivering. He never asked. It was for money, and after a while, it was for Badger. And Badger was good to him. He gave him cash, bought him CDs, meals, and even some furniture for his apartment. He would bring over flicks to watch on a secondhand Sanyo DVD player (once he even brought him some pornos) and got him his first leather coat for his birthday. Badger was cool.

Then, the fall had come. When he was twenty-one, Stickman had been arrested and prosecuted on drug charges. It was a shitty deal, and Stickman knew right away he shouldn't have done time for a first offence. The prosecution knew otherwise and convinced the judge that an example had to be made of the young man. He was going to Saskatchewan if he didn't give the RCMP the name of his supplier. Stickman had watched enough movies to know that the cops really wanted Badger and that the promise of prison was just to light the fire under his ass and to make him give his brother up. Stickman laughed in their faces. He kept silent.

And stayed silent for four years.

The Stickman had seen movies about being in prison and decided whoever the hell had written such untruths should be sent to one, themselves. There were no A-list actors there with Brad-Pitt looks, but there were plenty of mean bastards. It wasn't an R version like he remembered seeing on DVD, but it was hard core enough to make him become as paranoid as four years in prison will make a person. He was sent to the Shuckfort Provincial Correctional Facility in the flat province of Saskatchewan, where he was told a person could see an escaped con run away for days if one ever got out. Stickman believed it. After living most of his life by the water and surrounded by hills and forests, the plainscape where the land met the horizon in an almost perfect line totally weirded him out. He was raped on several occasions in his first year, to the point where his asshole burned when the soap hit it. His stick frame and small size made him a natural bitch for some of the hardcore types in jail. He submitted to survive.

Reflecting back, Stickman knew that he was meat back then.

But he had time to change things. And Badger did not forget him. It took him a year to show, but he finally did. The cops had tried to take him down but screwed up, or at least according to Badger, they had. They had him in a tight spot, and he told the Stickman the same, but they couldn't make their charges stick, and Badger had fucked them over gleefully. Now, it was payback time, and Badger called in some favors. One of them was the protection granted by one Gerald Burr. Burr had actually raped the Stickman in the shower with his gang, but that was in the past once he found out that the Stick wasn't just another stupid Newf from the Rock and that he was actually tight with Badger. After that, Burr was a guardian and even something of a mentor. Burr kept folks off the Stickman's back. And helped him weight train.

There was always one thing which little Crawford always wished to do, and that was to lift concrete and steel. There, in C-wing of Shuckfort, he had all the time, free weights, square meals, and, above all, *hate* to grunt, bark, and puke his own weight in the bench press. And then beyond. When Badger started getting him juice—steroids—Crawford's frame exploded to nearly two hundred pounds by the time he had served his sentence.

People might have scoffed at the mention of steroids as an enhancement, but it was funny that no one did so to Stickman's face. In the last year, Crawford was gone, and the Stickman was hammered into existence. The nickname, which was given to him in the first few months of his imprisonment, became a whisper often filled with fear. It happened shortly after he broke Burr's neck in his nineteen inch biceps, just after Burr had taught him a choke hold. Burr made the stupid mistake of wanting and trusting the Stickman to practice on him and believing that the rape of long ago was forgotten. Stickman remembered how Burr tapped his forearm for release and only got increased pressure. Stickman could not see the man's face, but he imagined Burr was thinking the man wasn't so stupid after all. Right up until the vertebrae in his neck snapped.

Crawford had become a monster, and the Stickman a thing of prison legend. No one dared cross the man for fear of seeing the huge, shit-eating grin and award-winning sympathy act. If you owed the Stickman money in the can, you paid as soon as you could, and *always* before the due date. After the death of Burr (where the authorities could find no witnesses to testify against the Stickman) most of the inmates walked carefully around the man. One Freddie Austin had borrowed cigarettes from him, and even ordered in a couple of Playboys from the Stickman's outside connection, yet when delivery time came, Freddie had simply smiled and shrugged, promising the Stick to pay up with interest in a week. Stickman had smiled back. He would allow the doubt. A week later, when he revisited Freddie and saw his smile, a condescending smile someone would give another person unaware of being run around, the Stickman simply smiled back again and offered another week.

Freddie was dead the next day. Slipped on some soap was the word. Broke his neck. The puzzling thing was that both of the man's testicles were evidently crushed in the same mishap.

The word became borrow freely from the Stickman, but only if you could pay him with certainty. Go ahead and order some fun from him. But when the time came to pay, pay the man. Have his fee ready when he came to collect, otherwise he would smile at you if you didn't, and tell you not to worry; he would return next week to settle up. If he told you not to worry, it meant he would see you when there were no witnesses around, and the settling would be made in blood, to the sound of bones and joints being twisted in directions that defied the original design.

Shuckfort took in a kid and released a killer. He went into the service of Badger. Badger had liked what prison had done to his boy. The Stickman became his terminator. His private cop. His angel of everlasting medieval agony if someone became ballsy enough to fuck around with him. Badger, himself, was scared shitless of the thing coming out of the cage, unsure of whether or not the man would remember who his employer was. Stickman did, though, and convinced Badger to further fund the man's training. He hired "Sensei" Bill Dutton, the local Kempo karate instructor who was also a rare disciple of Black Dragon Kung Fu and a fan of MMA. That all meant squat to Badger, but he was quick enough to have his killer trained by the best Halifax had to offer.

And the Stickman learned.

Badger never asked about the training. Never asked about the bruises on the man's arms or legs or face. There was no point as he could never fathom what Sensei Bill imparted upon the Stickman. He just paid for his soldier's lessons and kept him close by. It was comical at times as Badger was a full head higher. If the Stickman walked ahead of the other, it was as if a brick wall was protecting Badger's lower body. He praised his enforcer constantly, for in truth he was hugely impressed with the young man and the way he was turning out.

The Stickman owed it all to Badger. He was a father to him. He took care of the man's needs and all he asked for in return was to have his back. To cover his ass. Mind his interests. The Stickman looked down at the smashed form of his father ... who would be unluckier still if he regained consciousness. He studied the casts holding him together and pursed his lips. He couldn't even hold his father's hand because it was fucking crushed. So, the Stickman gripped the metal railings of the hospital bed with both hands and squeezed.

Badger had gone alone that night. He didn't have to, but he told the Stickman to get out and get laid that weekend. Have a good time. Meet some woman at the Palace and talk her up. Badger never mentioned what his plans were, and Stickman thought he was going to merely stay home and watch the Discovery Channel. He never questioned the wisdom of his general.

Now Badger was here.

And generals died in bed.

Stickman's knuckles were white now, and he had taken to twisting his hands slowly around the bars.

Badger was laughing in his mind the night before this happened. Badger was still able to laugh then. If he laughed now, the man would probably pass out from the pain of having a shattered jaw and cheekbones.

The Stickman's hands tightened further. A knuckle made dull popping noise. A second knuckle did the same, the sound punctuating the stillness of the room.

The hospital was the second to last place he had called. If Badger hadn't been here, the police would've been the last he would have called. But he found Badger in the hospital. He would have found the man eventually if the man was anywhere in Halifax. Or Nova Scotia for that matter. He would have found him.

The door opened, and a young nurse stepped through it. She had been on the job for all of five years now and had seen her share of sad stories: affection, hope and despair, and she always continued with her job. But the look she received from the man hovering over her patient's bed stopped her dead in her tracks. That one look spoke louder than any scream produced over a jacked-up, ultra-expensive sound system. Her breath caught in her throat, and she squeaked out an apology as she backed her ass up in reverse out the way she came. She would have slammed the door on her way if not for the pistons mounted above the frame to prevent such disturbances.

Stickman was glad she got the message. He might've done something stupid if she had come any closer ... like trading the railing for the softness of her neck, the hardness of the bone inside it, and continuing his slow twisting squeeze until her fucking eyes popped out. That would have been cool, at least, because now the Stickman found himself in the role of avenger. He would find out who had done this to the man he owed so much to.

A third knuckle cracked. Stickman grimaced upon hearing the noise. His jaw clenched. Impossibly, his grip increased.

He would find the perps. Anywhere between here and hell itself and under every rock along the way, he would search. And when he found the cocksuckers...

Another one of his knuckles creaked, and the Stickman let his breath out in a hiss like a locomotive of old just starting to pick up momentum.

CHAPTER 7

It was 5:00 when Tony left his mother's side and the hospital. The walk back to his car would not be remembered, not with his mind in such a numb state from hearing his mom's voice. The sight of her in his head, a husk of tight skin drawn over a skeleton. He wanted to cry, so he lowered his eyes, adjusting the peak of his hat just in case he did. Her eyes were dim and glassy like old marbles, and yet she knew where she was and why even though she was on enough pain killers to stun a herd of cattle. Unnatural strength, the doctors marveled in sorrow-filled tones. What they didn't say was that they wanted her to go as quickly as Tony did. To give up the fight and just . . . go.

It was 6:35 by the time he got back to his apartment. He had stopped off at the Atlantic Food warehouse and picked up two quick bags of groceries. It was a miracle that Tony managed to buy anything at all, but he forced himself with the reluctance of a person about to shove a needle into his eye.

Tony stowed the food away into cupboards, closed them when he was finished and cooked nothing. He probably would only eat in the morning when his body began gnawing on its own ribs for something to nourish itself with. To eat so soon after seeing his mother would fill him with a terrible sense of betrayal. His thoughts whirled around his head, and he flopped down on the sofa, placing both of his hands over his eyes as tears came and his breath hitched in his chest.

Outside of his apartment, across a narrow street and standing still against a lamp post that did not come on with the arrival of darkness, were two figures dressed in heavy winter clothes. They had followed their man since the hospital and waited for him while he was in the supermarket. They knew which apartment he lived in from the flickering life of lights as he entered his home. They said nothing as snow fell around them in huge lazy fluffs. They watched, unmoving, and if someone were to peer in their direction from any of the apartments, the onlooker would not be certain if they were even looking at the building. But Tony did not check, would not even look out the window, and the two strangers watched in silence. Somewhere in the city, a motor revved and moved away. Once the sound faded, there was little else except the hush of falling snow covering the concrete in white, making those fortunate enough think of Christmases past.

Darkness within darkness. The watchers did not stir, even after the light in Levin's apartment winked out, and the silence following midnight settled in. They did not move until morning.

At 10:00 p.m. exactly, with Suzie performing her very physical routine in front of a comatose scattering of patrons, Danny started thinking of getting home and getting a decent night's sleep for a change. The beginning of the week was always dead, but Tigh kept his office open. Sometimes the pay, which was pretty decent considering his and Boomer's workload, just didn't make up for the boredom.

The lights jetted over the tongue of a stage, and Suzie arched her back along its length, pushing her bare pelvis forward to give the onlookers in pervert row an eye-popping view of her clean shaven goods.

Danny idly scratched his cheek and glanced towards Tigh's office door. His boss was watching a hockey game in there, Detroit and Toronto. Boomer made his way back from behind the kitchen counter with his hands holding a full tray of munchies and a couple of cans of Moosehead. Boomer threw a look in Danny's direction and mouthed, "Thirty minutes," before giving him a maniacal grin and disappearing into the office.

"Fuck," Danny mouthed back after the big man had gone. Boomer said thirty, but they both knew how a period of hockey sometimes went. His eyes went over the empty seats, ignoring the half dozen or so full ones. He straightened up against the doorway. Dead night. Danny yawned into his hand and did not remove it until he had finished. Suzie wouldn't appreciate it if she caught him yawning during her act. She wouldn't understand. Danny thought she was a pretty girl. Beautiful breasts. But after seeing the same show night after night, it just didn't do anything for him anymore. Even her ample handfuls failed to interest him tonight. Danny wondered if she was feeling the drag of the winter, too. Suzie was a pro, but even she was straining to keep her face pouted and hungry for the customers. Tigh had some university students coming in Thursday night, apparently for a private audition. That would be interesting to see for all of a minute. They were usually too nervous to drop their drawers and shake their ass, or too sloshed to get it into proper gear. Tigh didn't want drunken dancers on his stage. But every now and again, he came across some raw talent. You just never knew.

Danny yawned again into his paw of a hand and cursed himself. He was too damn jaded for this business.

The outside door opened, and even though the inner door was shut, Danny felt the stab of cold air rushing in through the cracks. He'd have to put some insulating stripping down there somewhere. He didn't need a half dozen strippers complaining to him about how cold it was getting. He moved through a side opening which was the coat room. Tigh didn't charge a formal entry fee, but he did charge a $3 coat hanging fee, whether you had one or not. The face standing before the bouncer was a familiar one, and he declined to have his faded denim jacket checked but paid the fee anyway to enter. Danny allowed him, searching his memory for a name.

He remembered.

Danny opened the inner door. "Stickman," he muttered and dipped his head.

The Stickman nodded back. His eyes went immediately to the stage and Suzie's white ass jutting into the air.

"Here for the show?" Danny asked. He didn't care for the little big man in the least, and he sure as hell didn't like the way he was sizing up Suzie's pie. There was something grotesque in the way the Stickman regarded women, especially one on a stage. And Danny remembered how the girls would talk about how fucking creepy the Stickman was when he was watching. It was like he was jerking off right there without the meat and the motion. The women were right. They usually were.

"Hey."

Stickman blinked at him. "Wha?" he asked with a thick Newfoundland accent.

"What cha want?" Danny asked with a glare.

"'Ere t'see Mr. Tigh," came the reply, but his eyes were still on Suzie. Suzie felt the stare and noted him. Her eyes flicked away as if she had seen a bum begging for change.

"Ee in?" Stickman asked, an Exxon smile spreading across his features. He was liking Suzie a little too much for Danny's tastes.

"I didn't hear of an appointment with Mr. Tigh," Danny informed him with a hard look.

"Don't 'ave one, brudder," Stickman said in a distant voice. "Figured I could get in an' see da man. Find out oo bagged Badger y'know. Ee's inna 'ospital. Better off dead if'n ye ask I."

Suddenly Stickman was all Danny's. Suzie's package on the stage was forgotten.

"Da least ee could do I figures," Stickman said with a smile that would have made a shark give pause. Danny did not comment. The silence between the two thudded with the heady beat of Suzie's selected music, and each boom matched the quickening of Danny's heart.

"Don't cha tink?" Stickman said, and his smile abruptly disappeared. He sensed wrongness here. He could see it in the bouncer's obvious attempt to keep his expression neutral, and in doing so, he gave everything away. And the big man was taking too long to answer him. Stickman wondered why that was so. He read in an online article that liars sometimes took their time answering. They would take their time in collecting their thoughts and would not stare you straight in the eye like Danny Boy was now doing.

"Badge's done a shitload of work for da the big man, y'know. Maybe jus' as much as I's done for Badge. Like to talk to 'im, is all, 'im bein' the boss an' all." Stickman kept his unblinking eyes on the bouncer before him. He bunched up his shoulders and felt something *pop*. Danny's lack of eye contact was beginning to make him wonder about things. Stickman knew the man's reputation. There weren't too many around that didn't know of Danny and Boomer, the Twin Towers of Power, and Stickman didn't want to start anything on only a suspicion. Not yet, anyway.

Danny turned around and started for the door Stickman knew to be Tigh's office. This was more like it, and he began to follow when Danny whirled on him with an open palm raised. "Wait here," he ordered in a low voice.

"Sure ting, by," Stickman answered, as Newfoundlanders usually pronounce *boy*, meant in the same context as a casual *buddy*. "Sure ting." He felt gladness for the break in the impasse and returned to ogling the stripper on the stage. That glazed look returned to Stickman's face.

Lord above, Danny did not care for this little shit, and he made sure there were a few chairs and tables between him and the Stickman before turning his back. He knew the Newf's reputation, and he didn't like it. The Stickman was dirty in a way Danny couldn't quite put his finger on but suspected it was in the way a dog could turn on you in a flash the minute you stop feeding him like some kind of wild animal some people insisted on keeping as pets. He did not like the man, and he didn't like the way the Newf kept him on guard. You just couldn't trust freaks. He hoped Suzie wouldn't give him shit later for leaving the Stickman unwatched.

Stickman continued watching Suzie grind out her act on the stage that looked like a tongue. He figured that women probably had to watch their footing up there. His lips were moistened now and slightly parted. His tongue darted to and fro. He wondered if those breasts enjoyed being bitten—playfully, of course. He thought about Suzie having her arms outstretched and tied down to his bench press just like Christ on the cross. She probably had already done that before, though, so if Stickman offered up his cock to her gasping mouth while she was in that predicament, there'd be no hesitation to suck him off. Yeah, he was sure she had been tied up once or twice in her life. So, what could he do to liven things up for her?

On the stage, Suzie had no idea that the fucking song was as long as this. She had just stripped off her panties and covered herself with a blanket, which she would use to lay her back on as she spread out across the stage. The stage got to be as cold as fucking ice in the wintertime. She flicked her long legs up and out to keep the boys in perverts' row happy, but she knew she was being watched by him. Being watched in that way that made every dancer shiver and wish for the bouncers to throw the maggot out on his ass.

On her back, she closed her eyes and cupped both of her breasts and vowed to have both Danny and Boomer walk her to her car after work.

Stickman was wondering where he could buy some copper wire when Danny beckoned him over to where he stood before Tigh's door. His face was unreadable as the Stickman approached. Stickman took the opportunity to stare straight up Suzie's flexing crotch when the angle was at its best. That was one picture he would save in his mind for later when he was in the shower.

"Hold on here." Danny told him went inside.

Stickman could do just that, turning back to Suzie's act.

CHAPTER 8

Tigh's office was a small rectangular box filled with a leather sofa that ran against the far wall. A matching leather recliner was just to the left of the door, opposite the sofa and in front of Mr. Tigh's desk. At a glance, it looked like an office out of one those high rises in Purdy's Wharf, one of the classier business towers in Halifax. The desk was made of redwood and shone like slick ice in the light. A desk organizer was on top with prickly pens and pencils waiting to be used. Tigh was on the couch, while Boomer was in the recliner. Both men were hunkered over a coffee table covered with an open pizza box, the remains of a meat lover's extra-large, and a growing row of empty beer bottles. Both men were chewing and watching the wall mounted thirty eight inch widescreen LCD TV. Neither man seemed to notice Danny.

"That guy's got shit in his eyes," Boomer blasted over a half-eaten slab of pizza. "I saw him the other night ref'in' a game between LA and Washington."

Tigh nodded emphatically, chomping on his own and keeping his eyes on the hockey game. "Who won?"

"Washington. Good game, too. Anyways, he practically let Lindeman get speared right in from of the net. Cheap shit. I bet he's suckin' off the Bettman just to stay in the league."

"Gary?" Danny interrupted when he saw the chance. Tigh looked up from the TV, still chewing.

"You decided on who's going to work for me on Wednesday?"

"I'll give Levin a call and see if he's interested." A small piece of something flew from Tigh's mouth. "If he's not, I'll get Hillman. He's good."

Boomer straightened. "Not Roy Hillman, Gary?"

"Yeah, Roy Hillman. What's wrong with him? He's okay, ain't he?"

"Can't stand the guy," Boomer declared. "The man talks to his dick."

"What?" Tigh breathed in disbelief, wondering why Boomer always brought up such subjects while he was eating. "Fuck off, he does not."

"He does," Boomer nodded. "Swear to God. Ask Danny. The man talks to his dick. His own meat."

"Calls it 'Leonard,'" Danny said quietly.

"See," Boomer exclaimed, pointing a finger at Tigh. "A sick pup if'n you ask me. I was in the can one night last year when he was filling in, and I heard him come in. He was taking a leak, and I heard him talking to his pecker. 'C'mon out Leonard,' he's goin', 'help me out here.' Hell, his fuckin' bug eyes are freaky enough without having to listen to that. Talking to his own gear!"

Tigh almost choked on his pizza. He managed to control himself and swallowed. "You ain't going to be in the can with the man for Christ's sake. You'll be makin' your regular rounds."

"Yeah, but just knowin' he does that sorta creeps me out, y'know? I mean, jokin' only that's fine, but he didn't know I was in there until I flushed the can," Boomer finished in a conspirator's tone.

"What a dude does in private is not my concern," Tigh levelled at his bouncer, his eyes shifting to the hockey game.

"That's just it! It was in *public*! It was in the washroom, Gary! *Our* washroom! I bet he was just getting ready to grease ol' Leo up and have at 'im when I sent my chocolate torps out to sea."

"I'm eating here!" Tigh grated and regarded the man with wide incensed eyes.

"What? I can talk about a guy's dick and that doesn't bother you? But I mention I was squeezing some pipe, and you get all offended?" Boomer fired back, struggling not to be embarrassed by this breach of protocol.

"I don't wanna hear about dicks or shit or cock-sucking or *anything!*"

"Who said anything about cock-smoking?" Boomer threw out.

Tigh fixed the man with a look. "Boomer. Fuck off. Now. I mean it."

Disgruntled, Boomer switched his attention back to the game. "What about Lorne then?"

"Adam Lorne?" Tigh almost went into a spasm. "You want to work with *that* deranged perv? Jesus Christ, I wouldn't let that fuck walk my fuckin' dog in the *rain*, Boom! That guy makes chickens nervous. I don't need the knots in my tables punched out by permafuck. He's all over the girls. You forget the shit we went through last time? Half the reason I don't have him in here no more. All I need is another revolt by the girls." Tigh chewed thoughtfully for a moment. "Still, I don't have to pay Lorne to work . . ."

"And he doesn't talk to his dick," Boomer added.

"Surprised the man still has a dick. If he does, it must be hangin' on by a thread of meat. Fuck. Now, you got me grossin' *myself* out." Tigh threw his pizza down.

"Gary?" Danny asked from the door.

"What?" Tigh looked up. Danny gestured to the closed door.

"Right," Tigh muttered and wiped his face with his hand. "So, you won't work with Hillman?"

Boomer rolled his eyes.

"Why do you have to be so goddamn particular?" Tigh demanded. "Jesus Christ! It's only one night! Alright. I'm calling in the House and I don't wanna hear not one goddamn word about him. Be fucking professional."

That made Boomer feel just great. He shook his head slowly and let out a defeated sigh. He had traded in the whacked out Hillman and the living dick for the war child. House wasn't the kind of man you brought in for crowd control. He was the one you called in when you had a bad case of squirrels under your roof. He was a mark or two above Levin for the fact that the man had gotten too much of the taste for hurting others, lusted too much after the power of dispensing pain. Boomer thought the man was borderline wacko.

Maybe even psycho.

"What cha want Danny?" Tigh asked through a fresh mouth of pizza.

"Stickman here to see you," Danny answered, and gnawed lightly on the inside of his mouth.

"Stickman?"

"Yeah."

"He's *here?*"

Danny indicated the door.

"*Outside?*" Tigh demanded and got a solemn nod.

"Wants to talk," Danny reported.

Boomer watched Tigh stew where he sat for a moment. "Does he know who . . . wait. No. He knows shit. He wouldn't be here if he knew anything. He's just curious, is all." Tigh leaned in, chewing mightily on the pizza in his hand. He devoured the last of the food in three big, dog-like snaps. He took a sip of beer. Danny waited. Boomer waited. None of them cared for Badger's enforcer. The Stickman was simply bad meat in the sun.

"Aw, fuckit! Send the boy in," Tigh said, slap wiping his hands. "Let's have a chat. Period's over now, anyway. Hell, maybe I'll ask him to work on Wednesday."

The bouncers exchanged looks, and Tigh laughed out loud.

The Stickman was getting into Suzie's act, wondering where she got her music, when he heard the laugh from inside the door. It was loud and hoarse, and sounded like someone had a throat full of snot. Then the sound was gone, drowned out by the techno. The laugh made him lose all interest in Suzie. A scowl cut across Stickman's features. He slowly turned to glare at the door closed to him. What the fuck was so funny? If it was so goddamn funny, why wasn't he in on the joke? Were they laughing at him? Were they laughing at Badger lying near death in the fucking hospital? Stickman ground his jaw, and a vein popped into view on his forehead. They aren't laughing now, he noted, and the image of men behind the door grinning impishly formed in his mind. They *knew* he was out here, so what was so goddamn *funny*? Christ that bothered him. It set his nerves on edge when he heard someone laughing, and he didn't know if he was the brunt of the joke or not. Heat flowed into his cheeks. He remembered laughs like that from when he was in prison. Even when he was in high school, when his breath stunk because he never brought a toothbrush and his body reeked of sweat because there weren't any showers for the teenage boys after a punishing PE class. There were never any showers back then, and he had never had the common sense to bring any deodorant. That embarrassment, especially when he was reminded of his teenage weakness, was always quick to turn into anger. Raw and red and ready to get bloody if need be.

He focused on the door, ears tuning out the techno, concentration on full blast, searching, probing for an echo of the laughter he just heard. Stickman waited.

A song ended. Loonies and toonies pelted the stage. Suzie left the stage as fast as possible, letting Lou, the money man, come onto the stage to collect it all. She did not look in the Stickman's direction. That was all she needed. A surge of relief flowed through Suzie's frame as she got out of sight. God, how this job attracted the weird ones!

When the door opened and Danny leaned out, he was surprised to see the little shit not two feet from the threshold, grinning at him.

"Ev'ryting ok?" Stickman asked.

There was something greasy in the man's smile. It made Danny hesitate.

"'Kay?" Stickman asked again. It was the same face the Stickman wore before he snapped Burr's neck in the shower, goddamn the man's fucking soul.

Danny nodded and motioned for the man to enter, stepping aside as he did. His senses were alert now. He would be standing just to the side of this little snake. Just in case. He put his own "everything's cool" sleepy look on, as if he only gotten an hour's worth the night before. If the Stickman tried anything remotely brutish in there, he'd find his Newf ass sailing through fucking space and time.

"Tanks, buddy," Stickman grinned friendly enough and carefully stepped around the larger man, his hand at his sides, in plain sight. Nice and smooth.

Nothing hidden. But Stickman was thinking only of the training Sensei Bill had given him, and the way a finger strike to a throat could fuck a man up, if not kill him.

Once inside, he took a quick look around. Mr. Tigh had a nice little place. He nodded respectfully to both Tigh and Boomer, and saw the TV.

"Who's playin'?" he asked in a tone that almost convinced Boomer that the man could've been an actor.

"Edmonton and Boston," Tigh reported, sucking in his breath. "Boston's ahead by one."

"Ah, good," the Stickman said.

"Don't like the Oilers?"

"Can't stand 'em. Gets on me nerves. Likes d'Predators, meself."

"Nashville?" Tigh actually smiled. "Why in hell you like those guys? You like the underdog or something? They import their ice you know."

"Likes the name," Stickman answered. "Tons maggot."

Boomer arched an eyebrow. Tigh himself did not know what the man meant. Danny completed closing the door with the barest of clicks and put his back to it. Boomer leaned back in his chair, cool as black ice on a highway. His eyes flicked back and forth between the set and the Stickman.

"So," Tigh began, "what can I do for you, my little Newf?"

"Y' knows I's from the Rock?"

Tigh smiled coolly. "No one speaks English quite like the Newfies."

"I didn't know they spoke English out there," Boomer threw in and chuckled. Tigh snorted a laugh. Danny tensed for war.

But the Stickman only grinned. "Sounds like sometin', eh? I knows. 'Ave trouble understandin' meself sometimes."

Tigh nodded. The man was alright so far. "Well, you got a long wait for your Predators to get to the cup. Hell, if you told me there would one day be a hockey team in fucking Nashville of all places, I would have blown my gut from laughing. Right up there with purple elephants and pygmies in the NBA."

"And Newfs that speak English," Boomer threw in with an impish smile at Tigh. Tigh shook his head at the bouncer. Boomer could get on a roll at times. He didn't want to laugh anymore in front of the Newf. The man might start taking things personally. But a smile leaked out all the same.

Apparently not caring anyway, the Stickman only grinned wider. "That's a good one. Mr. Tigh, I really don't want to take up too much of yer time. Youse look busy," he gestured to the pizza. "I just wanted to know if'n ye heard anyting about Badger. Ee's in the hospital, y'know?"

Tigh did not hesitate. "Yeah, I know. Word gets around. Damn shame, too. Badger was a good head. Thick sometimes but a good head."

"Gave good head, too," Boomer stated with a sly look at his boss.

The Stickman chuckled and shook his head. Boomer felt uneasy. There was something he just did not fucking like about this little bastard. "*Youse* knows about *dat*, does yas?" he said, mocking the Newfoundlander's accent. "*Tree udder tings*, too."

The Stickman's hands came up in surrender, apparently not offended in the least. His smile widened, and he winked at Boomer. The bouncer ignored him.

From behind uninterested eyes, klaxons were ringing. Danny did not think Gary was going to reveal anything, but *already* he informed the Stick about knowing Badger was in the hospital.

Stickman pressed on. "Did ye 'appen to 'ear who did it?"

Tigh's face hardened for a moment. "I'm not going to bullshit you, Stickman. I never do, understand? That's why *my* boss likes me so much. I tell it like it is. And how it will be . . . everything being square and equal-like. You know what I'm saying here?"

His features soft and smiling, Stickman nodded his head ever so gentle-like, to show that he did so indeed understand. His hands went behind his back. Danny watched him clasp his hands together. In yin to the Stickman's yang, Danny let his own hands dangle at his sides. Just in case.

"Listen. I ordered the touchup on Badge," Tigh announced, speaking with his hands again and posturing them at his visitor as if he were trying to make him magically disappear. But the Stickman remained where he was and merely nodded his understanding again. His eyes blinked to the TV and back again to Tigh, his attention suddenly full of the lieutenant of Halifax's underworld.

"Badger was skimming on me, and I found out. You can believe I was surprised. I liked Badger. Still do. He's a good head like I said. But . . ." he let the word tick in the air for several seconds, and the Stickman counted every one, "he was taking a little more from me than he was entitled to. And he was makin' his own private sales on the side. Admittedly, only small ones," Tigh shrugged, "but what if he decided to take that one big chunk one day? Eh? Where would that leave me? That'd leave me with a big problem and a busy day getting together a fuckin' squad to hunt down his treacherous ass. Am I clear here? If he thought I wasn't noticing a pinch here and there. If he thought I was STUPID?!"

Even Boomer blinked at the sudden shout. Stickman cocked his head to the side, loosening up his neck.

"If he thought," Tigh carried on, "I was a total dolt, I'm sure he would have done just that. Probably wondered how I got to where I was today for being such a fuck up with the numbers. Do you see where I'm going with all of this? I liked Badge. I liked the way he did business for me. He has some pretty lucrative contacts for us. I was faced with the problem of having one of my valued own being led astray. Into temptation. Needing rehab. I ordered the touchup, Stickman. But *only* a touchup. I wanted Badger alive but marked for the errors of his way. And I wanted him to know that though he still worked for me, all of *any* fuckin' brownie points he had before he started this shit were gone. Used up. They bought him his life. Understand?"

In the absence of voice, the hockey game's commentators' lively banter filled the room. The shriek of a whistle. Someone called a delayed penalty.

Stickman, so slowly that his face might have weighed a ton, moved his chin up and down. Tigh liked that. At least the boy could think. He had heard rumors about this one, some of them incredible, some even coming from Danny and Boomer, and in all he understood that the Stickman was like a son to Badger. A devoted, unquestioning son. Newfoundlanders weren't the brightest of the lot, in his opinion. Hard maybe, but not bright. Badger was good with people though. Charismatic. A regular Don King. People like that were too valuable to be executed. It was better to try and reform their asses. And Tigh had the authority to make it so.

"But," Stickman said, quietly, cutting through the background sportscast, "Ee's in da intensive ward, Mr. Tigh." The emotion in the man's voice was striking. It was like a ten-year-old boy wondering why his parents couldn't afford to buy him the latest game platform when all the other kids had one. "'Is arms and legs are broken. Even 'is jaw. 'Is . . . *face*."

"I heard he was a mess," Tigh granted.

"Ee's a pap smear, Mr. Tigh," Stickman reported, his voice just a hint higher now. "The doctors say someting about trauma and such and 'ow it's a good ting ee's out cuz if ee *were* conscious, the pain would just shut 'is brain down."

Boomer shifted uncomfortably in his seat. The leather creaked.

"Don't y'tink the touchup was a little bit much?" Stickman asked.

"I do." Tigh replied in a solemn voice. "I've looked into the matter already. You don't have to worry about it."

"I mean like, somebody fuckin' *liked* kickin' the 'oly shit outta Badger. Someone liked it altogedder too damn much. Someone laid a fuckin' *drain pipe* across 'is face."

"I've heard about it all already," Tigh's voice rose up and over the Stickman's words, drowning it out. "I heard about it, and I'm looking into it. Like I said, I only wanted Badger bruised and not in pieces. I still want him to work for me."

Stickman's lips were drawn tight. "Well, someone took it upon demselves to do a little extra work. If it's okay with ye, Mr. Tigh, I'd like to know who did the job."

There was no hesitation. Tigh was firm. "I'm not telling you that."

Stickman's eyes fluttered and the expression on his face was one of pain. Tigh was once again reminded of a child who would have to stay home while others went off to the carnival. Tigh expected him to say something more. A protest perhaps. But nothing else came from Badger's enforcer.

"I'm looking after it," Tigh finally said when the silence became too uncomfortable. "Safe to say that the guy who did it won't be working for me again. Ever. I can't afford having people running around who hear one set of orders and go into action under another set. It's a screw up waiting to happen, and I don't let those things happen if I can help it. Understand?"

Reluctantly, Stickman nodded that he did.

"*And* you understand why Badger was punished?"

Stickman nodded again. His eyes were clear and staring and fully coherent by Tigh's judgment.

"And you understand I had nothing to do with the extent of the beating? I only gave the order for a scare and a couple of bruises. Not to be squeezed into soup."

And again Badger's enforcer nodded understanding.

"And you understand that I will take care of Badger's assailant pretty much the same way that Badger was done? An eye for an eye, right? That's my thinking."

For a moment, both Danny and Boomer sensed that the Stickman was going to go for it. They felt it. It was a change in the air, a feeling they mutually experienced together and talked about when they weren't on the front. It was from years of being bouncers. They could smell the trouble coming. There was badness just about to happen, something *verboten*. This little Newf was going to try something.

And then . . . the Stickman nodded, much easier this time, obviously realizing that things would indeed work out for the best. On the TV, the period was over and the replays showed the scoring highlights. The commentators were spewing forth statistics that Stickman did not hear.

"Tanks fer yer time, Mr. Tigh," Stickman said finally. "I'll go now."

Tigh didn't bother to stand. "You busy this Wednesday?"

"No."

"Wanna work? Just one night. Danny here has a hot date, you see, and I need another man to work the floor. Roughly seven or eight hours."

The man considered it for a moment but declined in the end. "Tanks anyway, Mr. Tigh. Maybe another time. I'd be too caught up in the action up on the stage anyways."

"You get used to it," Tigh said dismissively.

"Not in one night, sar," the Stickman grinned slyly. Neither Danny nor Boomer liked that rusty-razor smile. Tigh didn't like the look of it either. It stayed his tongue, which was going to ask the man to reconsider.

"Enjoy the game, Mr. Tigh," Stickman said and departed, respectfully easing around Danny's bulk and finding the door. He did not look back as he slowly closed it behind him.

The three men left inside were quiet for a moment before Tigh indicated to check the door. The huge man left and returned shortly.

"He's gone. Janice saw him leave," Danny reported.

"Fucking freak!" Boomer declared. "And why the hell did you offer him Wednesday night, Gary? I damned near shit myself when you did that!"

"I could smell it," Tigh said reproachfully, "but, look, it was a sign of faith, okay? A gesture of goodwill. I wanted him to know that I have nothing against him personally. Only business. 'S'all business. He seemed manageable enough anyway. Not at all what you two jokers told me about. Didya hear him call me mister the whole time he was here? Fucking polite for a stupid Newf."

"He's a freak, Gary," Boomer countered. "I only saw a guy that knew if he tried anything in here he'd be tasting his own balls in seconds. We'd have his ass in a fucking sling. And you know something else? I don't believe the face he had on for a second, and neither should you. That dog was wearing a muzzle."

"Where'd you hear that from?" Tigh wanted to know.

"From a book I'm reading."

"Oh. Any good? That's a cool line. I'm gonna remember that."

"It's not a bad book either, it's about this housewife, eh, and she's got this abusive shit of a husband, see. The kind you wanna just smash until yer arm drops and anyway, well—"

"I'll borrow it later," Tigh cut him off.

Danny stopped listening to the rest of the conversation. His head replayed the whole scene from the moment the Stickman walked into the office. Danny had to agree that the man had been wearing a face while he was here. Perhaps it was the three of them that kept him in line, but he somehow doubted it. The Stickman was a basket case, but it occurred to Danny he had half a brain, too. A part of Danny suddenly hoped the man did not. That would make him more than just dangerous. The Stickman was as creepy as a goddamn flying cockroach.

CHAPTER 9

On Tuesday morning, Tony was on the golf greens, again. He was down on all fours and close enough to feel the artificial fuzz prickle his cheek. A putter was in his hand. The sun burned overhead, perhaps thirty-two degrees, but Tony didn't feel a thing. He was as comfortable as a lizard here in the sun. And he was comfortable that he could sink his ball with a single putt. One putt and the prize was his. He couldn't remember what the prize was, but he knew it was good. Real good. Fucking *great*, in fact. All he had to do was sink this one miserable ball. Do this one shot from roughly one centimetre out. The ball was perched right on the edge of the hole, and just like his fucking girlfriend, it wouldn't get up off its fat ass and go down. Tony's brow creased. Where did that thought come from? He focused. All he had to do was *tap* the little fucker. Just tap it. And all would be fine in the world. Chocolate, milk, and honey.

He straightened up, dusted off, and leaned in. He looked to his watching fans. Nobody on the side-lines. Fuck 'em. It wasn't important anyway. Not in this match. He was sure the shot was being televised. They would see it. They would see him make it.

He bunched his shoulders and took a breath. He grasped the putter, being careful not to strangle the annoying piece of shit. He would *pull* the ball into the hole, not push. Pull! That's how he envisioned every shot. Pulled into the hole. Into a black hole.

Pulled.

And in this case, all he had to do was tap it to get things rolling.

He flexed, hunched over, and lined up the putter with the ball. Excitement fired through him but failed to overwhelm. His control was a thing of Zen. His focus, a laser. He gazed from the putter to the ball. It was a yellow one.

Laughter.

Tony shut out the ridiculing sound as easily as one would close a door. Laughter again.

"Not going to make it with that, you fucking dolt!"

The taunt made Tony jerk his head up. One the side-lines, stood a faceless figure dressed in white pants and a red shirt. A white sweater hung about the figure's shoulders. Tony could not see the face.

"You need a putter!" the voice insisted and broke in uproarious laughter.

I have a put—Tony balked. He no longer had a putter. He was holding a fencing rapier.

"What the hell is this?" he exclaimed. He didn't care in the least what his sponsors might think of his language. "What the *fuck*? I can't play with this!"

"You can't play with that either!" the voice rang out and giggled like a ten year old girl. Tony did not want to look down, but he did, the fencing foil still in his grip. When he looked up, a treeless land surrounded him. All was empty. Where was his caddy? Where were his fans?

"I can't play like this!"

"I agree with you," the figure said. There was light blazing past his head as if he were standing in front of a searchlight.

"They told me if I made the shot I'd get everything! I can't make the shot like this! With this!"

"Oh really?" the figure asked. Lord almighty, Tony wanted to see this guy's face. "And you believed them?"

"Yeah, well . . ."

"Hm. So, you can't make the shot then?"

Scowling, Tony looked back to the hole. Right on the cusp of the drop. Right on the edge.

"Nope."

"Then try another way," the figure sounded impatient.

That was a thought. How? "This is fucking stupid! Fucking impossible!"

They changed the rules on him right in the middle of the game. Bastards. Didn't even bother to tell him. Cock-nobbling *bastards!* If they gave him shit later, he would throw this entire episode in their faces. His thoughts raged for a moment. He finally dropped to his knees and hunkered over, reversing the foil and attempting to use the thing like a pool cue stick. It was awkward but useable. The ball was practically *in* the hole anyway. All he had to do was give it some love. Just a nudge.

Laughter, again.

"Will you, please, SHUT THE FUCK UP!" Tony roared.

"What kind of game you playing there, Elmo?"

"Elmo?" Tony straightened up on his knees. "You retarded or something?"

Then, Tony saw something he didn't quite understand but took perfectly in stride.

The hole was missing.

He blinked. It was still gone.

"Where's the goddamn hole?" he cursed. The figure was also gone. The grass around the flat green has risen up, creating a billowing wave like one might see if they were diving off a vibrant green coral reef.

"Still there," the voice said from somewhere in front of Tony. "Just not as big as you remembered it."

"This is fucked," Tony snarled and threw away the fencing foil, which was now a length of rope.

And Tony sensed the smile around the words "As is finding me . . ."

He woke up. Blackness. He was in bed. The door to the living room was open. A greyness that was not quite light marked the far wall. Then, he heard the giggle and the hair on the back on his neck stood up, and a shiver went through him. He strained to see something, anything. The giggle, again, soft like a child's, coming closer in the darkness at the foot of his bed. Oh, Jesus! "Who's there?" Tony demanded.

He got a giggle back.

Then the claws grabbed his ankles.

Tony woke up with a gasp and a sensation of falling. The rapping on his door became louder. Tony tore his face out of his pillow and sucked in air, hoping to God above he was awake this time. The pounding got louder.

"Yeah, YEAH! ALRIGHT!" he fumbled with the caul of his sheets before tearing himself away from his bed. He kicked the clutching sheets back. He stood and yawned mightily. It was black in the room. And it was cold. The air immediately chilled his bare flesh, bringing out goose bumps.

Tony took a step forward and crunched the smallest toe on his right foot into his dresser. He grimaced with pain and quietly doubled over, crashing off the corner of his bed and landing halfway out of his bedroom's doorway.

The knocking stopped. Silence listened.

"Don't fucking tell me you're gone, *now?*" Tony groaned, lying on his back. His toe felt as if he had driven it somewhere into the back of his foot. What good was that small toe anyway? He couldn't think of a purpose for that dangling piece of meat other than a brief appetizer for a dog. If there were a generic pain button on the entire human body, it was the small toe. He flexed it and grimaced again, taking in a huge gulp of air. It wasn't so bad. It wasn't broken, which was nice to know given how early in the morning it was.

Or was it still late at night?

Slowly, Tony sat up, hands before him. He groped for the wall, letting his fingers feel the way, and found his baseball clock. It blinked 5:38 a.m. Tony blinked back. It couldn't be that early. Who the hell was banging on his door this early?

His mouth suddenly went dry. It was the hospital. It was his mother. Oh, Jesus...

Tony rose to his feet and speed-limped to the living room. He grabbed his shirt and blue jeans from the sofa where he had thrown them down the night before.

"I'm coming," he hollered through the fabric of his white t-shirt. Red lettering swore that 'we don't have a split personality disorder.'

"I'm coming," he repeated. "Just wait."

Sockless, he reached his outer door and clawed at the three locks. Metal snapped on metal like a shotgun being readied. He pulled it inwards with a jerk.

"Good morning, Mr. Levin," greeted one of the pair of strangers standing at his door. Tony blinked at the pleasantry. The two men were dressed for winter, standing there bundled from head to toe in heavy charcoal black trench coats, toques and thick checked neck scarves. The one who had spoken regarded Tony with a "you ok?" look for the briefest of moments before smiling. He had a gash of a mouth with almost no visible lips. The man's face was hairless, smooth-looking and barren of any facial lines. It must have been a trick of the light. The man's face looked doll-like, but he was obviously older than Tony. He possessed almond-shaped eyes of a smoky grey, like the fog enveloping the city on spring days.

"Are you alright?" the man asked. The mouth hooked up on one side in a bad smile. "We heard the noise."

A nod towards his partner. His partner appeared every bit as hairless and erased of facial lines, but his head was shaped funny. It was oval and long as if it had been pulled out of a monkey's ass. The dude must've been teased fiercely as a kid with a head like that. But the man's eyes were different. His eyes were black. Tony took back his previous thought. There was danger about the man that Tony could sense. He suspected that if there were any teasing directed in football head's direction, there would not be enough plaster to mould the body cast needed for the offender.

It was much too early in the morning to have to deal with these two visitors.

"Mr. Levin?"

"Yeah," Tony said after a wary pause.

"May we come in?"

"Why?" despite the earlier pain, the word came out partially dunked in sleep. But Tony was waking up fast. And the pain was quickly subsiding. Tony was tough that way.

"Who the hell are you guys? And why the hell are you pounding on my door this time in the morning? You sure as hell better not be Jehovah's Witnesses, cuz I'll bounce both your asses to the curb and smile all the way."

The visitor with the football head straightened up and glared at Tony as he took one step forward. Tony instantly took one step back as if his spine were gripped by the tailbone and yanked on. The fear he suddenly felt was as reflexive as a gag on a piece of food in his windpipe. The man advanced three more steps into the apartment, and Tony matched him as if they were in an unrehearsed dance. Tony had his hands behind him, feeling the air for something, anything to stop his retreat. *And why was he retreating anyway?*

"Stop that," the first man spoke sharply, and the invader complied at once. He turned about slowly, his features twisting into an annoyed, questioning mask.

"Not that way," the first man continued with a derisive tilt of his head.

The second man stared at his companion for a few seconds. Then, the message understood, he arched his back again as if he were attempting to burst out of his current frame and regarded Tony anew. There was a quiet understanding in those black eyes.

"I'm terribly sorry about this, Mr. Levin," the first man said, and meant it. "My companion here is much more direct than need be. He doesn't have, or should I say, isn't used to small talk. He prefers being straight up, I believe you might say. Frank. Raw. Having you by your short and curlies . . ."

Tony backed up another step, placing his old faded coffee table between himself and the pair of necromaniacs in his apartment.

"Your short and curlies . . . ?" he said, expecting the worst at any moment.

"I'm different," the first man explained. "An opposite. Yin to his Yang. And I would be ever so heartened if you would allow us some time to talk."

The second man quickly sized up the apartment and screwed up his face in distaste.

"You guys get out now, or I'll start screaming for the cops."

The second man studied Tony again. This time his features morphed into amusement. Tony did not like that in the least. "Mr. Levin," First Guy said affably, "if you draw breath to scream, it will die in your throat."

The second guy took a step towards Tony behind the coffee table.

"JESUS!" Tony exploded and jumped backwards. His back cracked against the glass of his balcony window door. Second Guy halted his advance, but Tony still felt the aura of menace about him. It was the childhood fear of the bogeyman just behind the closet door or of an adult walking through an unseen spider's web with their mouth wide open. Or something grabbing you by the ankles in a dream.

Tony's hands came up in surrender. "Sure, come on in, then. Close the door too, eh? But you," he stabbed a finger in the direction of Second Guy. "Don't come anywhere near me, okay? You do, and I'll break your fucking head open. Got it?"

While he made his threat Tony took in everything within grabbing distance which could be a potential weapon to use against the two men. All he spotted was a phone book. The smirk on Second Guy's features was unmistakable. The black eyes narrowed in amusement in his pulled-from-a-monkey's-ass shaped head. Obviously, of the three people in the room, two of them were not so concerned with the threat.

"Mr. Levin," the first guy began, "he couldn't physically hurt you even if he tried. I promise you that. It isn't his nature at all—ah." First Guy abruptly raked the toque from his head, revealing a full head of short, spiky grey hair. "This isn't how I wished to speak with you Mr. Levin. Not at all. And speak with you, I must. I hope you pay close attention to what I have to say, but you cannot do that if you are distraught by fear."

"You can take 'fear' and stick it up your shitter, buddy," Tony barked back at the First Guy, noting how the man's features crunched up in slight confusion. "I ain't afraid of you or—"

Second Guy again made the motion to move.

Just a feint.

It was more than enough.

"JESUS H CHRIST!" Tony roared and flung himself to one side. He tripped over the coffee table and crashed landed into his sofa. There he stayed, looking up at the Second Guy with an expression of pure chagrin. "Don't *do* that! *Fuck!*" The man was like a spider dancing up your bare spine. A bare straight blade against your throat. Tony's tongue froze in his mouth. His heart crashed in his chest as if he had been injected with pure adrenalin. Panic so raw gushed into him like a faucet turned on full force. Not since childhood had Tony felt such fear, and even then, he could not quite remember an experience to compare with the terror this freak was invoking just by taking a single step towards him. Perhaps it was some kind of pheromone?

"Mr. Levin," came the voice of reason. First Guy met his eyes. "Just take a deep breath. Relax. It will be easier on your nerves. We're here to discuss many things of business. You are a locator of people right? Missing persons?"

"Yeah, so?" Tony gulped down air. "You want me to find someone?" he continued to eye Second Guy and his freaky football shaped head. The man was content for the moment to stand guard it seemed. He was looking at various things in the room and Tony was briefly amused to see the man settle his attention on his discarded ball cap "Bite Me," hanging from a hook in the wall.

"Yes. Exactly," First Guy said. "An associate of ours decided to leave work unannounced for entirely unacceptable reasons. We have no idea as to his whereabouts but we do have resources to find him. You are one of those resources."

The man sat down on the sofa next to Tony. It squeaked with the new weight.

"And so, we are here to make an offer."

"Who told you about me?" Tony wanted to know, his eyes narrowing. The notion of entrapment blossomed in his head.

"Ah," First Guy peered at the worn chestnut surface of the nearby coffee table. "Word of mouth, I suppose."

"Look," Tony said, "I'm no private investigator awright? I'm more of a bounty hunting deal. And I ain't agreeing to nothing until you two give me a name. It says 'BITE ME' okay!"

A startled Second Guy jumped at the shout directed at him.

"Mr. Levin." First Guy implored. "You do have neighbours, I believe. And they would appreciate you lowering your voice."

"I'd appreciate you coming back around noon," Tony countered.

"I'm afraid we cannot. Every second, every microsecond, every *nanosecond* is precious to us. In fact, the length of time it will take me to convince you of your task ahead will be far too much to expend."

"Uh huh," Tony grunted. His fear was slacking off now, even though Second Guy was giving him dirty looks. Fuck him too. "Give me a name then. Who sent you to me?"

"I believe it was a Mr. Tigh," First Guy answered.

"Really?" Tony's mouth hung open and he caught a whiff of his own putrid morning breath. "You guys didn't just happen to access a file or something didya?"

First Guy's eyes flicked towards an old yellow clock on the television set. The glow in the dark hands told him it was 5:44.

"Well, how about it then?" Tony demanded. "It better be a good story too. Else what I said earlier 'bout the curb becomes fuckin' reality. Give you a can of whoop—"

The fear was back and it killed the words in his throat. Second Guy's eyes were hard and glaring and Tony felt the press of an unseen but pointed weight, like icicles, pushing slowly into his head. Tony squirmed, actually whimpered, and pushed himself back into the small sofa. His eyes fluttered like window blinds in a gale. Weight, cold and God so heavy, pressed into his heart and lungs and he felt his ribs bending inwards . . .

And then nothing.

Everything was gone and the breath rushed out of him as if he had just spent a torturous minute underwater. Exhaustion crashed down onto Tony's frame and he collapsed on the sofa, feebly eyeing First Guy like a dying fish. He was too spent to look in Second Guy's direction.

"My name's Mr. Tim," First Guy introduced himself. "And that is Mr. Freddy," he gestured with an open palm at Second Guy. "We want you to find one Mr. Augustus D. Franklin, a missing associate of ours. He's been missing for an eternity, it seems, and we need him back almost immediately."

"What's he to you?" Tony mouthed, now feeling as if he needed a whole year of Saturdays to recover from what he had just experienced. "Steal something? Fuck your wife? Your daughter? Both? What?"

Tim appeared to mull something over, gnawing at the inside corners of his mouth. Tony had seen this behaviour before. He was taking his time, getting his story straight. His grey almond eyes were staring and Tony thought he was about to be fed a line.

"Mr. Franklin is in a similar line of work as yourself, I guess you could say."

"Oh," Tony breathed out, regaining his strength. "I could say that. Well, thank you. Like me, you say. Wow."

"Yes," Tim stated, and gave a little knowing nod, as if he had just checked a map and knew exactly where he stood. "He is a locator of people. And you could say, he ... well ... he ..."

Tim held out his hands, "he takes them."

This last statement struck Tony as odd. He was becoming less and less fearful of Second Guy now, and he felt the strength returning to his body and mind. He chanced a furtive glance at Second Guy, who stood at ease, glowering back at him.

"You mean—what? He kills them?" Tony directed at Tim.

"Yes, he does that," Tim allowed. "All of that."

"He kills them," Tony repeated. "You don't sound so sure right now."

Tim hesitated. "Yes," he said, sounding weak. "Yes, he kills them. He is what you say, a professional."

"So, he's a hit man?"

"Yes. A hit man. A raw realer," Tim said as if for the first time. "A whacker. A man in black. He finds people, and he cleans their clocks. Puts a ... cap ... in their asses."

Tony rubbed his face in thought. He needed a shave. "So, you're looking for a guy who will find this hit man for you? Why?"

Tim's almond eyes caught him again and did not move. Greyness, like a winter mist in March, pricked with blackness. "We need him back. No one is doing his job right now. There is a lot of work backed up, and no one can do his . . . thing."

"You mean hits?" Tony felt as if he were supplying the words in this conversation. He didn't like that. It felt phony to him.

Tim nodded. "Yes, hits. Contracts. He hasn't been working recently, and we want to know why. We must know why. But first we need to find the man. And that's where you come into the picture. He must be found as soon as possible and returned to us or, at the very least, contact us when you find him, and we will come for him."

"So, you don't need this guy dead? I don't have to kill anyone. I don't do that, y'know."

A smile stretched across Tim's face and he gently shook his head. "No. You wouldn't kill him. Only find him. It's all we require of you. Only find him and let us know. Bring him to us, or we'll come to you."

You wouldn't kill him. Tony didn't hear a challenge in there. Just a bright-as-day truth. "Just find the guy."

Tim nodded.

"No rough stuff?"

Tim appeared uncertain. "Rough stuff?" he repeated.

"Yeah. You don't need him having anything broken as a lesson?"

"You mean *assaulted?*"

"Yeah, whatever, assaulted, straightened out, fucked up."

Again Tim smiled. "Really, I don't think . . ." and he trailed off. "No. Nothing like that. Defend yourself if need be, of course."

"Of course," Tony agreed. *Fuckin' right I'll defend myself.*

Tim's smile disappeared. "Mr. Levin, the man we want you to find is extremely dangerous. Extremely dangerous. He is the taker of life the likes I have never seen before nor do I expect ever to see again. I could tell you tales around a campfire that would make your eyes explode out of your head. He is . . . Death himself. Do not under any circumstances fight him. He is dangerous—much more than even my associate here—and if he discovers you are afoot, there is a very good chance he will make you regret it."

"He's that bad, huh?"

"Very bad. I can't put into words how bad."

"Badder than freak boy over there?"

"Much badder," Tim said in a serious tone. Second Guy shifted where he stood.

"That must piss you off," Tony said abruptly to Second Guy. "Knowing that there's a guy out there who could take your ass."

Second Guy's eyes became slits. His shoulders tensed.

"Fuck," Tony went on, liking the reaction and feeling pissy. "I'd bring the guy back for free if I could see that. I'd enjoy seein' your white ass getting stomped on. Your hit man could take this chump right?"

Tim's mouth opened but nothing came out.

"Well," Tony wanted to know. "He could, right? Don't feel bad if you embarrass your temple slave here. You can talk about it back in the car or truck or however the hell you two got here."

"I suppose," Tim admitted uncertainly. Second Guy's eyes flashed with insult.

"I have it now," Tony went on, "Mr. Dick here is quite the lad at scarin' the shit outta people, but he doesn't have a clue how to take care of any other business."

"Actually, he can." Tim found his voice and began defending his companion, "but we prefer not to. Fred here,"

"Fred," Tony repeated, a smile on his face. Tim froze as if he said something inappropriate.

"Tim and Fred are in my home this morning," Tony declared, not saying anything about how totally fake these names sounded. He pointed two fingers at Fred, causing the man to tense up again.

"Why don't you say something there, boy? You can't talk or something?" He then shifted targets and directed his next question at Tim, "How much?"

"Five thousand dollars."

Tony liked that number. "When do you need him?"

"As soon as possible."

"Does the man have a family?"

"No. He's all alone."

"That's too bad," Tony said and meant it. That obvious lead was scratched. "Where's he from?"

"Nowhere." Tim answered him with that same stare again.

"Nowhere?" Tony repeated.

Tim nodded.

"Well, how do you get in contact with him?"

"Cell phone," Tim answered.

"You contact your gun for hire by cell phone?" Tony rolled his eyes in disbelief. "Fuck man, anyone could be listening in!"

"We talk in code," Tim assured him, but Tony could tell by the man's face that he wasn't so certain.

"Well, that sounds like fun," Tony scathed. "Ever have any screw ups? You know, popped the wrong guy?"

That made Tim pause. "No. Not really."

"Why don't you call him on the phone now then?"

"He doesn't answer anymore."

"Does he have any enemies? Maybe a contract was taken out?"

"Possible," Tim acknowledged.

"Do you think?"

"No."

Tony pointed a finger at the man across from him. "Don't play around like that," he warned. It was hard enough to think as it was. "There's no one out there that would want to put old Augustus into the dirt?"

"Anyone who might have is, well, dead," Tim said honestly.

The admission made Tony hesitate. "What?"

"He's extremely effective, you see. A hundred percent kill ratio. Nobody has escaped him really. He waits until the time is absolutely perfect and then, well . . . I can't explain it much more than that, really. In fact, I hesitate in sending people after the man at all."

"Hold on, what do you mean 'people?'"

"You aren't the only one."

"How many more people?"

"That isn't really important, Mr. Levin. I will say my particular organization is world-wide. We have operatives everywhere that are currently engaged in this hunt. At least one for every major city. We like to employ the local talent when we can. But keep that to yourself. Classified, you see. Just be clear that we are utilizing every means available to find Mr. Franklin. He is one of us, and as a result, he is proving very skilled in disappearing."

"Where have you looked?"

"Everywhere."

"You can't have looked everywhere, Tim. You ain't found the man yet. You ain't looking in the right places. Or you are, but it's at the wrong time."

"Possibly," Tim admitted. "But time is running out. He must be located. And very, very soon. Mr. Fred?"

Fred straightened, holding his mitten covered hands in front of him.

"Would you find me something to drink, please? Something cold? Not milk though," then he spoke to Tony with an uncharacteristic wink. "I'm lactose intolerant, you see."

Fred went to the kitchen without a word and began moving things about. It was clear that Tim was the chief here and old, freak-assed Fred was the muscle.

"There's apple juice in the fridge," Tony called out.

Tim's face brightened. "That would be fine."

While they waited for the drink to arrive, Tony looked about his apartment and saw the little yellow clock on top of his little TV. The glow-in-the-dark hands pointed out that it was still 5:44. Tony thought about that for a moment and decided that the batteries must have died.

"I'm afraid I can't tell you much more about your quarry, Mr. Levin. He drives a black jeep though. Of that I'm positive."

"A jeep?"

"I hear it's good in the winter."

Fear returned with a coffee mug of apple juice. Tim took it with a gracious nod. He sniffed at the drink before tasting it. Then he fished inside a pocket on his winter coat and hauled out a Japanese Nokia cell phone. It was black and looked like an old Star Trek phaser. He offered it to Tony.

"If you press the number key and then 00, you have his number. If you press the number key and then 01, you will ring me. Understood?"

"No trouble," Tony said, taking the phone.

"Contact us when you find him. If I don't hear from you in three days, I will assume something has happened to you, and I'll have to recruit more agents. Understood?"

Tony nodded. "Why should anything happen to me?"

Tim's almond eyes peered at him over the rim of the coffee mug. "I don't know, Mr. Levin. But you are going after a very dangerous individual. And... we have lost contact with other agents working for us. And we suspect Mr. Franklin does not want to be found. He may have silenced agents getting close to him, but we aren't positive of that. In any case, some very good people have gone missing, and we don't know why."

"Maybe they weren't that good?" Tony said.

"Their reputations are as good as yours," Tim said, his voice rising slightly in amusement. "Regardless, find him as soon as you can."

"But you have no leads," Tony said. "So, I hope you don't expect me to pull a fucking rabbit outta my ass here. What do I have to work with here? A black jeep? A cell phone? I mean, don't you have a picture or something? What does his guy look like anyway?"

The mug went up as Tim finished his drink. He carefully placed it on the edge of the coffee table. He took a shallow breath, then looked past Tony and exhaled with a long, weary sigh.

"We don't know."

"You don't fucking *know?*"

"We never saw his face," Tim said weakly.

"You don't know," Tony repeated, not believing the lack of material he was going to be working with.

"It was never our way to meet face to face you understand," Tim explained patiently but in a guilty voice. "It was safer to keep our identities unknown in case something happened that could endanger the network."

"Well, shit! I hope you have cash now," Tony said, shaking his head, "It's gonna take some cash to start digging out information on this guy. I have no address, no family, no picture. I have a phone number and a fucking black jeep that's good in the winter."

"He told me that," Tim said quietly, "while on the phone once."

"I have squat," Tony exhaled.

"You have my gratitude," Tim informed him in a gracious sounding voice. But Tony kept his less than gracious feelings to himself.

"I'll need a weapon," he finally said.

Tim shook his head. "There'll be no need for one."

"No need?" Tony repeated. "What the fuck do you mean 'no need?' You're just after telling me that I'm after the fucking terminator who's probably responsible for all your other servants being cut down, and you expect me to go after him without a weapon?"

There was a silence then as Tim simply sat and stared at the empty mug before him. "I don't think you'll need one at all, Mr. Levin. You would be only tempting fate. I do know that he doesn't use one at all."

"Well, how's he been killin' off your people?"

"I never said he was. I said our operatives had disappeared while trying to locate him. I happen to think they aren't dead," Tim suddenly became apprehensive. "Merely rendered inactive. Somehow."

"Uh-huh." *Inactive, my ass*, Tony thought. "You have any objections to me having a weapon then?"

"What kind?" Tim wanted to know.

"What the fuck do you mean 'what kind?'" Tony barked, causing the man across from him to flinch. "A fuckin' weapon! An honest to Christ elephant gun if I can get my fucking hands on one! Whatever I can dig up on short notice. Look. Don't worry, I won't kill your guy. Maybe mess him up a little, but I won't kill him."

Out of the corner of his eye, Tony saw Fred smile. The teeth revealed were pearl white and feral looking. Teeth for tearing things.

"What?" Tony turned on him. Fred shook his head, obviously amused about something.

"You only have to find the man and contact us," Tim said.

"I can, y'know," Tony directed at Fred, wanting to wipe that smirk off the man's face. "Especially if he operates like you. Fuckin' especially if he looks like you."

The smile on Fred's face broadened. Alien smile. Tony matched it with the monsters from those *Alien* movies. Big, fucking alien, shit-ass grin.

"Mr. Levin, please," Tim implored. "Ignore him. He isn't the one you want. Mr. Franklin is out there, and I hope you find him. If you must have a weapon, then do so if it'll make you feel better, but I'll stress again that you are only required to find the man and call us when you do."

Tony took a deep breath. No, sir. He did not care for Fred with the football-shaped skull. Not in the least. If he had had his bat in hand, there would have been most certainly a ball game and a short one at that.

"Fine. I'll use this," Tony held up the Nokia phone. "I'll do it. I'll find the guy for ya. For five thousand. I'll find him, and I'll call you. When do you want me to start?"

"Immediately," Tim looked immensely relived. That suited Tony just fine, and he took another look at his clock.

It remained 5:44.

"I'll need gas money too," Tony stated as an afterthought. "Expenses over the five thousand."

"Mr. Fred," Tim beckoned. Fred came forth. In his hands was a billfold thick enough to be a pillow. All hundreds.

"Been busy sucking, eh?" Tony said, pumping his fist in front of his mouth for added effect. He snatched the money a beat later, opening it and flipping through its wealth.

"That should be enough," Tim said.

Tony flexed his brow in agreement. "Should be. Anything I don't use I'll return."

"That's fine."

"Anything else?" Tony asked. He was feeling much better now that he had hard cash in his paws.

"No, I think that's everything."

"Don't expect miracles," Tony grumped. "I think I can find him. With this anyway. Just give me a couple of weeks."

"Time is a human measure," Tim said, his eyes crinkling at their corners. "I hope you are able to find him faster than that."

"No guarantees there," Tony said. He was wondering if the man actually knew anything about finding a missing person. If they were just missing, there was a better chance of finding them, which was a low percentage to begin with. If the person was dead or, even better, not *wanting* to be found, things got even rougher. But he was being paid, so he felt he should say something inspiring. "If he's on the continent, I'll find him."

For a moment, just a flicker of time, something in Tim's expression changed. It seemed like the man's face softened, as if he were a father looking upon his son. And then it was gone. "That's acceptable."

The man glanced at his standing companion. "Well, we'll be on our way then."

He stood up and dusted himself off. "Thank you for the juice."

Tony remained sitting.

"It's a cold morning, Mr. Levin. You'd do best to dress warm. Probably minus twenty five out there."

"I'll get out my mittens." Tony grunted. He was keeping an eye on good, old, egghead Fred.

"A good idea," Tim agreed with a nod. "Oh, and if you do manage to find our man within the week, I'm willing to add a considerable bonus."

"Yeah? How much?"

"Five thousand on top of your fee. An incentive if you like. Acceptable?"

"If I find him in a week? By next Tuesday?"

"Yes."

"I can just call?"

"Yes."

"You don't need proof?"

This made Tim smile. The glow could have warmed the old apartment for a year. "I trust you, Mr. Levin."

The pair of men moved towards the door, Fred with his head down. Tim pulled his toque over his head and smiled at Tony one last time, his grey eyes aglitter.

"Happy hunting, Mr. Levin."

With that, he opened the door and stepped through. Fred followed him out but paused just beyond the threshold. He fixed Tony with black shining eyes. Without a word, the man pulled the door closed. It went to with the barest of sounds, mindful of the neighbours.

Freaky, flashed in Tony's mind.

He immediately looked at the cash on the table before him. Five G's. Right there. Was there anything better than having a fistful of cash and a full day ahead of oneself? And a new cell phone to boot. He wanted one of those. He wondered if it had any games.

"Alright," he declared and snatched up the wad of bills.

Then he noticed the clock. The little hands had moved to 5:45.

Damn batteries.

CHAPTER 10

There was no time to waste and no point in lingering, so Tony immediately got to packing. He hauled out an old hockey bag and spread it open. Into this, he began lobbing clothes needed for two weeks. Seven pairs of assorted socks and underwear went into the bag.

Five thousand. Was he really on the verge of making that kind of money in a span of a week? It was a wonderful thought. What if he could make that on a regular basis? Five thousand a month would be grand. He was filled with the warm rush of dreamy financial freedom for moments. He would get on the road ASAP. A quick goodbye to his mom. He considered stopping by Tigh's and letting him know where he'd be, but in the end, he decided not to. Tigh wanted him to stay out of sight. What better way than to leave the city? He would call the man instead.

He finished his packing and zipped up the hockey bag. He threw it onto the sofa en route to the fridge and a quick bite to eat. He discovered that the fucking guy had drunk most of his apple juice. There was barely enough to slosh around the bottom of the quart. Lord above, he hated it when people did that.

He had a shower, shaved, and brushed his teeth.

He was out the door at 7:05.

The sky was cotton-grey and overcast, and Mr. Tim wasn't lying about the cold. Tony felt his flesh get goose pimply as he walked across the road to the parking lot. Snow squeaked like an alien life-form underneath his hiking boots. His winter trench coat was long, black, and warm. It made him look like a hit man, and it was also his last remaining possession that made him look as if he had money. Besides his car.

Tony slowed down. Freak boy was standing alongside the passenger side of his Mustang. Head-hauled-out-of-a-monkey's-ass freak boy Fred. His shoulders were all hunched up around his neck and dark eyes watched Tony as he drew closer. Tony stopped a good distance away from him. He noted, in annoyance, that Fred's coat looked a little like his own.

"Why you still around?"

"Mr. Tim said for me to go with you," the man said, his voice was coarse and gravelly. Black eyes, like those cut out of a spider's skull, regarded Tony and sent a chill through him.

"Who says I want you along?" Tony said, not liking the idea.

"Who says I want to be along?" Fred growled back like some bluesy singer with a bad case of tonsillitis. He nodded at Tony's car. "It's a piece of shit."

"Your *ass* is a piece of shit," Tony fired back. He hated it when people put down his ride. "No way you're going anywhere now."

Fred stared at him for a moment, not saying anything. Snow floated in the space between the two, making everything seem greyer than it should. Then Fred shrugged, the cold screwing up his mouth in clear distaste. He stepped away from the car. Taking the cue, Tony moved around to the driver's side and unlocked the door. He threw his hockey bag in the back, glancing at the Freak (as Tony now liked to think of Fred) every two seconds to make sure he stayed out of the way. It was too early in the morning to get into a fight, but they were outside now, and Tony would like to see Freak Boy pull the same shit he got away with in the apartment. There was room to move out here.

"You look like you're in a hurry," Fred said in that low if-rusty-nails-could-tear-flesh voice.

"I'm motivated," Tony said over the roof of his car. "Five G's will do that to a man. Another five helps, too."

"Money, eh?"

Tony fixed Fred with an indignant look. "Yeah, money. Man," he finished with a disbelieving shake of his head. He got into the car and had the keys in the ignition when Fred tapped on the passenger side window. Tony ignored him and started the car. The engine hoarked, coughed, and wheezed a few seconds, and finally came to life.

The tapping got louder. Tony sighed and saw Freak boy's midsection through the frosty glass. "What?" he shouted.

"Five thousand."

"What?" Tony hoped the car hurried warming up.

"What about another five thousand?" asked Fred, who sounded more and more like a poster boy for smokers for life.

Tony felt his face go slack. His mouth hung open. "Another five thousand?"

"Mr. Tim said for me to go with you. Said you might need my help." Fred still stood, and Tony saw the man pat his winter pocket. "And okayed the money if you were going to be a cunt about it."

He used the c-word. Tony had a cousin in Ontario who said she hated it when a guy used the c-word. As a result, Tony never used it himself, and looked upon those who did as toilet scum.

"Tim said it was okay to give me another five grand if I let you come along?" Tony demanded.

Silence. Only the man's midriff.

"Hey, fuck head!"

The motor hummed with warmth. The beast was coming to life.

"Rimmer!" Tony threw at the man outside. Nothing.

"Fuck," he grumped. He reached across and unlocked the door with a spiteful jerk. Fred slowly bent to get in, the snow dusting his frame and falling into the car.

"Let's see it then," Tony said, and held out his hand. "Right now."

Fred studied the other man as if he were an insolent child. With a low, exasperated sigh, he slipped a manila envelope from his coat and handed it over. Tony immediately opened it. A whole bunch of brown hundreds. Nice. This was turning out to be an exciting morning. His foot descended on the gas, and the Mustang breathed deeply. Never had Tony had this much cash on his person in such a short period of time. It was a little unsettling, and Tony found himself too willing to fight to keep it. He looked around the empty parking lot for lurking predators.

Fred sat down heavily in the passenger's seat. "No one's around. Let's get going."

"You got more of this?" Tony asked.

The black eyes narrowed, and Tony knew that they had to be contacts. He once saw a black guy downtown that wore contacts that were fashioned after a cat's, yellow and slit. Alien looking. They couldn't work on the chicks.

"What if I do?" Fred directed at him, his mouth an ugly gash, his demeanour ready to fight.

"You always walk around Dartmouth with this much cash on you? Dangerous, man."

"Like to see someone try and take it," was the response.

Tony smiled without humour. "You're the man, eh?"

"Don't you have somewhere to go?" Fred asked.

"Yeah, in a minute."

"Time's . . . a human measure," Fred stated in his rusty voice.

Tony thought for a moment. He jammed the money into his coat's inner pocket and placed both hands on the steering wheel. Snow covered the windshield, so he turned on the wipers. He stared ahead. Where *did* he go from here? He had a cell phone and a number that could be a lead if he pursued it enough. But how? He usually had something more to go on when he hunted down people, a place they hung out, an address, a photo even. He had squat on this one. Tony did have a friend at the telephone company. That would be a start, he supposed. And he had a name. A little digging might at least give him a direction. He also knew about the Internet and sites where all you needed was a name to help you find someone. That might be the way to go. Hang out in an Internet café somewhere and do a little investigating.

But...

His passenger sat in his seat, staring out at the grey morning. The wipers did a quick one-two across the windshield, clearing it of snow.

"Yes, by Christ we're moving now," Fred muttered. "Really speeding along here."

Tony ignored the man. It was his dream that suddenly took a hold of his attention. Premonitions were one thing, but he had a strong sense of direction with this one. It was really there, for whatever screwy reason. *A golf course.* He could not shake the image of a golf course from his mind and truthfully, with the way his morning was motoring by, it seemed like the best thing he could do.

"Whenever you're ready..." Fred said.

More snow gathered on the windshield. One-two. The wipers swished it all away.

West. The country was under a polar blanket of snow, but out west, Vancouver west, he heard that it rarely snows at all. Something to do with being on the coast. He even saw folks on TV playing golf out there in January. Golf! Now, there was a sign! But how the hell was he supposed to get all the way out to British Columbia in the thick of winter? Go west. But, Jesus, did that ever *feel* right. He considered going the other direction but a feeling in his chest, right above his heart, made him think something would burst out of there if he deviated from heading west. Was that logical? But how to explain his hunch to Freak boy was another question.

"You ever been out west?" Tony abruptly asked Fred.

"We're going west?"

"Considering it."

"Why west?"

A scowl came across Tony's face. "I have a hunch."

"A hunch?" Fred said with an unmistakable *you're shittin' me right?* tone underneath it.

"Yeah," Tony answered, ready to tell the man to bite it hard if the flack was forthcoming. He didn't want to tell the guy he didn't like to fly. Hated the thought.

"We'd best get going, then," was all Fred said.

That brought a look from Tony. Fred was staring ahead, watching the wipers flick back and forth, back and forth. Tony waited a moment more and realized Freak Boy wasn't going to say anything. A week. It would take more than a week to get to BC by car. Maybe Fred would help with the driving. Tony would ask him later. Right now, the less interaction he had with the man the better.

"Get your seatbelt on," he instructed the man, reaching around for his own belt and then placing both hands on the steering wheel.

Fred came out of a daze. He watched Tony buckle up, examined his own chest, then the windshield, and finally reached around and got a hold of his own seatbelt.

West.

We're going west, the words came to Tony, and disappeared in that cringing sound of wiper rubber on windshield.

CHAPTER 11

Wednesday night, and Hillman was getting into the music, his big shoulders moved to the beat like a hip-hop dancer. It was his lucky break that he got the call for work, and what a job! Anytime he had to watch over a bunch of half-drunks with a stage full of naked or near-naked babes on it wasn't really work to Hillman. This was paid vacation with a license to smack people around. And smacking around drunken bastards was the best if you were into smacking people around to begin with. They were easy to goad into taking the first swing, and after that, it was all game on. The fights were usually over much faster than they took to start, mostly because Hillman would strike to kill. He didn't give a fuck. If someone was throwing a punch at him, he would reply. His hands were toughened by years of construction work and punching a leather bag he had hanging in his apartment. When his fists connected with flesh, there was a distinct stoppage in play. Hillman could drop anyone with one punch. He'd like to take home Suzie, and drop her with one punch. That was one friendship he would love to work on. He reached into his jean pocket and discreetly adjusted his stiffening buddy there. Thoughts of Suzie were making his second-in-command come to dazed attention.

Boomer watched Hillman out of the corner of his eye as he strolled around the club, doubling as a waiter when need be. He didn't like him in the least. The bouncer wished that 'the House' was available for tonight's shift, but the man had a bad cold, and listening to him hoark and sniffle on the phone made Boomer wince. There was no other choice after that. It was Hillman or no one. And if it was no one and something happened in the club, he would never hear the end of it from Gary.

His route took him from the coat check room to the outer edge of tables, along the tables to a pause at the bar and a slow walk on past the door to Gary's office. He had a good view of things, and he didn't have to make small talk with Roy Hillman. The man was a big bastard, almost as big as Boomer himself, with an equally-sized ego. Boomer heard the man was once a rugby player but got tossed out of the league as he liked to *enrage* the other players to get them off their game. That included, as far as the stories went, Hillman jamming his thumbs up opposing players' asses in scrimmages. If he ever tried something like that on Boomer, the bouncer would quickly reciprocate with his size-thirteen boot up the man's ass—after breaking both the bastard's thumbs. Even the man's face was skewed up. His eyes were too big for his face, as if he were constantly choking on something.

Sensing he was being looked at, Hillman broke away from Suzie on stage and gave a cool *what's up* flick of his head.

Boomer ignored him. He was no comrade of his and did not want any such idea manifesting itself in Hillman's orcish skull. Then, on second thought, he made his way over to where Hillman was standing, who asked him a question.

"Just wave then," Boomer informed him, "but no jerking off in the toilet. You got that, man? And I fucking mean it."

Boomer liked the shocked expression on Hillman's face, knowing he pounded the nail hard on the head. He could read these unprofessional pricks like bad books. At least Hillman could be embarrassed at times. If it were Adam Lorne, the man would have probably offered Boomer a stroke or two. The thought made the big bouncer grimace. The people he had to work with. Why did House have to be sick? And part of him was sorry for not being able to get Levin for the night. Probably in some jail somewhere for kicking the shit out of someone. He could probably work with him. Levin hadn't completely gone mad-dog just yet, but he had informed them only yesterday morning that he was heading out of town. Heading to Vancouver on a job. Gary didn't ask any other questions, knowing that Levin was a freelancer. He just passed it along to Boomer that Levin was unavailable. It was probably best he was out of Halifax for a while anyway.

The music reached a chorus, and Suzie began gyrating around one of the poles on the tongue stage, her legs flashing out and scissoring up and down. She was a natural athlete, that one. Beautiful body, too.

Boomer scowled at Hillman. "Hear me?"

"Right, no problem," Hillman answered in an embarrassed voice.

Boomer didn't believe him, but he nodded grimly and moved on. Jesus, he hated working with the freaks. He hoped Danny got lucky tonight to justify the pain he was enduring here.

Hillman watched the bouncer go, his shock lingering in his head and chest. His eyes found Suzie grinding her pelvis up and down against the stage pole. His embarrassment was soon forgotten.

Boomer counted fourteen customers in the Beacon as he stopped by the coat check. Three of them were sitting right up in pervert's row. If no one got rowdy, then it would be a peaceful night, and that was just fine to him. It was uncommon to get so many on a Wednesday. Suzie's kibbles 'n bits brought them in any weather.

As if on cue, the outside door opened, letting in a gust of wind.

Along with the Stickman.

The man gave a wink and a nod at Boomer. Stickman paid the coat check fee and shrugged out of a leather coat. He wore a matching black turtleneck underneath, which accentuated the man's bulk. He was short, but then so were some of the toughest walls.

"Cold out dere, brudder," the Stickman said happily. "Is whatserface on tonight?"

The scowl on Boomer face showed up too quick. "*Whatser* face has a name."

"Suzie? I tink," the Stickman tried, appearing to think very hard on the subject.

Boomer did not want to let him in, but he'd already taken his coat. He flicked his head in the direction of the inner door. Stickman nodded and winked again at Boomer, and then he entered the bar. The tension in his body told Boomer all he needed to know about the little shit's presence. It was not good news. He wished he had Danny Boy around to watch his back instead of Hillman.

In the bar, Stickman caught Suzie's eye almost immediately. It was strange how the woman picked up on that. He supposed it was his animal magnetism or some shit. Maybe his pheromones or whatever they called them were acting up, and she could smell him. Suzie was already naked, and must've caught some of that wind from the outside. She looked all perky. A part of him thought it was too bad. The Stickman loved to see them undress up there. He went to the bar and ordered a Keith's Beer from a mouse of a man behind the counter. He then found a place to sit with his back to the bar and sat down.

And watched.

Anyone seeing him would have thought he was enjoying the show, but after the first hour, Stickman was still on his first beer, and had seen all he needed to see. There were a few too many people in here for what he wanted to do, but he wasn't too concerned about the patrons. He was interested in the burly figure standing by the far wall, who was watching the long-haired brunette called Alexia that came on after Suzie finished her act. Alexia pranced around the tongue stage as if it were electrified, and even looked in Stickman's direction a couple of times. So did Boomer. When Stickman caught their eyes, he calmly winked back. Alexia didn't seem to mind. The Boom was another matter. Boomer was the walker. The other bouncer was stationary. Stickman did not see Mr. Tigh around, so he figured the manager was in his office. He doubted he ever took the night off. And why would he with all the talent he had up on the stage? Man would be an idiot! All in all, there were three men visible to the Stickman. Two of them were threats. The bartender did not seem so unless he had a bat underneath the counter. He thought about the pair of bouncers. He wanted to catch them apart.

Divide and conquer.

He waited. He had his walls erected about him, or, as Stickman liked to think of them, his "force fields", invisible boundaries surrounding him that were sensitive enough to detect anyone approaching him. Sensei Bill had taught him a thing or two about elevating his sixth sense ability, his sensitivity as to who was inside his personal space. Most people thought such things were bullshit, but Sensei Bill demonstrated to the Stickman quite convincingly that such preconceptions could be fatal, especially to an attacker thinking he was sneaking up on a would-be victim. What was incredibly freaky was utilizing such abilities in fights where a person couldn't see. Blind fighting, Sensei Bill called it. The Stickman had learned quite a bit from Sensei Bill. Stickman had learned to elevate his ability to a level where, when he looked, almost always he would catch Boomer's eyes on his person. Call it paranoia, but Stickman's sensitivity to such things had saved his bacon a number of times. So, while he appeared outwardly calm to most, the invisible fields surrounding him were crackling with energy, and were as sensitive as a spider's freshly spun web.

Stickman waited. The chance would reveal itself.

The unknown bouncer eventually waved to Boomer, who nodded and sauntered on over to the coat check, making eye contact again with Stickman. Stickman smiled back, still trying hard to keep a façade of good humour, while in his mind, he was thinking how much he would like to hook both eyes out with his thumbs. Boomer calmly broke the stare and swept his gaze around the dark interior of the bar. Stickman noted the other bouncer heading for the washroom, disappearing behind the swinging door.

Stickman finished his beer, set the empty bottle gently down on the table, and waited for a minute. Exactly one minute. Counting slow, pacing his breath, and controlling the building energy in his body. He did not have to think about what he was about to do. He need only do it.

When Boomer's eyes were on him again, Stickman stood up and, with a wide smile, made the gesture of taking a piss. Boomer looked away with a disgusted look.

Stickman went to the washroom.

CHAPTER 12

"Breathe son, breathe," Hillman coaxed his pride, standing as if he were astride a horse and far back enough from the urinal that anyone walking into the facilities would have a generous view of what God had blessed him with.

"She's a fine piece of ass, that Alexia. Help me out now, and I'll help you out later, ok?" Hillman gave himself a quick stroke while looking down at the curved porcelain before him, willing himself to urinate. His gun was half-cocked as it was. He tried taking deep breaths to relax, to give him some slack, but the trouble was indecent images of both Suzie and Alexia double timing him back at his apartment were keeping the blood in his second head. Hillman considered going into the nearby stall and choking his chicken (to hell with Boomer and what he said—the man had to be dickless *not* to be affected by what was up on stage), when he heard the door open. That wasn't going to slow him down.

Stickman made to go past the positioned Hillman, towards the stalls, ignoring both the bouncer and the blue cake sanitary smell filling the room. The lad was enjoying himself a little bit too much, and Stick shook his head at the offensive scene. It justified what he was about to do. He moved past the two white basins next to the urinals and casually made his way to one of the two stalls in the washroom. Hillman paid the man no attention. The bouncer's eyes were closed, and a snarl of pleasure creased his face.

Stick felt the adrenaline surge into his arms, his engines. He felt the chemical sing through his powerful biceps and charge them up. With the bouncer preoccupied as he was, there was no need for silence. Stickman pivoted and took a quick two steps, bringing up a hand to clamp down on a pair of denim covered testicles. Hillman gave a muted wheeze of agony and actually tried to jump away, but the strength left his legs in a flood. He blew snot out his nose and grabbed the edge of the urinal with both hands. His knees buckled, and he dropped to the floor. He opened his mouth to vomit when Stickman wrapped both arms around his neck in a choke hold, crushing the blood flow in the man's right and left vertebral arteries. Hillman tried to suck in some air but got nothing. He tried to stand, willed himself to stand, but Stickman drove his knees into the back of the man's legs, and the big man dropped. Hillman's eyes bulged. His tongue shot out. Saliva trickled out of a corner of his mouth. His arms lashed out spasmodically, reached up and clawed weakly at Stickman's face. Under different circumstances, it might have been a caress. Then, the screaming of Hillman's testicles began to lessen, and his sight became black at the edges, as if his consciousness was being yanked backwards, away from the windows that were his eyes, to somewhere deep within his skull. Then, nothing.

Stickman didn't need to shift his weight in the least. Grabbing the bastard by the balls had done it. The choke was just the 'coop da grass', or however they said it in French. Hillman's neck had slipped into Stickman's grasp as easy as a single bolt locking a door. It took a little longer than maybe five seconds, and the man's struggles were little more than a child's resistance at being dragged out on the dance floor. He held on to the man for a few seconds more just to be certain. Then he released his victim.

"Ye wit me?" Stickman arched back the man's head and gazed into the eyes that were half closed, half rolled back. He held onto the man's hair and rammed his face into the hard porcelain of the urinal. Blood burst onto the white as Hillman's nose broke on contact. Stickman watched the man's body crumple lifelessly to the floor. He kicked the bouncer's ribs. Satisfied that the bouncer wasn't playing around, the Newfoundlander began hauling his victim into one of the empty stalls. Stickman wanted to place him on the toilet at first, but decided against it when he saw the front of the man's unzipped jeans. He had pissed himself, his penis hanging out like a fire hose peeking through a bird's nest of pubic hair. Stickman didn't want the man's piss on him, so he left him in the corner of the stall and closed the door. If anyone came looking, they would see the legs splayed out and guess the fucker had passed out over the can while puking. The subterfuge would last long enough to do the next part.

"Seeya, buddy," Stickman sighed heavily and winked at the closed stall door. That was one.

The next song was warming up as he eased out of the washroom. An old Bob Segar tune. He looked briefly at Alexia, taking in her pink parts. She was whirling around a pole in such a way that made Stickman think of the Olympics. But she didn't hold a candle to his Suzie. No, sir. Suzie was his gal.

He focused on the manager's door across the way, just beyond the last set of tables. There was no light seeping around the edges. No evidence of anyone actually being in the room, except he was. Tigh was in there. He was always in there. It was his lair. Stickman coolly glanced around and saw Boomer in the outer coat room. Some new guys were coming into the club maybe. Stick walked towards Tigh's door, feeling his feet hit the floor in perfect beat with the pounding music. He thought of the Crocodile Hunter, the poor guy killed by a stingray. He couldn't remember his exact name, but as he approached Tigh's office, with the music crashing down, he heard the man's voice in his head. *O've travelled quite a bit, but t'day, as luck would 'ave it, we've located the cave of a crime boss. A real focking bastahd of one at that! This particular breed is a Tigh, known exclusively for the amount of 'orseshite it can spit out—up to a distance of New Brunswick! Lethal stuff! A roight nasty cocksmoka, but today we'll 'ave 'im and see just 'ow far we can stick our boot up his leathery arse before it chokes to death on the polish. By crikey!*

Just loverly.

Stickman placed his hand on the doorknob, another quick scan registered no Boomer, and he cracked open the door.

With his feet propped up on his huge desk and his head deep into a Larry McMurty western, the opening of the door went unheard until the music found its way in. This made Tigh look up to see the Stickman slip into his inner chambers like a greased up shit-snake. The appearance of the man surprised Tigh to no end. He blinked once, as if taking a picture, then sat up. The Stickman closed the door.

And began walking towards him.

"What the sweet fuck are you doing in here, you fucking stupid Newf?" Tigh spat out, not believing his eyes in the least. He tossed the book down on the desk.

Stickman smiled. "Howya doin', Mr. Tigh. Taught I pay ye anudder visit."

"GET THE FUCK OUTTA HERE!" Tigh yelled, his face turning steam red. He stood up, posturing like a school teacher dismissing a naughty child and pointing in the direction to the principal's office. "RIGHT FUCKING *NOW!* How the HELL did you get past Boomer?"

Stickman spread his hands.

"Mr. Tigh, I'll ask ye again. Nice like. 'Oose da guy dat did the job on Badger?"

Tigh's face tightened in disbelief as if he were seeing an x-ray of his lungs, and death by way of cancer was unavoidable. He stabbed the air with his finger. "Now, you listen to me," he said in a much lower voice, "you little cumdrop—"

"Mr. Tigh," Stickman grinned hard, as if he were advertising a particular brand of toothpaste. "Tell me now, eh? If ye don't tell me now, I'll break ye in two. As gawd's me witness."

Tigh regarded the little wall of a man approaching him, open hands swinging at his sides. He fought down the urge to swallow. His eyes flicked to the closed door, the music noticeably muted as the guys who built the thing had promised.

"If you—" Tigh started and stuck his finger out again.

Stickman was close enough to grab it. He snapped it backwards, breaking the digit like a thick icicle. Tigh shrieked and tried to pull away. Stickman held on and twisted hard enough to drive the man to his knees. Tigh's other hand came up in worship. Agony scorched his hand all the way up his arm, shoulder, into his head and buzzed his brain like a jolt from a defibrillator. Nausea threatened to empty his stomach of the chicken fingers he gorged himself on an hour earlier.

"Dere's a good by," Stickman said, pleased with the results. He pulled Tigh closer. The crime lord whimpered, swearing loudly, his free hand covering his face.

"BOOMER!" he bawled out.

Stickman made a face and twisted again. The name died into a croak.

"'Oo did it?" Stickman hissed through clenched teeth, glaring into the pain filled slits of Tigh's eyes. "'Oo?"

"JESUS!"

"Mexican guy?" Stickman's brow made a single, curious hop.

"Oh, FUCK!"

This got on Stickman's nerves. He pulled closer, and Tigh came forward on his knees. The punch came like a torpedo from Stickman's waist, his fist twisting with power. Tigh's nose broke in a torrent of thick, dark poppy red. He crumpled onto the floor with his arm outstretched. Stickman did not let go. He wrapped his arm around Tigh's in an arm lock, and dragged the moaning man to the edge of his big, hardwood desk. He manhandled him onto its surface. Books, pens, and paper scattered. Stickman savagely arranged the prone body onto the table like an Aztec priest about to offer a sacrifice. He placed Tigh's elbow on the edge of the desk, straightened the limb out, and dropped his full weight onto it. The limb broke with a crack that Stickman felt through his clothes. Tigh screamed, once again. Sensei Bill would've loved this, Stickman thought. He sized up Tigh's arm, which was now a lazy L over the edge of the desk.

His grimace covered in blood, Tigh opened his eyes, and said nothing.

"Yer tough, Mr. Tigh," Stickman complimented the man. "But I 'aven't broken ye in 'alf yet. 'Ave a guess 'ow I'll do dat?"

Tigh bared his teeth. "*BOOMER!*" he screeched with all the energy he had remaining. Stickman's open palm, the heel first, crashed into Tigh's ear. Stickman landed two more punches into his sacrifice's ribs, each punch moving the man a little closer to the desk's edge. He stopped and flipped Tigh over onto the hard floor with a grunt. Tigh landed face down, blood bubbles bursting from his nose.

"Yer a wrestling fan, Mr. Tigh?"

Stickman landed on top of Tigh's back. The man was too heavy for Tigh to dislodge even if he had had the strength to do it. He was in terrible shape. The worst shape ever. His only chance was in getting Boomer. He summoned up the breath and was about to scream again when he felt fingers under his chin lacing together like steel cables. His yell became a caged thing, an agonized expulsion of trapped sound. Blood sprayed from his mouth, and his eyes cringed with the new pain in his lower back. "*Fuck!*" he spat/shrieked out through his clamped jaws.

"Yeah, dat's it. Da camel clutch. Ye know da one? Ever try dat out for real?"

With his fingers clutching Tigh's chin, his butt firmly in place on the crime boss's lower back, and his thighs up and under supporting Tigh's arms and upper body like a crucified prisoner, Stickman leaned back. All sound in Tigh stopped then, and his punch-dazed brain quickly became aware of its predicament. He felt his spine being bent slowly backwards. Stickman leaned back further, both feet planted firmly, remembering how the Saturday morning wrestlers used to do it, and wondering if it was real or not. A little grunt burped from Tigh's lips, followed by another.

Then the sound grew into a terrible, pain wracked howl through caged teeth.

Stickman pulled more, leaning way back, wondering if he would feel the snap of his victim's spine.

CHAPTER 13

Boomer's head twisted around. He had a sudden dismal feeling that a family member had just died. He patted Melinda the door person on the shoulder. She was a pretty, pear-shaped brunette in her forties with a cigarette glued to her mouth. She watched him go into the bar. Then, he was gone.

Light lasered back and forth, dazzling Boomer's eyes. The first thing Boomer *didn't* see was Hillman. The fact that the moron had gone to the can—what, five minutes ago?—Didn't sit well in Boomer's mind. Who could tell rain clouds not to pour down, and who could tell Hillman not to whack off? Boomer smiled grimly at the analogy.

It did not last.

Stickman was also nowhere to be seen.

That really bothered Boomer. He looked around the dark room, scanning the seated patrons enjoying the number jiggling on the stage. No Stickman. He took five big steps towards Tigh's office door, not understanding why, but feeling something was wrong in the thickening air.

Tigh had talked.

So, the Stickman released the pressure on his back and leaned forward. He wanted the man to be conscious for the next part. "So, da by's name is Levin, eh?"

His head still in the cradle of Stickman's hands, Tigh whimpered an affirmative. Bloody snot blew out his nose. He believed he had several discs in his back crushed. Squished. The entire length of his spinal column felt as if someone had done surgery on it with a chain saw.

"Where's 'ee at?"

Tigh sighed, and a bright wet ribbon of mucus flew away from his face. Another great shudder of breath went through his agonized frame. It was a question of will now and whether or not he wanted his death to be quick or not. He knew the Stickman was a killer. He knew the Stickman knew he was a man capable of bloody vengeance and that, if he was released, Tigh would indeed use every means at his disposal to hunt him down. Tigh knew the Stickman knew this, and thus, the Stick would not let him live. It was sound logic in Tigh's mind.

"To the States."

"Where?"

Nothing. A ragged intake of air, bracing for pain.

"*Where?*" Stickman demanded, tired of Tigh's bullshit.

The office door opened.

Stickman looked up. He forgot to lock the door.

Tigh whimpered in relief.

Amidst a thrumming beat of techno music, Boomer's eyes went from shocked disbelief to slits of terrible anger. "Let him up," he seethed.

Stickman was already complying, releasing the crime lord underneath him like a man releasing a broken sapling. He slap-wiped his hands and kept them loose at his sides, as if he were a sprinter about to take his mark. His eyes shined with dangerous mirth.

"No need t'call the cops here, I think," Boomer said, letting the door swing closed behind him and taking a step towards the man. His hands came up before him as if he were about to pounce on a rare insect. Tigh dragged himself slowly in the direction of his henchman and the door.

"Yer d'last, me son," Stickman told him with a sly grin. "I was gonna let ye alone. Nuttin' against ye, really. 'Ee's the one 'oldin' back d'info. And I gots the name I was looking for. I'm done 'ere. Ye can let me go."

He pointed at the slowly moving bulk of Tigh. "Maybe get 'im to an 'ospital."

Boomer shook his head. He stepped over Tigh inchworm-slinking towards the other side of the room, away from his attacker.

"You are so fucking wrong, man," Boomer said, his big hands getting closer. "You are *so* fucking *dead*. I'll fucking do CPR on you just to kill you twice. A third time for shits and giggles."

The bouncer was a full head and a half taller and every bit as wide as the Stickman. The man was a tsunami coming in hard. Stickman moved to his right, placing the edge of the couch between them. Music, muffled but furious, a techno war drum, permeated the room.

"You ain't runnin', you little shit," the bouncer swore.

"Run?" the Stickman smiled all the way to his eyes. "I's gonna *walk* outta 'ere, me son."

Boomer kicked the sofa with a groan of wood on carpet towards the Stickman. Stickman darted around it as nimble as a crab on speed. Boomer matched him and got close enough to unleash a missile of a punch, straight from the shoulder, at the other man's face. The smaller man slapped it away with an open palm, wrist flicking outwards. Boomer threw a combination of three punches, any one of them powerful enough to break bone. Two went for the head, the last sought a kidney. Stickman forcefully slapped the first two punches away as if Boomer were a child going for his grandmother's cookie jar. He moved back from the last punch. Stickman circled left a step, keeping his open hands before his chest, peeking up at the larger Boomer from just over the tips of his hooked fingers.

"'Eard ye were badder den dis, Boom me son."

"You'll know it," Boomer snarled, rolling his shoulders. He was just revving up his engines. The blood was surging into the places where he needed it, like multiple torpedo silos filling up with deadly ordinance. He was about to live up to his name.

"Yeah? When?" Stickman asked, stepping back to his right.

"When you feel my knee up your ass."

A storm of pre-practiced punches flew at the smaller man; a five-fisted combination targeting the face and body. Boomer exhaled spent air like the boxer he was as he moved in, wanting to corner this fuck rat and take his head off at leisure. But Stickman dodged left, keeping well out of reach. He bounced off a nearby wall and ducked under a swing meant for his head. Now, the desk was between the combatants, and they eyed each other with the techno pounding from beyond the door.

"Doubt it," Stickman smiled his slyness again.

"Yeah, that's right," Boomer snorted, deciding right then not to chase this little fucker all over Gary's place. He brought his fists up to guard. "You were in prison. Probably can take both knees up there now, can't cha?"

Stickman's grin frosted over.

Boomer knew he had hit a nerve and decided to shake it.

"Probably just fuckin' full of con jizim, too. How often your nose run there you goddamn, stupid fucked up Newf?"

Stickman lashed out, flat fingers stabbing for Boomer's throat. He blocked them with his forearms, but Stickman was in close now, and knife hands went for his adversary's windpipe. Boomer stopped them on his forearms again and punched out, grazing a forehead this time and knocking Stickman back, his eyes half closed with the contact. The man spun about and dropped low. A foot lashed out and swept Boomer's right knee. He cried out and crashed down. Stickman swooped in, his hooked fingers seeking the fallen man's testicles. Boomer kicked out his left leg and got a piece of his attacker's hip, stalling him in mid-flight. Stickman roared then, his eyes like livid cuts, his fingers like claws. He came in again low, slashing at the air like he possessed knives. Boomer got to his good knee and threw up his forearms to defend himself. Stickman's fingers drew bloody grooves in the man's flesh. Boomer twisted, furious with pain, and brought his arms about like a huge net. He missed his quarry, managing only to grab a brief handful of leather. Stickman flittered away, towards the door. He looked down and saw Tigh an arm's-length away. He drove a boot into the man's stomach. Tigh balled up like a dying insect.

"Yer not going anywhere," Boomer breathed, glancing quickly at the wounds in his forearms. Did the man have blades underneath his fingernails?

The Stickman only grinned. And attacked.

He loosed a frightening *KEEYAH* as he zeroed in, a series of short kicks snapping at Boomer's midsection and lower legs. Boomer sidestepped and dodged, but one boot glanced painfully off the meat of his right thigh. It went numb. The bigger man retaliated and jabbed a two-fisted combination at Stickman's head. The Stick darted backwards, impossibly fast, almost as if he knew where Boomer's punches were flying before he unleashed any. Stickman took another step backwards, almost up against Tigh's grand desk, and then charged back in, his hands, claws now, doing a furious weave in the air like an old fashioned lawn cutter's loose blades about to fly away. Boomer got his arms up to defend himself and a punishing storm of fists, strange strikes and counter strikes, thrusts and blocks erupted from both men. The breath escaped them like rutting bulls. They bared their teeth in the exchange even when the blood really started to fly. An open hand caught Boomer's jaw, smashing his lips against his teeth. Another punch made him bite down on his tongue. A fist caught the right side of Stickman's face, turning it a brazen red. A cut on his forehead channelled blood into his right eye, making him squint. A punch got through Boomer's forearms and caught him full in his left eye. Electrical pain crackled through a brain already reeling with multiple damage reports.

Then, another punch broke his nose.

They fought toe-to-toe for only seconds, but ask anyone in a fight about how a few seconds weighs like years on a combatant. Then Stickman whirled again, sweeping Boomer's weakened leg out from under him. The bouncer crashed onto the carpet, throwing his arms out behind him to break the fall. His head bounced on the surface. Stickman kicked him in the face, smashing an already broken nose. Blood splashed. Stickman snapped his kick out again, and Boomer did not even try to block the blow. Boomer was not registering much of anything except for the distant roar of surf in his ears. He shook his head, and it felt as if he were underwater. In slow motion, he watched the Stickman circle to his left. Instinct got Boomer moving. He pushed himself away from his attacker, backing up against Tigh's couch. The hate in his eyes made the Stickman pause. Boomer spat blood.

"Littlesumabitch," Boomer hissed in a berry-red froth. He got to his knees, managing to get his arms back to guard. "Gonna break all yer bones." He got to his feet. "Make sure I get yer favourite ones." Boomer swayed but his glaring eyes cleared. "Gonna be known as jellyfuck. Just like them blow-up dolls. 'Cept you'll be getting more orders on account of all that man service you sucked in."

Instead of a comeback, Stickman barked a hoarse laugh.

Then he was charging, his fingers straight out and seeking to scoop out eyes.

Boomer caught both of the man's wrists.

"Gotcha," he spat into the other's face. Boomer grinned evilly and twisted, knowing a little about joint locks himself. Boomer twisted the man's wrists down. The resulting mid-air somersault would happen to anyone not wanting their wrists broken. The effect was incredible. For a microsecond, Stickman flew. Boomer held on to one wrist as the man slammed into the floor. He kicked and Stickman twisted, feeling the man's foot hammer into his shoulder instead of his face. The kick was strong enough for Boomer to let go. Stickman got to his feet, rolling his shoulder. Boomer did not have the juice to press his attack. Breathing hard, swallowing blood, and limping, Boomer brought up his weary arms to guard, again. The little fucker had *chi*, but he didn't have the experience the legendary bouncer possessed. The two men regarded each other through swelling eyes and blood-filled vision. Both looked hard now. Both would look like surreal shit in the morning.

"C'mon," Boomer motioned, expending precious energy for that little gesture. "C'mon. Always wondered what a Tyson would do against a little Shaolin shit. Yeah. Tyson. You see him in prison? You his girl?"

Stickman grinned back, his teeth traced in red.

"Yeah, I can see you're a happy fucker. We'll see how goddamn chipper you are in the next thirty seconds. Hear me short shit? Thirty seconds. All you got. C'mon then. Bring that Jet Li shit across. Fuck you up."

Techno music pounded through the walls. The smell of blood was in the air. Gary remained curled up like a dead baby on the floor.

"Seconds, eh?" Stickman breathed. His head was ringing like a fucking gong, and his shoulder felt like a blow torch had been taken to it. He wondered if he looked anywhere near as bad as the corpse across from him. He drew breath from lungs that badly wanted to take the rest of the year off and sighed. He supposed he was stupid after all to think the Beacon's Boom would down go easy.

"Shut the fuck up." Boomer hissed. "You talk too goddamn much."

And Boomer lunged.

Combinations of fists and elbows pistoned out with the force of ten gauge shotguns. Some connected with maul-like force; others were deflected or dodged. The bouncer rained in his punches until he was close enough to grab his opponent. He wanted to wrap an arm around the little fucker's neck. He wanted to choke him until both of his fucking eyes popped out of his head. Choke him out, and then put the boots to his head.

Instead, they boxed around the room, heading into an unknown round.

Getting out of Boomer's way one too many times, Stickman's foot caught the corner of the couch. The bouncer saw him stagger and attacked. Technique was too much effort now. His punch was a straight over the shoulder thunderbolt right. It connected with Stickman's cheek, shattering it, spinning him round and showing the bouncer his back. Boomer grabbed him then, his heavy arm wrapping around the smaller man's neck. He lifted him up, and in the fury of the techno, Stickman's feet went up, kicked at the florescent light above and knocked it from its ceiling mooring. The light fell and swung to and fro, and the room spiralled in brightness and shadow. Stickman's face went crimson.

"This's *it*," Boomer breathed into the man's ear, holding Stickman up off the ground by his neck. "I'll make it hurt."

Boomer squeezed and panic surged through Stickman's body. The panic that comes with knowing that imminent disaster is rushing in. A stream of images exploded in Stickman's mind then, of a young man named Crawford, naked, in a crowded shower room, self-conscious of his nakedness. Other men shoving him, touching him, pulling at him. Men with bulging bellies covered in hair and ropey wet penises. Slippery soap. Gerald Burr's voice cutting through the steam lathered air, buzzing in Crawford's ear just as the shoving finishes and his arms are grabbed from behind. His legs are kicked out, and he's forced to the shower floor. Water beats against the concrete like wild rain and is sucked out by a black drain. All of Crawford's limbs are seized. His legs are spread apart. A forearm presses down across the back of his neck, further immobilizing him. Hot soap enters his rectum. Terror widens his eyes, but otherwise he cannot move.

"That's it," comes Burr's voice close to his ear. "You fight."

And the tungsten pain of being invaded.

That one episode, so long ago but never forgotten, instilled a primal fear of anyone—especially a man—pressing themselves up behind the Stickman. It made him ferociously paranoid of small cramped places. He could only do elevators if he got on first and put his back to a wall. Even public transportation, especially if he were standing, made him sweat with all of the close bodies. But being *held* from behind, being *grabbed* . . .

Like now . . .

Stickman freaked.

He shifted his hips to his left and clawed upwards into Boomer's crotch. Frantic fingers hooked into soft testicles and ripped with as much force as possible. Boomer's voice became a breathless wheeze as if he had just jumped into freezing water. The blood came like a burst water balloon. Paralyzed sick with agony, his knees buckled. Boomer felt his grip go on his prey. Stickman spun about and drove an elbow into the man's temple. Another foot crashed into the man's groin.

Boomer went down hard, hands instinctively clutching at his broken balls.

Stickman landed on top of him. His knees pinned the big man's shoulders to the carpet.

"Take yer picture," Stickman grated and drove a wrecking ball fist straight into Boomer's face.

The music had stopped, but the beating went on. And it continued for several long, wet seconds. It went on long after Boomer stopped moving. It went on long after it felt as if Stickman were punching a bag of meat pulped with shards of marbles. It went on and on and on.

And after Stickman tired of punching, he stood up and began stomping.

But by this time, Boomer's consciousness had long since left the continent.

From where he lay, Tigh heard the blunt sound of flesh on flesh. After what seemed like years, it stopped. Then, stillness. There was no music from the outside. There were no voices above him. Just pure stillness. The storm had ended. Boomer had saved him. Boom would get him to a hospital, too. Then, they would get back to the little shit known as the Stickman.

Footsteps. Near his head.

Movement. Very close.

"Now den," came a weary voice that made Tigh cringe and whimper and caused tears to seep from his tightly closed eyes. "Where was we . . . ?"

Tigh set his jaw before wet hands began working on him. He knew then that the storm had not passed as he had hoped.

He had just sailed into the eye of it.

CHAPTER 14

It was early Tuesday afternoon, long before the battle at the Beacon, and Tony slowed the car down. It was lunchtime, and he thought about eating something, feeling guilty for just thinking about food. He wondered about Fred, as well. Freak boy Fred who had not said a word since the hospital's parking lot after Tony had said his goodbye to his mother. He just sat there, listening to the radio and DJ Jeff's coffee high. When they became further out of range of the signal, Tony played with the dial until he found a classic rock station. Fred never said a word. He simply sat there and watched the landscape blur by. At first, Tony thought the man was pissed at him for some reason. Maybe the cracks Tony made at Freddy's expense were taken to heart. Not that that worried Tony in the least. Fuck the freak. Then it became blissfully clear to Tony that the man was simply not a conversationalist. Try driving along the highway in open country, and see if you can resist talking to the person beside you. Unless the man had no tongue, Tony figured that it couldn't be done, but, as fuck was his witness, Fred was doing it. He could almost clap the man on the shoulder for his silence, for a job well done, but that would send the wrong message. It was better for Tony this way.

He felt his stomach get cranky.

He finally decided that it came down to a test of will. Fred wasn't sleeping over there in the passenger seat. He was watching gas stations, scattered houses, and the odd tourist shop roll by as they travelled towards New Brunswick.

By three in the afternoon, Tony decided that old Freddy had won. And it was after lunch.

"I'm hungry," Tony stated as he sighted the next Irving Station, convenience shop and restaurant all rolled into one.

Fred said nothing.

"How about you?"

"Me?" Fred's eyes never left the road.

"Yeah, you. You hungry?" Tony asked as he pulled into the parking lot. "You eat earlier or something?"

Fred thought on that for a moment. "No," he said finally, perhaps answering both questions.

"Well, I am. You better eat something, too, cuz I'm not stopping until bedtime after this. Not even if you have to use the shitter."

"I'll wait here," Fred said, staring ahead at the lot.

"Fine, then."

Stubborn bastard. Tony parked next to a teal green SUV and unbuckled his seatbelt. He got out of the car and breathed deep of the cold air. The land was frosted in white underneath dark cement grey clouds that threatened to fall any moment. There were flurries in the weather forecast, but Tony hoped that he could escape Nova Scotia into New Brunswick before anything started. He figured he was an hour or two from the provincial border. He glanced around at the carefully snow-cleared lot and the row of white snow-capped trees behind the Irving station.

Driving.

When he had the cash, driving was the only way to go. Felt good to go. He stopped first at the men's restroom, made his way into the diner part of the station, thinking that he would fill up the gas tank as well when he got back out. The waitress standing at the cashier was named Cecile. She gave him a nice smile as she pointed to an empty booth near the back with red vinyl cushions. A frosty picture window gave a clear view of the wintry forest behind the station. Tony sat with his back to the wall, gave the scene outside a moment's consideration, and plucked the menu from the table's rack. The waitress that visited his table after a minute was a woman in her forties named Irene, who apparently tried hard to camouflage her years. Tony wondered at times why women wore any makeup at all. It occurred to him that maybe they wondered why they wore makeup.

"Let me know when you're ready," Irene told him after she deposited a glass of water on the table. Tony thought she had a nice smile, too, despite the overdose of cosmetics. Then, his stomach demanded attention. He decided on a hot turkey sandwich and tried very hard not to think of his mother in her hospital bed. He did not want to think at mealtimes. Not those thoughts. And then there were the moments when he would gorge himself for no reason at all, feel terrible after, and not eat anything for a day or two, or however long it took for the lightheaded weakness to set in.

It was all so damn unfair.

And now he was driving across the country on a feeling to find a guy that did not want to be found, who was apparently pretty dangerous.

The sigh that left him was full of self-mockery. How did he ever get himself into this one? Then, he remembered the hard wad of cash on his person and half smiled. He studied the hair on the back of his hands, noting that his flesh still looked young. Still looked good. And he still had his hair. All of it. And other than the nagging little whisper scraping on the inside of his skull like a blunt chisel on hard wood, he believed he still had a grip on things. Most things anyway.

Irene returned and took his order. He thanked her and meant it, and the smile he got back told him that she believed him. He wondered how Irene thought of herself at those times of self-reflection, when there was nothing on the television, the radio was off, and the silence hummed to itself. He looked across the way and saw a businessman in a blue suit glossing over something in a newspaper. The headlines were big enough for Tony to read. A parachutist had fallen twenty thousand feet and lived. Hopefully the poor bastard had insurance.

Tony looked back the other way, and there was Fred.

Tony jumped, slamming one knee up against the underside of the table. "Jesus! You're a quiet one, ain't cha!"

Fred was content to say nothing. He watched Tony's fading fright with those weird black eyes of his. Tony wondered if the man had some Asian blood in him.

"Yeah, well, you can flag her down then and order your own damn meal," Tony told him. He wasn't paying for it.

Without invitation, Fred sat down across from Tony. He slid a menu out from the table rack and opened it, slowly, like a child turning the first page of a Christmas book, his brow arching upwards with genuine interest at what he read. Tony wondered yet again if the man wasn't somehow retarded.

"See anything good?" Tony remarked, not really expecting the man to answer.

"What is poutine?" Fred asked, screwing up his mouth as he said the word.

Was the man from the States? "Fries covered in gravy and cheese. I hope to hell you don't eat with your mouth open. Or lips smacking. That shit gets on my nerves. If you do, you can move your ass to another table."

Fred held up his hand and caught Irene's attention. The waitress came over, and Fred pointed to what he wanted. He nodded and shook his head at her follow-up questions. Irene placed a glass of water before him and walked back to the kitchen. Tony watched the whole episode, and it bugged him that the man said nothing to the waitress.

"You could've thanked her, y'know," he grumped.

"Could have?" Fred asked, returning Tony's hard look.

"Yeah, God only knows how many asswipes she has to put up with in a day. And an honest to gawd *thank you* would be appreciated. Make her feel better and not like some damn android. You make sure you leave her a tip, too, since you're paying for all of this. Call it a business expense. You can claim it on your taxes."

Large black eyes studied Tony as if trying to decide where he should bite.

"Fuck you," Tony fired first in a low voice.

"Fuck you, too," Fred muttered back.

Tony rolled his eyes. "Sweet Christ on a telephone pole," he sighed. "You gonna run off and cry to mom that I pushed you off a swing or something now? Just do me a favour and don't talk to me, okay? Just don't talk to me. If you do, we'll have issues. Just remember that."

Without saying anything, Fred leaned back in his chair as if he were a smoker about to let off a puff towards the ceiling. He kept his narrowed eyes on Tony. Tony ignored the freak. Why couldn't he have been the one whose chute wouldn't open? Being suddenly stopped after a nice vertical drop from 20,000 feet would do wonders to the man's present features.

Irene brought them their food. Tony's hot turkey sandwich was served up with a yellow hill of corn giblets and a log jam of French fries. Everything was glazed with light brown gravy. It looked and smelled wonderful.

"Have a nice meal," Irene said more to Tony than to Fred. Tony thanked her.

"Thank you," Fred blurted out a little too loudly. Irene paused and smiled at the man.

"You're welcome," she said.

Fred did not smile back. It was becoming quite clear to Tony that the man was socially inept. He did not want to think any more about Freddy. The turkey sandwich called to him, and his knife and fork flashed and clicked to attention. He said a quiet prayer for his mom and dug in. The first bite was the best. The turkey was hot and tender. Tony could live forever on turkey. At least once a week. Chicken, too. Fuck beef. It turned his stomach. Fowl, now that was a whole different meat.

Across the table, Fred watched the man devour his food. He considered the bowl of poutine. It was like a child coming to grips with the idea that if he wanted his dessert, he was going to have to eat his vegetables first. Fred finally took up a fork and held it overhand style with his elbow sticking out. It made Tony think of shovelling. A knife joined the poised fork, hovering just over the cheesy surface, and Fred made a thorough study of just where to stab and cut, from this angle or that. He eventually inserted the fork under the cheese and lifted, peeking at what lurked beneath. He dropped it back after a moment and, with his knife, pushed the cheese back like a layer of snow. He inspected the exposed fries underneath. He replaced the cheese, turned the dish around to the opposite side, and did the same thing: lift the cheese, peer in, replace, and turn the dish back to its original place.

Tony stopped eating.

Fred did not notice he was being watched. With his fork, he hoisted the edge of cheese up and pried it back far enough so that it would not slip. He placed a knife on the cheese fold to ensure it stayed there. Then, he got his fork and carefully selected a fry that seemed the appropriate size for his mouth. He stabbed the fry, fished it from the gravy and melted cheese, lifting it high from the dish and marvelling at the cheese string clinging to it. Holding the fry around forehead level, Fred moved in, birdlike, focused on the now sagging cheese string, his mouth opening slightly. He blew on it. Twice. Then, with a shy tongue protruding, touched it as if it would burn him.

Tony glanced around. No one else was watching, and he supposed he should give a fucking silent player to rosy Jesus above just for that. As of that exact moment, Tony was convinced that old Fred was indeed developmentally delayed.

Fred wrapped his tongue around the cheese, and pulled it into his mouth as if he were a centuries-old Colombian tree frog with an arthritic jaw. The man then sucked the strand in, taking deep breaths and stretching the cheese further as he went along. A look of stern concentration crossed his features as he drew the meal up and into his mouth as it were a fucked up rescue rope of some kind. After getting it all in, he chewed, swallowed, and nodded at both the cheese and a performance well done. Then, for whatever reason, he made with his fork to tap his glass full of water.

"You fucking ting that glass and I'll hit you."

The words made Fred blink in surprise. He fixed Tony with a sudden glare that froze the other man. It was like knowing that a double barrel shotgun was tapping ever so gently at your testicles, just to let you know it was there and ready to operate, and Tony was distantly aware of his mouth hanging open, too terrorized to scream. He wanted to fling himself back from the table, flip over onto his belly, and scratch crawl his way, ass high, out the nearest door. He clenched his fork and knife, and drops of perspiration beaded on his forehead. His eyelids fluttered out a weak tattoo. He felt his lower stomach turn sick and curl over itself like some unearthed worm being scorched by the sun, and Tony knew then he was about to defecate himself right there.

Then Freddy turned his eyes back to his meal, and Tony collapsed at the table as if Darth Vader himself had just released him from an invisible strangle hold. He landed on the red vinyl cushion of the booth, white-faced and drooling, taking deep breaths. His fingers gouged the cheap vinyl upholstery of the booth, and he held onto it out of sheer fright. It was a concrete ledge to him and below was a fifteen storey drop.

The man in the business suit looked over, an expression of concern on his face.

Fred focused on him.

The man in the business suit blanched and jerked his newspaper before him like an unstable shield. But it did not stop there as the wave of fear blew back towards the counter and the kitchen beyond. It caught Irene as she was filling the coffee pot with water. She spasmed and dropped the glass pot. It shattered on the floor. She grabbed for the counter for support, to try and control the room from spinning faster. Grey haired Robbie in the kitchen felt his fifty-year-old frame become suddenly cold as if an entire parade had just marched over his grave. The hamburgers frying on the grill sizzled and begged to be flipped, but he paid no attention to the sight, sound or smell of cooking meat. He stepped back and slammed up against the unmovable cutting table set into the middle of his kitchen. He held on to a corner and tightly shut his eyes, fighting for control of his stampeding heart and pulse rate.

Then nothing.

As quickly as the feeling came on, the sense of sheer terror pinched off as neatly as a kid playing with a garden hose. Relief poured over Robbie in the kitchen, with one hand on his cutting table and the other feeling for his testicles (thank the Lord, they were still there). They felt like they had been hauled up inside of him higher than a church's steeple. Irene gulped for air and slowly became aware of the broken glass and mess of water on the floor. She went about searching for a cleaning cloth immediately, still feeling her hands shake. The businessman behind the newspaper stayed there. The day's headlines did not drop, and no doubt, the poor guy would not move until he was good and ready. Or until Irene finally peeked over the lip of the paper, stared into his wide eyes and asked in a very careful voice if he were okay.

Coming out of his own wave of fear, Tony slowly turned his head towards Fred. Fred had taken the first bite of his poutine and chewed on it with barely a sound. Black almond shaped eyes met Tony's gaze and delivered a thunderbolt of a message: *don't fuck with me.*

Tony willed his desert-dry mouth to work. He sat up with effort and reached for his glass of water. He downed it in seconds and returned the glass to its resting spot, fighting the tremble in his hand as he did so, willing it to stop.

Fred cut himself another bite of his meal. His eyes stayed on Tony, waiting to see if there were some smartass comments forthcoming. There weren't.

No real surprise there. It was all Tony could do to keep himself from shaking. When Fred finished his food, Tony finally looked down at his own turkey sandwich. In a voice that was barely a whisper, full of memory of what had just occurred, Fred instructed him to eat it.

Tony gripped his knife and fork, and cut at his cool lunch and shovelled the tasteless sustenance into his mouth. He chewed because he was told to do so. He managed to finish it against a stomach undoing its terrified knots. He passed on the offer of dessert when Irene came around and ignored her questions on what had just happened. He barely heard her at all. She was talking as if through a squeaky glass and soon gave up, moving on to the businessman with his newspaper.

"Go out and start the car," Fred told him after a while. Tony did so, ignoring other people in the restaurant and how their own recoveries were progressing. He left Fred to pay the bill, the bill being the farthest thing from his mind. Tony left the restaurant, entering the cold air again, and walked mechanically towards the Mustang. The growing wind in his face caused the blood to rise to his cheeks, and Tony stopped alongside of his car to breathe it down. A car pulled into the Irving Station's lot, and a white minivan zipped by on the winter highway.

Tony stood and sucked in lungful after lungful of air, and with each breath, his memory allowed him to reflect on what happened just moments ago. With one look, Fred reduced him to a shivering, useless lump of flesh. And as far as Tony knew, there was no one on earth that could do that trick, to anyone, in the middle of the day over a hot turkey sandwich.

Not one goddamn person.

But *he* did.

And Fred not only did it to him but to everyone else in the place. With just a look, he had scared the piss out of everyone. Was such a thing possible? Tony didn't believe it was—knew it wasn't possible. So, what was it then? What caused that one second of absolute terror that affected everyone except Fred? He stood there in a cold that quickly made its way through his winter clothes, looking like a person puzzling over where his keys might be. Snow gathered around his ankles, and he continued to stare into space.

Until Fred appeared on the other side of the car.

Tony blinked but kept his face neutral, not wanting to trigger another tsunami of fear. Not wanting to feel that utter helplessness ever again.

But the hard case in him wanted to know.

"What happened in there?" Tony demanded, his words becoming steam. Fred stood quietly for a moment with one corner of his mouth hitched up in a snarl. If there wasn't a car between them, he might've tried to slap Tony.

"What was it?" Tony heard his mouth say and felt his balls rise up again, anticipating another salvo any instant, and yet still wanting an answer. "What was it? What the hell could make a crowd of people feel that way all at once? But not you? What?"

Fred did not answer. He looked across the highway and the white plains beyond.

"Are you . . ." Tony began, his face whitened, "are you, like . . ."

"Get in the car," Fred commanded, not bothering to face him. "If you say another word, I'll make you shit yourself." With that, Fred got into the car.

Tony suddenly did not feel like driving anywhere. He didn't feel like much of anything except maybe running as fast as a pair of freezing legs could carry him away from this oval headed freak. In his pocket, he felt the reassuring lump of cash paid to him for services he agreed to carry out. He very much liked that bulge in his pocket. He did not want to give it back. But was it enough to continue on?

In a sudden lapse of reason and a show of balls, Tony hunkered down and slipped behind the wheel of the Mustang. He fired up the engine, the beast coming to life with cough and a snarl. A tune up might be in the car's future. The thought made Tony smile weakly. After what he had just been through, he still worried about his piece of shit Mustang. He clung to that. It took his mind off his passenger, and what he was capable of.

What was he capable of?

"Where to?" he asked Fred, surrendering all lead to him.

"You know where," Fred said. "Don't ask me. Just drive. And what were you smiling about?"

The defiant part of Tony did not give an answer. The car was starting to move now. Tony looked over his shoulder and guided the beast back into the frozen country's circulation. If freak boy wanted to scare him now, he would have to grab the wheel and take control of the car, and Tony wondered if he could do both things at once. The thought popped into his mind as he slowly brought the car out of the Irving parking lot and towards the highway, the car's brake lights coming to life and the breath of an old dragon growling from its rear.

CHAPTER 15

Danny got the call from St. Mary's hospital in the afterglow of the last bout of sex with Glenda. He wasn't going to answer at first, but somehow, he knew that it was one of the boys. He changed his mind on the fifth ring. Glenda stayed unmoving when he did. The nurse on the other end informed him that his name was taken from a Mr. Tigh's wallet and he was to be called in case of an emergency. Danny was already moving as she informed him that it would be prudent to come on down to the hospital. He told Glenda to stay in bed, stay as long as she wanted. He told her that the hospital had just called. He told her that his friends were in the emergency ward.

And then, he left.

Danny jumped into his Toyota Celica. He thought himself lucky he didn't ram anyone driving through Halifax as fast as he did. At the hospital, he still managed to greet the nurse behind the reception desk despite the fear he was feeling. He was led to an emergency room where doctors and orderlies swarmed over the bloodied and very still forms of Boomer and Gary. Danny towered over the nurse, and he distantly heard the details of how they had been found and the list of injuries they had sustained. Gary looked incredibly bad, but Boomer looked as if a train had been dropped on him. They were covered in plastic, gleamed with metal, and wired with tubing. Neither would be going anywhere for some time.

"His lower lumbar has been snapped," a doctor was telling him. The nurse laid a hand on Danny's shoulder. "Along with most of his ribs and his right arm broken, and hairline fractures in his skull. Most of his fingers have been broken as well . . ." the doctor went on. Bones broken. Internal injuries. Something about a spleen. A *perforated* scrotum. Ruptured testicles. It occurred to Danny that it would probably save time if the man just told him what was *still working* with the two men. The doctor said something about a police report and how they would want to talk with Danny. He said something about the perpetrators being apprehended soon. As soon as possible. Justice would be served here.

The doctor, a middle-aged man with a tuft of black hair that he secretly dyed, wanted to tell this giant of a man that in his ten years of working at St. Mary's, he had never witnessed such an extent of injuries sustained by two men. And the doctor had seen some pretty freaky things, enough to drive him to indulge in a little wacky tobacky once a month—twice if he really needed it. Burn victims, crash victims, methane explosions, and just plain bad luck accidents. Like the kid who had fallen into his family's septic tank and broken both shoulders going in. He once even removed the salt and pepper shot from the ass and hip of a hunter whose drunken companion had thought he was a two-legged deer.

But these two . . .

The doctor lavished medical terminology on Danny's ears, but all Danny needed to know—could see for himself—was how totally fucked up both Gary and Boom were. No matter how the doctor phrased it, they both had the living shit kicked out of them, and it amazed the fuck out of the medical staff they were still breathing.

They had the living shit kicked out of them, glowed in Danny's mind as if some branding iron had pressed the message into the soft greyness of his brain. He answered the pair of RCMP officers' questions to the best of his ability, and was told there was no evidence of any cash having been stolen or any other wrongdoing. Did he know of anyone, *anyone* at all, capable of perpetrating such a brutal attack? Danny answered "No". He didn't know anyone capable of doing this. No one at all.

And, surprisingly, the officers let him be. The hospital allowed him to remain with his friends, and so he stayed in their room while medical staff swarmed about them.

Boomer was perhaps the worst. His head looked like someone had stomped on it, the only thing keeping the shards of skull in place was his skin, and the effect looked like a cloth bag full of broken crockery They were transporting him to another hospital with better neurosurgical capabilities, and Danny got the feeling that ol' Boom would not be coming out of his coma anytime soon. He heard the words concussion, intracranial haemorrhaging, and hematoma. Judging by the looks on the doctors' faces, it would probably be in Boom's best interest if he stayed in a coma. Danny hoped his friend's passing would be painless. He got the feeling he should pray for it.

They moved Boom, but Gary remained behind, hooked up to machines whose purpose was a mystery to Danny except for the IV and the beeping, bouncing line that told him that Gary was still alive. White-jacketed personnel moved around him, and Danny stayed in the back of the room, hoping that his boss and second closest friend—probably soon to become best—would be fine.

Around 6:30 in the morning of the following day, Gary opened his eyes, and in a perfectly lucid voice asked what hospital he was in. Danny was by his side in a flash, having insisted on remaining near the man's bedside. He didn't call the nurses from their station yet.

"St. Mary's," he informed his boss.

"Good," Gary breathed, his voice becoming a whisper now, as if he had spent whatever energy he had simply breaking the surface of consciousness.

Danny nodded.

"It . . . was . . . Stick," Gary slowly got out, grimacing with every word now as if he were in a gym and powerlifting something beyond his strength.

"Okay," Danny said, placing a hand on the man's pillow. "Okay."

"I . . . can'tfeelnuthinin!" Gary hissed out through clenched teeth " . . . in my legs." He sounded as if he were in pain from everything else. Danny wanted an increase in whatever painkiller was being pumped into him.

"Dan."

Danny leaned in close.

"Dan," Gary breathed again, on the brink of losing consciousness. "Make the call. Kill . . ."

A laboured breath rattled out of Gary, and his eyes became slits and finally closed. Danny's throat tightened, but then, he realized the machine was still beeping. The boss was only out. Thank God for that. Thank God.

Danny watched his friend slip back under the black tide of unconsciousness, trying very hard not to leak any tears. It was only a day ago the three of them had been sitting down at the Beacon and enjoying breakfast together. And now, Gary felt nothing in his legs. Boom was pulp. Danny seriously considered what was going to happen if they both died. God help him, as much as he loved both of them, piss-poor table manners and toilet humour aside, he hoped they died in peace. And soon.

He growled as he wiped his wet eyes. The last time he had cried was during that *Lost* episode where Hurley lost his potential girlfriend. That truly sucked. Before that, it was Tom Hanks being on a deserted island with only a fucking volleyball to keep him company, which he later lost at sea. Danny thought it took a pretty damn good actor to make a person get misty over a fucking volleyball. Boom had thought otherwise, but then again, Boom still liked action over the chick flicks.

Action with revenge themes.

Danny finished wiping his eyes. He cleared his throat and breathed deeply through his mouth as his nose was full of snot.

They had talked about *"what if"* one time, if one of them or all of them were somehow knocked off. What would the dead want of the others? Boomer's answer had been expected and joking joke, but Gary was stone cold serious. He told them both that if he were ever killed or somehow incapacitated, the others had permission to use whatever funds Gary had in his not-so-secret retirement fund—a load of hard cash done up in bundles of twenties, fifties, hundreds and a few purple thousands (he even had nice bars of gold in there). Use the money and find the fucker who did him in. Find them, tell them who had wanted them to die, and then kill them. Gary had also provided them both with a name of an individual that was a myth on the East Coast. A man that did such professional contracts without suggesting neither Boomer nor Danny had the cajones to actually kill someone. Gary personally thought they didn't, but he never said that to their faces. He gave them the name of the person whose business it was to make people disappear.

Danny stood up. He remembered the name as easily as someone recalling 911. He informed the nurses of Gary's brief surfacing and left. He made his way to his car. Memories of his friends were in his head, being slowly replaced by what they were now. The Stick. The Stickman did both of them in and fucked them up bad enough that death would be a release. Danny got behind the wheel of his car. He had a man to call.

Danny would see to it that the same courtesy would be extended to the Stickman.

CHAPTER 16

In Miyagi prefecture, Japan, in the mountainous city of Sendai, a celebration was beginning in the Sunny Hills Retirement Home. Fumiko and Natsuko Aso, identical twins, had their wheelchairs rolled into a common room filled with the pleasant grassy scent of brand new tatami mats. They were wrapped in white, flower-sprinkled blankets for extra warmth, and the instant they came into the room, they were surrounded by their remaining children, grandchildren and even great grandchildren. They gazed up with once-deep-brown eyes at the bright decorations one might see at a school party. The women were steered through the room towards a centre table with a huge cake on it and decorations of red and green roses. Peals of laughter enveloped them. A three digit number stuck out of the white frosting, burning lively and throwing sparkles into the air. Hands were clapping, and the masses broke into song. Fumiko bared her unnaturally white teeth, new, only a year old, while Natsuko stared at the flaring numeral with eyes that looked immensely tired. She never asked for this. A smoke would have done her just fine. Her sister could have all the parties she wanted.

Camera flashes went off from both family and the press. The owner of the Sunny Hills Retirement Home, a Mr. Saito, beamed at the ladies from beyond the gathering of their relations. He left the families and the two newest centenarians to their birthday cake—which the children would devour—and the more traditional rice cakes that the sisters were much fonder of. He retreated without anyone noticing, the sound of applause dappling the halls of the retirement home. He knew of the sisters. And he remembered how they had asked him not to allow such a party to take place. They did not want one. Did not require one like some other people. Yet, ever since they became centenarians, thirteen years ago, they were given one, against their secret wishes. Each year, the lustre of the day of their natural birth was a mark in time of not things to come, but of memories lost. Both had lost their husbands decades ago, and Natsuko had even outlasted one of her own daughters, a terrible loss to her, and something Saito did not like to dwell on. How could a person watch their child grow up, marry, have children, and then keep on watching as their child grew older and older and finally passed on?

Regardless, Saito loved the twins. They were a living testament to the care he and his carefully selected staff routinely took in their work. The ladies were in perfect health for their age. Their diet was carefully monitored, and they lived as actively as their brittle forms would allow. And they lived on. Soon, the day would come when the twins would not be with Sunny Hills, but Saito did not want to think of that either. Perhaps it was the love of the grandchildren that kept them in this world, wondering just how old they were, or how they felt, and asking about the past with eyes shining so bright and new.

The twins, own eyes were old now, no longer as resplendent, and rolled from here to there to take everything in. These days, their eyes watered almost constantly with the strain placed upon them. Their fragile frames were hunched over, always felt chilled, with their faces marked and sucked dry by unseen years. Yet, while their bodies were old, their minds were still sharp. They could remember the birthdays of their children before them, and although some memories made their eyes water even more than usual, the images they recalled warmed them better than any pretty blanket. If asked, they could remember Nagasaki, even before the bomb destroyed the city.

One of Fumiko's most vivid memories was of how they sent their children to school, to huddle there while they clawed raw vegetables out of a scorched earth. Despite the almost total destruction of the city, the school's walls had been untouched. The roof of the school had been blown off completely, like the top of a toy house.

And on one day in the winter, the children in school looked to the heavens and smiled.

For it began to snow.

Great powdery puffs of snow fell magically into the school, and the children thought this to be the greatest thing. Those days and the images of smiling children gazing up at winter through a missing roof to watch rare falling snow were one of the treasures in Fumiko's old head.

Snow. As white as the not so sweet frosting on the cake before her. It was interesting what thoughts would come to her these days, and the times when they came. She realized then where she was and looked at her sister. Natsuko gazed at the cake, her mouth cracked opened ever so slightly. She did not have her teeth in today, and she wondered how many tiny bites she could manage before her stomach turned on her. There was a time when she could eat as much of anything as she wanted. She missed those days. Fumiko did, as well, but she did not dwell on them.

Then the people around them sang a birthday song that ended with a great *omedeto gozaimasu* and an applause that sounded like monsoon rains. It lifted the twins' spirits. They were with family today. They were amongst people who loved, cared for and honoured them, and it was that warm rush of emotion that kept the ache of their years at bay.

And it was yet another moment in their long, long lives.

CHAPTER 17

At 8:45 in the morning, Danny sat in Gary's office, behind the great desk. The police allowed the big, grief-stricken man into the office and did not protest when he closed the door to the crime scene. Danny quietly went to the safe set into the base of the desk. It wasn't hidden. No one ever expected the Beacon to be hit. And the Stickman hadn't been interested in the contents of the safe. It was untouched. Danny regarded the safe with half-opened, dead-serious eyes. Never did he think there would have been a day like this one. Never. And yet here it was, smack damn in the middle of his face. He sighed and entered the combination on the number pad. He opened the safe and took out two of the six brown envelopes within. There was a brown wooden box next to the envelopes, and Danny knew that was where Gary kept his gathered gold. How many ounces, he didn't know and didn't care. Gary might have been a crime boss, but he was a friend. Instead, Danny plucked the white enveloped marked for either him or Boomer.

Boom.

Coughing from the swelling of emotion in his throat, Danny tore open the envelope. He tapped it with a finger, and a white card fell onto the floor. It was blank except for one long telephone number. Not caring if the cops could do anything with the telephone or not, Danny got into Gary's chair and removed the receiver from its cradle and began to dial. He had an idea who he was calling. He remembered Gary talking about the number and the man on the other end. Danny did not care. This was his friend's last wish, and he would see it through.

The voice that answered was not alert or careful sounding. It sounded bored. It asked questions, and Danny gave the best answers he could. There were pauses on the line, in that other place, and Danny wondered in those moments just where that other place was. More questions and pauses, muffled, as if someone were covering the receiver and conversing with others nearby.

The voice finally asked Danny for his cell phone number, which he gave. He was then told to go home and wait.

In a blue daze, Danny did just that. When he got home, he asked Glenda to get dressed and go home. She asked why. Danny didn't give her an explanation. She started to ask again, but Danny silenced her with his big brown eyes and the pain therein. He told her he would call when he could, and she said okay. He saw her to the door, and once she was gone, he went back to the bed smelling of strawberry shampoo and perfume. He lay down and stared up at the ceiling, the phone nearby. He thought about better times with the boys.

Sometime later, his phone buzzed. He answered it. A different voice gave him instructions, a time, and a flight number for that evening. The voice asked if Danny got everything, and Danny said he did. The connection broke. Danny went back to staring at the ceiling.

There was no going back now.

Crew placed the latest *John Grisham* novel into the magazine pocket in front of him. He would leave it there when he left the plane, amongst the magazines and the *Where's Waldo* illustrations for aircraft emergencies. He started reading the book two days ago and while it wasn't up to par with *The Street Lawyer*, his favourite to date, it was still a decent read. He'd leave it for the next person to sit here if the attendants didn't find it first. He never stockpiled his books. What was the point? You buy the thing, read it, and pass it on if it was any good. Why hoard it? Read it again? Movies could be watched more than once if they were exceptional, but who had the time to read a book twice? Those who did had too much time on their hands in his opinion. And the second reading would be diluted anyway, just like a movie would be. You knew what was going to happen, but at least in a flick, you had music to sort of make it work. Not in a book.

Still, some folks derived something from it. Crew just didn't get it. If life was that boring for some, then they should just die and get it over with.

Or at least buy a new book.

There were plenty out there.

The fasten-all-seatbelts light blinked on, and Crew felt the aircraft turn to the right. He adjusted the blanket he used to cover his legs with, using it more like a giant drop cloth than for warmth. He looked across the two empty seats. He had been lucky today. Out the window was Halifax, Nova Scotia. A city that once was flattened by an explosion that made God's own teeth ache.

What would he find down there?

At thirty-seven years of age, Crew—nicknamed 'Wrecking'—found himself asking that question more and more often with each job he took on. What would he find? Who would be found? What would be the hunt and where would it lead?

Who would die?

He was getting older, and those musings floated inside his skull. He managed to keep in shape, exercising four to five times a week, weight training and aerobics. He remembered Abbot giving him a hard time about the aerobics until he bet the man five hundred he couldn't keep up for fifteen minutes in the class. Abbot actually managed ten—surprising Crew as it was the advanced class he had chosen for the bet—but the man was white-faced, trembling, and sweating like he was about to drop right there on the floor. He might have even puked in the dressing room. Abbot never mocked Crew about the class again. He even admitted the women there were pretty hot and wondered if Crew ever took a run at any of them.

So, he was in shape, still had his hair, and only a few wire stripes of grey in the otherwise black military cut hinted at his age. He dressed well, if not tame. For this trip he opted on beige pants and a denim shirt buttoned to the throat. A coal black winter coat was overhead for the cold. Nothing fancy, but serviceable. He always maintained eye contact with the female flight attendants, always thanked them, and always left them feeling easy. He sometimes caught them sizing up the horizontal scar on his right cheek, a brazen two inches long. He didn't mind that. He made the scar look good, and made it look hellish when he needed to. He didn't like to draw too much attention to himself, but the number of phone numbers he sometimes collected spoke otherwise.

So, fuck age, though he knew the nagging in his skull would return soon enough. After all, he would be crazy to be in this work still when he hit forty. And did he really want to be part of the Abbot's old guard then? Part of the permanent fixtures adorning the man's estate? The equivalent of a cop's desk job after a bloody career of servitude to a crime lord? Crew felt he was too educated, well-read—if one considered John Grisham and Stephen King being well-read—and had invested his money intelligently with the goal of getting out when he wanted to. Just disappearing. The question was would the organization let him? Crew did not know of anyone actually getting out. But he did manage to keep from becoming a full member. He was more of a contract cleaner, taking on work concerning folks outside of New York State. All he needed from whoever was contracting him was a name and an address. If there was no address, that was fine too. Crew enjoyed the challenge of finding someone as much as the next person enjoyed a crossword puzzle. He was a roamer, so he liked the travelling part of the job. He never allowed himself to work more than one hit at a time, never initiated small talk with anyone other than the Abbot, and kept as much information about himself as confidential as possible. The Abbot once mentioned that working with Crew was like signing on a ghost with an attitude. Crew liked that.

"You think all that's going to protect you if we really have to find you?" an associate named Jones had once asked him over the phone. Jones sometimes talked to him if the Abbot wasn't around. Crew didn't like talking to Jones. The man always wanted to talk, and when Crew didn't, Jones would fill in the silence with what he thought Crew thought.

Honestly, Crew did not know if all the precautions he had taken over the years would be enough to save him from the organization if they really wanted to slag him. He believed he had enough fake aliases to disappear. He had money in multiple offshore accounts and was thinking about either Mexico or the Philippines for retirement. He stayed offline. He had no permanent address. He used disposable phones. He tried very hard to be the ghost people thought him to be. And when the day arrived when he did disappear, he would still have a plan B prepared just in case of any visits by old, unwanted associates.

Problems. He possessed enough of them. Besides his eventual retirement, as he identified it, one was that he had enough money to get out today and live a life of luxury if he died at exactly sixty. If he died before then he would have thousands untouched. When to quit was a mystery to him.

There were also hints that the management *would* want to meet him face-to-face someday. Something which Crew considered a very bad idea. He wanted only to work, to do the job, collect his fee, and move on. But the ride was going to come to an end. He could not ignore or side-slip the request for personal meetings forever.

He had a final problem, too. He enjoyed what he did. He enjoyed the hunt. If the target was outside New York and had to die, he enjoyed being contacted to do the deed. He liked what he did too much.

And quitting was going to be a bitch.

CHAPTER 18

The plane landed with a soft thump, and the ground outside his window streaked by. The edges of the runway were white with snow. He felt for his heavy gloves and coat, all black, and a grey ringed toque if he needed it. He had brought a change of clothes good for three days. He had brought no weapons. He had his two hands and had no problem using them. If he really needed a weapon, he would pick up a hunting knife somewhere. That would be weapon enough.

He left the seat and book, and departed the plane with pleasant goodbyes to the cabin crew, catching their eyes for brief moments before moving on. He passed through immigration without any trouble although he inwardly hoped that one day he would be contracted to knock off one of those ill-tempered bitches or bastards. Perhaps the airport hired these people with that character trait in mind.

He made his way through the arrivals door with the rest of the passengers, crossed the threshold, and stopped just a step beyond. He inhaled the fresh floor polish, and the overhead florescent lighting made the white tiles gleam like bare bone. Travelers were greeted by family or friends, or simply moved on to the parking lots and bus stops. Crew glanced up at a big LED clock and read 6:35 p.m. on the nose. He went to the baggage area, retrieved his one bag, a blue duffel job, and waited until all the others did the same and were gone. Then he saw his contact, a tall black man that could have easily made a career in football. The dark winter clothing he wore made him look bigger. After the crowds had dissipated, he was the only one still hanging around. Their gazes met. Crew approached the man after a short moment. He hoped to God the man didn't speak Ebonics or whatever the fuck it was. It turned his stomach to hear smart people talk stupid. *And da wuz d' troof.*

"Danny?" Crew asked quietly with a cocked eyebrow.
"Yeah, that's me. And you are?"
"DJ," Crew informed him without a smile.
"Okay. You got much stuff?"
"Only the one bag."
"Travel light, huh?"
"Travel light," Crew answered.

"Well, let's get going then," Danny said and started walking towards the exit. Crew was content to follow, measuring up the big man from behind. In his mind, it struck him that Danny was polite enough as he made his way through people, excusing himself here and there, and avoiding playing 'chicken' with anyone smaller than him. Crew liked that. Most of the guys his size, like Jones for instance, used their weight too goddamned much, and suffered from what Crew labeled as 'Big Man Syndrome.' Every person coming their way had to move first or get a glare, a glare that suggested a willingness to get physical if the smaller person wanted to. The smaller folks rarely did.

Crew was glad Danny did not display any signs of BMS. And he was glad the man spoke normally. Another plus.

They stood in front of the rotating door that led to the outside, listening to the steady beat of the whirling glass as if it were the gills of the airport. In the reflection of the glass, Danny sized up the man just to the right and behind him. Crew was of regular height, in good shape, dark complexion, hair and eyes, with a bitch of a scar across his right cheek. A knife wound? Or maybe it was made with a nail or something. Quiet little guy as well, which suited Danny fine. For the life of him, he really did not know what to say to a person who killed people for a living. Danny was an enforcer, but he rarely had to fight. His size and reputation had plenty to do with that. His appearance could diffuse a situation in moments, and if the shit really looked like it was going to go down, Boomer was almost always at his side. Any of the fights he had been in were short, and usually with drunks, made both brave and stupid by their booze. And in truth, Danny felt like shit if he did have to thrash a drunk. Sometimes he and Boom would have heated debates on whether or not he had been in the business too long and was going soft.

He wanted to ask DJ if he had guns. Or knives. Or something. He read some spy novels where the guys wore wire around their wrists that could serve as a garrote if needed, but DJ had no adornments that Danny could see. And if he did have anything, he wanted to ask how he got the shit through security. But such questions seemed professionally uncool at the moment.

They took turns heading out the revolving door. They exited the airport and entered the cold of a Nova Scotia winter. The air was chilling and sobering, and tasted wonderfully pure. It was also cold enough to turn Crew's nipples into diamonds. His one thought was a teeth chattering *Jesus!* He looked ahead and saw in the distance a dark and frosty tree line illuminated by road lights. Danny kept a few steps in front, weaving his way through parked vehicles with the snow drifting up between them. He finally stopped in front of his car.

A 2001 Toyota Celica.

A black one.

Crew sized up the small sports coup and then studied the man before him.

"You fit in that thing?"

"Just barely," Danny said with a reflective smile as if there had been some difficult times in the past. "No one sits behind me when I'm driving."

"You mean you haven't taken out the front seat yet?" Crew said seriously. "Holy shit."

Not bothering to answer, Danny unlocked the car door. He reached inside and popped the trunk. Crew hoisted it up and threw his bag in.

"Nice country here," Crew remarked.

Then Danny did something that would have inspired David Copperfield. The big man lowered himself and disappeared inside the tiny sports coup. It impressed the hell out of the New Yorker. The passenger door opened, and he got inside.

"Man," Crew said, wondering how in the hell Danny could fit in the driver's seat. "If you stretch out, your legs'll be chewed up by the engine."

"Yeah," Danny replied in a weary voice as if he had heard it all several times before. He started the engine and jacked up the heat. The powerful glare of the dash caught Crew's attention. It was a gorgeous interior, and the lights blazed at him. Danny turned on a techno tune with soft violins and adjusted the volume so they could talk. The music hit Crew from the front and back. If he were into cars more, he could've appreciated the Celica's charms, but as it was, it was simply 'nice.'

"Did you bring a picture?" Crew suddenly asked.

This brought a sigh from the big man behind the wheel. He looked down into the gentle glare of the dash lights. "No. Nothing."

That wasn't good.

"A name then?"

"Crawford Ryan. They call him the Stickman or Stickman. Or just Stick sometimes. Short guy. A little shorter than you, but built like a wall. Did some time out in Saskatchewan. He's the main guy for Badger. He was the one working for Mr. Tigh." Danny always referred to Gary by his last name when talking to business folks. He went on and explained the background of Badger and how events came to putting him in a hospital. Danny told the man all he knew.

When he finished, Crew was staring out at the night, looking though a windshield reflecting a diamond's sharpness of dash lights.

"Some fuckheads just don't get it," Crew shook his head. "It pays to stick with college grads in this business. Definitely higher than high school."

This made Danny nod sagely. Stealing from a boss and then sticking around certainly wasn't the smartest thing to do. No, Badger wasn't the brightest bulb, but how bright was the Stickman? Danny drummed a finger on his steering wheel as he peered ahead. He didn't think the man was overly intelligent, but the word *cunning* came to mind. The man had to know that hitting Gary in his office would bring about retaliation, and he was hunting Levin against a clock now, before he was taken out for his attempted kill. So, he would probably be heading west after Levin, but would he be coming back? If he was smart, probably not.

"I know what he looks like," Danny said quietly. "And where he's heading. I want to come with you."

There was no response from the other man, and for a moment, both of them sat while the motor quietly warmed the interior of the Celica. It was no real surprise to Crew. He supposed he would do the same thing, *if* he allowed himself to get close to any of the people working in the organization. And he tried very hard not to let that happen. That was a conditional that he could not allow. Not if he wanted to retire clean one day.

"So, you a bouncer?" Crew asked him.

"I prefer 'peacemaker' myself," Danny informed him with the barest of smiles. "And you're a . . ."

Whatever, Crew thought. Fixer. Cleaner. Stain Remover. He once overheard someone call him the Ghost of the Sea. Another once referred to him as the last magic show the condemned would ever see, and many people had disappeared when the show went on the road. But that was stateside. His reputation was there. This was a different country.

"You know where he's headed?" Crew wanted confirmation, ignoring Danny's question.

"A general idea," Danny said.

That was fine for Crew. "Usually I get all the information I need in a brown business envelope. You're a little bigger than that."

"I'll probably talk more, too," Danny said. "So, what's the verdict? You okay with me coming along."

In the illumination of the dash, the cogs of Crew's mind slowed. He did not like having travelling companions. The more people that knew his identity, the greater the threat to his peaceful retirement. If he had to, he would kill this man if he became such a threat. He did not go into a long lecture about being careful.

The truth was if Danny did become baggage, he would be terminated after the Stickman. Sooner, if Crew could identify the man on his own. He hoped he would not have to do such a thing. He hated collateral casualties.

Still, word from the Abbot spoke highly of the one called Danny.

"You packed?" He finally asked.

"Everything's in the backseat."

This made Crew glance around. Right there, in the middle of the rear seat, darker against the darkness, were two small overnight bags.

"Drive on then," Crew said and knifed a hand at the windshield.

CHAPTER 19

The evening was clear and cold. The edges of daylight were just turning a beautiful orange as a bruised, blue, '85 Mustang growled its way northwest along Highway 2. The car had passed the Saint John River, going by the provincial capital of Fredericton. It motored by Exit 259, heralding in the darkening winter evening, and ignored the sign for the Living History Museum of Rural Life, also known as King's Landing. Inside the car, Fred's eyes took in the billboard sign briefly before turning his attention back to the road. Rural life did not interest Fred.

Nor Tony, who gripped the wheel with both hands, concentrating on the snowy road and wary for black ice. He said nothing to his passenger, and Fred, in turn, said nothing back. For Tony, New Brunswick's section of the Trans-Canada was hell's version of a Sunday drive going on into eternity. It was a long twisting highway with few straight sections where a driver could really burn asphalt. It was a road where some drivers found it necessary to pull over and rest from its rolling monotony. Tony was not one of those drivers. He had a live wire of fear coursing through him that would not allow him to relax. There were some houses along the road and snow drifts, but he paid them no mind. The fear kept Tony on course, and threatened to make him rip the steering column from its housing. He was on edge. He felt like he might've downed a bucket of espresso, then been strapped into a Lazy Boy and asked to relax. He wanted off this road. He wanted out of this car. He wanted to be away, so very far away, from fuckhead on his right. He was going to freak soon. He could feel it. The pressure building up in his loins and heart felt like a dentist's diamond drill spinning on a raw nerve and sending up tendrils of smoke. If freak boy Freddy pulled another one of his shock treatments, as Tony now thought of them, he would probably slam the brakes on and just see how far the Mustang would fly. What would it be like if the ache in his lower legs just kept building and building, like a car pushing 200 kilometres an hour, but locked in neutral? Would he know if he snapped? Would he be grinning like Jack Torrance in the *The Shining*, peeking through the jagged hole he had just made in the door with a fire axe? Would it sneak up on him or simply snap into his mind like a poisoned quarrel?

Tony felt like it might do the latter.

They did not stop for dinner. They did not stop for a piss. They did stop for gas twice, but both times, it felt like a hurried pit stop where Tony did not dare get out from behind the wheel. Freak boy always paid for the gas and listened to the music of the radio. He seemed to be enjoying it, and anything that diverted his attention away from Tony was good. Perhaps it was the music helping Tony keep all of his marbles. Perhaps, if the music stopped, the ache he currently felt would triple in intensity, and he would simultaneously shit, piss, and puke himself with volcanic intensity the very instant it did.

Tony concentrated on the road, his nose getting a little closer to the steering wheel as he did.

Highway 2 became Route 185 as the Trans-Canada continued into Quebec. Any other time, Tony would be overjoyed. The maddening twist of the New Brunswick highway was behind him, and he could look forward to flooring it down the straight as razor strips along the mighty St. Lawrence River. Night dropped on them like a black, starless avalanche, and the Mustang's headlights illuminated a blacker road shouldered on the right by massive walls of freshly cleared ice and snow. Gravel mixed with salt covered the snowy mounds like excessive maple sprinkles on ice-cream. Road signs peeked out of snow drifts and flashed by, screaming out short messages.

"Pick her up," Fred abruptly said.

This caused Tony to frown. "What?"

But Fred did not repeat himself.

Fucking asshole.

Fred did not repeat himself because he hated to repeat himself when people clearly heard him the first time. Yet, some people would still ask simply out of reflex.

"Pick up *who*?" Tony blinked into the darkness rushing towards him. On the right, the reflective squares nailed into the guard rails zipped by, but otherwise, there was nothing out there except road and snow and night. It had to be minus twenty out there. No one would be out here tonight. Especially a single woman hitchhiking at night in the winter!

But then there she was, blinking into existence like a skinny tree, facing them on the shoulder of the highway. Arm outstretched, and a backdrop of snow behind her. He could see her breath steaming from her mouth, a grimace in the glare of the Mustang's lights.

He put a foot to the brakes. "Whatever, man," he muttered, wondering if there was something *else* he had to worry about now. He cursed himself for feeling even a drop of amazement. Not after this day. Fred was simply too goddamn unreal. Predicting a hitchhiker and commanding him to pick her up before Tony even laid eyes on the woman was nothing compared to what went on in the restaurant.

Hell, *everybody* gets a lucky guess once.

The Mustang zipped by the figure in its deceleration. The car slowed and finally stopped. Tony looked over his shoulder. In the red glow of his tail lights, like afterburners, he saw the woman run towards the car. In seconds, she was thumping on Fred's window.

Fred scowled and adjusted himself in his seat.

The dark figure outside his window tapped again. She was wearing red mittens.

"You gonna let her in?" Tony wanted to know.

Fred ignored him.

"You were the one who wanted to stop, so you let her in," Tony grumbled under his breath. He hoped that she wasn't half the twist-pack his friend Freddy was. When Fred failed to open his door, Tony shook his head, finding his balls for the first time since the restaurant. "Man, you're something else."

He opened his door and got out.

"Hi."

Standing there, smiling bright enough to shame the sun, she gave Tony a little wave that struck the man as both endearing and gawd-awful cute. She wore a black leather jacket with a bee's bottom striped toque. Her face was almost perfectly round with dusky skin and dark Asian eyes. Black straight hair with the barest of ripples fell about her face, highlighted by a ribbon strip of hair that had been tinted snow white.

"Hey," Tony said.

She unleashed the full might of her smile upon him then, and it stunned Tony. It could have been minus *fifty* on that gash of asphalt in the middle of the night, but the warmth in that smile simply enveloped him, and left him grinning stupidly back.

"Thanks for stopping," she said. She had the most adorable nose, too.

"Hey," Tony said again through half frozen lips that his mind continued to ignore. "No trouble. Uh. It's, uh, weird, actually. My—" he caught himself. He was *not* about to call Fred his friend. "Uh, Fred saw you before I did."

"Oh," she said, her chin rising as she spoke, her smile dimming by degrees. "This Fred?" she inquired downwards with a red mitten.

"Yeah."

"He changed his mind awfully fast."

"Yeah. You can get in on my side though."

"Really? You aren't gonna change your mind, are you?" and her smile turned into an irresistible half pout.

"Ah, no," was all Tony could manage.

She did not move. "You guys aren't freaks are you? Or pervs? There are two of you. You aren't gonna try anything, right? Or get weird or anything?"

"Huh?" Tony blinked. "No, no, course not. No, I'm not gonna do nothin.'"

"You're sure?"

"Sure, I'm sure."

"That's good cuz I sure wouldn't want to have to fight you," she adjusted her bee bottom toque, pulling it lower on her forehead. Tony wanted to do it for her. He smiled in spite of himself.

"Okay," she said brightly. "I believe you."

She came around the front of the car and Tony saw that she wore high, white boots with fur frills and black jeans. The boots reminded him of a poodle for some reason. The jeans were tight, and he did not scrutinize any more than a glance would allow. The red mittens were, however, the old fashioned typed. Hand knitted and very warm looking.

"Aren't you cold?" Tony said, wanting to ask her *something*.

"Sure am. I'm lucky you came along when you did. Nobody's been along this way since it got dark. I could've died out here!"

Tony opened his door and pulled his seat forward for her to climb into the car. He made a quick inspection of her heart shaped bottom as she went in. He waited until she was settled away before pushing the seat back.

"Get in quick!" she cried. "It's *freezing* out there!"

He had to agree. In the short time he was outside, he felt he could use his balls as wind chimes. She was right about one thing: she would have died out here if they didn't pass along. He climbed in and slammed the door, hoping the damn thing wouldn't fall off with the force. He checked his mirrors and blind spot out of instinct, and eased the Mustang into drive. Snow crunched underneath the tires as they picked up speed.

"What's your name?" she asked from behind. Tony caught the undisguised roll of Fred's head. In that one motion, he made it clear he despised the new passenger.

"Uh, Tony."

"Anthony?"

"Just Tony."

"Anthony is nicer."

"Tony is shorter."

"Anything nicer is worth a little more effort."

"Yeah, well, anything is better than asshole, too," Tony said. There was an abrupt silence from the darkness back there. Tony knew in an instant that she did not care for the word "asshole", and he suddenly felt very conscious about using it. He felt an invisible hand of *"What the fuck?"* snapping him on his forehead. What was happening to him?

"Can I call you Anthony?" she asked to Tony's relief. He did not want to be on this one's bad side. He had a lifetime's worth of ugly vibes from monkey boy on his right.

"That's fine," he said. "But Tony is fine, too."

"Nice to meet you, Anthony," she said as if not hearing. "And thank you for stopping. I'm Lucy."

Tony nodded into the rear view mirror.

"Hi, Fred," she called out musically, surprising Tony.

Despite himself, Tony caught Fred's expression go from sulking silence to one of absolute sickness. As if the greeting were the most sarcastic words Lucy could have ever spoken to him.

"He doesn't talk much," Lucy noted.

Tony looked into the rear-view mirror and saw only darkness underneath that bee bottom winter hat. Then, he could see her eyes as if she had closed them for a moment. He quickly looked back to the road.

"No, he doesn't," and damn if Tony didn't want the squirrel fucker to start talking now. What was the man's problem? He wanted her picked up, and Tony had done so. If only Fred had gotten out of the car to let her in on his side. Tony would have left the bastard behind in the night.

It occurred to him that perhaps Fred suspected he would do exactly that. Smart fucker.

Freak? Definitely. Stupid? Not enough.

"Well, that's fine by me. We'll just talk by ourselves," Lucy went on.

"I'm listening to the radio," Fred rumbled, and Tony felt the all too familiar crackling of ice seizing his innards. He choked the steering wheel with both hands and felt the blood pound in his ears.

"You can still listen to it," Lucy told him, and like a shot of hot whiskey, her voice melted Tony's freezing core. He took an unrestricted breath and relaxed his grip on the wheel. Just like that, whatever spell Fred had been concocting was dispelled.

Even more incredible, Fred became all the more miserable shifting into petulance as if he has just been unjustly scolded by his mother. He sank into his seat, hooded eyes fixed on the road ahead and black with poison. For the first time since the restaurant, Tony felt somehow liberated. A smile spread across his face in the glow of the dashboard lights, and he searched for Lucy's face in the rearview mirror.

"Lucy, I like you," he said, and meant it.

"Most people do," she informed him and smiled so sweetly that Tony found it difficult to return to the road. "In fact," she continued, her eyes downcast now, "all people do. I haven't met anyone yet who didn't like me. That might sound bad or conceited or something, but I think it's true. Don't think badly of me, Anthony."

"I won't," Tony assured her. Just seeing old Fred boy shrunk up like a chilled buffalo scrotum was enough to make Tony love the woman.

"I try to be a nice person. Really," Lucy paused for a moment and looked out at the blackness beyond the glass. "Where are you guys going anyway?"

"West," Tony told her. "Vancouver." *I think*, he wanted to add but didn't. She would probably be long gone before they got to Vancouver anyway.

"Hey that's great!" Lucy pealed. "*I'm* headed for Vancouver!"

From the passenger's side, Fred rolled his head again. He had already had enough of this bitch.

"Would it be too much for me to tag along?" Lucy asked in a pleading voice. "I'm not being too forward I hope. I have money. I can help pay for gas. Well, some anyway."

The smile on Tony's face got wider. "We just picked you up remember? Only a minute ago you were asking if I was a freak."

"That was a minute ago. But point taken. You could still be a freak. I guess it wasn't too smart of me to say I have money, right?"

"Nope."

"Well, sugar," Lucy cursed.

"But you didn't say how much exactly, so I think you're safe." It was hard not to smile when talking to this woman.

"You're right, I didn't. Well, let's just see how the next little bit goes, and I'll decide then if I'll go with you to BC."

"You'll decide, will you?" Tony *really* liked this chick.

"Well, you're not going to force me to get out in the middle of nowhere, are you?"

Tony shook his head in reply. He'd kill Fred first.

"Would you, Fred?" Lucy addressed the quiet man with the barest note of challenge. A friendly challenge, but with the funk Fred was in, any challenge, no matter how good-natured, would probably feel like a thumb up his ass. And as Tony expected, Fred declined to answer.

"Would you?" Lucy asked again, and the silence that ensued made Tony think of the endgame pause on the last second on a bomb, between nothing and detonation. And instead of fright in his heart, limbs and guts, Tony felt nothing but ease. It was the damnedest thing.

"Fred?" she persisted with a tease of a smile.

And then, to Tony's disbelief, Fred mumbled something. It was completely incoherent, but he responded to her.

"What was that?" she asked.

Fred heaved out a breath like it was a fifty pound weight. "No, I suppose not."

"Oh, good!"

Oh good! Tony thought. It was as easy as that. The beast rolled over and exposed its belly. He found himself shaking his head. It couldn't be *that* easy to bring Freddy down, could it? 'Course then again, Tony wasn't a hot Asian chick in the back seat. It made him shut up for the next few seconds.

"So, you're from Nova Scotia?" Lucy asked Tony, wanting to chat.

"Huh?"

"Nova Scotia? Your plates said that."

"Uh, yeah. You?"

"Nah. Visited there lots though. Nice place. I especially liked Bridgewater. Beautiful town. Nice and quiet, y'know. I could raise a family there."

"That so? Where you from then?" Tony slowed the Mustang's speed ever so slightly. He didn't want to rush while speaking with Lucy.

"Everywhere and nowhere. My Dad was a salesman, so we got to move around a bit. We lived in the States for a while, too. Know Appleton?"

"No," Tony shrugged.

"Well, you'll check the map next time, won't you?" she smiled at him. "You'll win a prize if you do."

The rearview mirror displayed the little "*oh really*" jig Tony's eyebrows did.

"That's a nice town, too, but if I had a choice, I'd still go with Bridgewater, especially in late September. The nights there are *soooooo* comfortable. Summer's cooling off, but it's still warm enough to sleep outside. We had a boat there, too, when I was a little girl. Nothing fancy, just a big fat speed boat to scoot across the water on."

"Anyone with a boat must be doing well for themselves. What did your Dad sell?" Tony asked.

"Industrial equipment. The big stuff they use in mines or whatever. He only needed to make a couple of sales a year, and he'd be set. It was pretty international, too. Got to travel a lot. Even went to Germany once. And Japan. That was freaky."

"Wow," Tony muttered and meant it. Who would have guessed it from a hitchhiker on the side of the road. "You speak any Japanese?"

"Yes, I can," she said merrily.

"Let's hear some."

"Nani o iimasu ka?"

"Whaaaa?" Tony said, impressed. "What's that mean?"

"Essentially, I asked, 'What do you want me to say? Sorry. I'm not too creative at times, especially on nights like these. All the creative juices are frozen."

That was his opening. "So, what happened out here? You break down or something?"

"Don't own a car, so I guess it's 'or something.' It's a little private, and I really don't feel right talking to you about it, seeing as we just met. Sorry. You okay with that?" She ended on an apologetic note that made Tony burn with self-hate for even asking such a question. He immediately forgot all of his other questions.

"Hey, no trouble," he huffed out. "Sorry for asking. Just a little strange to see something like you—some*one* like you on the shoulder of the road. But never mind. None of my business."

Highway reflectors nailed into three foot high road posts flashed by marking a wall of snow.

"It's been a strange couple of days," she said in a sad, reflective tone. Tony could understand that, especially when he had fuck-head Freddy as a co-pilot. And speaking of the man who was quickly becoming a legend of absolute fucked-*upped*-ness in Tony's mind, Freddy turned around violently and fixed Lucy with the most serious of looks.

A moment passed before Lucy asked, "Did I say something?"

Freddy screwed up his mouth in annoyance as if another person's child was challenging him, and he was powerless to slap it.

"Did I?" Lucy asked again, and this time there was authority. Perhaps it was always there, but Tony was too charmed by her to notice.

Freddy's face slackened. "No," he said and turned back, slumping in his seat.

Two for two! Holy Shit! Tony *really* liked this chick!

"I mean," Lucy said quietly over the hum of the car, "if there is a problem, I can get out. There'll be other cars coming along."

"You're fine," Tony jumped in. He'd fucking push Fred out the passenger window before he would let Lucy out. "Just fine."

"You're not fine to me," Freddy said ominously.

"Yeah, well, *fuck* you Fred!" the words left Tony so fast they might have just have been pressurized. Ever since the morning at the apartment, the roadside Irving restaurant and in his own car, Fred had be scaring the shit out of him and paralyzing him with whatever black magic shit he possessed, and the words 'tired of it' did not encapsulate the river of emotion flowing through him at that precise moment. Being able to tell Freddy to fuck off and not feeling fear was like kicking free of the cement shoes dragging him to the extreme depths of Halifax Harbour and surfacing into sunlight. And that was what Freddy had—some sort of jizzed up power that induced fright. Perhaps it was a gas or something? Or he was a hypnotist? Whatever the hell it was, it wasn't working for the twat now, and it felt so good to unload those words on Fred, to sling them in his face for invoking whatever evil mojo he had working for him.

The effect was astounding. Fred appeared as if he had just been slapped. Hard. It reminded Tony of Tim back in the apartment and how he had a leash for Freddy—the same leash that Lucy was slipping around his neck right now. Around his balls too, and truth be told, Tony hoped Lucy gave him one or two good yanks, just to keep him in line.

"I'll talk to you later," Freddy vowed in a spite filled voice like a brother talking down to a smaller sister that had just squealed on him.

"Like fuck you will," Tony looked at him for as long as he dared while driving. He gave him "*la look*" he used on people that truly pissed him off.

"Sounds like a fight," Lucy observed from the backseat darkness. The sound of her voice swept aside the whoop ass intent swelling up inside Tony like a broom to dust. "And I hope you don't. I hate fighting. Really."

Outside the car, it began to snow. Great free floating flakes smacked into the windshield and splayed themselves across as much surface space as possible. Tony flicked on the wipers. They groaned on the first pass. He didn't want Lucy to be pissed at him. "You caught me at a bad time. This asshole prick has been riding me most of the day and night, and I haven't been able to . . . to . . . say *shit* to him!"

"Why is that?"

"Why don't you just stay out of this?" Fred snapped at her. "Just sit in the dark and shut the fuck up!"

"You shut the fuck up!" Tony snarled at him. Then to Lucy, "I'll say this much for you. Fucking Giggles over there hasn't said that much all goddamn day. Like he's super pissed at something and just fucking waiting to unload on the poor bastard that just *looks* at him the wrong way."

"Oh, I don't like guys like that," Lucy drew in air.

"I'm warning you," Freddy spat out. "Just shut the fuck up. You're in the car now, so just shut up and take the ride. If you can't—"

"Hey."

Tony's right hand left the wheel and clamped down on Freddy's throat, fingers gouging into the flesh around his tender Adam's apple. Freddy's eyes bugged, and he pressed his chin down, his hands going for Tony's wrist. Tony slammed the brakes on, halting the car in a long shuddering skid that threw their frames against their seat belts. The sound of ice-slick highway and winter-rubber trying to ignite and failing filled Tony's ears. He twisted and pulled Freddy towards him. Eye to eye, a feeling of utter viciousness fell over the man, and he peered into Freddy's pain filled face.

"I've had enough of you," Tony hissed into his passenger's face. There was no fear in him at all now, and the *knowing* of it filled him with a power that smashed up against his senses like a tsunami. There was a second explosion of rage, and Tony welcomed it as it scorched and melted whatever shackles Freddy had on him. He had the digit by the *throat* for gawd's sake! He felt the rage rising up as fiery black as nuclear smoke, and as he did, something inside him was putting the suffocating foam to it, trying to fight it back, contain it. And part of him welcomed that, too. Tony had felt that rage before. He was potentially murderous when he did. And it always frightened him just how easy it was to flow.

The car stopped moving.

"You got a choice," Tony pulled a gagging Freddy in close. He stared the man straight in the eye and for the first time all day, did not flinch. "Get the fuck out of my car. You get out, and I won't break your arms. Think about that. You'll need them if you want to flag down the next ride. Be pretty fuckin' silly if you have two snapped arms. And it's winter out there, but I don't give two shits to Tuesday about breakin' *anything* of yours. So, you get out all peaceful and shit, and you can keep your arms. Use them all you want. See if you can wave some poor bastard down. Bless them with your company."

Freddy stared him back, positively livid. Tony could see it plain as paint, and he knew then that he would probably have to snap *something* in order to subdue his captive. He would not give it a second thought if he had to, and he brought up a very large fist to signal his intent.

"Gonna try for teeth too, are ya?" Tony spoke, his fist parallel with his cheek and thrumming ever so slightly in the air.

"*You . . .*" Freddy croaked through his pinched throat as his eyes rolled in the direction of the back seat, "*did . . . this.*"

"I did this?" Lucy stated calmly, watching with a very doubtful gaze. "He's the one that's got you by the throat."

"Goddamn fortunate I didn't grab him by the balls," Tony breathed. "But I figured I'd go for the bigger target, y'know."

"*You . . . need . . . me,*" Freddy wheezed out.

"You get the fuck out of this car. Right now," and with that, Tony released the man, shoving him against the passenger door. "And I don't need you. I still have the cash your buddy Tim gave me. You can be sure I'll be tellin' him of all the shit that's gone on since you've been with me, just so there're no secrets between us. Now, get out. Get."

Looking like a demon poised to re-establish its dominance over its host, Freddy's form tensed up, and he bared some very white teeth. He felt his throat and massaged it briefly, and then decided it was best not to say anything. A smart move, Tony figured. If he had, Tony would have smacked the living shit out of him right then and there. He was barely keeping his whoop ass in check.

Shaking with suppressed fury, Freddy reached up and unlocked the door. "You'll see me, again."

"Five," Tony started.

A frown creased Freddy's face. *He* was getting a *five* count?

"Four."

Shaking with anger, Freddy got out of his seatbelt and flung it back. Metal clipped off glass.

"*Three*, and if you cracked my window, I'll do a such fuckin' river dance on your flat ass you'll feel as if you're squeezing toothpaste every time you take a shit."

Freddy opened the door and got out. The rush of winter wind took some of the heat out of Tony, but he still wanted to be free of this prick. He was trying really hard not to get out and go after him. Not with Lucy in the car.

"And don't you slam that door either," Tony jabbed two fingers in Freddy's direction as if lasers would shoot out from them. "Don't even think about it."

Freddy obviously did think about it; however, in the end, he did not slam the door. He took one last furious look at Lucy and closed the door. Beyond the glass, he straightened up against the cut of the wind. Only his midsection was visible to those within the car.

Tony took his foot off the brake.

"Fuck you, too," he muttered and gunned the gas. They shot into the void of a very cold night, taillights illuminating red snakes swirling on the asphalt.

Freddy watched the twin afterburners fading into the freezing night. He watched until the lights winked out, as if they had never existed at all. He stood there on the black surface of a frozen highway, in absolute darkness, and thought briefly that there probably wasn't anything darker than a winter's night. A shivering wind came up, flinging glacial chips into his face. It howled in his ears, trying to freeze his nerves as well as flesh, and wanted nothing better than to see this piece of meat go mad with the desperation of being left alone in the middle of nowhere, at night.

Freddy inhaled deeply, hoarked and spat in its face. Frighten him? *Take your best fucking shot*, he thought savagely. He bared teeth, and dusted off the snow that had already gathered on his toque. He took the first step into the mouth of the building wind, marching right down its freezing throat. He meant to follow the highway as best as he could to wherever.

And damn if he didn't hate walking.

CHAPTER 20

No more than five minutes after leaving Freddy behind, Tony decided to speak. "You can sit up front here now, y'know. If you want, that is."

Back there in the darkness, two eyes flickered at him. "No, thank you," she said simply, her voice sounding like muffled Christmas bells.

Suit yourself, he thought, but was glad of it. He wanted time to purge Fred's reek from his personal space. To have the passenger side filled again so soon would not be wise.

"Wow," Lucy finally said in mild awe. "I suppose he had that coming? I mean, for you to just dump him like that. At night too. Out there. It's pretty cold out there."

"He had it coming," Tony assured her.

"What did he do?"

Tony tried to focus on the road. He squinted. He didn't want to answer the question.

"Anthony?"

"What?"

"What did he do?"

A tired smile spread across his face. The kind of smile that happens after a crisis has passed. Freddy's supernatural ass was gone. And this one in the back was more than a welcomed replacement.

"It's really not my business, but considering you did just leave the man on the side of the highway, it would make this passenger feel a little better. Actually," she paused for a moment and looked up at the ceiling, "a lot better. If you explained it to me. If it's not, you know, not too touchy."

This one was not about to leave him alone. Tony sighed and checked his speed. What the hell, he figured. "He . . . scared me."

Lucy allowed herself a moment to digest this. "He scared you?"

"Yeah."

"Threatened you?"

Tony glanced out his side window. "No. Well, yeah. A little."

"Did he have a gun or something?"

"It's hard to explain."

"No gun, 'eh?" Lucy nodded, and then decided to let the matter go. "We still going to Vancouver?"

Good question. "Yeah."

"I haven't decided yet if I want to head out that way with you or not," she said.

"Ok, fine. You think about that then," Tony said right back. He wanted a little bit of silence for the next few minutes regardless of how utterly delightful he thought her voice sounded. Christmas morning bells. There was a sentimental merriness in her voice. A note of innocent excitement. It actually made Tony consider turning around and picking Freddy up. He decided against it. If Lucy had anything to say, he figured she had already said it, and that was great. She didn't know about Fred or that fucked up talent of his to make a person shit themselves without even looking at them. Tony still wasn't sure how he managed any of it, himself, but he knew this: he felt better and stronger the further he drove away from freak boy Freddy. Hell, he might even be able to eat something at the next roadside Irving if he could find one that was still open. He wasn't certain of the hours they kept outside of Nova Scotia.

"How long you guys been riding together?" Lucy decided to start again.

Shit. "You like to talk, don't you?"

She smiled then, a slow smile that reminded him of fine tasting dark chocolate for some unfathomable reason. "My father would say the same thing. Must be true. But if you don't want to talk, then I understand. But it is a long ride to BC, and I hope we'll be chatting a lot more than you and Freddy there. It'll be even longer if we don't."

"Yeah," Tony said in a tired voice. He suddenly realized that he was exhausted. The fear had left him and was replaced with a bone deep weariness like he had been hauling bags of fifty pound shingles up a forty foot ladder for eight hours straight. He wanted sleep. "I could use a good sleep first. I'm pretty wiped here. Been driving all day non-stop. There has to be a motel along the way here somewhere."

"Not afraid of Freddy catching up and finding the car?" she asked him.

"No," he replied. "Not right now, anyway. Too tired to give a damn. Maybe I'll feel different later but not right now. And anyway, if he did, I'd find him first."

"Oh, really?"

"Yeah."

"So sure?"

"It's what I do," Tony said, glancing at the gas gauge. "Always been lucky at finding people."

She said nothing, and when he glanced back minutes later, he could see that she was asleep.

Roughly one hour later, the fastest hour Tony had ever driven it seemed—he turned off on Exit 177. The snow had stopped falling for the moment, and the clouds overhead had moved away to expose a diamond-studded night. He drove on, looking for someplace to sleep, and saw the glowing sign for the Best Western Hotel. The building looked expensive and a surge of apprehension went through Tony. Where the hell was the Comfort Inn when you needed it? Then he realized that he had an expense account of sorts, and decided to test Mr. Tim's credit line. Tony didn't think there would be a problem with staying one night in luxury.

He parked the Mustang in a well-lit but practically empty lot.

"Where are we?" Lucy suddenly asked from the back.

"Have a good sleep?" He asked her, he peered into the mirror and was rewarded with catching Lucy in a modest stretch. God, he loved it when women stretched.

"Mmmmhmmmm," she smiled. "It's too cosy back here. So, where are we?"

"Hotel. I need to sleep. Especially now that Fred's gone. Maybe get some takeout as well."

"Place looks expensive," Lucy said. There was a tinge of uncertainty there. Tony suspected it wasn't about the cost.

"Listen, we'll talk about the travel arrangements in the morning, okay? But right now, I tell you what: I feel pretty good about ditchin' old Fred back there. And I think you had something to do with that. So, I think I can spring for your own room. That okay?"

Lucy's mouth dropped open. "But this place . . ."

"Hey," Tony interrupted. "I'm not cheap while on the road. But if it makes you feel better, I'll be looking for a pizza place or something nearby. Doubt if the restaurant in this place is open now anyway."

"What time is it?"

He realized he was blocking the dash clock. "Almost 11:30. Time sure as hell went fast. Jesus, I'm wiped. Could've sworn that it would have taken longer than this, too. So, anyway, you want that room or not? No strings attached. You can have it on the other side of the hotel if you feel better about it."

"Thank you, Anthony." Lucy said with an appreciative smile. It was bright like the light under a closed door. "I can really have my own room?"

"Yeah," he said, smiling back but nowhere near as cute. "Let's go."

Lucy sat for a moment. "Okay!" she finally let out in an adorable burst. "I guess I can always run out on you in the morning, too, if I want."

Tony nodded at this. "If you want."

He hoped she didn't, though.

They got out of the car, and Tony retrieved his bag from the trunk. He noticed then for the first time that Lucy carried no bag. Strange, but he kept the thought to himself as he offered the room free and full of nothing but good will. He didn't need a background check on the young woman. He had a good feeling around her, and if there were a story, then he would wait until she felt comfortable enough to tell him. And truthfully, with the passing of the day, the need for pure, uninterrupted sleep, the grizzly bear kind, was the only thing Tony wanted.

They signed in minutes later, obtained different rooms in opposing wings and parted ways in the main lobby. Tony walked down the soft illuminated corridor of the second floor, appreciating the stillness of the place. He liked staying in hotels when he could. There was something comforting about it. Some folks didn't care for sleeping in beds people might've fucked in the night before, but Tony had no problem at all. Once in a while, he was one of those people.

He arrived at his door and used the passkey to unlock it. He flicked on the lights once inside and stepped out of his shoes, closing the door behind him. Two double beds covered in brown, soft-looking comforters stood before him. A beautiful hardwood set of dressers, night tables and closets filled the rest of the room. A big flat-screen was in a corner, and a PC terminal was on a table in front of the curtains. He glanced into the washroom and saw a shower and bath cleaner and much nicer than his own. The towels were as thick as carpets. He would have to take a few to replace the frayed rags he had at home. Part of him regretted signing in so late. One night wasn't enough to fully appreciate all this. He sighed and tossed his bag onto one of the beds and sat on the edge. He faced the TV and decided to turn it on. Late news wrap-up. An irresistible weariness pulled at his frame and eyelids, but he managed to see some of the newscast: some guy down in Michigan had gashed his thigh with a chainsaw while cutting a hole for ice fishing. Some kid had blown away half his head in a game of Russian roulette and had survived. Another story from Pakistan where thirty people had been crushed under rubble when a bomb went off in a nightclub. Scenes of shocked survivors moved across the screen in a soupy slow motion. Gruesome scenes of destruction. Tony reached out and turned the TV off. Christ. Wasn't there any *good* news on? He dropped back onto the bed, feeling the freshness of the covers. He felt the downy softness of the bed, and a huge sense of sleepy relief seeped through his person.

He thought about undressing and getting underneath those seductive blankets, but then he was already asleep.

And he dreamed. In the mesh of images that were real and yet weren't, he found himself drifting, moving across a sunny plain he couldn't identify but sensed he somehow knew. He was walking towards a sign, a big sign, billboard size. He could read the words and willed himself to remember them as he read it; it could be a message of some kind. The words were cheery green on white, *"Partly Cloudy"*. Then the sign was behind him, and he moved over the brightest golf greens he had ever seen. Forest curtained the edges of his vision. A golf course. He was on a golf course, and the smell of spruce and pine filled the air. He suddenly felt a terrible sadness soak into his heart. On such a beautiful day, in such a beautiful place, how could he feel anything but good? He could see roman numerals standing side by side, chatting away. Then, they were no longer numerals; they were men. With golf clubs.

And one guy topped off with a black White Sox ball cap was lining up a ball. The other men watched, chatting all the time, and yet the other golfer said nothing to them. There was a smile on his face. He flexed and did a weird little bird dance on the spot, slipping into a golfer's stance and smacked the ball in what seemed to Tony to be the fastest wind up he had ever witnessed. And Tony could see the ball flying a distance measured in a squinting glare, heading towards gigantic white saucers that were sand pits. But these sand pits weren't pits at all. They actually were the saucers you would find at carnival booths, and if you managed to keep a penny in one of those things, you would have the stuffed animal of your choice. And the animals were in Tony's dream except they were spectators behind the partition ropes marking the course. That was really fucked up. Then the golfer was back in Tony's sight. He was bouncing on his knees. He stuck a finger into his mouth and then jabbed it in the air, making mental calculations beyond Tony. His companions were speaking in tongues now, and Tony somehow understood it to be about the beauty of flamingos dancing along the lakes of the Huron. The golfer had another ball ready to be whacked; apparently, the other guys were merely supporters. He took aim with his club, which was a mallet now, and did the same little dance as before. And then he swung.

And missed.

The mallet flew from the man's grasp like a dove bursting from a cage and flew into the sun. The men behind him were numerals, again, now, and the chatter of the stuffed animals on the side-line grew louder and louder, their button eyes glassy and staring.

"*AND ITS ALL YOUR FUCKING FAULT!*" the golfer suddenly shrieked at Tony.

He woke.

He was still dressed but had shifted in his sleep onto his belly. He blinked slowly and saw sunlight around the edges of the closed curtains. Tony groaned. Nothing like a screwy dream to cap off a sound sleep. He glanced at the digital clock on the night table. Eight in the morning. Tony rubbed his belly. In a place like this, the hotel probably had a bitchin' breakfast. Thoughts of his mom darted around the edges of his mind and made him pause. He would breakfast on something simple, perhaps cereal. He could not control, however, the sudden image of steak and eggs popping into his waking mind. Then, sausage and eggs. With toast. He sighed, shook his head and decided to get moving. He changed his clothes, and did not shave. In a minute, he was walking down the corridor towards the restaurant.

She was waiting for him in the main lobby, dressed in the same clothes. "Good morning," she said brightly. "Going to breakfast?"

"Morning. And yeah, I am."

"Can I join you?"

"Sure, though you might be paying for this one. Your own, that is. Not mine." Generosity was one thing, but some people, after tasting too much of that particular sweet, turned into parasites. He had no desire to have this one leech off of him, cute as she might be.

"Actually, I was going to offer to pay for yours," Lucy informed him, her shoulders swinging to and fro.

Tony's surprise showed on his face. "Really?"

"Yes, I have money."

"You said so before."

"Then, shall we?"

Tony dipped his head in the direction they were to go. They moved into a pristine dining room covered in so much white that Tony felt the roof must have been rolled back during the night to let the snow in. Silverware glistened and the crystal sparkled. A waitress in an exceptionally sharp-looking black and white uniform brought them menus. Tony ordered Sugar Crisps and toast. Lucy ordered the continental breakfast. The waitress took their orders and thanked them, the barest of a French accent sweetening her words.

"I like the way she talks," Lucy said after the woman was gone.

"Me, too," Tony said. He had half a boner to prove it. But it was more for Lucy, however. The woman had beautiful mocha skin. Tony wanted to ask if she was part Japanese or something, but did not dare. He had a bad experience once with a woman who was of Indian descent, and Tony asked her, innocently enough or so he had thought, what was the origin of her name. Looking back, perhaps it was somehow insulting to her, but Tony still, to this day, didn't mean anything by it. Regardless, he was not about to make the same mistake with Lucy.

"Can you speak French?" he asked her.

"No. You?"

"Mais qui!" Tony let out. "Le grunt, le pew. Avec!" He growled in a deep morning voice that made Lucy giggle. The sound made him think that a glass of water could not produce a cleaner, purer chime. Not even if there were a hundred of them.

"Avec," he repeated, in a more sombre voice, and answered her smile with one of his own.

"I know what that means," Lucy said. "What you said doesn't make any sense."

Tony shrugged. "It sounds good when you're throwing something out a window, though. Try it sometime. You'll see."

"Maybe later."

"Not in the car, though, okay?"

"Okay," she said.

Tony shifted in his chair. Did that mean she meant to travel onwards with him?

"You sleep well last night?" she asked him.

"Yeah, except for this weird dream."

"A dream? You remember it?"

"Naw," he said, shaking his head.

"You should write your dreams down," she went on. "They're very important. Some give you messages. Could be trying to tell you something."

"Le grunt."

"I'm serious," Lucy said, feigning insult.

"Well, since you're serious then, what are you going to do today? Still heading west with me?"

"You going to keep on paying for my motel rooms?"

"Ah, probably not. But I'll give you the first choice over where we can stay. Probably won't be like this, though."

"Probably not, but I like this place," Lucy commented.

"Me, too," Tony agreed. "Ah, to be able to afford this day after day."

"Yeah," she drew out, deciding on something. "Well, if you are heading towards BC, then I'm in. Can I help pay for gas?"

It was the second time she surprised him. "No trouble here. I was just wondering how to ask that."

"I have money," she said. "And I'm not a cheapie."

"That's good."

"But I probably won't go all the way to BC. I just might decide to get out earlier. I'll let you know."

Where was she going? But Tony did not ask her. She would tell all in her own time. He was confident in that. Was she running from something, though? From someone? There was a pause in the conversation then, and both of them simply sat and looked about the dining room. They were the only ones there. Then her dark eyes, ever so slightly curved upwards at their corners, studied him, waiting.

And then the moment was gone.

"So, is that okay with you?" She asked innocently.

The words flashed him back to a time and a gay guy called Jimmy. Being somewhat homophobic, Tony still thought of Jimmy Bridges as being a nice man. A great man in fact. He owned a little franchise coffee shop down on Halifax's Hollis Street. *That okay with you?* Everyone had a certain catch phrase and that was Jimmy's. He'd also say *phenomenal!* quite a bit. 'It was *phenomenal!* The movie was *phenomenal!* Oh my Lord, he looks phenomenal!' Jimmy looked to be in about his early forties at that time, and he was always bright to the customers. He'd even come over and talk with Tony at times and eventually recognized Tony as a regular. He called him Anthony, as well. He always called his mother Mrs. Levin, and he personally served her whenever she entered the shop. It was Tony's mom that had got him into the place, and even though Tony eventually felt comfortable with Jimmy, he could never quite let his guard down for fear if he did, if he appeared too comfortable around Jimmy, the wrong signal would be sent out. Tony didn't want that kind of embarrassment, but his mother continued to insist on Jimmy's whenever they were down on Hollis. She declared that Jimmy's sandwiches and the cheesecake were the best around.

And they were.

That okay with you?

That image of Jimmy, smiling at everyone.

And in that moment, Tony remembered sitting down at the counter at Jimmy's place with a newspaper in hand. He remembered seeing an older Jimmy moving a little slower than usual back there. Wearing thicker layers of clothing to protect him from the coming Halifax winter. His hair a mousse mass of silver. Eyes that watered constantly when he read a paper, smiling at him.

But is that okay with you?

Tony wasn't going to ask Lucy the questions on his mind because he wanted to eat and enjoy his Sugar Crisps as much as he could without thinking of what his mom would be eating. He wanted Lucy to enjoy her breakfast. He convinced himself that she probably did want to talk about her present or her past. Sometimes, you just couldn't handle the information those questions hooked. Or the kind of trouble a person could bring on themselves for asking. If you cared.

Across the table, Lucy waited for a response.

He gave one.

"Yeah. That's okay with me."

CHAPTER 21

In British Columbia, Fire Chief Ralph Maia got up at around the same time as Tony and Lucy had been on the road for an hour. Maia had decided to sleep at the fire station, taking a night shift, and camped out in his office, on his steel frame cot. His metal hammock. It usually delivered a great sleep, better than his mattress at home, but this morning he got up sensing trouble. Ralph Maia had learned a long time ago to pay attention to his instincts, and they were all a-flutter this morning, just like a mosquito buzzing around his ear in complete darkness. He had the same feelings back in 2003 when a forest fire had devoured Kelowna. That fire had proved to be the alien queen bitch of a bunch of blazes that threatened to ravage the whole province. When they finally extinguished that monster, the feeling of relief that washed through those hundreds of firefighters and thousands of civilians was heartbreaking. Many of his own men, both regular and volunteer, had been simply too exhausted to do anything more than just smile after that killer had been officially vanquished. The destruction caused in the blaze was monstrous. One of the worst in BC's history.

And to see it. To feel the heat from that beast.

Maia sighed. It was something *wonderful*.

He once preached this great nation had the Americans beat on firearm safety, but he muted that praise by telling the masses Canadians liked to burn things. They enjoyed their fires too damn much. There were estimates that the number of fires in Canada were only a few percentage points behind the States. And that civilian deaths in both countries were the highest amongst the industrialized nations What did that tell you? It told Maia that folks were quite simply fucked up when it came to turning on the kitchen stove. One day close to retirement, or perhaps when he was simply fed up with public appearance, he would say just that. Those very words. Some shock therapy to sober up each and every individual. Maybe it would cause people to be more careful . . . but, more than likely, not. He didn't know much about psychology, but he did know people, and people in a mass could be as thick as cattle being led into a Mickey D's. It put a furtive smile on his face.

Maia got up and moved about his small but orderly office. He made his way to the head, right across from his door. Trucks were to the right, a small but respectable and shiny fleet. The sleeping quarters for the men on duty was down the hall on the left, and old Ralphie was right in the middle, across from the toilets.

The story of his miserable existence.

For where is the worst and yet the best place for a sociopath murderer to hide if not at a suicide prevention clinic? What is the worst situation for a soldier if not peacekeeping? Where was the worst place for a burner to exist—and exist as a *leader*—if not a fire department?

Torment. Endless torment.

And yet, Ralph Maia deserved an Oscar for his performance to date. He possessed a talent to beguile the masses, to appear as a ferocious advocate of fire safety. He brought in the masses and toured them around the burned sites of buildings razed to the ground, black and smoking like a roast left too long on a spit. Commanded them to look, just look at what carelessness could do to a community. Of how a single act of negligence could unleash something that would consume everything. He was like a priest of old, preaching sermons of prevention at every venue he could manage during the day and then wishing for some of the worst blazes by night.

There should be some measure of reward for the act.

But there wasn't.

And now the beast was running free again in the greater Vancouver area. Unchecked and unreined, like some drunken imp full of flame jumping from house to house. Maia shook his head. The fire crews in the city had their hands full and it wasn't even summer. Already there was a dramatic increase in fire accidents for the month of March, and if someone didn't start doing something soon, people might just start asking questions. Not that Maia would ever be suspected. He only burned something when he absolutely had to. When the urge could *not* be suppressed any longer. And there were plenty of accidents and amateurs out there to take the blame.

Maia breathed out. The Kelowna fires had been an act of carelessness, and the man responsible had come forth to confess to the deed. That really pissed Maia off. A lesser being actually apologizing for birthing such a monster *by accident!* It aggravated Maia to think about what he could unleash upon the world with a solid plan, the right materials and the knowledge of fire that he possessed. But he could not. Not until he got permission. And when he did occasionally get permission to let off steam, to burn something, it had to be controlled. His or his firefighter's involvement had to be completely covert. And if he or any of the others *did* burn, he was still bound to defend these cattle called people. Instead of revelling in their agony, instead of prolonging their agony, he had to call out his forces, including those responsible for the fires, to save the masses and put down the beasts.

He had to protect them.

And he was a *burner*, goddammit, a *burner!*

He faced his reflection in the mirror. The washroom was empty, the showers silent. Maia was alone as he gazed at his body. A skinny pear, but pear-shaped all the same. But if anyone really wanted to probe, they would discover a bear's strength rippling under his layer of fat. His thin goatee gave him a vampiric look, and he basked in it. He thought he looked cool. Yet it was a false face to fit in with the Mundanes. It was *his* Mundane face. He hated it so. He hated his day to day existence. He had convinced them all, and he so badly wanted to burn it all down. Torch the whole lie.

In frustration, he placed his hands on either side of the sink and hung his head.

"*Pain is upon the world.*"

The words made him jerk his head up. Maia stared at the reflection in the mirror. It snarled at him, baring white teeth. The voice was the sound of a striking match.

"*And there are those that wish to find the Boatman.*"

Maia stood with enraptured eyes, locking gazes with his reflection. The mouth in the mirror moved while his did not. The eyes therein burned red.

This was the first time such a message had been delivered to him from beyond. After so many years, was this the sign he had been hoping for?

"What . . ." Ralph paused, thinking for a moment. His eyes were wide and uncertain. "What would you have me do?"

"*Do not allow them to find the Boatman,*" his reflection commanded, in that striking-match sound. In awe, Maia stroked his black beard. The reflection did not.

"Is this . . . the *word?*" Maia breathed, barely able to believe it.

"*The word is . . .*" and here the apparition in the mirror paused with a sinister air. When it spoke, again, the voice was abyssal-deep and choked with filth. "*Do not allow them to find the Boatman.*"

"For how long?" Maia asked, barely able to contain the excitement in his voice.

"*Not long,*" said the thing in the mirror, its face blackening like cooking meat. A look of childlike smugness swept over it for the barest of seconds. "*Not long.*"

The thing in the mirror vanished then, without sound or smell, and Maia staggered and grabbed at the white porcelain sink as if he had been held by the throat. His breath heaved as if he had just run a marathon. He looked at the mirror and saw his own face looking back. Disappointed, he waited for something more, but nothing came.

He gripped the basin hard enough to make something crack in the wall. With a huff of breath, he released it and stepped back. He thought of smoke.

And where there was smoke . . .

"Stop them," he repeated to himself, nodding and rubbing his hands together eagerly. "Stop them. If the Boatman isn't found, war will come."

War would ram itself home.

Ralph Maia's normally stoic face split into an ungodly, ferocious grin. Elation ignited his core. It was not the word that he had been expecting, but anyone could plainly see that the real word was not far behind as long as the Boatman remained unfound. The longer he did, the closer the word came into sound.

Maia slapped his hands together like a titanic sumo wrestler before battle. Lightening had not been called down yet, but the thunder could be heard in the distance. And it was coming Maia's way

Coffee. Ralph needed coffee badly. Just one cup to fire up his engines. Racket up them highs only felt by pilots and speed freaks. He had preparations to make and no time to lose.

The orgasmic bliss known as War was coming like cannon shot.

CHAPTER 22

"So what happened?" South Carolina State Trooper Dean asked the biker on the ground in front of him. Behind his mask of neutrality, the trooper felt more than a little satisfaction from seeing this road shit quivering like he had just jumped into a winter river. Dean recognized the biker who had no particular gang affiliation; he had chased the fucker enough times to recognize the back of his head from fifty yards out. He let his eyes drift past the man and inspected, for the third time since the troopers had arrived, the roadside bar called the Crazy House. It was Redneck heaven. Paramedics swarmed over the worst of the unconscious lot, big burly bikers and assorted road scum, wearing grease streaked blue jeans, sleeveless shirts, and torn denim vests or ripped leather jackets. Thick arms and hairy paunches were marked with laughing skulls, daggers, and barbed wire entangled with roses. The screamers of the highway, an entire pack of them, perhaps twenty or more, and here they were writhing about on the ground with a growing list of injuries that sent one medic to radio in for a helicopter. One first responder believed that a train must have struck the whole lot, when another later clarified it was a bar fight. He got that from the owner of the Crazy House; a bar fight which had torn apart damned near two dozen brawlers, including the bartenders.

Trooper Dean had seen this shit before. Usually it was a fight over a woman, or a bike. Perhaps one of them didn't back down fast enough, and the wolves fell on the offender. Bad drugs or booze made a normal man unreasonable sometimes. They could make a bunch of animals like this become cannibals.

Of the many who were suffering from broken bones, concussions, torn ligaments, missing teeth, ruptured eyeballs, punctured organs, or even internal bleeding, only one biker looked to be in any condition to give a statement as to what happened. And whatever drugs he had been on during the fight looked as if they were running out. Dean didn't like talking to the guy as a medic had him on his belly, trying to ascertain why the victim was bleeding profusely from his rectal area. Dean shook his head. It was looking more like a bomb went off in the bar.

Trooper Dean decided to stoop down so that he could both hear better and not see the paramedic gingerly spread the man's ass cheeks apart. "Well? You feel like talking any?"

The victim's head was right before Dean's black boots. Dean remembered the guy's nickname. They called him Squirrelshit. Right now, he looked like it. Not only was Squirrelshit's ass gurgling blood, his right knee had been twisted around so that his boot toes were pointed at his right shoulder. *Jeeezus!* Then there were his arms, both of which were snapped back at the elbows. The right side of Squirrelshit's face looked like the royal blue steak that Dean had eaten the night before, pulped and bloody. There was an imprint there that could be a boot print as well.

And this miserable survivor was the only one that was conscious and lucid enough to talk.

Squirrelshit's left eye, the one that had escaped the mash of the boot, moved about like a fish's. It looked like it wanted nothing better than to be free of this wreck of a body, especially before the drugs in its system wore off.

"A fight," Squirrelshit slurred.

Dean could see the man's teeth. The air slicing across that broken window smile would just add to Squirrelshit's approaching joy of sobriety. *Jeeezus!*

"A fight," Dean smirked and shook his head. He gazed around the war scene and wondered if Bosnia or Somalia could produce worse. Maybe a herd of cattle had run through the place. Hell, perhaps even a missile strike. But a fight? Somehow the word did not fit the carnage around him.

"I was . . ." the eye seemed to recognize the law officer now, "drinking."

"Uh-huh."

"Clay was behind the bar."

"Right. That Clay?" Clay was currently holding his jaw in place. It looked as if someone had tried to rip the thing from his head with a meat hook. A leg had been broken too, by the odd angle of the limb. There weren't enough medicine men around to see to him yet. They were tending to the worst-looking ones of the bunch.

The eye rolled in the direction of where Dean was looking. "No. That's not Clay. He's by . . . the cooler."

This made Trooper Dean scowl. He looked to the man lying by the cooler and wished he hadn't. *Jesus, Joseph, and Mary.* Clay just might get the 'Most Fucked Up' award if he survived his wounds.

Squirrelshit took a breath. Spawny, red drool leaked from his mouth as he exhaled.

"Dewy was at the end... of the bar. Got his fingers caught in that... wooden piece that... goes up and down. Clay closed the piece down on Dewy's hand. Didn't see his hand there... Crushed it... Heard the clap of wood as... it came down. Fucker screeched. Getting your... balls caught in a Harley's spokes... would be worse."

Squirrelshit's forehead rested against the gravel ground, and Dean almost felt a pang of sympathy for the amount of pain that had to be assaulting his brain. But the man talked on.

"Dewy's hollerin'. Can't move his fingers. Clay pulls the countertop back up. Dewy's fingers are... shredded, man. One of the bar bitches goes for ice or something... and then... then... he came out of nowhere. Big fucker. Looked like a skin... head. Like a wrestler. He grabbed Dewy by the fingers and ripped them off..."

Squirrelshit started to giggle. More bloody froth gathered on the ground.

"Something funny?" Trooper Dean wanted to know.

"Dewy didn't know what hollerin' was... till that fucker took his fingers off," another rusty giggle. "Right off."

"We got up... everyone in the place. Everything came out. Pool sticks, knives, guns, broken bottles, knuckles, tire irons, *everything*. We were... we were... gonna kill the rat fuck bastard. See how many... pool sticks we could shove up his ass. Gonna make him a fuckin' urban *legend* man..."

"And?" Dean prompted when Squirrelshit looked to be about to go to sleep.

Squirrelshit smiled the grin of a desert skull. "The fuck came... at *us*, man. *All* of us. Our bitches ran... when Cruise went down..."

Cruise. Trooper knew the bastard. He was the one over yonder with the broken back and the potato-mashed testicles.

Squirrelshit began to cry.

"He picked Cruise up and brought him down... across the counter... four or five times... then threw him out the window. Then... then... he came for..."

Squirrelshit's eye squeezed shut, and for a moment, Dean thought he had died.

"*Me!*" The biker's eye flew open. Whatever pain sedative was in the man's system looked to have finally worn off. Squirrelshit started to thrash. The medic working on his ass yelled for assistance. Squirrelshit's eye found Dean. It was redder than before. "AND HE WAS LAUGHIN', MAN!! HE WAS LAUGHIN'!"

Red spittle flew from his lips, and Squirrelshit began to scream. Another paramedic dropped on him, trying to contain the thrashing form. Dean stood up and away, fixing his hat and letting the professionals deal with fix the broken biker. He would not ever admit that Squirrelshit's rant unnerved him. Squirrelshit continued to shriek until one of the medicine men jabbed something into his ass and arm. The biker began to relax almost immediately, but Dean did not see this.

Trooper Dean was heading for his car and the radio there.

CHAPTER 23

After the battle of the Beacon, the Stickman parked his Chevrolet Sunbird in the parking lot of an Irving Service Station along the Trans-Canada highway, with the window rolled down just a crack. He tried to sleep. To heal. He was covered in blankets that he had stashed in the trunk of his car, a lesson taught by his uncle Marty: always have blankets in the trunk when driving a long distance in the winter. Stickman found it amusing—the little things that stuck in one's mind as time marched on. His eyes opened and closed in a dreamy haze. It was night outside, and the light from the station illuminated the ceiling of his old Sunbird. He was in the back seat, wearing a pulled down ski mask and heavy gloves underneath his blankets. It was a tight squeeze, lying down as he was with his legs bunched against the far window, but it beat paying for a room somewhere. Something that he could not quite afford. The wind would rise and fall, moving around the car like some deep sea current seeking to suck it away into the night. He was medicated on Methadone tablets—the strongest shit he could get his hands on at such short notice. The fight with Boomer at the Beacon had wrecked the Stickman, and he would hurt even more if not for the drugs. His face looked like a piece of tenderized steak, and his head felt as if someone was trying to pitch a tent inside his skull. But he was still walking, which was more than he could say for the likes of Boomer and Mr. Tigh—and wondered why he still thought of Mr. Tigh as a 'mister.' Stickman's injuries were only bruises, and they would heal in time. They always did.

He thought about the fight. It had been a good one. He was glad he won it. He wasn't so happy he had to fuck up Boomer and Tigh, but if they hadn't given him the run around in the first place, none of this would have happened. Stick could understand why Tigh had protected this Tony Levin guy, but Stickman was after blood. Badge was going to get *revenged*.

As always, Stickman did most of his thinking and recollecting when the lights were out. The cold that crept into him wasn't that uncomfortable, and he wasn't sure if it was actually cold or simply too much painkiller. With each drifting breath, he relaxed a little more, and his mind disconnected. The winter wind encircled the car, moaning to his last bits of consciousness, and Stickman wished it would fuck off. It was the darkness that allowed him to think. The darkness covered all visual distractions. It was comforting to him. He thought of Badger, lying in his hospital bed near death. It was a shitty way to go down. If Stick had been around, he would have covered his ass, but Badge could be thick headed sometimes. Stickman should have been with him that night; cursed the fact he wasn't. Then, he was thinking of the Liquor Dome, the drinker's paradise.

Five separate bars all under the one roof, and a guy with a full wallet could not find a better place to lessen the load. The festivities began around nine, and it was a Friday night. Badger had brought him to the place, and a pitcher of beer later, the man was up wandering the dance floor. Stick followed, and together they slipped through the masses of gyrating bodies like connected beads of mercury. This was difficult to do for the Stickman; he did not like so many people being around him, and if it hadn't been for the beer, he would probably have eventually snapped. Stickman only managed to hold onto his sanity because of Badger and the beer.

And Beverly.

The night was ripe for mingling. And mingle they did. Stickman, who believed he had less than zero sexual attraction—except to soaped up convicts in showers—felt a soft, exploring hand cup his pec from behind. It gave a squeeze before running down the tracks of his ribs. He was wearing a Break at Moose-head t-shirt and blue jeans, and he supposed the clothes were snug, like the hand that was slinking downwards. When it reached his waist, it disappeared. Stickman whirled about, intent on targeting someone and pounding the shit out of them. Badger was forgotten, lost in a pulsing tide of flesh and loud music.

Standing before the Stickman was a woman, an exceptionally fine woman. She was a brunette, permed, with well-done makeup, and wearing a white t-shirt and black bra underneath. Stick made it a point to gawk. He wasn't up on small talk. Didn't know how really. But somehow, he had hooked her, attracted her, and she was a pretty piece of pie. She sized him up for seconds, the music thumping in the air like orkish war drums, and took a small step towards him with a smile on her face. Stick remembered that smile. Remembered the wetness of it. Even now, he could not fathom the depths of his luck in finding her. She could easily have any man in the whole place, and yet she gave him the quick rub down. She saw his face and stayed. She stepped in closer. Stick leaned forward as well, close to her ear, and shouted loud enough to be heard over the industrial beat.

"YOU'RE NOT A MAN, RIGHT?"

Thinking back on it, it was then that disaster *could* have struck. But it didn't. Instead, her face lost its lustre for a moment, as if wondering if she had just been insulted or joked with. Then, she saw the fear in Stick's face, and her smile returned, a little clouded.

"No. I can prove it."

And she had.

She stepped in close to him, close enough for him to cream his underwear in a flash and pressed her breasts up against his tight chest. She shouted in his ear if he could feel those.

He could indeed.

Her hand took his and guided it to her centre, right there amidst all of those gyrating savages. Could he feel that?

Yup.

Any other questions?

"He'll be back in a moment, babe," Badger suddenly yelled as he yanked Stick away from his goddess. Her expression showed as much surprise as Stick's.

"Can't leave you for a minute, can I? Jesus!" Badger shouted as he hauled his man towards the bar, leaving the woman of Stick's dreams to be swallowed up by the crowd. Stick felt as if his only friend had just shot him in the back, and continued to feel that way even after Badger bought the fifth round of beers for them both. Stick remembered buying the sixth round, mostly because he was numb by then and felt he should do something, from a tall sleepy-looking waiter who walked about with his mouth open. Stick handed the guy a twenty. The waiter inspected the bill, stared at the Stickman for a quick moment, and plucked a bill from his waist pouch and gave it back. Stick took the beer and the money.

"What are you doin'?" Badger suddenly roared.

"Huh?" Sleepy Eyes abruptly became alert, caught like a kid doing something very wrong, like snooping around in his parents' closet just as both mom and dad walked in.

"You fucking took a twenty. That was a twenty he gave you," Badger said loudly, smiling evilly at the accused. "Give him back the ten."

"Huh?" None too bright either, or bright enough to play stupid.

Badger stepped in close to the man. "I fucking *saw* you take his twenty and try to pass off a five. You choosing your tips these days?"

Stick remembered the five in his hand. He remembered moving in to flank the waiter. The waiter recognized the mass of the Stickman.

"I was heading back to the bar for change," Sleepy Eyes said. "I wasn't doing anything bad."

"You didn't tell him you were going back for change. You were just going," Badger's smile got wider, amused at this little shit's pathetic lie.

"My mistake man, here, maybe I have a ten on me," Sleepy searched himself and came up with the cash fast. He offered it to the Stick.

Badger stepped in closer. "You, walk on now, and forget this. If you give us a reason to, you'll spoil our night and by fuck, I'll make goddamn sure you'll never do something like this again. Get the fuck away from me now, and don't try this shit again."

There were no bouncers in sight, and Sleepy Eyes looked alone and scared. He looked caught. He backed away from the pair of men, and the crowds swallowed him whole.

Badger shook his head and yelled in Stick's ear. "Pretty fuckin' good scam if you ask me. Fuck knows how often he pulled that shit in the past. Mistake my ass. Should've slapped the prick's balls for that. I was watchin' him the whole time. He pulled that fiver outta his pocket. He figured you were too wasted to notice."

Stickman remembered he was.

"But I saw him. You can count on old Badge, son. I got yer back. I got it," and he grinned then and pulled Stick close by the scruff of his neck until they tapped foreheads together. "Never worry about that, young man!"

Stick never did.

"Now, that reminds me, hold on," and with that Badger disappeared, leaving the Stick to mull over his Moosehead.

Badger came back five minutes later, dragging the goddess with him.

Her name was Beverly.

Stickman remembered that night, dreamed about it in the back of his car while a winter gale howled around him. He saw the shadowy form of Badger in his head. Body broken. Machines beeping. Sadness welled up. He did not have Badger's back. He could only do the next best thing.

"Always count on ye, Badge me son," the Stickman mumbled in his sleep, coming very close to waking.

"Always."

CHAPTER 24

Danny and Crew rose at 7:00 the next morning. They had stayed at a Comfort Inn Motel near the border of New Brunswick and Nova Scotia. Danny paid for the rooms out of Gary's emergency fund, and both men were grateful to get off the road. They ate breakfast in silence, not looking forward to the hours that lay ahead, perhaps hoping that somehow luck would give them a break and they would find their quarry soon enough. They finished their meal, collected their bags, and stepped out into the maw of March's winter. The sun was bright but cold. There was no wind, and the roads were dry.

They checked the parking lot the night before, but they checked it again in the morning. Crew met Danny back at the Celica.

"You see anything?" Crew asked squinting in the sun's light.

Danny shook his head.

"Can't be many blue Mustangs around here," Crew commented. Danny noted how dark the man's eyes looked, a hunter's eyes.

"Just thank God for the TCH man," Danny said.

"The yellow asphalt road?" Crew looked in the direction of the nearby highway. "Goes from ocean to ocean?"

"Coast to coast," Danny affirmed with a sigh. "If Tony's going to BC, he'll take this. And the Stickman will, too."

"Why do they call him the Stickman anyway?"

"Because he's built like a brick shithouse."

"Oh." Crew said. He could appreciate the contradiction.

The morning traffic streaked by, and the noise of the passing cars sounded liked low flying rockets. Crew watched it for a moment, and then snarled at the sun. "Alright let's get going then. Starting to freeze here."

Danny's expression hardened. "Ain't cold at all. When you can feel your nipples, that's cold."

"Yeah, well, my nipples could cut glass right now."

They got into the car, and Danny fired up the engine. He allowed a little smile when Crew jacked up the heat as far as it could go. He let the motor warm up before pulling out into traffic. "You get used to it," he said to his passenger.

"Jesus, and I thought New York was cold," Crew muttered. The car wasn't heating up fast enough for him.

"You from New York?" Danny asked casually.

Crew did not answer, and the sudden tension in the air made Danny feel as if he had done something wrong.

Crew clarified his feelings right away. "Listen, don't ask me about where I'm from. No personal questions at all. Nothing. Okay? The less you know, the better for both of us. That cool?"

Danny never took his eyes off the road. "Cool. Gonna be a pretty boring drive then, if you don't want to talk."

"You can talk. I'll listen."

That made Danny chuckle. "See, I'm usually the one that listens. Never was one for talking. Even with the ladies. Maybe that's why they like me."

"Got a woman, do you?" Crew asked. He was scouring the sides of the road and traffic for an old blue Mustang.

"Yeah. A good girl, too." Danny shrugged. "Least, I think she's mine. We're just starting out. I got a good feeling about her. She's studying to be a chiropractor. That's a good job. Things work out, I'll never have to worry about my back again."

Crew gazed out at the wintery road ahead. The sun was strong and Crew wished he had some sunglasses. It hit Danny as well, and he popped open the compartment at his elbow between the seats and fished out a pair of wire frame sunglasses. They looked like goggles to Crew. They also made Danny look incredibly monstrous. And ruthless.

"She a stripper?" Crew asked.

Danny nodded "She had a couple of shows. 'S how we met. But she only worked for her tuition. She's a waitress now. Makes good tips all round. I tell her I'll drop by in my leather sometimes. Freak her out. Wouldn't though. The thought of her getting mad at me scares the shit outta me."

"Chiropractic." Crew was impressed. "Good area to get into."

"Mmhmmm," Danny agreed. "Nice to have someone with goals like that."

They drove by some snowy-looking houses and one or two people shovelling out their driveways.

"Got a question for you."

"What did I say about asking questions?" Crew said in a neutral sounding voice.

"Nothing about you," Danny assured him.

"Alright, then. What is it?"

"How you going to do it?"

"Do what?"

"Kill Stickman. Or is that a personal question?" Danny kept his eyes on the road.

Crew thought about it for a moment. "Yeah, it is. But I'll tell you anyway. When we find him, I'll decide then."

"No guns or knives?"

Crew studied the man's profile. "No guns or knives."

Danny thought about that for a moment. This guy wasn't like any of the hit men he had seen on TV or the movies. Hell, in some stories, you'd see hit men operating in packs or alone but with all the latest high-tech hardware. Hardware that would make Danny look shit up on the internet and see if he could actually find the make of the guns he saw in the picture. Guns, knives, that funky strangling wire that one guy wore around his wrist like a piece of jewellery. Thin knives that one guy would stick down the crack of his ass. One guy had a boot that he could click off the other and a four inch blade would pop out of the toe. Those were the international killers who really took the cake in Danny's book. Then, there were the mob guys who went around in packs with suitcases filled with combat shotguns they would piece together before going to work. One flick he watched had a four-man hit squad with bags go into a hotel and rent out a room two doors down from their target. Once there, they pulled out shotguns, handguns, and guns that looked like mini-Uzis. A Hollywood-style hit squad. They later tore into the suite where their target was waiting with his bodyguards. In the end, the hotel needed a shitload of screen doors and windows.

Anyway, those pros all seemed to be carrying *something*.

Yet Crew did not.

Or he kept it hidden well enough.

"You study some sort of martial art?" Danny asked him.

"I did."

"Which one? Kempo? Taekwondo? That one where a guy tries for your leg or arm and hauls you to the ground before fucking you up?"

"There are lots like that," Crew said disdainfully.

"How many are there then?"

"Lots."

"Which one you know then?"

Crew sighed. "It's a good thing you're the quiet type. I'll tell you I don't know Taekwondo."

"No? Why?"

"It's an Olympic sport for one," Crew explained. "Second, in close quarters, it's too flashy. Useless."

"No good for the street?"

Crew shrugged. "I think it's okay for the street depending on who you're fighting and how many you're up against. And whether or not the other guy knows how to fight."

Danny leaned over. "My buddy and I watched mixed martial arts on pay-for-view."

"Me too," Crew said.

"Yeah, it's from the States. Anyway, you don't see many straight boxers in those fights. I mean, like, never. Zero. You see some, but they get their asses kicked pretty bad."

"It's not like Hollywood, is it?" Crew threw in.

"No, it's not. Shit, there's some quick knock downs. But anyway, we'd be watching and got around to asking 'Why?'"

"I've seen a few, but they wind up like your sumos."

"Why is that then? Boxing is tough, man. The conditioning is hell." Danny glanced left and right out of his windows, watching his blind spots. The heat was really coming through now, and he turned it down some. "Your belt? Is it black?"

The American was silent for a moment, and Danny felt then perhaps he had spoken too much. But the shit was interesting to him. He wasn't pumping the man for information. After a few moments, Crew decided to speak. "Yeah, it's black," he said and decided then he had talked enough. "What about you? You're a bouncer. Ever have training of any kind?"

Danny kept his face straight. "Boxing. Only a bit, though. Not really any good at it. But against drunks and someone who don't know what they are doing, I get the job done."

Crew was nodding. "And it helps to be the size of a house, too. Ever face anyone with training of some kind?"

"Tyke Ki Do."

"What?"

"Tae Kwon Doers," Danny glanced in his rear view mirror. "Boom and I call them Tyke Ki Doers. Lots of 'em in and around Halifax. I don't think I came up against anyone that was any good though. Maybe a yellow belt. Or green."

"The worst kind," Crew commented and meant it. "So, what happened?"

"Thursday night. Average crowd, but one of these lanky guys got into his beers a little too deep. You always get one in a week, but chances are not much will come of it. This guy though must've just signed up for his Tyke Ki Do lessons. A little beefy. Average height. Like a smaller version of Steven Segal. Even had the pony tail."

Crew could picture the type. Christ.

"Anyway, he starts mouthin' off at the women on stage. The usual shit: 'I love you'; 'Your shit is bad'. Whatever, but he keeps on and starts to piss the ladies off to the point where they start looking to me. So, I move a little closer and start watchin' him, just off to the side where he can see me. Usually that's enough. Just to let you know you got my attention, and the smart ones usually shut up. But this one doesn't. Hell, he gets worse. Starts calling the girls bitches and sluts and whores."

Crew winced. "Once knew a woman that said the worst thing you could call a woman was a slut."

"She got it right then, but this little Stevie didn't stop there. He keeps right on goin' and starts shouting louder, well, even worse than before. Gary's pretty strict about that kind of shit. I mean, the girls get up there and show off their goods to Lord knows what kind of individuals, including university fucks and losers in business suits. They expose themselves daily to that kind of shit, but they don't have to take no verbal abuse from them."

"Customers know that?"

"Sign right by the coat check. Anyway, the second he starts going on about seeing some fuckin' twat, I put my hand on his shoulder and tell him 'Sir, that's not necessary,' to which he says 'What, asshole?' 'Swearing at the dancers,' says I. 'These fuckin' salt flaps are dancin'?" he says back to me and I give him the look."

"The look?" Crew asked, glancing sideways at Danny.

Danny winked back. "Warning look."

"Show it."

"Naw."

"What? C'mon, show it here."

Danny shook his head. "I can't, man. Not angry now. It's one of those things I can summon up only when I'm mad or something. And I'm drivin' here. Drivin' always relaxes me out."

Crew allowed him that. The big man seemed nothing but relaxed behind the wheel. He liked that.

"Anyway, this guy throws off my hand and gets to his feet. Sticks his hands out like they're knives or somethin'. The music goes off, and he tells me to back off. 'Back off, motherfucker!' he goes. 'Just back the fuck off!' and on and on about how'll he fuck me up and yada yada yada. So, he's gone in my book. Now, it's a question when, where, or if he wakes up."

Danny paused then, caught up in the recollection of his story. He shook his head, remembering how it went, and smiled. "We should stop somewhere and pick up something to drink. Snacks, too. You like beef jerky?"

"Yeah, I do."

"We'll get some of that. I love that stuff. Anyway, where was I?"

"Where and when and—"

"Oh, yeah," Danny nodded. "So, I tell him to step outside, but he's pretty much shitfaced and a Tyke Ki Doer. He's already got his leg cocked back, and I *know* he's gonna kick, but I'm wonderin' if he's just fuckin' *stupid* enough to try, and guess what?"

"He's stupid enough?" Crew ventured.

"Yup," Danny replied. "Saw the foot comin' in slow motion, man. I mean, I had time to think 'He's really going for it,' as he's doing it. The foot's coming around the mountain, gathering steam. He's even hollerin' that KEEYAH shit they shout to release the extra energy or scare the guy or whatever. He's fuckin' KEEYAHIN' like he walked into a hen house and forgot the axe. And the foot's still in the air, coming round, and his eyes are all lit up, looking at me, going even wider when I step back. He goes over the table. And I'll give the little bastard this: he was a *nimble* little squirrel fucker. He lands on both feet and brings up his fists, and he's still Keeyahin' like he's the fuckin' *originator* of the Keeyah. And he's got plenty of room cuz there ain't no one around him, so he flips over a table and urges me on. It was a parody of fuckin' *Bloodsport*, I tell ya."

Crew was smiling. "So, what'd you do?"

"Well, he flips the table, still Keeyahin' like he's got bionic lungs or something, and he does this little focusing thing in the air with his fingers. Like making little triangles. So, I let him. I'd have to pay money to be this fuckin' entertained any other time. Little Stevie does his finger focusing thing, slaps both of his hands together and slaps his thighs, bends over like a golfer and fuckin' spins on me! But by this time, I ain't entertained no more. I step back, dodge the foot and step in. Popped him square in the nose—the off switch—and he crumpled. Boomer comes around and picks him up and throws him outside into the dumpster. I guess little Stevie upchucked on himself, too, so Boom has to flip him on his belly, so the little moron doesn't choke to death on his own vomit. Nasty shit, that part."

"That is nasty," Crew laughed. "Funny shit, though."

"Yeah," Danny agreed. "Funny shit." The big man paused for a moment, letting the remembered time play itself out in his mind. Crew did not disturb him.

That was good of him, sensing when not to break a silence, when a silence was the best thing to hold.

"Anyway," Danny started after a while, "that follows what you were sayin'. About a decent boxer being able to take a not so good Tyke Ki Doer."

"Martial artist."

"Right."

"But he was drunk," Crew noted. "He could have been better sober."

Danny made a sour face. "Nah. That one was all wind and asshole. You get 'em. All shapes and sizes. I just hope to gawd I never hurt the dumb bastards."

This interested Crew. "Really? You? A bouncer afraid of hurting someone?"

"Oh, yeah," Danny stressed. "Don't need that on my conscience. Now, there are some that get off on that, but Boom and I never did. And we hated working with the ones that do. They were the ones you had to be careful about."

"You ever think about being a cop?"

That brought a smile to Danny's dark face. "Don't got the grades. Got everything else but the grades. Might have a chance these days, though. I hear that the RCMP are looking for folks with life experience. I got that," he rolled his eyes with comic effect. "But, nah. I think they get even less respect than a bouncer. Where I am is okay for now."

Was okay, but Crew did not say this.

It was on Danny's mind, however. Where would he go after this? Gary had no family. Boomer did, but they were in PEI. A mother and a father. The idea hung in his head like a flickering exit sign on its last leg. What would he do if those guys didn't pull through?

The silence returned, and Crew honoured it this time, staring out at the snowy scenery rushing by. He hoped he would spot a blue Mustang soon.

CHAPTER 25

They were driving. Tony told himself that. They were driving and talking. He was driving and glancing out ever so casually, checking his mirrors, his blind spots, switching lanes and stealing looks in Lucy's direction whenever he felt she wasn't watching. Sometimes, he would look anyway, just to make eye contact. To let her know that he was becoming more and more interested in what she had to say. He was very interested in what she had to say. Extremely interested.

The only trouble was that Lucy was being so goddamn boring.

She would not say a word about her past or why in hell's name she was on the highway at night in winter when they—*he*, (Tony corrected himself. Freak show could go fuck himself with a telephone pole)—picked her up. She offered no explanation of any events leading up to that particular junction in time. Nor did she talk about any family. Tony couldn't recall anyone, not one person, ever engaging him in conversation and not mentioning *something* about someone.

The news on the radio interested her, however, and she became pensive at times as the radio spewed out reports on the hour. It all concerned miracles, people surviving some terrible mishap or accident and living to talk about it. There was a report on someone's 100th birthday, and Lucy speculated aloud what it must be like to be a hundred years old, to see one's family grow up and even die while the centenarian lived on. Tony knew the news could be morbid, but with Lucy, it became even more depressing. Two people had their legs crushed when their van went off a highway and smashed into a tree. A swimmer off some Florida beach was run over by a speedboat and lived despite being shredded by the craft's fiberglass hull. A local Ontario man slipped and fell on his chainsaw. A university student playing Russian roulette blew away a chunk of his skull and then walked into a hospital.

"Amazing," Lucy breathed. "There must be something left over from Christmas. They all should have died."

"Yeah," Tony rumbled. He hoped to God above that something perky in the way of music came on soon. He'd even listen to French pop music right now.

The music did finally come on, and sensing a real need for more quiet, Lucy did just that. She sat there on the passenger side with her bee bottom's toque on, black jacket, jeans, and white boots. She began humming in tune with the music on the radio. Highway signs cautioning them went by. Towns passed by. Cities passed by. Faceless shapes that might have been people blurred by the Mustang's window, and Tony paid them scant attention. Time seemed to stretch, and the weirdest sensation of movement began to overtake him. He compared it to *déjà vu*, except it wasn't. He knew he had never driven this far outside of Nova Scotia before, and yet, something was going on here. Something was *transpiring*. He glanced over at Lucy. She was still humming. More signs flashed by, green streaks in the air, reminding Tony of a superhero's fist before the impact. Low flying meteors just outside his starship. White supernovas.

Then, it hit him. He felt as if he was warping ahead, and everything outside of the Mustang was being stretched into a featureless flat band before disappearing behind him. And for the life of him, he could not remember the last sign he passed. He couldn't recall the last town, the last city. Tony's eyes squinted together in concentration.

What *province* was he in?

Had they stopped in Quebec? Or had they driven on through to Ontario?

"Lucy?"

"Yes?"

"Do you feel . . . I don't know . . . funny?"

"No. Why? You?"

"Yeah?"

"Are you sick?" Alarm in her voice. Probably thinking he was about to puke.

"No."

"Are you sure? Pull over if you think you're going to throw up."

"No, I'm fine. I'm not sick. Just . . ." he trailed off, and even the fucking music on the radio seemed to echo to Tony now as if he were hauling ass in the opposite direction of the concert, except the concert was still right before him. Puzzlement flooded his person. Trippy.

His eyes suddenly went wide. Was he *high*?

He looked at the dash clock. It read 3:25.

Was it *that* late?

Wasn't it morning a moment ago?

"Anthony? What's wrong?" Lucy's voice seemed to come from miles away.

"Nothing," Tony lied, and his voice sounded slurred to him. "Just sleepy."

The sun was dropping in the sky now like a blazing ball, like someone filmed its descent and later sped the footage up. But it was dropping towards the east.

The clock said 3:25.

No fucking way, Tony's mind stated in a truly awed tone. This was some serious fucked up highway hypnosis. But he was looking all around now. And Lucy seemed fine to him though she was looking worried. Sweet. He really wanted to see her naked.

Then, he felt sick in his stomach. A cold sweat popped out on his forehead, and he felt the colour drain from his face. A tide welled up within his stomach, and Tony had been a drinker long enough to know that feeling.

"Lucy," he gasped, and hunched over the wheel.

"Yes?" A voice came from over hills.

"I have . . . to . . . pull over."

"Okay."

He decelerated, feeling what pilots might have called *G's* pulling at his seatbelt, cutting across his gut. There was a Comfort Inn sitting brightly below the highway, just off ramp. Tony aimed for it, knowing he was going to barf well before he got anywhere near it. And he knew he was going to spray all over the interior of the beast, in front of this angel. Blank white that was formless before slowed and became ramparts of snow piled higher than the car. The white had a soothing effect on Tony's eyes and his stomach. The feeling of nausea lessened. Hills appeared. Lines fattened themselves and became long plains. Icicle trees sporadically spotted the frozen stretches of ground.

Open plains?

The Mustang pulled into the parking lot. A wind battered the sides, and Tony could feel the force through the steering column. Then there was nothing. Tony clawed at his seatbelt, released himself and flung the door open. He fell out onto the ground, mouth yawning and popping his ears like skin stretched too tight over a drum. The frigid air made his nostrils dry out immediately, and on his hands and knees and facing icy asphalt, he gulped down purifying lungfuls.

And he did not empty his stomach onto the ground.

His senses returned. He felt hands on his back, rubbing it. "You okay?"

"Yeah," Tony said. He felt the returning rush of wellness you feel after ejecting whatever foreign substance had made you ill in the first place. He looked at the ground. Nothing. He switched his attention to his ass. Nothing. Didn't shit or piss himself. That was all good. He dropped to the ground. The cold seeped into his chest and body. He was on ice. Just like a beer. It felt wonderful.

"You okay?" Lucy's hands continued to rub his back. When did she get out of the car?

"Feel strange, but better," Tony whispered in a weak voice. "Queasy."

"You gonna throw up?"

He thought about it again and shook his head.

"All I need is fresh air."

"No more driving," Lucy informed him.

"Okay."

"You can pay for the rooms, again, too." There was a smile wrapped around her words. That, alone, made Tony feel immensely better. He rolled over and stared up at her.

She was beautiful.

"You're too goddamn perky for your own good," he said to her.

Lucy smiled and snow blew about her face. "Okay. I'll pay for my room. You pay for yours. But I will pay for dinner if you can manage to eat something. That okay with you?"

Tony smiled back. It was.

They signed in, in different rooms, and had dinner in the motel's small restaurant area. Tony had forgotten about his early sickness. He had a hot turkey sandwich, which he wolfed down, silently asking his mother for forgiveness. Lucy picked at a lasagne and took much longer. In the end, she offered the remaining half of it to Tony. He discovered, with only a margin of guilt, he had no trouble with downing that as well.

Lucy paid for the entire meal. A white clock hanging on the restaurant wall stated it was 8:40. She gazed at the clock for a moment, and then turned her attention to Tony.

"There's a bar here, you know. Care for a drink?"

"Sounds good. Let's go."

They made their way down a brown corridor that seemed to have carpet growing up its sides to knee height. The road of carpet ended at a door with a neon sign that read in white letters "Da Double". Tony liked the name and wondered how the bar got it. He let Lucy go in first, entering into a lounge almost the same size as the Beacon back in Nova Scotia. Centred in the area was the bar itself, a dark bastion of sparkling spirits encased in shiny hardwood and trimmed with armrests of dark leather. A single bartender stood underneath a ceiling of crystal beer mugs, and he gave them both an affable nod. Tony noted how his eyes lingered on Lucy just a second longer and felt a stab of jealousy. He realized it was jealousy, as well, and the notion made him set his jaw. He was getting too attached to this woman. Christ almighty. How long had he known her?

"We're early," Tony said, keeping his eyes on the barkeep until he dropped his stare.

Lucy walked ahead, turned, and wriggled a finger for Tony to follow. They moved past the bar, and avoided the many tables surrounding the glittering fortress of alcoholic merriment. They chose a more private booth near the back where the walls were padded with great black plumes of vinyl. They looked fine from afar, but up close, Tony could see that they were worn. The seats were exceptionally comfortable, and he sighed when he made contact with the cushion. Lucy sat across from him and turned down a paper pyramid adorning the table. The pyramid displayed the bar's specials for the month. She gave it a quick look and hid it from Tony.

"My treat. If you see the price you might feel like you might want to chip in. Can't have that."

"I'm not going to argue if you really want to pay. I love it when the lady foots the bill," Tony said and flexed his eyebrows.

They ordered a pitcher of beer and talked only now and then. Tony sensed Lucy was waiting for something, but he could not guess what. She watched him drink from over the rim of her tall-necked glass. Asked him if he had ever been this far west before. Tony believed she had asked him the same question earlier, but answered her anyway. He found those dark eyes of hers mesmerizing, and he caught himself twice staring into them for too long a time. Lucy did not seem to mind, and she eventually shrugged out of her coat. Tony averted her eyes while she did so. When he looked back, she locked onto his gaze like a current of electricity.

The bartender put on some soft rock. They listened and the conversation became even quieter. Time flowed as easily as the beer. Tony glanced at his glass. It was his fourth now and the second pitcher. He was beginning to feel pleasantly buzzed. Lucy was on her fourth as well and seemed just as relaxed. She looked in the direction of the bartender. The man was cleaning glasses. He worked with his head down, each movement in time with the music. She looked back to Tony and smiled softly.

"How do you feel now?"

"Better. Weird, but I feel much better now. Must be the beer."

"Must be. And the company."

Tony smiled. "Probably has something to do with it."

She smiled back. "You gave me a scare back at the car. I thought you were really sick."

"I feel fine now. And I'll sleep fine tonight."

"Me, too."

"Not going to sleep in the car?" Tony asked her. This seemed to amuse her.

Tony cocked an eyebrow. "An old girlfriend of mine looked just like you do now when I told her I stopped buying and wearing silk underwear."

"Really?" Lucy frowned. "Why?"

"I had to. I was feeling up my ass too damn much."

The laugh that came from Lucy was adorable. She made it even more adorable when she clamped both hands over her mouth to quiet herself.

She sobered up then, and looked straight into Tony's eyes. "Anthony, do you know what time it is?"

"Yeah, it's—" he remembered his watch and started to look at it. Lucy reached across the table and covered its face with her hand. Her touch froze Tony. Blinking, he glanced around the bar, searching for a clock. "Well, near eleven anyway."

Lucy did not seem pleased with his answer. "Yes, around there. When did you pick me up?"

"Yesterday," Tony sipped on his beer, trying to remember. "Maybe around nine-ish? Nine-thirty?"

"And where are we now?"

Tony shrugged. "Just into Quebec maybe . . ." he trailed off. He had no idea. "Why? Do you know?"

Lucy nodded. She reached over, gently took off his watch, and placed it face down on the table. Tony did not resist. She had folded the paper pyramid up and down during their beers and now she began folding it in upon itself. "How are you about surprises?"

"You mean if I like 'em or if I can handle 'em?"

"Both."

"Okay, I guess. Depends on the surprise. If it's like a birthday kind of surprise, then that's fine. If it's something else, then I dunno. If it's like your mom has just been diagnosed with terminal cancer, then that's a different matter. But I can handle it. If that's what you mean. I don't freak out easy."

Lucy digested this stoically. She took a sip of her beer and pinched-wiped her mouth with two fingers. It was obvious she was contemplating something heavy, but Tony could not guess what. Was she finally going to open up about her past? Was she a single mom on the run from the mafia and heading west to start a new life? Was she really a man? Christ, Tony hoped he was wrong on that one.

She flipped up the paper she had been folding. It was a tourist advertisement. There was the bluest river before a city with a high tower topped off with what looked like a flying saucer. Mountains glowed next to it, and tiny people were skiing down their faces. Golden words were etched brightly across the fabricated sky. *"See Calgary! See How We Live!"*

Tony studied the ad for a moment. "Where you get that?"

"It was always here."

His eyebrows went up in an '*oh really*' expression.

Lucy was not smiling anymore. "Really."

"So . . . what?" Tony shrugged.

"We're in Alberta," she informed him.

"We're in Alberta," he repeated, not believing her and trying hard not to grin at the ridiculous notion.

"We passed Calgary a ways back," Lucy told him.

"Hm," he simply said, looking off into space and wondering if the wench actually believed she was being convincing. The thought made him shake his head again.

"You don't believe me?" Lucy asked, sad.

"No," Tony smiled. He didn't want to, but he could not help himself. At least he managed not to laugh in her face.

"I see." She looked in the direction of the bartender. "Excuse me!" She yelled.

The man's head bobbed up.

"Where are we exactly?"

"On highway one. Almost two hours outside of the city."

"What city?" Lucy asked, glancing at Tony to see if he was listening. He was. Sort of.

"Calgary," the man answered. "You folks not from around here?"

"No," Lucy replied. "Thank you." She fixed Tony with a '*you see*' glare.

Tony smirked. "So, you paid the guy or something."

"You didn't see the calendar in the lobby? The plates on the cars in the parking lot?"

"I was getting over being sick. I didn't notice," Tony said truthfully. "Should I have?"

"Go take a look."

"*Now?*" It was cold outside. "I'm not going outside!"

"Ask about the time, then," she instructed him.

Tony scowled. She was going too far with this. But he did so anyway. "Hey buddy, what time is it?"

A pause. "11:10."

Tony thanked the man. "Alright Lucy. It's 11:10."

She handed him his watch. It said 2:10. He studied it for no more than a second. "You changed this or something?"

The man was handling it quite well thus far, but Lucy was nowhere near the drop. "With one hand? Right in front of you? I think you'd notice."

"I think so, too," Tony agreed. "So, how you do it? You work in a casino once or something? Tell me. Seriously. Light up the mystery. Damn good trick so far though, I'll give you that."

"It is something of a trick," she admitted, "but that part isn't really important right now. Right now, I have to convince you that we are in Alberta. On the other side of Calgary. That weird feeling you had earlier. That's part of it. And you'll feel it tomorrow when you get behind the wheel. You'll feel that way because, well," she looked him straight in the eye, "time is very important right now."

"I bet. A question, though."

"Go ahead."

"Why aren't you feeling weird then? Feeling sick? You were in the car, too. What's up with that?"

"I'm different," Lucy said simply.

Tony had been around a lot of liars. He had a pretty good idea of how to detect someone in the middle of stretching the truth. And, as far as he could tell, there was nothing in her tone, her body language, or her eyes to suggest a lie. She was telling the truth, as far as he could tell.

"Okay, you *believe* you're different, then." People from Quebec were different too. "And you believe we're in Alberta."

"Let's step outside for a minute." Lucy was already pulling on her coat.

"Why do I want to step outside? It's *cold* outside, man! It's *warm* in here! You can go outside if you want. Just leave the beer, okay?"

"Just for a minute. A minute. I'll prove to you that we are in Alberta."

"No," Tony smiled at her. He wasn't moving. He raised his mug.

Lucy studied him for a moment, debating something. "I'll give you a blowjob," she announced finally.

The words stunned Tony faster than a Taser to the heart. He blinked over the rim of his beer. He forgot to swallow. He finally did and lowered his glass to the table. "Wow," he muttered in blunt amazement. "Did you just say—"

"You heard me," Lucy interrupted, her eyes never left his.

Tony sat in silence for a moment. "You're serious," he eventually stated.

"Yes."

"If I go outside with you, a BJ is mine."

"Yes."

"No questions asked."

"No."

"Only service."

Lucy expelled an impatient breath, "You want the blowjob or not?"

Tony sat blinking for all of three seconds, three thudding heartbeats, and then he was getting to his feet as if his ass were on fire.

They got up and moved towards the exit. Lucy led the way. Tony trailed behind as if he were on an invisible leash. He was too shocked to say anything. He met the eyes of the bartender as he went by.

A blowjob? The guy mouthed wordlessly to him, equally shocked.

Tony only nodded.

The bar guy slowly shook his head. Then, he nodded his approval. Like Tony needed it. He was stunned by the proposition, but he was coming out of the thaw very fast. He liked the prospect very much. Lucy was an exotic dish. Part of him already envisioned her generous lips servicing him. He wondered if she was a sucker or a stroker or both. Did she cup balls? Then, he realized he didn't care in the least.

They stepped outside, into the freezing cold of the late winter night. The ploughed snow made ramparts around the edges of the parking lot. There were cars in the lot, and a few pickups, all dark and shiny under tall lights. Lucy marched towards the vehicles.

Reaching the front of the first car, she whirled about and pointed at the license plate. "There!"

It was clearly an Albertan license plate. "Alberta. Wild Rose Country," it read.

"Well?" Lucy demanded after a moment.

"Well, what?" Tony countered. "Don't mean anything. They could be tourists. Or on a business meeting or something."

"It's from Alberta because we're in Alberta," Lucy stomped in the snow to the next car as she spoke. She jabbed at the plate with an open palm. "See this?"

It also read Alberta.

"So, it's a convention." Tony said calmly. "We're not in Alberta, and I think you owe me something."

Lucy ignored him. She wasn't too happy with his reluctance to admit what was obvious. Tony didn't care as long as he got what she said she would give. In the back of his mind, he knew he wasn't going to get anything, and he certainly would not force the issue, but he was buzzed just enough to have a little fun.

"Here," she said, stopping in front of the next car.

"Alberta." Tony declared loudly. "Big convention. Funny though that the bar was empty. I figure folks from out west would all be big drinkers."

"Step out here," Lucy ordered him. She moved closer to where the parking lot met the highway. The snow was piled up chest high.

Lucy whirled on him. "Tell you what. I'll guess what the next car is. If I get that right, I don't have to give you a blowjob."

Already Tony's head was shaking, "No way, man. I specifically came out here for a blowjob. And I'm here. And it's cold. You have any idea what happens to a guy in weather like this? And why would I risk a sure thing anyway?"

"If I'm wrong, you'll get more than a blowjob."

Sweet Jesus. "More?" he asked, dubiously.

"More," she repeated, the challenge glowed in her face and stance.

Tony cleared his throat. "How much more?"

Her eyes locked onto his. "Everything."

The word *everything* was a little slow piercing Tony's brainpan, however, once it did and understanding set in, the slow nod of his head became more energetic. "Let's do it."

"You only get it if I get the car wrong."

Something bothered him. "The next *five* cars."

"Deal," Lucy said immediately. That did not bode well, either. She was too sure of herself.

"Hold on." He glanced about to see if there were any hidden parking lot mirrors. He couldn't see any. No camera, either, however the hell she could work that to her guessing five cars in a row.

"Are we doing this or what?" Lucy wanted to know.

The light poles were empty, too, and Lucy was standing with her back to the road. She couldn't see anything. The cars would be past her before she did. And she looked ready.

"Five cars." Tony wanted her understanding in this.

"Five."

"Makes and colours."

Lucy made a face. "General makes and colours. I don't know that much about cars, Anthony. A hatchback is a hatchback, okay? A truck is a truck."

"That's a little too general," Tony mulled.

"I have to guess five cars! Five! I think the odds are pretty much in your favour."

"Me, too," he said, not checking the grin slipping across his face.

"Then, shall we?"

"Year of make, okay?"

"ANTHONY!"

He held up both of his hands. "Okay, no years. Go ahead, then. Work your magic. Dazzle me."

A corner of Lucy's mouth hitched up into a dirty smile that Tony did not like in the least. He stepped in front of her, looking over her head, to ensure that she could not see a goddamn thing. Then, he thought of Gretzky. The Great

One had exceptional peripheral vision. Lucy could be the same way. The prize was too great to chance it.

"One second," Tony said, pulling her bee bottom toque down around her eyes. She did not resist. "Okay, anytime you're ready."

Lucy's wonderfully full lips pouted in distaste, and Tony wanted very badly to kiss them. He could tell she didn't like the blindfold. Well, he wouldn't require her to wear it for the blowjob. Or whatever other naughtiness he could come up with for later.

"Yellow Camaro," Lucy said almost instantly.

A split second later, a yellow Camaro drove by the motel.

Tony's mouth dropped open, his eyes staring in disbelief.

"Black hatchback," Lucy declared, barely before Tony's mind could fathom the first correct guess.

The black hatchback zipped by.

Tony blinked in stupefied amazement.

"Black pickup, red four door sedan, and blue four door sedan," she listed off and like comets racing across a black sky, each named car blazed by.

"That was a black sedan," Tony cleared his throat.

"It looks black under this light. In daylight, it's blue," Lucy told him.

"That was black as God is my witness," Tony protested calmly.

In reply Lucy drew breath. "Red pickup, cherry red four door something, black and chrome transport truck."

The vehicles snapped by like noisy lasers, and with them, whatever words of protest Tony might have mustered.

"Well . . ." he began in an extremely calm voice. Then, he changed his mind. "*FUCK!*"

Lucy rolled up her toque. She was smiling.

Tony glared at her. "How the hell—"

Lucy kissed the air in front of him. "Guess I win."

"Horseshit," Tony spat out. "It wasn't like I was really expecting anything."

"Oh, no?"

"Course not. You're not the type."

"But you believe me now?" Lucy was serious.

"That we're in Alberta? No," Tony almost laughed.

Lucy rolled her eyes at him. "It was easier to convince people fifty years ago. No, make that a century ago."

That sobered him. "What did you just say?"

"Come here." She marched towards the main doors of the motel. Tony followed, grateful for getting out of the cold. He was beginning to wonder just how detailed this joke got. The ad was fine, and it was easy for her to get the bartender to go along. But fuck him how she managed the traffic. That was incredible. They would *have* to get to Vegas. Then, it suddenly occurred to him: Why was she going to all the trouble? Why the big effort about convincing him he was in Alberta, anyway? It was too damn cold to joke about such a thing.

They stepped into the motel's lobby, the winter air shrieking in and wrestling with the warmth beyond the threshold. Directly across from them was the front desk. The elderly lady behind it reading a paperback, immaculate right down to the bread bun of hair tied on the back of her head, gave him no more than a second's appraisal.

"See there," Lucy said in a suddenly gentle voice as if this were the final proof she needed to convince him.

Tony walked by her, thankful to escape the deep-space cold outside. He could feel his testicles clinking together like a pair of frozen wind chimes. He wiped his feet before closing with the front desk. He could see from here what Lucy was pointing at. It was the bronze frame and ceremonial plaque firmly establishing the opening date of the motel.

In Alberta.

Tony stopped in his tracks and stared at the words for almost a minute. The lady at the desk eventually decided to take notice of him again. "May I help you, sir?"

"No," Tony replied very quietly with both hands resting on his hips. There was a chill coming up his lower legs. His testicles hoisted themselves up when it reached his crotch, like white mice trying to escape a rising river. He took in the front desk, and his mind blossomed in shock.

Pictures of the Rockies.

A wondrous wilderness shot of Banff National Park.

Listings of possible trips and their destination prices: Wintergreen; Lake Louise; Rabbit Hill.

A pile of community newspapers.

The day's copy of the Calgary Herald.

A picture of a group of smiling people standing in front of a castle-like structure called Mewata Armouries; a dark green tank just to the group's right.

Every drop of spit in Tony's mouth evaporated. It suddenly became drier than a nun's hooch laid out buck naked in the middle of the Sahara. A hand on his arm tugged and pulled him away. He was guided back to the bar. He didn't say a word, nor did he resist. The time of resisting was long past, now. Now, he was aboard the dream for wherever it was going, whatever it was worth. They sat again and beer was placed before him. Lucy was speaking to him, her voice low and melodious like a soft song on the radio. She promised she would explain everything. She promised answers to all of his questions. The important thing was for him to be strong and to not be afraid.

It was goddamn easy for her to say.

She obviously accepted the fact that they had driven two thirds across a very big country in a day. Instead of the more realistic eight or even *nine* days.

Tony sipped on his beer.

"Are you going to be sick?" Lucy asked him. Her voice echoed in his head.

"No," Tony said truthfully.

"Are you sure? 'Cuz if you—"

"I'm not going to be sick," he told her in a stern tone. He did not want to talk right now. Lucy respected the silence he invoked. She watched him sit and hoped he didn't get sick. It happened sometimes when the impossible got wrapped around their world and was pulled tight. That kind of tightness made gullets heave and eyes bulge. So far, with the exception of the day's travel, Anthony was holding up fine.

He took a breath and rubbed his eyes. Another deep breath, a plunging, clarifying one, and then he zeroed in on Lucy. She appeared genuinely concerned with his frame of mind and health.

"Okay," Tony's eyes narrowed, and his mouth puckered up like a sucker on an octopus's tentacle. "I need to ask some questions . . . First . . . how did we get here so fast?"

Lucy nodded. "We drove, of course."

"Of course," Tony said in a smartass tone. "But what the fuck else happened there?"

That didn't impress Lucy in the least. She sat there for a moment before answering. "It was, well, time that was altered. Hours becoming minutes so to speak. That sort of thing, anyway."

"I see," Tony said blindly. Then, as an afterthought. "Bullshit."

Lucy winced. "That's what happened."

"How?"

Another smile, dear and utterly sympathetic to his confusion, spread across her smooth features. "It's difficult for you to understand."

In a sarcastic nod, Tony's head bounced in agreement.

"But that's how he works," Lucy said.

"He who?"

"I can't tell you his name. Not his true name, anyway."

"Why not?"

"Because," her eyebrows flexed, "your head would explode."

Tony balked, his beer half raised to his lips. "Excuse me?"

"His real name would make your head explode. If you can accept that you are in Alberta now, you'll have to accept the other. I can tell you what you call him though, and you've already met him. He's Mr. Tim. He's, well, Time."

If this was supposed to surprise him, he did not let it show. In fact, he just stared on. After a moment, he cleared his throat. "He's done this."

"Yes."

"Why?" Tony asked. His beer was forgotten now.

"Because we have very little of your time left. Very little. We have to find who you are supposed to find and very quickly. This was the fastest way since you wouldn't fly."

"Find this Frank guy?"

"Is that the name Time gave you?"

"Uh-huh. Augustus Franklin."

"Then, he's the one."

"Why didn't you know the name? And fuck, while I'm at it, how do you know Tim? And now I'm on it, I bet you know fucked up Freddy, too! Am I right?"

Lucy's face became drawn then. Every time Tony said the F-word, she became a little sadder. "There really isn't any need to swear."

Tony did a fine impression of feigning shock. "Oh, I think there is every fucking NEED to swear right now. Jesus and Joseph humping Mary! Every last goddamn fucking syllable to come out my goddamn fucking mouth could be Jesus Christ's name in vain, and since I find myself in goddamn fucking ALBERTA..."

Tony let that hang in the air for effect. Lucy did not attempt to interrupt.

"I think I can get away with it," Tony finished. He raised his glass, drained it and banged it off the table. The bartender did not appear to notice. It was a lover's fight as far as he was concerned, and as long as the guy didn't start whacking his missus, all was fine.

"You're only making this harder for me, Anthony," Lucy said quietly. "Please."

Her wonderfully dark eyes met his.

"Fuck that," Tony waved his hand about as if warding off whatever magic Lucy was trying on him. "Start talking. And you better get a goddamn move on, too, if my time is so goddamn important. What I do fucking care about is wrapping up this pigfucker of a cock-sucking headache I'm getting from all of this goddamn bullshit. And it's grade fuckin' A prime bullshit, too. So, give up some more. Oh, I'm sorry, am I offending your goddamn sensibilities with all of this?"

Lucy sprang up and ran. She crossed the bar floor in a matter of seconds and disappeared out the door. The bartender, dry wiping a mug that had occupied his attention perhaps a little too long, looked up in the direction of Lucy's wake. He did not look at Tony.

Tony made no attempt to go after her. He had no inclination to. Fuck it. He was quite content to just sit there and stew. He did exactly that. He fumed over the situation he was suddenly in, in a province a long way from home. He raised his mug to his lips and realized he emptied it moments ago. "Shit."

He refilled it with what was left in the pitcher. Drank that. Since Lucy was no longer around, he drank the rest of her beer, as well. No sense in letting it go to waste seeing as it was all paid for. The beer placated him long enough to think. He thought about the conversation, replayed the entire thing in his mind, and thought, with a growing distaste, that he had been a prick. The whole picture hadn't even been explained to him, and it seemed Lucy was about to before he exploded. Before he bawled her out. Lovely Lucy.

A heavy sigh shuddered through his frame. He was a prick. He thought of the blow job, and he shook his head. No chance of that now. Not even any sympathy service. Fuck! Double Fuck!

Your time, her words came back to him. *Your time.* What in hell's pisspot did she mean by that? Tony sat with a full blaze smoking up the timber frame of his mind. It was clear to him what he had to do now, what he had backed himself into. Shaking his head and swearing at himself, Tony got to his feet.

"Smart move," the bar guy said as Tony walked by. "Go apologize. The lady's too fine to stay mad at."

Tony ignored him. He didn't need the advice. He knew what he had to do. He left the bar, keeping the growls emanating from his throat low.

Minutes later, he stood outside her room. He thought that things were too fucking weird for him. A part of him screamed to just get the fuck out of there. Get out of the motel, get into the beast and drive. Forget Lucy, forget Tim and Frank, *especially* fuckhead Freddy. Things were weird. Really weird. And if he knocked on that door . . .

CHAPTER 26

The door opened.

"Come in," Lucy invited quietly. "And take your shoes off. The carpet is too nice to ruin."

"I always take my shoes off," Tony muttered with a frown, looking incredibly guilty. His mother had driven that discipline into him. If he ever ventured into the living room with his outside footwear on, his mother would unleash unholy hell. He slipped out of his shoes and moved past the TV and bed, towards the small table where Lucy sat and another chair waited. Two cans of beer were opened and waiting.

Tony pointed to the beers. "Figured I was coming, did ya?"

"I guessed."

"You're pretty good at that."

"The best I know," Lucy dipped her head, but there was no smile on her face.

Tony sat heavily, sized up the room and reached for a beer. He fondled the cold Molson for a moment. "What's your name?" he finally asked her. "Is it really Lucy?"

She shook her head slowly. "I can't tell you my real name. If I did . . . your head would explode."

Tony sighed and drank. "So, who do I owe my formal apology to?"

She smiled then, and the room lit up like a star had just exploded. A smile that would thaw any freeze the longest winter had to offer. "Lucy is fine."

"Lucy, then. I'm sorry. I shouldn't have lost it back there. I shouldn't have yelled at you. I'm sorry for . . . for swearing. I'll try to do better."

While he spoke, she watched him over the rim of her own beer. Her dark eyes glittered.

"That was nice," she finally said. "I believe you."

Another sigh left Tony. "Good."

"You don't like apologizing, do you?"

"No." He tossed his head to the side. "Who does?"

"True," Lucy agreed. "Necessary sometimes, though. As is the truth I have to tell you now. We no longer have any of your time left to let things go their natural course. Other pieces are in action."

"You said 'your time' again," Tony pointed.

"Time is," Lucy's eyes strayed to the closed curtains of her room, "a human measure. A mortal one. You made it. You abide by it. It's yours."

"A mortal measure?" Tony's nearly squeezed shut with the question.

"Mmmhmm."

"So . . . you're not . . ." he shrugged, "human?"

Lucy removed her toque. She shook her hair loose. It looked wonderful in the dim light of the room.

"What are you?" Tony whispered.

Her eyes strayed then, thinking on how to answer the question. Thinking on what she *could* tell this . . . *man*.

"I'm the help," she finally said with a tight lipped smile. "And that's good enough for now."

"Another one of those words that'd make my head explode?" Tony inquired good-naturedly.

"Can't chance it. Not here. The drapes are too nice. And I like the carpet too."

The carpet was maple beige and thicker than most hotel carpets he had seen. She was right. It was nice.

"So, why are you here?" He finally asked.

"To help you."

"How you gonna do that?"

"For one, setting you straight about everything. As I said, things are moving very quickly now. We have to move with it. There are those who don't want Frank to be found. They want him to stay missing."

"Alright. Fine. So, why do we have to find Frank anyway?"

Lucy drew breath, and Tony knew right then she was going to let him have it. The punch to end all punches. She knew she had to give it as well. The moment she got aboard the blue Mustang, she had known she would tell all. At least, he was accepting that he was in Alberta. That was a big start.

"You've been following the news?" Lucy asked him.

"You asked me this before, I think," Tony said. "Yeah. A little. Why?"

"What's happening in the news?"

"Aren't you supposed to be telling me something here?"

"I'm getting there," Lucy told him with infinite patience, despite the urgency inside. "So, what have you been hearing?"

Tony shrugged. "Same old shit. Stuff, I mean," he smiled an apology then. "Politics. Sports, robberies, people getting killed."

"What was the last news story you heard? Can you remember?"

"Ah . . ." he shook his head. "No. Sorry."

"It's ok," she said. "Let's watch some TV."

She turned it on. The channels flipped until she got what she wanted: CNN. She backed up and perched on the edge of the bed. Tony watched her move the whole time in silence. He noted her cheeks were shaped like little apples.

The news announcer was a familiar face to millions, but one that Tony could not place. He didn't watch the news all that much. He could not be bothered. And the news was so damn depressing anyway. Today was no exception. A pickup had nailed a five year old kid on a motorbike (stupid fucking parents had actually *bought* the kid the bike, so they could make home movies). Some woman swimmer had been resuscitated after being hooked out from under lake ice for forty five minutes. A power man had been zapped by a fallen cable for ten thousand volts. Five German peacekeepers in the Middle East had been badly mauled in a car bomb blast.

Nothing. Same shit. Only thicker.

"What are we looking for here?" Tony asked.

"Don't you see?"

"No."

"Keep watching," Lucy instructed him in a whisper, as if they were trying to spot something moving in the night sky.

Tony sighed, but did as he was told. Fifty four people in the English Channel on a sinking ferry that caught fire. All were fished out of the water. All suffered terrible burns and smoke inhalation.

Then, it was the weather.

Lucy frowned, then, while sitting only four feet in front of the TV, she pointed the remote at it and changed the channel. A movie was on. With an irritated grunt, she switched the TV off. She returned to the table and her warm beer, and faced Tony.

"What did you see?"

"Nothing really."

She held up a silencing finger. "Oh, no. It was there. C'mon, now. You're more observant than that."

"Not really."

"Try, then. Think on what you just watched. Think hard."

Taking a breath, Tony tried. The news reports were like a scattered jigsaw in his brain, and he was hunting for the edges—the frame pieces. Build the frame first. That's how his mom taught him. Then group the colours. The rest would fill itself in. The obvious.

"The obvious," Lucy whispered.

"A lot of people were hurt," Tony said after a moment of serious thought.

"Yes."

"Hurt bad," Tony continued, his brow knotting in concentration. He thought of the lady under the ice. That was pretty damned lucky. And the kid on the motorbike hit by the truck. Also fortunate. Peacekeepers. Incredibly lucky. He had seen pictures of the devastation a car bomb could do. It was fucking depressing.

Then it dawned on him. "They all lived."

Lucy slowly closed her eyes and opened them. She was pleased. "What else?"

"They all lived," he repeated. "Those were some pretty bad happenings, but they all lived. Really lucky. Miracles."

Tony drew back and slowly placed his beer back on the table. He looked at Lucy in revered awe and in a small voice said, "Are you . . . an angel?"

"No," Lucy replied with a lazy smile. "I'm not that lucky."

He closed his mouth. "Well, anyway, that's my guess. They were all miracles. They didn't die."

This wiped the smile completely from Lucy's face. "Were they miracles?"

"Well, yeah."

"You just said it then," Lucy pressed. "They didn't die."

"Yeah. Really lucky."

"Well, that's the problem, you see," Lucy said in a soft, slow voice like rich chocolate. "They *should* have died."

Tony stared at her. "That's a problem?"

"The biggest kind."

"What are you talking about? Those people got a second chance!"

"No, Tony," Lucy said gently. "They *had* their chance. Their games were over. Yet, they live on. Brain damaged, broken, crippled but all still aware of the terrible pain that is waiting for them once they regain consciousness, or are in right now; in the purest agony because they live when they should have died. Those people floating in the channel when the rescue boats came for them. Some were cooked, Anthony. Their flesh was black on the outside like a well-done steak. They practically had to be hooked to get them onto the boats because to touch these still living corpses with melted faces would cause whatever skin remaining on them to slide off. And when the boats found them, they were still screaming. What the report didn't say anything about was how eighteen of those people were burned. Melted, in fact, right down to the bone, and yet, they still live. Children, Anthony. Cooked children," Lucy finished with a sniff. Her eyes were welling up with tears. Tony fidgeted in his chair. *Burned alive.* And still living when they *should* have died.

"They . . . still have a right to live," Tony said weakly.

"Yes," Lucy said, a tear slipped down her cheek. "But this isn't about rights, Anthony. This isn't about what is right or wrong. What you saw there" —a nod towards the TV— "was only some of the highlights of today. In this province and around the world. Anthony, what would you say if I told you that *no one* has died as of three days ago?"

"What?" Tony stretched out in disbelief, his face crunching up.

"Just that. No one on the face of the earth has died. No one. Anywhere."

"That's impossible."

Lucy barely heard him, his voice was almost gone.

"Like being in Alberta?" She asked him.

"That's different," he said feebly, wanting to say more but clearly out of words to express himself. "But why is it bad? People want to live."

"Do they?" Lucy's eyebrows arched upward.

"Yeah, just like in that movie where the guys could only die when they got their heads chopped off."

Lucy reached across the table and touched his hand. The contact made Tony go very still. "What if I told you that immortality, in this case, would indeed allow you to live forever. But you would still age physically. Still grow old. Your organs would still deteriorate. Your vision fail. Your sex drive wilt. But you would not die. Even after your frame has shrunk, and your bones are no more than twigs. Your flesh, the colour of the yellow pages in the telephone book. And still you live on. What if those realities were pressed upon your immortality? Would you still embrace it?"

"Fuck, no," Tony whispered, forgetting about the profanity. This time, Lucy did not seem to mind.

"No, most would not. And then add to it whatever pain and suffering you are living with and would still have to endure. Eternally living like a roasted piece of meat. Not being able to die even when you *want* to? Or even just when you've had your fill of life? When you are simply too tired to see another sun rise?" Lucy paused for a moment, "but it won't come to that anyway, Anthony."

"What? What do you mean?"

She paused for moment, searching his face. Extreme concern and worry flooded it. "What I mean is that a lot of people are celebrating birthdays when they shouldn't be, while watching the same five o'clock news full of miracles. No one suspects anything. Some might, but they'll be scorned and mocked by the others. At first," she finished in a warning tone.

"And then?" Tony asked, but not wanting to know.

"You'll get your crazies that will start putting their suspicions to the test. People will start jumping off buildings, driving cars over cliffs. Shooting themselves or whatever just to see. And they will. They'll all live, Tony. It will only take something truly horrible to put the nail through that people can no longer die. Then . . ."

Lucy's face was true. "Chaos."

"Chaos?" Tony tasted the word as sour as cheap booze.

"Yes. What do you think will happen when people realize they can't die?"

Images and sensations blurred through his mind, all stamped with the word chaos. It sure as fuck would be chaos. And that was putting it lightly. He took a deep breath and fixed her with a look devoid of hope. "So, what do we have to do?"

"*We,*" Lucy stated quietly, another tear slipping down her face, "have to find Frank."

CHAPTER 27

Fear hated walking. Fucking despised it. Walking was for losers, and he was getting more and more pissed that only losers walked. Only *losers* walked. The short message replayed itself in his head. He took a few steps and cursed walking as walking was, again, only for losers. He was far from being a loser. Yet, here he fucking was. Walking.

Why didn't he get a car? He could afford it. Easily. And one with a goddamn better sound system than that rat-fuck Tony had in his piece of shit car. Fear could not believe his luck. Of all the wonderful sound systems available in cars today, he had been stuck in a fucking *antique*. And a *Ford* at that! How the hell anyone could drive anything made by Ford these days was beyond him. He was a firm believer in Toyota. The Japanese knew their cars. And the Germans. It struck Freddy as odd then that the two losers of the second Great War were putting out the best cars. Almost like a very quiet "fuck you" one might try to disguise in a cough. And you could buy beer practically anywhere in both countries.

The fires in Fear burned mightily as he trudged onwards through the blackness of night on that lonely strip of highway. Freezing wind smacked him in the face, and snow lashed his flesh, melting on contact. He had been on the road for hours, it seemed, and four cars travelling past had not stopped to pick him up. Anger. Fear was so *incredibly* pissed off. Pricks. They were all pricks. Two cars had slowed down, but they had only slowed down for a moment before bolting like discovered deer. Almost as if they had sensed who he was at the last possible second.

Freddy did not give a rat's ass. Not a ball's deep donkey fuck.

He was Fear. Fear walking. Fear incarnate in godforsaken flesh.

And on this cold night in March, in total darkness made only deeper when watching the red receding lights of cars drive away, Fear was *totally* consumed with rage.

Walk it off, he told himself. Walk it off. Turn the negative energy into something positive. He saw it on a health show once. Anger Management. They had suggested yoga and meditation, too, but like fuck Fear was going to get into a lotus position out here. Fuck that. FFFFFFF—and he really could not stress the 'F' sound enough—*FFFF*UCK that.

And it was all because of Tony. And that bitch Lucy. Fear was actually more pissed off at Lucy than the Mundane. The bitch. Picking her ass up did not allow her to get him kicked out of the car in the middle of nowhere. And kicked him out she had. She nullified the control Fear had put into the little shit Tony. Tony had been all his, and it was just like her Highness to stick her ass down where it wasn't needed or wanted. Fear could have completed the task without her. And what was she doing out there on the road anyway? Did Time figure someone else should accompany Tony? If he hadn't wanted Fear to go along, then why assign him in the first place? Jesus, it was infuriating to be subjected to such inefficiency. Hate wasn't an emotion unknown to him. In fact, Hate and he had done quite well together in cards. But Fear did just as well on his own without Hate. Fear did just fucking fine.

He stomped his way along the Trans-Canada, in the night, stopping several times to bellow "FUCK THIS!" at the blackness surrounding him, and then kept right on walking. He walked on for what seemed to be an eternity and that got him thinking about Time again. Why hadn't he manipulated time for Fear to make this little stroll go faster? Someone was going to have a serious goddamn talking to once Fear got home.

He kept on thinking black thoughts even as he came to an off-highway exit. Fear did not acknowledge the sign. He just walked down the slope, steaming his way through the gathering snow like some prehistoric machine. He paused once at the base, roared *"FUCK THIS!"* and continued on again.

Traffic increased along this new strip of road, but not one slowed for him. It was well past midnight. Fuck them too.

Fuck them all.

He eventually walked into the edge of town, the lights of the houses glowing in the distance. He saw the glow of the Black Bear, a roadhouse bar, and marched towards the war-bunker shaped establishment. The place probably looked its best in the winter when it was covered in snow with a background of black timberland. Bars like this on the fringe of town always made Fear think of the clientele it served, so-called hicks and hard asses. Townies. Fear didn't care. He was pissed, and he wanted a shot. He made his way toward the Black Bear. As he drew closer, he saw how the exterior paint was old and how it lacked windows. Obviously the owner didn't give a damn. The signal sign in orange light illuminating "The Black Bear" hung to the upper right of the doors. A snow-covered veranda lay to the left of the doors. Fear thought the whole place would probably have been torn down and replaced by a condo the next time he was in this part of the country.

Just then the double doors burst open, and two of the local boys stumbled out into the night air, laughing and swearing loudly. One tried to slam the doors, but the spring mechanism mounted at the top of the frame would not allow it. With a drunken roar, he heaved his shoulder into the door. It closed immediately. Someone shouted from within.

"Fuckin' whatever!" shouted the one that did not attack the door. His friend giggled hoarsely at that, the same kind of high pitched giggle that marked the annoying sidekick of a bad 80's movie bully. Both men squared off at each other, then, like apes pushing for territory. They started swearing.

Stupid fucking apes.

Fear walked towards them, hands shoved deep into his pockets. One of the apes, a young college boy type perhaps already flunked out of university due to excessive drinking, saw Fear approach. His red eyes opened wide at the potential amusement here.

"Hey Stevie, lookit!"

Stevie. Fear despised it when grown men insisted on ending their names with an 'ie' or a 'y'. It sounded stupid to him. Davy, Stevie, Terry. The bile started to rise just thinking about it. No doubt the monkeys ahead thought it the coolest thing.

"Lookit, Stevie! A bald night owl!" and a finger pointed. The man drew breath to laugh.

And Fear unleashed himself.

The monkey that had been smiling suddenly clamped its jaws shut. His eyes bulged and he staggered—flung—himself backwards. Stevie did the same, pushing himself away from the night owl with a terrible, mindless energy only reserved for when one was truly in mortal danger. Stevie's buddy fell back five feet and landed on his ass, arms and legs still moving, still trying to put distance between him and Fear. Stevie launched himself into and over a wall of piled up snow, his legs swimming in the air as he took himself out of sight.

Fear's being hissed. Fear was *power*, even over those as blasted with spirits as these two. The fact that they had been drinking enabled their dull senses from being utterly paralyzed by the blast Fear sent in their direction. They should have been curled up on the ground, vomiting whatever was in their stomachs onto their silk shirts.

Fear, the mortal equivalent of his true name, marched by the helpless men. They were no threat to him or anyone for the rest of the week, and many people would be wondering how they got their premature grey hair. Fear was power. Fear was control.

And right now, Fear was pissed off with existence.

As he entered the Black Bear, cigarette smoke enveloped him and accosted his senses. The drift of pot was in the air. He made a face at the smells of sweat, tobacco, booze, and puke, and the parasitic partying accompanying them. The doors closed softly behind him, still functioning despite the earlier battering. People looked him over once, people on the dance floor glanced in his direction as well, and then went right back to their mindless courtships and revelries. People ringing a pool table looked him over. They went back to their game. People mingled and mashed together underneath the roof of the Black Bear, completely oblivious to who had just entered their midst.

Fuck them all, Fear griped and made his way towards the bar. He wasn't in the mood for concealment, and he projected a steam shovel of terror before him. The mortal mass of bodies parted for him like a greased zipper. Where there were packed people standing shoulder to shoulder at the bar, now there was only an empty space and the bartender. Fear cleared elbow space equal to about three bodies on either side of him. Behind him, the dance floor raved on to some music where the beat was louder than anything else.

The bartender, a big man in his forties and covered in a mass of black pubic hair, stared at the strange newcomer with the oddly shaped head as he stepped up to the bar. Fear regarded the man. Perhaps this was the black bear himself? He looked fierce enough.

Fear pushed, and the façade of the man split like cheap plywood.

"Whiskey," Fear commanded, placing a single finger down on the bar where he expected the drink to appear.

The Black Bear steadied himself, and blinked at this character's gall, doing an admirable job of fighting down his fear. Fear allowed him so that he could be better served. The Black Bear reached for a bottle of Jack Daniels. Fear saw the bottle and approved. He was a fan of Jack's. The man did good work. Fear could feel eyes on him still, but no one dared approach. At the end of the bar, a drunken man kept himself upright through blind determination alone. A pay phone was on the wall, and the receiver was practically in his mouth.

"DO YOU SCREW?" he shouted into the device. "DO YOU SCREW? I SAID DO YOU SCREW?"

Fear shook his head. It was fools like this that gave Mundanes a bad rep. And it was fools like this that gave him the most resistance. It was always the spirits they drank. Call it confidence or courage, but Fear knew it was really a lack of intelligence and willpower to simply give oneself up to the drift of alcohol or any other vice.

"*DO YOU SCREWWWW?*" the drunk wailed into the telephone. He became angry with the telephone then, and slammed the receiver back into the cradle. Black Bear turned at the noise, pausing in the preparation of Fear's drink. The drunk glowered at the bartender, "FUCK YOU!" he lurched, sticking his chin out.

The Bear had stopped pouring.

That irritated Fear.

Fear fixed the drunken man with a look. The drunk saw him, and his frame sucked in air, no doubt to spray forth another 'fuck you.'

Fear unleashed himself at the man like a missile.

Not even the bullet proof amount of booze the drunk had consumed could protect him from that single concentrated beam. The man's head backed up on his neck as if smashed by iron. He fell backwards, crashing into patrons behind. He landed on the floor. No sooner was he on his back that he vomited, a dark geyser that fountained upwards and covered his features. Like Fear when he entered the bar, the people around the downed drunk pulled back from him.

"Christ," the Black Bear exclaimed, placing the shot of sour mash whiskey exactly where Fear wanted it. The Black Bear motioned for his bouncers to move in on the downed drunk. "Not even Friday," Black Bear said sourly.

Then to Fear he said, bravely, "That's five fifty."

Fear paid the man. He paid when he owed. He may have been many things, but he paid when he owed. It balanced him.

"New around here, ain't cha?" Black Bear shouted at him over the house music. Fear looked him straight in the eye. The look made the barkeep much more interested in whatever he had on tap, and he immediately busied himself with other customers. That was smart of him, Fear thought. He sipped on his drink and felt its fire. Good.

Fear was power. Perhaps that was what Time was trying to prove by making Fear walk. He could do a lot of things but he could not shorten or lengthen time while he was in mortal form. It wasn't his talent. And in this, at a time where speed was needed most, Fear found himself stranded in goddamn nowhere land and removed from his charge. The charge he never wanted in the first place, but to strand him out here pissed him off. Why get him to go so far with the punk if they were going to replace him with Lucy? Did they disapprove of the method in which Fear motivated the Mundane? Could that be it? Jesus Christ! Hypocritical! How did they figure they were any different? It just irked him how they threw their talents around, and after a mess or two, just stood back and pleaded innocence. Fear was what he did. Everyone knew it. And in the coming days, he was going to be extremely busy, which was yet another reason for him to be angry. Yet they wanted him to take care of the Tony tool like a fucking nursemaid. Did one place a shark in an aquarium to guard goldfish?

Fear ground his perfect teeth and slammed back the last of his drink. *Fire.* Jesus, that was good. He bared his teeth at the burn and surveyed those about him. Meat. All of them. Yet, he needed one to transport him west. For all of his power, Fear could not drive. He cast his gaze about the bar.

Who was going to be the lucky one?

CHAPTER 28

Ten minutes past midnight, Ralph Maia switched on the lamp in his office. Eight men stood around his desk, dressed casually. All of them waited for their chief to speak. They had been summoned to the station with the rest of the night crew, and they had been ordered to form up here before Maia. However, unlike the rest of the night crew, only these eight stood before him now while the others slept. They waited for Maia with the air of school kids waiting for an authority figure to announce something important. Something like a *school's out*. There was something to this night. They could all sense it. Maia felt their growing excitement and decided to let it build just a few seconds more. One man's dark features were on the verge of exploding. Peters always was the most excitable and one of the most dangerous. He possessed a wiry frame and a temper which was as short as the fuses on the fire bombs he constructed. He believed that if he couldn't feel a twinge of danger over something so destructive, then he just did not want to do it. The others understood Peters, but they were wary of the firelight dancing in his black eyes, the potential for chaos on a spectacular scale. Some of the men present had no preference over who they burned. Peters did. He liked children. How he ever restrained himself from frying the world and all of the kids in it would forever be a mystery to Maia. The men thought of him as crazy. Maia regarded him as unstable as nitro, and never to be used until the gloves came off.

There was Bull Wash, the door breaker. Bull had come from northern British Columbia. Big, blond, and silent; his shoulders were rounded and bulging like great boulders, and the force they generated was something of firehouse legend. He still travelled north for the occasional felling of firewood and to partake in the local lumberjack competitions. He always came close, according to the media. Maia knew the man was simply holding back. Like Peters,

Wash's eyes held a craziness, a total abandonment if a dangerous task was to be performed. If challenged to a fight—few would really dare to take on the blond giant—it would be to the death.

Both Peters and Bull Wash were Maia's favourites, the two he could count on. They were his rooks in a greater game of chess. There were the others as well. Saunders was reliable but itched constantly to torch something. He controlled his impulses, but, frankly, the fire chief was glad the man would not have to hold back much longer. Maia would sometimes placate both him and Peters by allowing them to ignite some house blaze. Planned arson was something close to Christmas to them all, and catching old folks or kids in a house fire was a thing to riverdance about.

Then there were the Hansons, bespectacled brothers with frames like retired welterweights. The muscle and speed were still there. If Peters and Bull Wash were rooks, then the Hansons were the knights.

There were Marvin and Edwards. Both revelled in forest fires and perhaps would be better suited for hooks and pitchforks rather than extinguishers and fire hoses. Edwards also enjoyed electrical fires and rigging device failure. His greatest scalp to date was a catholic priest out in Calgary, whose trapped car consumed him like a candle wick being flashed with napalm.

Finally, standing behind them was Northman. Grey Northman was new to the group and not especially talkative. When they did talk, it was said that he was a jack of all trades. He seduced smokers to light up in bed, he enticed children to play with matches and aerosol cans. He took a particular interest in watching fat fires consume a kitchen. Though all of the Minions present maintained the masquerade as stand-up firefighters and even family men in their community, laughing at the Mundanes they walked amongst and often toyed with, all of them perceived Grey Northman as an oddity. He was middle aged and had no family—something that had proved to be useful to the Minions. He did not laugh at the others' trophy kills, but rather quietly judged each of them as if grading for some unknown purpose. Northman was ordinary looking, average-build and as educated as any of the Minions, yet there was something not quite right about him. Peters found the man creepy in a mad scientist kind of way, which he confessed to Maia. The admission amused the hell out of the fire chief, especially coming from the likes of Peters who would probably, personally, put his wife and new-born daughter to the torch when the time arrived.

The Minions enjoyed starting fires for the sheer delight of watching those hungry ribbons of orange feast, unleashing the fiercest beast of all at the simple strike of a match. Northman was different. He dabbled as if testing something or searching for a result of some kind; the kind of character that would stuff a cat into a microwave and record the predictable outcome. A Minion he was, but he was perhaps the most sinister where the others were borderline mental cases. He was the most reluctant to talk about his past, to talk about anything in fact, even to the fire chief.

He kept order, however, and Ralph Maia was glad of it. As Minions went, all had their quirks. He was fortunate his cell's quirks did not reveal their identity. They were all close to the edge, however, and maintaining the illusion of protectors was becoming more and more difficult with each passing day, like sharks muzzled and then being forced to swim in blood. There had been others who could not maintain the lie, and their final act of pyromania usually included themselves, the desire to unleash the beast finally overwhelming their tortured minds. If their monster did not consume them, Maia or someone like them would ensure that the unhinged Minion would be put down with extreme prejudice. Ultimately, their deaths served the remaining Minions' masquerade. Maybe that was the thing troubling Maia about Grey Northman. Perhaps Northman was very close to the edge. Perhaps, even now, he was entertaining ideas of self-immolation, becoming the heart of a monster of fire and smoke.

Maia would have to keep an eye on him from now on. Just in case. Nothing could be at risk.

"Gentlemen," Maia spoke as he beheld the gathered firefighters around him, "I have received a message."

They became still then, listening for his words, hoping for the *word*; the word to burn everything down. And with the command came the end of their false identities, free to shed their skin for their true forms. They all longed for it.

Maia was evil enough to let them wait and suffer with suspense before saying, "But it was not the word."

The disappointment in the room was as despised as heavy rain. Several eyes glowered at the floor and the desk's surface as if stares alone could ignite it all.

"But," Maia added sweetly, "I expect the word soon."

How a few sounds could transform the mood, the fire chief reflected. Hope now surged in their faces. Even Northman's usually indifferent expression had been replaced with a glow.

"How do you know?" Peters wanted to know, his voice full of awe.

"The Boatman is missing," Maia informed them all.

Silence from the now stunned Minions.

"How," Northman squinted at Maia, "can this be? What do you mean, 'missing'?"

"He is gone. Haven't you noticed?"

Northman's head slowly arched back as if sniffing the air. His eyes, cold and dark, stared down the length of his nose. "Yes," he said finally, "I sense it now. Faint . . . but it's there."

"It'll get stronger soon enough. Just like flesh left to rot in the sun," Maia grinned at him.

Northman did not grin back.

"So, we can unleash the beasts?" Peters asked for them all.

Maia shook his head. "No. Not yet. We don't have the word. We do have a task given to us. We must see to it that the Boatman *stays* missing. There are those who are searching for him. Everywhere. They are legion, and there will be some here soon enough. We must find them before they do—yes, that means the Boatman is here somewhere. He has taken up residence in some bag of flesh *here*, but don't concern yourselves with him. Focus your efforts on the ones coming. They are searching for him, and their time is short. All we have to do is stop them." He met the faces of his Minions, one by one. "Just long enough for the Mundanes to smell the same thing we're smelling now. Long enough for them to taste it and rip everything apart in their panic. That's all we have to do."

Bull Wash appeared confused. "But, if the Boatman is missing..." he paused as his brain turned itself over, "how do we to stop them? Kill them?"

Maia grinned again, a wide vampiric cut of a smile. "Any way you want. With the Boatman gone, the suffering they'll experience will be . . . exceptional. The word will probably come within days or hours. No longer than a week. I'm certain of that."

The Hansons smiled at one another with evil understanding. Northman looked as if schemes were already forming in his skull. Realization that the word was near brought impish eagerness to the faces of them all.

Then Peters spoke again, "What about the others here tonight? The rest of the crew? The Mundanes?"

Still grinning, Maia stepped back and reached for something out of sight, behind his desk. He held up a fire axe.

"I'll prove to you the Boatman is gone," the fire chief said. "Right now."

The gathered Minions smiled like skulls.

CHAPTER 29

It could not have been any more than an hour on the road. An hour and twenty minutes tops since they had left the motel that morning under a cold overcast sky. Tony felt the same rush from the day before, except this time it wasn't as strong; it was diluted somehow. He didn't get sick.

He stood on the Trans-Canada highway, facing west. A brisk wind blew in from the north and made him squint against its chill. He stared at the asphalt, grey and snaking with white swirls of snow. Couldn't have been more than ninety minutes. This time he tried his best to measure what happened. Tried his best to just grip the wheel and see the land blur by as it should have.

But here he was.

On the shoulder of the road, he stood before a sign with thin white socks of snow gathered around its posts. It was a big yellow and blue one. "Welcome" was printed over a rising sun, coming up over a blue mountain range. Beneath that, against white that Tony assumed to represent snow, read "British Columbia," with a side note Tony had to tilt his head to read— "The Best Place on Earth." There was a chill in his feet now, and he wasn't sure if it was the cold or not. But he didn't get sick. He swayed a little, shoved by the wind, but stayed in place, staring at the impossible. What he knew was impossible.

And yet, the impossible was right smack before him.

It was certainly funky, and better than flying, as he could still pull over when things got too much for him. The shock of folding time made him think of what a shot of adrenalin to the heart might feel like. No more than ninety minutes on the road, and they managed to cross the vastness of Alberta and pause right on the provincial border.

Fucking incredible.

He stood for a moment more, considering the road sign and the mountains in the distance. He had never been to British Columbia. Always said that when he had the money, he never had the time, and when he had the time, he never had the money. Now it seemed as if he gripped both by the balls and they were howling at him . . . and here he stood.

If only all things in life could be so simple.

The cold bit him again and forced him to return to his growling Mustang. He left the motor running for Lucy. He closed the door as softly as possible once behind the wheel, not wanting to disturb the magic he felt. He gripped the wheel as if he were on the edge of something impossibly deep. His knuckles went white.

"You okay?" Lucy asked him softly from the passenger side.

"Yeah."

"You don't look okay."

"I'm okay."

"You looked spaced out," she went on gently. "Can you tell me if you feel funny?"

"I'm okay," he repeated in a whisper. "Really. Just . . . give me a minute to take this all in. I'll be fine then. Just a minute."

A great sigh left him, and his shoulders slumped. Lucy looked away, granting his request. She did not want to push him any more than necessary. Under the circumstances, he had handled all she told him the night before quite well. When she finished, Anthony asked if it was okay to just listen to the radio for a while. He needed time then to take it all in, to digest it like a man just given a huge meal after surviving a desert. He had watched the morning light up the sky. He watched the morning news and the coverage of multiple near-death accidents and miraculous tales of life. No one perished during the night. Not one soul. One terrible head on collision on a local town road and yet not one person died. The drivers of both cars had been crushed. *Crushed.*

Yet, they lived on.

Whisked off to the emergency ward like slabs of bloody meat on magic carpets.

When? Tony asked Lucy then. When would people begin to realize that dying was no longer an option? How would the masses react when they found out about their new immortality? What could they do? There, on the corner of Lucy's bed, he held his head in his hands and dropped his gaze to the carpet. He even threatened to jump from the roof, just to see. Lucy scolded him for that. How many, did he suppose, would begin to test that very question? How many sick people—the crazy ones—would go through with their suicides and wake up from their overdose of pills? From their gunshot wounds? How many would simply hang from whatever they attached the hangman's noose to, kicking and twisting in the air until someone discovered them? What would be the ripple effect from these otherwise tried and tested methods to end one's existence? A greater harm to life? Crime perhaps? Or would people just go insane? As much as Tony tried to imagine what would happen, he also thought about the obvious.

Life everlasting.

But to continue to age until your bones were so brittle that a sneeze would rip you apart. Your flesh thin enough that a handshake would feel like an executioner's lash.

All sorts of punishing thoughts ran through Anthony's head, and Lucy comforted him as best as she could.

"Christ," he muttered at the steering wheel. Lucy did not say anything and waited for him.

"Where to from here?" he finally asked.

"That's up to you?"

"Huh?"

Lucy peered at the mountains. "Why here, Anthony? Why did you come here? You picked me up, but it was you that said you were going to BC. You were chosen by Time for a reason. Why? Why you? Why here? What's your lead? Why do you think this Frank is here?"

"Just a guess."

Lucy shook her head. "A guess? You've driven across a county to get here. All this way on a guess. Was it really a guess?"

"Sorta."

Lucy waited. She did not look convinced.

"I dreamed it," he admitted with an embarrassed sigh.

"You dreamed you found him in British Columbia?"

"Maybe. I dreamed—I *have* been dreaming of some guy playing golf. And the grass was faded. I only guessed that, if you could play golf anywhere in winter, it would be BC It seemed real enough. Weird."

"Very weird."

"But, then," Tony added, "after picking you up, everything's kinda gone that way."

"Yep," Lucy said, popping the 'p.'

"So, what do you think?" Tony abruptly asked her.

"Me?" her smile was both sympathetic and hypnotizing. "Doesn't matter what I think. I'm only here as an aide. A co-pilot. Like Freddy."

"You're not like Freddy."

"Thank you."

"I mean . . ." he was about to swear at the enormity of it all but caught himself. It was a ridiculous long shot finding anyone anywhere, a needle hidden in a haystack amongst a football field of identical haystacks.

Tony released the wheel. Felt the ache in his hands. What the hell was he doing here? It was official. He was officially in klicks over his head.

"You okay?" Lucy checked.

Tony didn't answer.

Lucy kept quiet for a moment, and then decided she had something to say. "You know, for all that's happened, and what will happen, despite all the mysteries left unexplained or the forces walling in reality as you know it, there is one thing that remains constant. That is, simply, you. People. Whether you believe in us isn't really important—well, maybe it'll become important, but when things were working and people were dying regardless of their time on earth, we always existed for you. We watched you, and we believed in you, often when you did not believe in yourselves. You are not the only person searching for Frank, Anthony. You are not alone in this. There are others, and they are also being aided by those like me to help them accomplish what needs to be done. Whether or not we succeed is not known, but we are here to help, and we will always be here, behind reality. We believe you will succeed, and we're here to help. We always will be. As weird as it sounds, we believe in you, and we're just amazed that, despite all of our abilities, we can't solve this problem *without* you. *Without* any of you."

Tony looked at her, his eyes red rimmed. He was absorbing it better than the night before.

"Believe me," Lucy went on, "if we could do this alone, we would. Who wants to . . ." she struggled for a moment, searching for the right words, "Who wants to use children as soldiers?"

"So, why me?" Tony asked.

"You? You're special. All of you are special. Think of yourself as a bloodhound. And there is something else." Lucy hesitated for a moment. "You have conditioning against pain."

Tony made a face. He wasn't sure he followed.

"You're tougher than most," Lucy tried to clarify. "You have a high pain threshold. You can take a beating, and not feel it as bad. Isn't that right?"

He nodded reluctantly. He could indeed take a punch. Several punches. It was never about how hard he could hit, but how hard he could get hit, how much punishment he could sustain before his legs dropped him out of a fight. He had never been knocked out. He had sustained deep knife cuts, caught fingers in car doors, hard knocks from accidental falls, and every time, he would simply grimace where others would scream out. He always thought he had nerve damage. His mother shared the same toughness.

"That is why Tim—Time—chose you," Lucy whispered and smiled at him. "You are very special to us."

"Sorry about all that," Tony said and meant it.

"It's okay. You didn't completely freak out on me."

"Has it happened before?"

"Mmhmmm, you would not *believe* the things people will say or do sometimes. Or maybe you do?"

"Maybe."

"Well, anyway. You were chosen for those reasons. Following your instincts is exactly what we need. A departure from logic. Believe me, if it were as simple as placing a phone tap we would have done it already."

That made Tony think. Lucy became quiet, recognizing the magic of thought when she saw it.

"Let's find a phone booth," Tony finally said. "Find a listing of golf courses. There can't be that many around. And there can't be that many open in March."

"Do you have a name in mind?"

"Yeah," Tony answered as he put the Mustang into gear. "Anything to do with clouds. And Lucy?"

"Yes?"

"Let's drive slow this time. No more warp? Okay?"

Lucy winked at him and smiled. "Okay."

They drove deeper into British Columbia, looking for a phone booth. They found a new-looking motel just off one of the ramp ways. A huge sign framed with unlit bulbs said "Happy Site." Tony parked the car, which coughed and sputtered bad enough for him to get a wondering look from Lucy. He was thinking it, too. The beast was sick. Hauling ass across the nation just might have taken its toll. They left the Mustang on the parking lot and went to the Happy Site's reception desk. He asked the receptionist for a telephone book, which the young man produced without a word. Tony took it and sat down on a cushy chair, near a window with a view of the parking lot. Lucy joined him, sitting with her hands between her knees, and watching him with interest.

"You got a pen and paper?" Tony asked. She immediately got up and went to the receptionist. She returned with both and handed them over.

Tony wanted to ask her if she went that far for nothing, how far would she go if he actually offered something. It was an old joke, and he kept it to himself. He took the pen and paper, and wrote down what he found. "Mountain Greens," he muttered in a light but clearly impressed tone. There was an address for Partly Cloudy Road.

"Got something?" Lucy asked.

"Yeah, maybe," he answered. He tucked the paper inside his jacket. "Follow me."

They left the motel without looking back at the receptionist and walked briskly to the car. The seats were still warm.

"Well?" Lucy demanded as she sat next to him. "What's up? Are you going to tell me or just leave me hanging?"

"Sorry," he said. He didn't want to keep anything from this one. "Can you play golf?"

"Golf?" she repeated sceptically.

"Yeah."

"Still thinking about your dreams?"

"Yeah."

She nodded slowly, understanding softening her features. Truly, she thought, who could really understand where these wondrous creatures came up with their ideas. But, given how they were prone to be wrong with their predictions, Lucy learned long ago to hold her breath. This time though, she felt no doubt at all.

She felt quite lucky instead.

"You have an address?"

"Yup." He held it up, over the steering wheel. "Shouldn't be too hard to find. It's a golf course after all."

Lucy smiled. "Have you ever played?"

"Golf?" he perked up. "Once. Well. No. I went walking around the greens with a buddy once. He played. I watched. Just there for the exercise. And it was summer. Just shootin' the shit, y'know."

She frowned slightly at the word. Tony liked seeing the crease between her eyes.

"How did it look?"

"Boring. Much rather club a seal. But I was with a buddy, so it wasn't bad. I knew nothing of the game really, and I remember asking him how long it was going to take to play. Two or three hours, I figured. He laughed at that. Five hours later, we were done."

"Oh, well," Lucy said, not impressed. "Maybe I'll try it sometime."

"You can swing a club?"

"I can swing anything," she grinned.

Tony grinned back. "I bet you can. Let's drive."

One hour later they arrived at the golf course—there hadn't been the slightest bit of fast time, Tony thought. Perhaps 'fast time' was only for the highway driving. There were no walls barricading the course, only open fields that could be seen from the road. The greens were more crab apple yellow, and deserted.

But Tony had a hunch. A mighty powerful hunch. He felt it when he first saw the ad. He felt that if he had his eyes closed and were just tracing the page with a finger, he would have stopped on that same ad. The feeling was that powerful. He opened his door and glanced at Lucy.

"We're here," was all he said.

CHAPTER 30

The world.

Against a plain of yellow.

That was how the golf ball looked to him, staring down at it as he was. A world against a nebula of dull gold. Or a moon. Yes, moon was better. Craters and all. And this little moon at his feet was about to have the living shit whacked out of it. The driver almost came into contact with the ball, but then backed off. Almost made contact again . . . and backed off. Concentrate. Tiger Woods. Be Tiger Woods.

He swung.

Too hard, the ball flew off into the sky like an ice chip, slicing to the left and dropping out of sight into a copse of evergreen trees.

The man calling himself Frank watched his ball disappear.

"SWEET FUCK AWMIGHTY, YOU GOD . . . *DAMN* PIECE OF SHIT!" he roared, beating his driver into the yellow covered earth again and again as if trying to execute the very ground. Oath after obscene oath scorched the air. Frank abruptly paused and stabbed his attention in the direction of the trees, wishing he had a fucking flamethrower to point and spray. He stomped in a circle as if attempting to summon up a storm god that would bury the copse in a white sheet of flesh-ripping hail.

He eventually stopped and stood, reflecting on just what it was he did wrong. Just behind him, yet well enough out of his way, stood two figures. They knew their companion well, and exchanged looks between themselves—careful not to look at each other too long. If they did, they would start to giggle. In fact, they would probably laugh until their holes dropped out of their asses. In Frank's presence, it was never wise to laugh.

And it was blatantly stupid to laugh at him while he was playing golf.

So, they only glanced at each other for a second, and tried to focus on anything else while Frank continued to heat the air with looks alone. He was fixated on the ground now, just daring demons to rise up so he could kick the unholy shit out of them.

One of the onlookers cleared his throat, almost like a soldier fixing a helmet to a stick, and poking it partially up over a wall to see if any snipers are about. When Frank kept his silence, the man decided to take the chance.

"You can go again, Frank," he offered.

"Yeah, man," agreed the other. "Go again. It's only a game."

The air dropped a nipple perking ten degrees with the glare Frank launched at his playmates. In that instant, neither of them dared to breathe for fear Frank would come at them with the driver. He would not think twice. He would probably feel a helluva lot better if he did.

In the deep-space silence that ensued, Frank released a heavy sigh. "It's okay?"

"Sure, man," they both said at once with encouraging nods.

"You're sure?" Frank asked again, warming to the idea now.

"Go ahead," said the first.

"We don't care," insisted the other.

Frank decided to take them up on the offer. He had conquered mini-golf and practiced driving on the gym simulator. The real stuff was only a few swings away.

"Thanks," he muttered and slipped back into Tiger-Woods mode. He dug out another ball from his pocket. Another whitey. He cued it up and kissed it ever so slightly with his driver. He was Tiger Woods, again. He paused and considered the wind coming in from the northwest. Nothing to really worry about there. He placed both feet wide of the ball, slipping into his stance. He was the hammer to this pale earth at his feet. He was Armageddon, and his driver was the meteor to slam the ball into the sun. It would fly true, it would fly true. He was Tiger Woods, again. It would most certainly fly true. The driver kissed the ball, again, testing its reality. Frank looked up, willing it to arrive in the place he wanted it to be. It would be there. It would. Will it, and it shall be so. It will be there.

He drew back and swung.

The ball snapped off the tee and sliced like an off-centre cannon ball blast into the same copse of trees.

"GOD . . . *DAMMIT!* GODDAMMIT! SWEET MARYFUCKING DONKEY COCKS! DOGBALLS! DOGBALLS! GREAT GREASY DOGBALLS! PIG COCKS! YOU STUBBORN, COCKEYED SHITSTREAK OF A PISS POT! GODDAMN YOUR SOUL TO CRAB HELL! JESUS NAILED ON A TELEPHONE POLE! JESUS! JOSEPH! And MARY you BITCH! *FUCK!*"

Frank thumped his driver into the turf with a force hard enough to bend it. He slammed it again and again before finally flinging it at the trees like an out of whack boomerang. "PIECE OF SHIT! PIECE OF SHIT! YOU FUCKING JIZM STREAK PIECE OF SHIT!"

The first onlooker about-faced completely to hide the blazing grin on his face, striking a pose as he did so.

The second onlooker did not dare to look at his companion, whose very frame shuddered with the force of will being exerted to contain his laughter. He would lose it if he did. He knew he would. He would lose it, and Frank would kill him and that would be the ending to an otherwise chilly day on the not-so-greens. Laughing now would condemn both of them to a fate worse than Augustus D. Franklin, and just the thought of it almost sent him over the edge of gut-stabbing, hysterical laughter. It was all he could do now not to split into gales as he watched Frank stomp out a Neanderthal-like dance on the yellow greens. He waited until Frank calmed down or at least appeared to have calmed down. He kept his head down, his fists on his hips, looking as if he had just lost a loved one.

"You can go, again, Frank," the second onlooker offered.

"Fuck you," Frank shot back.

The first onlooker's shoulders trembled at this exchange, but he kept his back to both of the men, and kept his own head down.

"And fuck you too, H2," Frank fired at the man's back. "I see you over there. May crabs the size of turtles crawl up your ass and snap your fucking spine in two."

"No, really," the second onlooker tried again, and his smile broke out. He clamped down on it like a man trying to suppress a gunshot wound. He tried to coke off his laugh and snot shot out of his nostrils. He immediately turned away, his hands covering his gushing nose.

"Godammit!" Frank swore at himself this time. "The last fucking time I have either of you out for a game. A little company is all I ask for, and I get the fucking snickers brothers. No fucking wonder you guys are so goddamn popular with the kids. Both of you can go fuck yourselves."

"Awww, c'mon, Frank!" pleaded the man who had cleaned his nose but still grinned in spite of his efforts not to. "Don't be like that. You just take the game too seriously, is all, man. We both can see it."

"Listen, H," Frank directed at the speaking man with a finger. "You see that tree over there? That's the one you can shove up your ass. Ever hear the story of the angel on the Christmas tree? You'll be able to relate."

"You take the game too serious, I'm telling ya." H went on. "People play this game to relax. Not to blow the tops of their heads off."

"Like hell, they do," Frank retorted. "They play to win. Either to beat themselves or the other guy. Don't fucking stand there, you tweed-covered dolt, and tell me otherwise. They may say they play to relax, but deep fucking down, they all play to win. Why do you think there are so many goddamn suicides, eh? If people only played to relax, you think there would be so many suicides?"

H inspected the palm he cleaned his nose with. "We still talking about golf?"

"Same field, different game." Frank stood, one fist on his hips, glaring in the direction of where his club might have landed.

The third man turned around, his laughter fully under control now, and decided to join the conversation. "Man does have a point," he muttered, "though I like to think—"

"Shut the fuck up," Frank snapped without looking. It was all he needed. H2 talked too goddamn much. Some people had the gift of the gab, and H2 was an Olympic god when it came to gabbing. The only way to swerve out of the way of that tri-athlete tongue, as revolting as it sounded, was to shut him up before he started. Fortunately for Frank, he knew all of H2's lead-ins like "I'd like to think . . ." or "It would appear to me that . . ."

If he heard any of these, Frank would take the necessary evasive action.

"Just shut the fuck up," he warned H2.

H2 did as he was told. He did not seem to mind.

"I'm going in," Frank declared and moved towards the gold cart parked a few feet off the yellow green. "Get a beer or something."

At once both H and H2 began to follow. Beer was something they both appreciated. They kept quiet. Neither wanted to walk back to the clubhouse, and Frank was legendary when it came to being pissed off at nothing in particular.

"Oh, Jesus," Frank said and suddenly stopped.

"What?" H asked, looking around. Then, he saw the approaching figures.

H2 saw them as well. "Who are they?"

"Fuck if I know," Frank said, anger still seething.

"We're supposed to be the only ones on the course today," H threw in. "I saw to that myself."

"Well, you didn't see to all of it," H2 accused him.

"Goddammit, H," Frank closed his eyes and wished for peace. "I told you I wanted the greens to myself today. Just fucking me. It was bad enough you morons wanted in."

"You can't get much clearer than this," H informed him.

"Then who the hell are they?" Frank pointed with his chin.

"Oh, shit," H2 muttered, recognizing one of the people getting closer.

Frank recognized her, too, and shook his head in disgust. "Well, fuck me," he stated in a defeated voice. He placed both hands on the gold cart and closed his eyes. "How the fuck did *she* know we were here?" he grated.

H wanted to know that as well. He looked at H2, whose hands simply went wide in a questioning *"What?"*

Frank composed himself and focused on the approaching couple. The H's flanked him. Of all the folks he knew and associated with on a semi-regular basis, this particular individual had a knack for getting into just about anything and everything, and still coming out smelling sweeter than a field of roses. He hated that kind of luck. But there would be no escaping this time, and he suddenly realized he was looking forward to the confrontation. The H's understood his feelings.

Sort of.

"If I find out either one of you two hole lickers had anything to do with this, I'll personally make sure you're ball-less going through the remainder of the ages. You get me?"

H spread his hands. "Jesus Frank, I had no—" but Frank raised his hand, silencing him. He looked at the newcomers. One of them was made, but who was the tough guy? Frank scrutinized him as he got closer. He could scry nothing on the man. Then, the answer smacked him between the eyes.

"Mundane," he seethed, as if no greater insult existed. He planted his feet as if bracing for a storm.

Tony and Lucy walked side by side as they approached the trio of men. All were well dressed in fall colours: beige dockers, deck shoes, and sweaters. All looked to be in their early forties. The men on the sides wore sweaters, one all red and the other all yellow, with plain white ball caps. The guy between them wore a black sweater with a single white stripe across the chest. A White Sox baseball cap was on his head. None of them looked happy, and Tony felt a strong weight bearing down, trying to keep him away from the three golfers. Or one golfer. He did not see the other men's clubs. And where did they get the cart? Everything had been locked down at the clubhouse. There wasn't anyone working at the gate or office. The course was closed for the winter, so how was it that these three managed to get on the greens with a cart?

"Hey," Lucy greeted when they were close enough. Tony stopped when she stopped and gave her an uncertain look. Lucy did not notice him.

"Hey," the man in the black cap grunted. Tony tried to catch the guy's attention but it was centred all on Lucy. His eyes were as black as volcanic rock and hard.

"I'm Lucy," Lucy said.

For a moment, Tony did not think any of the three men would answer. None of them looked very talkative, especially Mr. Brightness in the black sweater, a sweater looking thick enough to deflect a knife thrust.

"You guys have names?" Lucy finally asked when the silence became painful. "Or should I just call you by what I think of you?"

"You . . ." the man in black hissed. "Just like you to show up with the likes of *him*."

"What's wrong with him?" Lucy asked.

"You know what's wrong, you fucking wench."

"Hey," Tony's finger came up. "You better apologize right—"

"It's okay, Anthony," Lucy told him. "Really, it is. He's talking loud here, but there are rules that even he has to abide by. He'll introduce himself, won't you?"

"You want my real name, Lucy?" the man in black suddenly smiled, and the air around him became as cold as the deep Atlantic. The question froze Lucy, and her mouth hung open. She did not expect him to make such a threat.

"He's Frank," said the man in the yellow sweater.

Frank rolled his eyes. "Why am I not surprised," he said aloud, and fixed the man with a menacing look.

"There are rules, Frank," H stated quietly.

"Fuck the rules," Frank spat out, "and fuck you, and you, and especially *you*." His finger branded them all but lingered on Lucy. "You," he spoke as he switched to Tony, "I know you, but the question is do you know me?"

A breeze blew up then, filling the quietness. It made Tony think of winter winds and old houses that creaked.

"Yeah," he said, nodding and feeling a chill. "I know you. You're Augustus D. Franklin. You're Death."

There was a stunned silence on the course. The H's both looked at each other in absolute surprise before regarding this Mundane with new respect. Even Frank seemed a little taken aback. But only for a moment. Hostility soon seeped back into his gaze.

"Well, well," he said acidly "looks like you got a real winner here, Luce."

"What? You mean my head didn't explode?" Tony said to Lucy.

"No, it didn't," Frank chipped in before she could say anything. "Death is the name given to me by cattle like you. And while it's nowhere near my true name, it's fine by me. A fucking nickname. But a nickname that carries a little more respect than what you just gave. Jesus Christ, Luce, where the fuck do you dig these dogs up? Back up, douchebag, else you tax my patience. I do have a question for you, though. How did you know it was me? Huh? Did old Luce there have something to do with it?"

"I guessed it," Tony informed him. "Just lucky."

Frank was not impressed. "Luck is being born with a second asshole. Or maybe you think that's a good thing?" He aimed his next barrage at Lucy. "What have you told him, Lucy? Hm? What? Probably your side of the story. I can smell it off you. You haven't told him shit about my side. Goddammit. Just like a fuckin' PR person, ain'tcha? Give just enough to get the job done. When were you going to tell this Mundane, huh? Tonight? Tomorrow? Next week? You think you got the time to wait that long?"

"You're a real fucking asshole," Tony stepped forward.

Frank did not back up. "That's a problem then, ain't it? I'm the asshole here. I'm a real fucking asshole. Probably the biggest one on this course. And I don't give a shit anymore. Not about Luce there or any one of you fucks, for that matter. I just want to be left alone for a while, but can I get that? Better I camped out in Hell for the day. I'd get more peace."

Frank revealed a perfect set of teeth as he spoke, and his face darkened. He glared at Tony, considering this mortal man standing not three feet before him.

"You really have a clue as to what's going on?"

Tony's smile was frosty. "People aren't dying."

"So, they aren't," Frank said without pity. "What do you think about that then, eh? People aren't dying."

"I think it's pretty shitty."

Out of the corner of his eye, Tony noted the man in the yellow sweater rub his face and look plainly uncomfortable.

Frank merely smiled and shook his head in disbelief. He muttered something foul under his breath, but Tony didn't catch it. Frank appeared ready to implode, his hands clenched and unclenched.

"That's the problem right there, isn't it, Luce? Isn't it? And you bringing one of them around just strengthens my resolve. You," he jabbed an open hand at Tony, "can go fuck yourself."

That was it for Tony. He stepped forward even as Lucy yelled for him not to. His hands shot out to grab Frank, meaning to shake the ever-loving shit out of the cocksucker. He grabbed the front of the sweater and felt the cold. The godawful, freezing *cold*. With a scream of pain and terror, Tony released the man and drew back. He held up his hands, hooked into claws, and looking as if they had been exposed to the deepest reaches of space. Grimacing, he backed away, and stumbled to his knees.

"You idiot!" Lucy screamed at Frank as she grabbed for Tony's hands, rubbing them frantically.

Frank smiled. "What did I do? You saw him. He wanted a piece of me. Ask me, he's fucking lucky he grabbed only wool instead of flesh. I'd be cracking his hands off me like fucking icicles."

"Why are you doing this?" Lucy demanded.

"To prove a point," Frank shot back. "I don't care for these little shits anymore. That's all they are. Little runny, complaining shits! That's what I've had to endure since I don't know when, and my job is hard enough without the disrespect I get from them."

Frank paused and drew in breath. He shook his head to clear it. "*Jesus*, I'm pissed off now! I'm going for a beer."

He boarded the golf cart. H immediately climbed in alongside.

"You stayin'?" Frank demanded of H2.

"Yeah."

Scowling at what he regarded as turncoat behaviour, Frank started the cart up and drove off, pushing it to whatever speed it could muster.

H2 watched the little vehicle tear off across the greens. An expression of sadness hung on his face. He glanced at his shoes before turning his attention to the couple still crouching on the ground. His shoulders hunched up in a shrug before he walked over to them.

"Sorry about that," he said. "Frank wasn't in a good mood to start with. Bad day on the course. I'm H2."

He offered his hand, and Tony stood up and reluctantly took it. They broke contact, and Lucy gripped both of his hands, again. He could smell her hair and the strawberry shampoo she had used. It all made Tony feel tons better.

"Bad day, huh?" Tony said to H2.

The man smiled. "Yeah. Frank sucks at golf."

H2 was slim and dressed something like a brand name dork, Tony thought. He spied the little horse on the left side of the red sweater and the classy looking deck shoes. He was clean shaven and relatively handsome. A hint of a five o'clock shadow gave his dark eyes an even more seductive edge, and Tony figured he played up those eyes every chance he got.

"When did you get here, Lucy?" H2 asked her, full lips pouting. "And why didn't you call me?"

"I was watching this guy," she informed him gently, exposing her beautiful teeth.

"Forgot about me already then," H2 said. "Y'know, Lucy, I've never quite forgotten how you left me in that New York restaurant. I thought you were a little better than that."

A different kind of heat suddenly flared inside Tony now, and he barely managed to look at Lucy, still holding his hands as calmly as possible.

Lucy gave H2 a wry look. "I am a little better than that. I guess I just got a little tired of all the touchy-feeliness going on."

H2 drew back, mortified. "I hardly touched you! Well, your hand, I'll grant you that."

"I'm talking about the maître d'. The brunette with the C-cups."

This caused a look of careful thought to appear on H2's face. "Oh, *her*! You mean *Victoria*! She was just a friend."

"You nibble on your friend's ears, do you?" Lucy asked, frowning.

"Some of them," H2 smiled warmly and looked to Tony. "My apologies. Old adventures being demystified. Happened years ago."

Tony could only nod. Old adventures? The heat was scalding him inside now, and he fought to control his features. His back straightened altogether too straight, his eyes looked too uncaring. And he could sense it. He was screwed.

"He," Tony indicated H2, "he uses our time," he said to Lucy. He did not know what else to say after the brief exchange between the two . . . what? Old lovers? Oh, Jesus Christ, he hoped not.

"I never said we don't use it," Lucy explained, still massaging his hands. H2 noticed it as well and smiled again. Tony did not like that smile. It made him think of what a horny coyote might look like.

"If you're into hand massages, Lucy, I'd love to be next," H2 said in a slick voice and matching smile.

"Sorry," Lucy said, but the smile she returned him made Tony's insecurity geyser. "I'm busy. And this one seems to be just about done. Feeling better?"

"Yeah," Tony said as she released his hands.

H2 assessed him for a moment, dark eyes sly with confidence. "Ain't much of a talker, is he?"

"He talks when he wants to," Lucy told him.

"He knows what's going on?" H2 asked.

"Yep," she replied, popping the 'p.'

"How did he take it?"

"I'm right here," Tony said a little too testily. "You can ask me."

H2 nodded. "But I'd rather speak to her if you don't mind, chief."

Tony was really beginning to dislike H2. Not only for the way he spoke to Lucy and for the jealous vibes he invoked, but for calling him "chief". Tony hated people who, just after meeting you and forgetting your name, would go on and label you with a pleasant sounding buddy-like tag as if they knew you were a swell person.

"I'd rather you speak to him," Lucy said, hands now on her hips. Tony almost leapt for joy.

"Very well, then," H2 said, as smooth as butter. "Good guess there with Frank's name, by the way."

"You mean Death?"

"Yeah. You took him and the rest of us off guard there. Not too often that happens."

Tony sure as hell didn't see that at the time, but thinking back, he guessed he did surprise the man.

"Lucy told me," Tony admitted.

"I know," H2 smiled, implying there was no other way Tony could have come up with Frank's name, or any other solid line of deduction for that matter. "But it was worth it to see. When you've hung around *The Reaper* as long as I have, you start to enjoy the little slips and shocks you people give him when his guard's down."

"You people?" Tony asked, frowning.

"Mundanes," H2 clarified, chuckling as he said it.

That made Tony glance at Lucy, who did not say anything. He regarded the man in red. "Y'know, I think I might know your name, too."

H2 paused. "My name?"

"Yeah."

"I've told you my name."

"No," Tony countered. "You've told me a name. Not your real name though."

"Oh, really?" H2 almost sneered. "So, what is it?"

"I know your name," Tony repeated, looking at H2.

"No, you don't," H2 replied, grinning at if he were talking to a child.

"Yes, I do."

"No, you don't."

"Yes, I do."

"Say it then."

"And have my head explode?"

"I thought you explained things to him," H2 asked Lucy.

"She told me enough," Tony answered for her, and hoped, in a quick afterthought, she would not be pissed with him for doing so.

"Then," H2 aimed at him, "you know you can't die."

The words made Tony blink as they entered his head and rattled around. *Then you know you can't die.* Holy squirrel shit! That applied to him!

"I can't die?" he asked Lucy, amazed.

Lucy shook her head.

The thought took time to sink in. "I can't die," Tony repeated to himself.

H2 shook his head in disbelief.

Tony stared off into space. "That's fucked up."

"I wouldn't say it, anyway, Tony," Lucy said. "There are plenty of people who are alive these days but are brain dead."

"But they still have their heads?" Tony asked.

Lucy faltered. "Yes," she answered uncertainly.

"So, how can my head explode and I not die?"

"It's . . ." she stretched the 's', "difficult to explain."

"She could be lying," H2 threw in.

Lucy flashed him a look of annoyance. "You can stop it right there, buster. I know what you like to play at, and I'm not having any of it right now. And you should be ashamed at even trying any of it. Especially in these times."

The unexpected barrage from Lucy caused H2's smile to melt off his face. A schoolboy expression of shame appeared. Tony had to admit the boy was good. He almost felt like rushing in and apologizing for something he didn't do. It struck him then that this H2 character was an incredibly dangerous and manipulative man. Two good reasons to fuck up that face.

"So, lay off!" Lucy jabbed a finger at him.

H2 was quiet for a moment before apologizing. "You're completely right. Sorry. I'm sorry."

"That's better," Lucy said.

Tony kept his eyes on the well-dressed coyote, thinking that farmers just might have the right idea—and solution—with shotguns.

"Now," Lucy took a breath "let's get back to the job at hand."

"I'd rather get back to a hand job," H2 smiled evilly.

"Which is?" Tony asked, ignoring H2.

"Getting *Franklin* to start killing people again," H2 said out of the corner of his mouth.

An exasperated sigh left Lucy. "He doesn't kill them. He saves them. Or steals them. Depending on which argument you take."

"What d'you mean?" Tony wanted to know.

"Death will tell you," Lucy said, looking at him. She studied him for a moment. "He'll tell you a lot of things, I think."

"Shitloads," H2 added.

"And there'll be plenty of *stuff*," Lucy emphasized with a black look in H2's direction, "that'll you'll probably not want to know."

"Like what?" Tony asked.

Lucy shrugged. "I don't know. He's Death, Tony. He's bound to know a few things, and right now, he's angry."

"And why is he angry, again?" Tony asked. "Shouldn't I be angry at him? I mean, he's letting all these people live and suffer, right?"

"We are all frustrated with him," Lucy blurted out and stopped herself from saying more. H2 grinned wryly at her. She ignored him, "and we've told him so, but he only gets angrier at us."

"Why would he get angrier?" Tony asked, suddenly confused.

"Because," H2 stepped in, "he thinks he's right."

"Is he?"

Both Lucy and H2 were silent.

"Well?"

The silence went on.

"Why is he right, then?" Tony demanded.

"It's because of you, Tony," Lucy began. "People. Mundanes. Mortals. You've—excuse me—you've been blaming Death for centuries for so many things now that he's fed up with you. He's like a kitchen hand tired of cleaning up after the cooks and being needled and ridiculed and jeered at and hated for doing nothing more than his job."

"A necessary job," H2 added pensively.

"He's angry at all of you for, well, running his name down into the filth," Lucy finished.

Tony could not believe what he was hearing. "But . . . he's Death for Christ's sakes! I mean, how the hell can *he* be offended?!"

H2 looked concerned. "You sure your boy here is ready? Sounds to me like he isn't."

"I'm not some—what?—head shrink! You're telling me I have to fucking *apologize* to Death?" Tony demanded.

"Yes," Lucy said, allowing the four-letter swear words to fly like buckshot. Under the circumstances, she supposed it was okay.

"And why me, again?" Tony strained to understand.

"You're mortal," Lucy said, her eyes flicking to H2 for the briefest of moments. "Frank doesn't want to believe or hear us anymore. He won't listen. He wants you to see how life is without him around for a while. He's willing to let people suffer to prove his point."

Tony clasped his head. "He wants an apology from me, and he'll go back."

The pair exchanged looks again. "We think," H2 said with a little smile.

"A sincere apology, Anthony," Lucy said. "You have to convince him that you speak for all of your kind. You have to convince him to come back."

Tony shook his head. "Alright, fuck it. I'll apologize. Sure, why not."

"Anthony," Lucy met his eyes, "it has to be sincere. You have to convince him that you are being true."

This made Tony pause. "I dunno, then. I mean, I'm a brawler if anything. I don't know if I can sweet talk him like you want."

"A blow job might do it, then," H2 threw in.

Both Lucy and Tony regarded the man with dangerous looks.

H2 shrugged. "What? He said to me that fellatio fascinates the hell out of him. I'm trying to help here."

Lucy's disgust was evident in the way she slowly looked away from him.

"Think of your mom, Anthony."

Tony's back straightened with shock. "How do you know about my mom?"

Lucy's voice was full of sympathy. "It's kind of my job to know these things, Anthony."

"I'm starting to get really suspicious about your job, Lucy," Tony almost barked. His nerves were jangled now.

"Look," H2 said calmly, "you need motivation. She's it. He hasn't come for her yet, right? And with him being the way that he is now, he's not going to anytime soon. And if he doesn't get back to moving people really soon, none of this will mean shit because we'll all be—" H2's hand flopped around in the air, gesturing at everything around them. He didn't finish what he wanted to say. He did have a little spot remaining for Lucy and her sensibilities.

And although he didn't say it, Tony suddenly felt . . . fucked as if by a telephone pole.

His mother.

If he convinced Frank to return to work, his mother dies. How did he feel about that? Wouldn't he be responsible then for killing her? No, he would be releasing her. He would be bringing back what should have happened naturally long ago. But it was his mother. He couldn't bear the thought of letting her go. Not her. Not letting her go to . . . *him.*

"Tony?" Lucy's voice.

"Yeah?"

"You okay?"

"Yeah. Fine." Tony looked at her. "Didn't you say before there were others like me looking for this guy?"

"Yes."

"So, if I blow it, maybe another one will do it?"

"Possibly, but you are the closest now, Anthony. You could end all of this by tonight. But. We. Must. Go. *Now.*"

"Where?"

"'Tis three in the afternoon," H2 smiled at him. "Old Frankie boy will be thirsty after all that swearing. He's going to the Paradise Lounge for drinks."

"Death drinks?" Tony said, mildly surprised.

"Like a school of fish," H2 informed him, his smile widening. "Good thing he's Death if you ask me. The man should be dead himself the way he slams them back. I could tell you stories."

Lucy glowered at him.

"But I won't." H2 drew up and coughed uncomfortably "Not today anyway. Like the lady said, we gotta go."

"You're not coming," Lucy told H2.

"I thought you'd never ask," H2 grinned at her.

"I mean it."

"But I *have* to go," H2 was serious now, "It's three! Truth be told, I drink like a school of fish, and Frank will be wondering where I am and hey, anyway, I want this whole mess cleared up ASAP just as much as you. Doesn't do my business any good for him to be tempting the—"

H2 clamped his mouth shut.

But it wasn't fast enough. "Tempting the what?" Tony wanted to know.

"Nothing," H2 said. "But you still need me."

Lucy frowned. "He does know where this Paradise is."

The slick grin came back.

"I can find that in a phone book," Tony retorted, pleased at seeing the man's smile falter.

"We might need him anyway," Lucy said, looking disappointed.

"I'm really starting to dislike you," Tony pointed a finger. It made H2 grin again.

"Wait 'til you get to know him," Lucy said.

Tony flashed wary eyes at the man. "C'mon. This way. The sooner we get on with this the better."

The three of them began walking back to the parking lot. The desolate course was full of dampness. Unlike the rest of the country that was struggling through the last white coughs of winter, this part of British Columbia was experiencing unusually warm weather. Tony heard the province was one of those places a person could fall in love with. He supposed, glancing around, he wasn't in a particularly affectionate mood. They reached the parking lot and moved towards the car. At one point, H2 slowed and stopped in his tracks.

"You didn't drive up in *that* piece of shit?"

Both Tony and Lucy turned about to see the man's mixed expression of horror and bewilderment.

"That piece of shit's gotten me 'round for years," Tony said, feeling the heat coming into his cheeks like a pair of stove burners. He didn't like anyone mouthing off about his car.

"So, I see," H2 stated, nodding.

"Look, if you don't like it you can—" He remembered Lucy. "You can walk."

"Probably get there faster," H2 commented, sizing up the beast with a look of amazement. He came closer, stopped and dropped to his hands and balls of his feet. He peered up underneath the vehicle. "Christ almighty. I think I see a dead cat."

"Fuck you." Tony grated. That was enough. "You can walk then if you're this fucking righteous."

"Tasteful is more like it," H2 muttered back. He hopped to his feet and slapped his hands clean. "Really, I thought I saw a dead cat. Or a squirrel. Something with a tail anyway."

"Fuck off, I said," Tony seethed.

"You do a lot of country driving? Or just like running over things?"

Tony turned an exasperated gaze to Lucy.

"Yes," she informed him. "he usually is like this."

"Lucy," H2 pleaded, "I picked you up in a limo for God's sake. A limo. Leather interior and champagne a push button away. DVD's if we had the time. You want me to ride around in this?"

"In the back," Lucy told him.

"I don't want you along," Tony threw in. "Remember that. I'm really starting to dislike this fucking loser."

"I'm a loser?" H2 preened and smiled. "Lucy. Maybe we should get some of the other Mundanes for this job. I doubt this one could follow directions on a soup can. And he's going to talk to Frank? Try and convince him to get back into the field?" He slowly shook his head. "I don't think so."

"I do," Lucy declared. "You wanna make a bet he can't?"

For a moment, Lucy and H2 regarded each other with the coolness of professional Vegas poker players, and Tony felt the pull from both of them. It only took a moment to weigh in the amount of confidence Lucy was placing in him to make the wager. He recalled their bet only hours earlier it seemed, and how Lucy won it hands down. Hands down was the understatement of fucking infinity. How *did* she manage that anyway? He got the impression Lucy rarely, if ever, lost a bet of any kind to anyone, and the look on rat bastard H2's face confirmed it. The man's chiselled features, particularly the way his jaw twitched from the pressure of grinding his teeth, told Tony H2 knew she rarely, perhaps *never*, lost a wager.

Never lost a wager. Jesus. He'd have to convince her to get to the casino in Downtown Halifax. Or legendary Woodbine in Ontario. Do some betting on the ponies.

That made him pause. It suddenly occurred to him that this exquisite woman who made his stomach shiver possessed a great deal of faith in his ability to bring Frank around. He wondered why. Confidence was not something he had in his speaking ability. Unless he was speaking in two- and three-punch combinations.

H2's hands came up over his head in surrender. "Alright. Alright! You command here. I'll ride in that. But I sit up front."

"You can sit on the toe of my boot," Tony quipped.

"I get the front," H2 insisted.

"I'll put you on the fucking roof if you keep this up, you complaining prick."

"Lucy, you're not going to make me ride in the back of this thing are you? It'll ruin the crease in my pants!"

That made Tony grin.

"Yes, I am," Lucy put in forcefully. "You sit in the back."

H2 sucked his breath in between clenched teeth. "You know what you do to me when you give me orders like that."

Tony struggled hard not to say anything, and instead, turned and got into his car. Lucy allowed H2 to climb aboard on her side and she got in after.

"Awfully cramped back here," H2 squirmed to make himself comfortable.

Feeling evil, Tony reached down between his legs and adjusted the seat, ramming it further back. He was going to make the bastard's ride back there as unpleasant as possible. He made a mental promise to hit every pothole or speed bump he could see along the way.

"Hey!" H2 squealed indignantly, "You just put the seat back further, man!"

"I got long legs."

"Your legs ain't that long!"

"I'm the driver, man," Tony warned him. "You're baggage."

"You hear how he's talking to me, darling?" H2 directed at Lucy.

"Yeah, I do," she replied with a little smile at Tony, "and I'm liking every syllable."

Tony smiled back, and then turned his attention to the growl of engine starting up. When he fired up the beast, H2's expression became one of worry. He realized his seatbelt didn't fasten properly either.

From across the road, standing with his hands in the pockets of his black parka and looking nothing like an agent longing for the release of total chaos upon the world, firefighter Peters watched the Mustang swing around and cruise off towards distant traffic. The car backfired at one point. Peters dug his sneakers into the yellow grass covering the shoulder of the road. He looked at the ground where he left a scuff mark, memorizing the blue vehicle for the coming hunt. When he looked up again, the car was gone. Things were moving along now, faster than Maia had anticipated. There had been five, then there were three, and the threesome was driving off. Two of the three were Entities. Peters believed he could take all of them, but he suspected they were headed towards Death and the other one. Peters recalled the way Maia was talking as he was doing up the sleeping firefighters with the axe. There was a lot riding on this, and the thought of it made him hesitate to act alone. Fighting four Entities would be too risky. It would be better to bring in reinforcements. Peters would not be the one who would be remembered for botching up the Apocalypse. Fuck that.

Digging into his coat jacket, he found his cell phone and speed dialed Maia's number.

CHAPTER 31

They sighted the Holiday Inn within the border of New Brunswick and Quebec, and agreed that it would be a luxury after a day spent on the road. Danny parked the exhausted Celica, and they got a double bedroom. They saved a little cash by eating at a nearby McDonald's, although Crew made it a point to have a decent breakfast in the morning. McDonald's twice in one month was enough for him. Two days in a row would just not do. He likened it to one night stands: one can live off it, but it isn't healthy. Danny promised him something good in the morning, even if it meant dining in the expensive restaurant of the hotel.

The hotel also had an ample bar and both decided that a couple of beers before calling it a night would be a good idea. Take the edge off. The place was dark, full of polished wood and tables, and practically deserted apart from them and the bartender. The bartender was from Quebec, and Danny surprised Crew by speaking French to him. He was a young man, clean shaven, and his eyes brightened for a brief moment before answering, "Oui, oui," to Danny's orders. They made themselves comfortable at a table well away from the bar and settled in for the first round. Crew heard of the brew they made up here, but he had never really tried any of it. After two bottles of Moosehead, he was thinking of importing it.

"Good beer."

"Not bad," Danny shrugged. Crew thought the man was a mountain about to fall over.

"Where'd you learn to speak French?" Crew asked.

"School," Danny answered, eyes downcast.

"Really? Learned Spanish in mine. Had the option to do Japanese, too."

"Spanish is a cool sounding language."

"So is French."

"Aw," Danny drew out, "it's okay. Not too much opportunity to speak it though. Sometimes we'd shoot over to New Brunswick there and speak a few words to the locals, but that's it. Nothing big."

They talked for another hour during which Crew drank another two beers and the room took on a fishbowl quality. He also noticed his words were becoming slurred in some places. No wonder Buffalo and Detroit teens were making runs across the border to get at this shit. To wait until you were twenty-one was a crime.

"Good beer," he commented.

Danny nodded. "You keep saying that. How you doing over there?"

"Pretty good," Crew said, leaning back in his chair and making it creak. He drum-patted his belly. "How about you?"

"There's a snap on, alright," Danny admitted. "Must be all of the driving getting to me. Haven't done that before. Sometimes, after the bar closed early, Gary—I mean Mr. Tigh—Boom and I would slam back a few Mooseheads. Many a good soldier would perish on those nights."

Crew listened to the music playing in the background. "They're good, aren't they," he stated, referring to the two men.

Danny met his eyes. "They are . . . my best friends."

Crew held up his bottle, and Danny met it with his own. The bottle necks clicked together. "

"To finding the prey," Crew toasted grimly.

Danny nodded. They drank, and for a moment, Crew believed the big man was weeping. Crew looked away, suddenly interested in the nearby tables, and downed his beer. He then signalled the barkeep for two more.

"Two more for the toad—I mean road?" Crew asked.

"Yeah," Danny said rubbing at the side of his nose. "You watch 'Star Wars?'"

Crew's brow arched with interest. "'Star Wars?' Yeah, I've seen it. The old ones, right?"

"Yeah, episode four."

"Then yeah, I've seen it."

"What cha think of the music?"

"The music?"

"Yeah."

The bar guy came over with their beers and placed them on the table. Crew paid the man before answering. "Good, I guess."

"Boom would say that's music to have sex to. That and 'Superman.'"

A smile spread across Crew's face. "That so? Yeah, I guess it would be."

"Next time you hear it, you'll be thinking of it. Guaranteed. I've tried it, actually, and the man has a point."

"Superman, too?"

"Nah, not superman," Danny scoffed. "That'd be too much. I can see my lady's eyes rolling over now if I tried some shit like that. 'Star Wars' is acceptable."

Crew swallowed a mouthful of beer and chuckled. "What about the music from the cantina part, then? That good for sex, too?"

"Foreplay," Danny answered, and they both smiled. "Got you thinkin' now, eh?"

"Yeah, you do," Crew chuckled. "I liked all them movies though. Except episode six. 'Return of the Jedi.'"

"What was wrong with that?"

Crew leaned forward. "Okay. You got this planet right, and the new Death Star's force field generator down there, and the Emperor's got a legion of his finest stormtroopers down there guarding it. Ass kickers to the last, and they get fucking pummelled by a bunch of spear-chucking teddy bears. How the hell does that happen?"

"Merchandizing," Danny sympathized. "Boom and I argued over the same point."

"What point?"

"How the stormtroopers could get stomped by a bunch of teddy bears."

"So, he agreed?"

"Nope. The other way. He figures—and this is his opinion only—that we only saw glimpses of a mass attack. Thousands of the little Ewok bastards swarming over the stormtroopers. The white boys just didn't have a chance."

Crew considered the idea. "He's got a point there. But you don't see it well enough in the movie."

Danny pointed a finger at the man. "My counter exactly. You don't see it well enough in the movie. You could do it now with all of the CGI stuff going on. I mean, look at 'Lord of the Rings'. Great stuff."

"Not exactly the kind of debates I expect from a couple of bouncers at a strip club," Crew stated thoughtfully, squinting at the other man.

"Shit, we talk about everything there. Politics to sports. World Events. Hell, I even have my own website up."

"Really?"

"Selling sports' paraphernalia. Cassius Clay's first set of boxing gloves. Stuff like that."

"*What?*" Crew did not bother covering up the amazement in his voice.

"Hell, yes," Danny nodded. "Can't work at the Beacon forever. I got boxes of old baseball cards and hockey cards. Plan to retire on the money I make off the shit. Plan to just travel around to conventions, selling my merchandise, and picking up whatever I can for the best price I can get. Even selling some of it on eBay."

This was impressing Crew no end. "Sounds good to me." He took another shot of beer. This Moosehead brew got better by the bottle.

Danny watched him. The beer was making him talkative. "Oh, yeah, I could retire in a year, I figure. I got enough stock to keep me going."

"Stock?" Crew almost laughed.

Danny nodded slowly in earnest, a very sly expression on his face.

"So, why are you working at a strip joint?" Crew wanted to know.

Danny smiled. "I enjoy my job. You should see some of the ladies working at our place. Mr. Tigh brings in some pretty talent." He sighed heavily.

Crew could only grin back. "I bet he does. Bet he does."

"So, what about you, then?" Danny turned over. "What retirement plans do you have?"

The beer bottle suddenly fascinated the hell out of Crew, and he turned it round and round watching the beer inside slosh about. "That's something I can't talk about."

Danny chuckled. "Should've waited for beer number six."

"Maybe you should've," Crew agreed, but what he left unsaid was, no matter how drunk he got, he always remembered what he did the night before. And he would certainly remember giving away any personal retirement plans. His retirement meant disappearing. Up and into the wind like a baby's fart. And he would not dare consider letting his own mother know what his plans were, let alone the bouncer and part-time sports' stuff collector across the table from him. As much as he was beginning to like this Danny character, Crew did not want to tell the man anything he would later regret.

Things he regretted had a way of dying.

They both had a sixth beer, and by that point, Crew knew he would be a hurting unit in the morning. In truth, he suspected he was going to hurt after the fourth beer. Number six was there in hopes of making the pain go away.

They talked on into the night. Though quiet when sober, Danny could talk on and on when he was buzzed. And his anecdotes about drunken patrons at the Beacon were amusing to say the least, if not hilarious at times. The stories went on until midnight when they both decided to call it a night.

"You driving tomorrow?" Danny said as they went back to the room.

"Hell no, you're driving! And not too fast, either."

"Beer's good, eh?"

"Way too good. Shit." Crew staggered a bit in the soft lit corridor. "You don't snore, do you?"

"No." Danny shook his head. "Not me. Not that you're going to hear anything."

"Got that right."

"Boom could snore. That boy has a buzz saw in his throat. Nasty deboning shit like someone having their spine ripped out."

Crew grimaced. A memory popped into his head of another place and time where a chainsaw was involved. And the victim that died by it.

They got to the room without accident. Danny unlocked the door and closed it when they were both inside. They fumbled about as drunken men do before falling into their beds. Crew undressed down to a pair of dark satin boxers, and collapsed on his bed face down. In the darkness of the room, his muscular back looked intimidating. He muttered something which caught Danny's attention as he was heading for the can.

"Yeah, man," Danny answered. "I'll get you some water." He believed that Moosehead number six was just landing on the wasted surface of Crew's brain. All his systems were shutting down in stupor. Danny looked at the man for a moment, then hauled off a beige blanket from his bed. He covered Crew up with the blanket and moved the garbage can from the bathroom to his bed, right below his head. Just in case. Crew mumbled something again as Danny set the can down.

"Yeah, sure," Danny said.

Another slur of words as if the man's tongue was in a snowy river full of slow moving ice.

"Yeah, don't worry about it," Danny assured the man. He didn't have the slightest idea what Crew was talking about. He was a quiet character, but opened up when the beer started to flow. He reminded Danny of himself. He also reminded him of a Halifax cop by the name of Rod Crouse. On a blue moon, Rod would appear at the Beacon and chat with both Danny and Boomer. An affable enough person, Boomer had characterized the man in a second.

"Nice enough guy, but watch what you say around him. He's off duty when he comes here. Give him a reason to come here when he's on duty, and we'd see a different man. He has a job to do and if you become part of that job, the bad part of that job, he'd take you down without thinking. Maybe he'll feel like shit afterwards, but he'd still take you down cuz that's what he does. So, just watch what you say around him. He don't want to hear about it, anyway. And don't let no one know he's a cop. He's just a regular guy here enjoying a T-show."

Danny got into his bed. He folded his hands behind his head and stared at the ceiling. Somewhere outside, phantom engines went by every now and again. His eyes got used to the dark, and he eventually closed them. Boomer's words were still in his mind, and his friend's smile was behind Danny's closed eyelids, keeping him awake. *Just like the bastard, too*, Danny thought as a tide of weariness pulled him under.

At 4:05 in the chill of the morning, a black Toyota two-door pickup pulled into the parking lot of the hotel where Danny and Crew were sleeping. Brake lights flared red, illuminating the exhaust like the breath of a dragon. The truck did a slow slanting ninety-degree turn and parked itself next to Danny's Celica. The engine rumbled, sighed and went to sleep. With the motor dead, the interior quickly chilled. The cold did not bother Fear. He sat in the darkness of the truck and stared out at the street lights blazing like yellow stars against the night. He would wait until morning, until the pair of men emerged from the hotel and got aboard their car. He would then commandeer the vehicle, and the three of them would spite time and travel to British Columbia, which reminded Fear that he would have to make a phone call.

He turned to his driver. The pussy-beard had become a frosty, lifeless white as had the man's hair. The man's eyes darted in his passenger's direction as if he were about to be given the beating of the century. He pressed himself up against the driver's door, huffs of breath bursting from his nostrils, picking up speed. A snot bubble exploded in one nostril, but the man was beyond caring.

"You have a cell phone?" Fear asked the terrified driver he had hijacked back at the Black Bear.

There was a frantic nod.

"Give it to me."

The driver almost tore his coat pocket off in his frenzied attempt to get it; his hand was shaking so hard the nerves were thrumming. He dropped the device into Fear's hand as respectfully as he could manage, given the state he was in, and jerked it back as if he had come into contact with something unholy.

Fear ignored the man. He flipped the phone open and dialled a nine digit number. It went through, and while Fear waited, he regarded the cell phone's picture of a golden Labrador retriever.

Fear hated dogs.

"Hello?" Time answered. "Who is this?"

"It's me."

A pause. "What do you want?"

"I need to get to BC"

"Now?"

"Soon. In the morning."

"Have you seen something?"

"Two things. Two men. I'm waiting for them. When they get here, we'll go."

Another pause on the line.

"Lucy is in BC" Time said.

"Bitch."

"Well, she didn't say that of you."

"Whatever."

"They found Death."

It was Fear's time to fall silent. He considered the information. Old Tony the tool was the ticket after all. Damn.

"They'll need me," Fear said.

"Yes."

"And soon."

"Yes. Very soon."

A car drifted by Fear's vision. "How long do we have?"

Another pause. "Not long." Time sounded worried. "Already there are those that suspect. Some have already tried, and it's just a matter of time before they are discovered. Or . . . their remains are discovered."

Fear screwed up his face at the thought. Fucking cattle-minded Mundanes. "I can do what I can."

"It'll be difficult now that the fear of death is wavering. Chance will bear a lot of the weight. But you must press on."

"She's still with Levin?"

"Yes, but she will manage. She has to."

"They're trying already?" Fear wanted to know for certain.

"Yes."

"Fucking idiots," Fear spat out, shaking his head in anger.

"I know," Time said seriously. "Why anyone would risk their lives to take that chance. I mean, it's their lives. Their . . . *existence!*"

"Fucking dolts."

Time sighed into the phone. The weariness in his voice was unmistakable. "Well, where are these two men now?"

"Sleeping."

"How do you know about them?"

"All things are connected. You know that."

"Can you wake them?"

Though Fear would never admit it, the concern in Time's voice worried him. He thought about it for a moment, and then he shook his head.

"No. Let them sleep for now. I'll be pushing them hard enough in the time coming."

There was silence on the line, and then, "How did it ever come down to this?"

"You know how," Fear told him. "We all know how."

They were both quiet for a moment. Finally, Fear sniffed and broke the spell. "I'll go then," and hung up. His request was put in. He did not want to listen to Time anymore. Time was too hopeful while Fear was black and white. Cut and dried. They balanced each other, but now that they were apart, Fear had no stomach to argue or debate or even listen to Time. They would either succeed or they would not. Hope could do little for them, or so he believed. Part of him wondered what his existence would be like without the Mundanes. The others worried about it constantly.

He did not care.

Mundanes were a noisy, complaining herd of cattle.

A part of him thought that the cosmos would probably be a quieter place when they were all gone. For him, certainly.

He placed the cell phone on the dashboard before him, flicking a disgusted look at the man he had come to call Pussy-beard.

"Fucking idiots," he swore, and went back to staring at the night sky.

CHAPTER 32

Funabashi City, Chiba, Japan.
 Hiromi gazed down past her twitching bare toes, past the Seiyu's department store's eight floors of steel and concrete, and wondered if she would feel it when she hit the pavement below. If there was a greater power amongst the heavens, it would grant her the little bit of relief of feeling no pain at all. Life had been agony to her, so at least death could be painless.

A gust of wind blew the black skirt of her high school uniform up past her white knees. Modesty made her press it down before the wind could lift it higher. The thought she was about to kill herself didn't make her worry any less about the wind blowing up and exposing her secrets to the world. She didn't care after she was gone, but for now, while she was still drawing breath, her skirt would remain three fingers below her knee.

She set her jaw and gazed out over the cityscape of Funabashi-shi. She had lived here all her life, and hated every fucking millimetre of its steel bones and concrete guts. The people in the city were indifferent to her plain looks, to her short bangs, to her eyes spaced just a little too far apart. Her acne had turned both her cheeks into the surface of mars, and her mother allowed no makeup as it only inflamed the skin more. In the movies, a person with her lack of physical appeal would usually make up for it in school grades.

Not in Hiromi's movie.

Her exam scores smacked of mediocrity. The prestigious high school her parents wanted her to enter for so long would not take her. All the pressures of studying had been endured for nothing; all the nights when she could only sleep for three or four hours, if sleep came at all, had been for nothing. She knew what her parents would say. Their words would shame her to the spot. It was better this way. Get it over with. Reboot. Leave an apologetic note. She was so sorry to have been a disappointment, to her mother especially. Hiromi could care less about her salaryman father, whom she barely saw at all. He worked even harder than she did, starting with a two hour commute every morning and every night to and from Yokohama. She didn't know the man. All she knew was that he gave whatever money he managed to make to her mother.

And then there was Yui Okikawa.

Kazuo had been the only boy that had ever showed any kindness to her, that ever showed any interest in her, until Yui stole him away. That theft left Hiromi both livid and miserably depressed. It happened just before her exams to make matters worse. Yui was beautiful in Hiromi's opinion. She was beautiful enough to have any boy she wanted, but she decided to lay Kazuo above them all, the only boy Hiromi ever had any feelings for, and later boast about it in the girls' locker room. Just to show Hiromi that she could. Hiromi didn't know what she had done to incur Yui's wrath. Perhaps she saw Kazuo talking to her and that had been enough. That would be enough for someone like Yui. She demanded the attention of all the boys.

Hiromi pushed it from her mind. She pushed everything from her mind. The only thing she concentrated on was the ground, so far below. This life was over for her. She wrote those exact words on the note she sealed in a plastic bag and stashed in her vest pocket. She looked down again and wondered what it would feel like to fly for mere seconds, and then hit the hard ground. She tried to imagine it, succeeded somewhat, but then gave up. Reality was but seconds away. All she needed to do was take a step, one foot and then the other, as if she were descending steps.

Her bare toes edged over into air, pressing against the concrete. Fear flared up in her, trying to make her stop. But it wasn't enough. She thought of Yui and Kazuo. She thought of her damn acne, she thought of her parents and how disappointed they would be once they saw that their daughter would not be getting into the school they wanted.

She stretched out her arms and stepped into air.

The rush of wind and nothingness smashed into her resolve to kill herself, and in an instant, Hiromi's fear exploded in her head and heart. She shrieked. She did not want to die. She had made a mistake. Windows flashed by like silver in the sun. Her stomach went up into her throat, and she screamed again. This was not right! She wanted to take it back! She fanned her arms, attempting to slow her fall, but the earth sucked her down. Pavement rushed up to meet her.

And she smashed into it.

The people nearby heard the heart-wrenching scream. They looked up in time to see the shape of a person freefalling against the glare of the sun, and they heard the wet, bursting splatter not unlike a balloon filled with water.

As they drew close, they could see that she had landed on her back, arms and legs flung wide. Lines of blood like the tails of doomed comets left the starburst pool of blood surrounding her. Blood spilled from her eyes, ears, and nose. Her skull looked like an egg dropped to the floor, crushed on one side. Bone shards stretched a blackening scalp. Her face was paint white, and while some simply stood in shock at the blood blooming before them, others speed dialed 119.

One man, thinking more of the women and children passing by in the street, took off his runner's jacket. He meant to cover up this poor girl, to give her some dignity rather than leaving her on display for the death watchers. The ambulance chasers. It was with great effort that he summoned up the nerve to approach the mess of a human being before them all.

He only got three steps, his jacket spread wide in his hands, when Hiromi opened her mouth and moaned.

CHAPTER 33

Paradise wasn't exactly what Tony expected when he pulled into its parking lot. It was a roadside bar, brown, with its windows full of faded tropical islands and trees. The double doors were just closing as the Mustang parked itself, and Tony wondered if the place was busy so late in the afternoon.

"Paradise," H2 announced from the back seat. "Looks like a shithole. But you warm up to it."

"I really wish you would not talk that way," Lucy said.

"I am what I am. Therefore," H2 snapped his fingers in what he probably thought was cool. "Am I wrong, chief?"

"Fuck off," Tony said clearly. He wondered if the man actually forgot his name. He glanced over at Lucy, mouthed a silent 'sorry'. The man did have a point, however. The place did look like a shithole. A brown caked one. The thought made him smile, but he did not share it with Lucy. She already controlled him, and he liked it. God above help him if they ever got together once this was all over. She'd probably have him wearing couple's clothing. And liking it.

"What are you smiling at?" Lucy asked him.

"Nothing."

"I know what he's smiling at," H2 chided.

"Fuck you squared," Tony fired off, and grimaced at Lucy, "Sorry."

"Oh, whatever," Lucy threw up a hand. "You're both going to do it, anyway. Knock yourselves out. When it really starts to bother me, I'll just leave. So, there."

"We goin' in?" Tony asked.

"Yeah," Lucy said, and looked at him, concerned. "You ready?"

"Yeah," but he wasn't. He delivered messages with his fists. Not with his brain.

"Good," H2 declared. "'Fraid I wasn't going to be able to walk if I stayed back here any longer."

"That would be a shame," Tony sneered.

H2 got the jab and was ready. He had two eyes. "But you'd take care of me, wouldn't you Lucy? Just like that time in the hot tub down in Boracay?"

Lucy rolled her eyes and did not reply. The words made Tony set his jaw. The man in the back had his number, and he knew it.

They got out of the car and walked into Paradise. Tony glanced at his watch. It was 5:30. There was no one on the door. They went inside, and the smell of marinated steak and onions hit them. Tony loved bar food. *Loved* chicken fingers. Back in Halifax, he used to be a regular at the Thirsty Duck and the cheap Chicken Finger Night there. Then, there was Pedlar's decadent hot turkey sandwich with a hill of golden corn giblets on one side and a mound of home fries on the other; all deep in gravy. Heaven.

He hadn't had bar food in a long time. Not since his mom. He couldn't. How could he enjoy eating when she couldn't eat anything? When he finally did eat, he felt guilty. Tony set his jaw and tried hard to concentrate on what lay ahead.

They stood at a nexus in the bar and turned right. They moved past a long, lacquered, wood counter top complete with beer taps and spouts all gleaming and longing for the lights of Las Vegas. The two bartenders behind the counter wore black and blue t-shirts, and greeted the new customers with smiles. The three of them moved past high bar tables, all empty, and down a short flight of stairs into a pit area lined with alcoves and filled with tables and cushion chairs. At the far end of the room, a decorative fire place made the room quite looking, except for the chicken wire covering the unlit fire logs. To the right of this, in one of the alcoves, Frank and the man called H were sitting and talking. Tony saw the man he had come to talk to. Frank sensed the gaze immediately. He looked at Tony and shook his head. H looked in the same direction, his expression unreadable.

Nodding their heads in greeting, Lucy and H2 moved to a neighbouring alcove. Lucy went in first, and Tony blocked H2 from following her. With an evil smile, H2 sat down on the other side, placing Lucy between them. If she noticed this, she did not let on.

She snatched up the menu on the table. "Mmmmm, they have chicken fingers. On special, too. And a happy hour. I like Paradise already."

"Let's get a pitcher," H2 said.

"OK," Lucy agreed and waved for a waitress. "You want some of this?"

Tony frowned. He did not want to think of eating. Not even chicken fingers. "Maybe just some water. I'm driving."

"Dickless," H2 commented with a disapproving shake of his head.

"What did you say?" Tony said, leaning forward.

"I said 'titless,'" H2 cupped his hand to his mouth and coughed. "The waitress."

This drew a frown from Lucy. When the woman arrived, Lucy did the ordering. The waitress wore a pink casual shirt with Labatt's written above its breast pocket. Tony thought it was cute and not at all titless as H2 had said.

"Full of shit," Tony muttered.

"What was that? Lucy asked.

"I said he's full of shit."

"Frank?"

"Him, too" Tony said, ignoring H2's glare. "I'm going over there now and getting this shit over with."

"Wait for a bit," Lucy said, placing a hand on his. The contact made Tony become very still. "He's a lush when he drinks."

"What?" Tony made himself say.

"He's a cheap lush," Lucy told him. H2 was nodding. "He was on a pitcher when we came in. Let him finish it. H won't drink much cuz he's with us. He knows Frank can't drink much, either."

"We all know that," H2 remarked with contempt.

"Even Frank," Lucy went on. "But he doesn't care. He likes his beer. So, wait until that first pitcher settles in."

"I'd even consider holding off until the second round is over," H2 said.

Tony was astonished. "Death's a *drunk?*"

"I didn't say he was a drunk," Lucy was quick to correct him. "I said he's a lush. He likes to drink when he has the time. And when he drinks, he drinks a lot. Like anyone who likes to drink but doesn't do it too often, he doesn't have the tolerance built up, so it hits him fast when he does drink. But he's far from being a drunk."

"I have to *wait* until Death is shitfaced before I can speak to him," Tony shook his head in growing disbelief.

"He'll be more agreeable," Lucy said.

"He can still be a prick, though," H2 nodded with a knowing expression.

"As you might have guessed." Lucy said, scratching at the table's surface with a fingernail.

"So, I hold off," Tony said, not liking this new information in the least. He didn't want to talk to a smashed Death. He hated dealing with drunks anyway. They were way too unpredictable; either being way too goddamn silly or being too goddamn violent. There was no middle ground.

"I think it's a good idea," Lucy suggested softly.

And she knew the guy.

"Alright," Tony conceded reluctantly. "When he's a pitcher in."

"Two pitchers, chief," H2 winked and flicked up two fingers. He then dropped one and wagged the finger at Tony. Tony did not need to have H2 flip him the bird. And he hated being winked at. It was gay shit. Yes, Tony figured that, at this particular juncture in time, it was safe to say he hated H2's fucking guts.

"Yeah," Lucy agreed. "Two pitchers to make sure. That's a safer bet I think."

"So, what do we do in the meantime?" Tony asked her. He wasn't going to talk to H2 anymore if he could help it.

"Wait," H2 answered for her. Lucy gave him a stern look.

"And eat chicken fingers," H2 smiled back at her.

Tony sighed heavily. Two pitchers in. Great. It was times like these he wished he had a drug habit. He was in drug country to think of it. As far as marijuana and ecstasy went. He heard crystal meth was pretty popular out amongst the Albertan rig pigs as well. He wondered if the meth had gotten to BC. Music flowed in and around them while he thought his thoughts, but it was low enough that it was still easy to talk. And what day was it? Wednesday? Friday? If it was, he wondered how busy Paradise got going into the weekend.

Then, he started thinking about Frank.

The food came: two serving baskets with a beautiful pile of chicken tenders and two accompanying saucers filled with honey mustard dipping sauce. A pitcher and three frosty-looking mugs were placed before each of them.

"Thank you, Debby," H2 said, holding her gaze. Tony thought the man looked as if he could lick shit up off the floor if he wanted to.

"How did you know my name," Debby asked, a little wary, but meeting his gaze with large blue eyes.

"Heard the bar guy mention you when we came in," H2 answered.

"Oh," she smiled briefly before retreating to the bar. H2 watched her go.

Lucy rolled her eyes. "Struck out there."

"Think so?" H2's brow crocked up in a challenge. "She'll be asking me for my phone number before this night is through. Right now, I'm on her mind."

"Oh, yeah?"

"Yeah," H2 said. "And I noticed you didn't say anything about making a bet. Why is that, Lucy my dearest?"

Lucy chose not to answer him. Instead, she pulled a chicken strip from one of the baskets closest to her and dipped it into the sauce. She nibbled on it and sighed.

"Mmmm, try some."

H2 was pouring the beer. He thrust his chin out to Tony. "I see no water in that mug there, chief. Want some of this?"

The beer looked like gold to Tony. The chicken smelled wonderful. His stomach rumbled and never felt emptier. Again, he thought of his mother back in the hospital and the guilt hit. He eventually nodded and slid his mug over to H2, who filled it. One mug would take the edge off.

H2 filled Lucy's and his own mug then, and raised his in a toast. "To Tony there," he said.

Tony was mildly surprised. The prick remembered his name after all. He did not raise his glass, though Lucy did.

"To Tony," H2 repeated. "May Lucy blow him sooner rather than later."

He took a huge gulp of beer, leaving his drinking companion behind.

"Can't be nice for a second can you?" Lucy said as she laid an arm across a rising Tony. She could tell what he wanted to do, and she couldn't allow that right now.

"What do you mean?" H2 asked in defence. "That was nice! Wasn't that a nice toast there, chief?"

Tony drained almost all of his beer.

"Only lookin' out for ya," H2 said, and then to Lucy, "I bet she's a screamer," nodding in Debby's direction.

"Why couldn't you have stayed in the car?" Lucy said.

"What? And miss Debby's victuals? I don't think so," H2 replied, taking a drink. Lucy watched Tony sitting with the last of his beer. He had a nice profile when he turned his head. She grabbed another chicken finger and dipped it. She couldn't really enjoy them under these circumstances, but she had to give the appearance of some confidence. She had to look calm at least. It would be disaster to look any other way and for Tony to see it. She felt a medicine ball lump of sadness for the man. There was a goodness in him, but it was up to its neck in trouble and bad luck. She liked him and would have to be blind not to see his growing affection for her. But she had been down that road before. It would never work. She would never tell him that. She hated confrontations of that nature. When the time came, she would just disappear and become a memory. She drank some beer and left half a glass. God above, she was worried this time around. Frank was really pissed off. She decided to keep quiet and let Tony prepare himself for what he had to do. She told herself to ignore H2.

The Entity did not notice her, however.

H2 was too interested in the curves of Debby's jeans.

CHAPTER 34

They emerged from the hotel at 7:30, squinting at the sun and a field of freshly fallen snow. Fear watched the men come out into the light. He sat on the hood of the Celica, arms folded. They walked slowly towards him like frozen gunslingers with their hands dangling at their sides, careful of the ice glazing the parking lot. They exchanged looks and regarded Fear at the same time, the puzzlement plain on their faces. This clearly was not on their list of morning things to do.

Well, shit happens sometimes, Fear thought.

"That's my car you're sitting on," the bigger one said, raising a finger.

Fear did not move a muscle. He wanted them both a little closer.

"Would you mind getting off the car?" Danny asked politely. He was feeling the effects of last night's beer. There was potential for a serious headache in his future if he didn't get to a convenience store. The guy on his car did not seem in a hurry to move. Danny sighed. He wasn't in the mood for this.

"He asked you to move," Crew said in a low voice as crisp as the cold morning air. "Now, I'm telling you to move."

Fear smirked.

"What would you call this?" Crew asked of Danny.

"Trouble," the other replied.

"Well, between you and me, I think we gave fair warning."

Danny's chest heaved again. "Yup."

"Let's do a sound check just in case," Crew focused on the sitting man. "GET THE FUCK OFF THE CAR!"

Fear's eyes widened. The little one caught him off guard with the blast.

Crew nodded to himself. He surprised himself as the beer had not hit him as hard as he thought it might. But it did nothing to improve his mood to see an ignorant tit spoiling for a fight so early in the morning. "Well, his hearing seems fine to me."

Crew started walking towards the man, studying him for any concealed weapons. Years of the trade made his skull suddenly buzz with danger, yet he could not see anything. Danny stepped away, instinctively doing what Crew was about to tell him to do. That was good. Between both of them, the joker on the car would not prove to be a problem.

But goddamn if Crew did not like the way the bastard's smile was growing.

Fear watched the men draw closer. He watched them split apart, just in case he was going to shoot them. This was the part he always enjoyed, letting the Mundanes have their way, being as cautious as they wanted to be, just before he unleashed the shit storm. The thought made him smile, and his smile made the men pause.

Too late, Fear mused.

And, without any pity or remorse, the essence that was Fear lashed into the two men with tsunami force.

And swept them both away.

CHAPTER 35

That same morning, the Stickman woke up in the backseat of his Sunbird. He slowly opened his eyes and stared at the ceiling. He wondered how the *heel* it got so dirty. He didn't smoke, but what were those stains the colour of phlegm doing up there? He opened his mouth, smacked his lips without shame, and wanted something to drink. His throat was all raw and sore. Shit. All he needed was to come down with a cold. With a breath, he propped himself up to a sitting position, heaving away the thick blankets he had brought along specifically for camping out in his back seat. His chest hurt. His face hurt. His windows were fogged up with his breath so bad that a passerby might think he had a hooker inside. He thought about Beverly and wondered where she might be this morning. Probably married now. The girl was a catch for anyone.

Stick inhaled deeply and pushed the thought aside. He rolled down the backseat window. Cold wind clawed at his face, making him squint. Squinting hurt like hell. He looked at the Irving Service Station and saw they were open. Some cars were already pulling up to the pumps for their morning chug of high priced gas. No one had called the cops and that was good. He figured the money he saved from not staying at a motel would buy him a half decent breakfast in the roadside restaurant of the service station. It was too bad he wasn't working for the government. He once knew a guy who talked of a guy who worked for the province and who always got cash for gas, food, and lodgings when he travelled. If he remembered right, it was something like nine dollars for breakfast, fifteen dollars for lunch, twenty for dinner, and another twenty for 'incidentals'. Then there was money for every kilometre travelled. And that was only the provincial level. The feds got more. Stickman wondered how much school a person needed for a job like that.

Rubbing his chin and feeling the need for a shave, the Stickman got out. He did not want to shave, however. The hurt that Boom put into his face would not allow a clean cut this morning, so he would allow his bruises to sprout roots. He walked towards the convenience shop section of the Irving Station. The cashier did not acknowledge his entering, and Stickman ambled past the counter towards a white looking hall and the washroom signs within. There was no one inside the men's room which made him glad. For a few moments, he could pretend the place was his.

He had his morning dump without incident. No one walked in on him. When he was finished, he flushed, exited the stall, and placed both hands on the sink to get a good look at his morning face. He snarled at what he saw. *Christ*, he looked fucked up. Black and blue and blood crusted in places. He smiled in spite of it all, and thought about the mess that used to be Boomer. He abruptly jettisoned the thought and got on with his morning ritual. He had brought along his tooth brush and floss, and saw to his dental hygiene. Afterwards, he removed his coat and shirt, and washed his face and armpits. He considered his hair. He had no shampoo. Muttering curses, Stickman regarded the liquid soap dispenser on the wall. The public washroom soap always smelled like shit to him. "Fuck," he swore. He wasn't going to use that. He did not want to smell like cheap-ass soap for the rest of the day. He ran a hand over his dark hair and thought a haircut would be in order. He should have gotten one before setting out on his mission. Oh well, for now, he would run his head and hair under the faucet and clean it as best as he could without soap. The faucet was fixed high enough for him to get under it. He ran the hot water, and massaged it into his scalp as gently as he could. He knew he would have that unwashed hair feeling immediately afterwards. It was enough for him to want to seek out a Shoppers' Drugmart somewhere. Or, shit, he could have checked out the convenience shop out front. They would have shampoo too.

The moment he had the thought, he lifted his head, forgetting his temple was right under the metal edge of the running faucet.

In training with Sensei Bill, who professed to dabble in Jeet Kun Do, Stickman had learned of the one-inch punch. Bruce Lee had mastered the one-inch punch, and Sensei Bill was determined to, one day, focus his chi and produce the same effect as old Bruce: the ability to strike a blow powerful enough to drop a foe without a wind-up and, thus, without warning. To think a punch or a strike from one inch out could render a person senseless was something that Stickman had trouble believing.

When his temple connected with the metal faucet, a firm part of a washroom unit not going anywhere, the idea of the one inch punch exploded in a white light of pain. Stickman grimaced and hissed like molten iron meeting cold water. He pulled himself out from underneath the faucet and stood hunched over the sink, his breath hissing in and out. *Christ almighty*, he dinged himself good that time. He kept his eyes clenched shut, but when he opened them, he fully expected to see blood in the sink. If there wasn't any blood, there would be another damn impressive welt. Despite the pain, he smiled. He wouldn't need any coffee this morning.

After a few moments, the lesson began to subside, and he peeped into the sink. It was still porcelain white. Relief for that little mercy flooded through the Stickman. That was good. Now for the mirror.

There in the reflection, just over his shoulder was a grinning man. A *big* grinning man with a shaven head. He had a shark's open-mouth smile. A Great White Shark on the hunt like the Stickman had once seen in National Geographic footage.

"Da fuck y'lookin' at?" Stickman winced. Fucker must've walked in when he clocked himself under the faucet. The Stickman did not like being surprised, and he did not like big men standing behind him. He whirled to face the intruder, but the big man jabbed a fist into the Stickman's kidneys. The connection robbed Stickman of his breath, and he doubled over. Like clockwork, he doubled over to meet the stranger's powerful uppercut. Stickman's lower back crashed into the edge of the counter and sink. He lifted his arms to defend himself, but they were slapped away and then grabbed. Stunned as he was, his attacker spun him around, pinned his right arm up near his shoulder blade and slammed Stickman's face into the black countertop surrounding the white porcelain. He felt the accordion crunch of his nose, and the starburst of pain. He tried to free himself, but his attacker locked his wrist, and hooked his armpit with his thumb, forcing him to continue kissing the countertop.

"You okay?" A voice purred into his ear. Stickman felt a groin press up against his backside and, through the fog of agony, the old fear of being raped welled up.

"Fuck you!" Stickman shot back, and squirmed. He still had one free arm. He reached backwards, clawing for the bastard's balls.

But his attacker gouged his thumb further up into Stickman's armpit, finding a bundle of nerves and drawing a muffle grunt of pain from his prey.

"How about now?" the man asked.

The pain made Stickman clench his teeth so fast he could taste blood. "I'm gonna ki—"

The man twisted Stickman's arm and his words strawberry swirled into an agonized growl.

"Okay now?"

"YES!" Stickman blurted out. "I'M OKAY!"

"Good, cuz I don't want to kill you. Understand that? I don't want to hurt you anymore than necessary, and right now it's necessary." The voice took on a matter of fact tone. "I need you. Do you understand that? You're looking for someone, right?

No answer.

The Entity known as Pain twisted the arm he held a little more, feeling muscle, already taut, begging not to be twisted any further. But Pain demanded attention. Pain demanded prompt attention, and he would teach this Mundane just that.

"Yeah," came the barely contained reply. Stickman wanted to scream out. Pain could tell.

"Good, then we're going to hunt together. I'm looking for the same man you are."

"You . . . are?" Stickman asked uncertainly.

"Oh, yes. He's in British Columbia now. I'm going there. You want to come with me?"

"BC?" Stickman panted. "'Ow's 'ee in BC? Chrissakes, y'can leave me me arm!"

"He drove," Pain ignored the Stickman's request.

Drove there?

He drove across the fucking country in two days?

Im-*fuckin'*-possible! Stickman's mind shrieked in rage. Not even if Levin had a jet engine strapped to his ass!

"I want to help you find this man," Pain told him. "I want you . . . and I to find him together."

"OK!" Stickman blurted out. He was ready to agree to anything. His goddamn *arm*!

"You're going to drive me to BC. It won't take long. I'll make a phone call."

"BC?"

"No, no," Pain said slowly, enjoying the time he took speaking, knowing it was torture to the Mundane. "To a friend who owes me a favour. Well, he's going to owe me a favour because he's doing things that I don't think are fair. But maybe you don't understand? Let me explain . . ."

"NO!" Stickman retched through bared teeth and a red face.

At that time, the door creaked open. An Irving man stuck his head in—the cashier from out front. "Everything okay in here?" he asked timidly, not knowing and probably not wanting to know what was going on.

Stickman did not see what happened next. He heard a voice growl, "Get the fuck out of here."

Stickman heard the door quickly close, and he closed his eyes in defeat when he did.

"Now," the voice went on very close to his ear. He felt the groin press up against his rump. "You were about to agree to help me help you, right?"

"YES!"

The voice paused. "Y'know, I don't believe you. In your position, I guess I'd say just about anything to get out of the predicament I was in. Just about anything."

"JESUS H. CHRIST!" the Stickman blurted out in agony. He did not see the face behind him close its eyes in pleasure.

"Yes, just about anything." Pain went on smiling. "So, you won't mind if I ask a few questions to, uh, satisfy my suspicious nature."

"YES!" Stick's eyes widened in sudden fright at what he'd just said might be taken as defiance. "NO! NO!"

"Good. So, you'll give me your word that you'll do as I say from here on in?"

"YES!"

"My every command?"

"YESYES!"

"Every*thing?*"

"YESSWEETMARYFUCKYES!"

There was a laugh of someone who had two great lungfuls of phlegm. Even in Stickman's agony, the sound of that buttery rattle made his tongue curl.

"I guess that's enough," the voice chuckled. Then, it became lethal sounding. "But remember this. I took you easy. I can do it again."

The pressure on Stickman's arm and shoulder was released, and he snapped around like a coiled spring. For a moment, he considering tackling the bastard and thrusting his thumbs into his piss-hole eyes. He considered it. He considered his arm. It was still on fire. He sighed, "Y'know Badger?"

"From way back."

"Why didn't ye say so den?"

The man shrugged. "I had to domesticate your ass first."

That made Stickman hold his tongue. He didn't like to be talked to like that at all.

"Listen," the other said, smile disappearing. "I apologize. I overreacted. One reason why I don't work for Badger anymore is that he sent me away. But I remember things he did for me. I heard you were looking for the guy that put him in the hospital."

Stickman held up his good hand. "You 'eard dat? Where from?"

Pain smiled. "Around."

"Yeah, where?"

"The same place I heard where Levin is heading."

"Y'know where 'ee's goin'?"

"I do."

"And ye wants I to go wit ye?"

Pain nodded. "He has company with him. You'll even up the odds."

"Two's better, eh?"

"Maybe," and a skull smile.

A frown formed on Stickman's features. He sure as hell didn't trust this dick, but if he knew where Levin was, then a partnership would be a smart thing. "Alright," he said, massaging his shoulder. *For a while anyway.*

Pain smiled at him. His eyes were no more than blots of tar.

"So, what's yer name?" Stickman asked.

The grin got wider.

CHAPTER 36

Paradise.

Paradise was sinking.

Or so it seemed to Tony who, despite not really intending to, drank a pitcher of beer over a span of sixty minutes. So much for resisting the impulse. He felt so much better for doing so except that now, Paradise was sinking. And spinning.

A different waitress appeared before their table. "Another?"

"You got anything else?"

Lucy exchanged looks with H2, who was also feeling his beers. The man gave a half cut smirk.

"Cocktails."

"Cocktails?" Tony repeated stupidly. "Paradise has cocktails?"

The waitress winked at him. "Paradise has everything, honey."

Lucy had something she wanted to say to that, but H2 placed a hand on her arm. He wanted to see what Tony would do.

"You have any . . . daiquiris?" he asked.

"Strawberry ones."

"I'll have one of those."

The waitress took the empty pitcher away from the table. The plates had been gathered up a while ago.

"We'll have another, too," H2 said. "Stuff's too good. Almost as good as you!"

The woman frowned good-naturedly and took the empty pitcher away from H2. "You guys sure like your beer."

"Our friend here has discovered his thirst for life, it seems." H2 pointed at a red-faced Tony.

"The beer is good," Tony remarked, getting more and more buzzed.

"Yes, it is," H2 nodded, "but a girly drink?"

"Fuck you."

A little drunk smile appeared on H2's face. "Starting to like this boy of yours, Lucy."

Lucy had her own glow on. "He does start to grow on you after a while, doesn't he?" she said as she looked at Tony with a growing red-faced fondness. Her dark hair hung loosely about her shoulders, and Tony thought she was the most beautiful creature he had ever seen . . . recently. The last word made him giggle, prompting Lucy to look at him with an unspoken question.

Death passed in front of their table. He cast an annoyed look at the trio, but did not slow down. He moved towards the washrooms. This amazed Tony. Death had to *piss*! He actually felt the *need* to void himself! In Tony's buzzing world, it was the coolest thing to realize. Then he remembered he had a job to do.

"There he goes," he said like a man who had drunk a bit and was aware of it. "Gotta do it now. Gotta talk to him."

"Wait for him to come back," Lucy advised. "Don't try talking to him while he's peeing."

"I wasn't going to," Tony said.

"Looked to me you were," H2 said. Lucy pointed a *you see?* finger at Tony.

"Well, I wasn't," Tony said, defending his honour. "I was gonna wait until he got back."

Then the man called only H appeared before them. "Hey," he greeted with a heads up.

"Hey," the three chorused back.

"Guys feeling good?"

"Yep," Tony said.

H regarded him for a moment. "He's feeling good, I see."

"Oh, he's fine," Lucy said, sipping on her beer.

"When you coming over?" H asked, looking at Tony.

"Soon," H2 answered.

"I wasn't talking to you, wingnut," H fired back.

"Soon," Lucy nodded agreement. "We're waiting for him to come back from peeing. He's gone to pee."

This display of intoxicated cuteness had no effect whatsoever on H. He regarded them all with the look of a police officer wishing to fuck that he wasn't the one on duty to have to deal with these drunken teens.

"You didn't call her a wingnut." H2 protested with a sloshed smile.

"She isn't. You are." H told him stoically, levelling a *"don't fuck with me"* glare at the man. "If you are coming over, make it soon. I think he's gonna want to head out somewhere for pizza next. He's been waiting for you, y'know."

"He's waiting?" this amazed Tony.

"Oh, yeah," H nodded.

"How many he's after having, H?" Lucy asked.

"Two pitchers."

"In under two hours?" Lucy asked. She was a little surprised. Frankie was downing them faster than usual.

"And all the while he's been waiting," H informed them. "You know he isn't going to cross the floor. And you know he's not going to make any first moves. And if you don't make it first, he's going to say fuck it and move on."

"Pizza?" Tony asked.

H regarded him. "Doesn't like big crowds. But you do have one thing going for you. I think he's going to make a move on one of the waitresses here."

"Which one?" H2 demanded, looking a little agitated.

"Debby."

"She's mine!" H2 said, even more agitated.

"Didn't see your name on her," H informed him calmly. "Take it up with Frank if you want. I'm not interested."

"Maybe I will," H2 jeered.

"Yeah, well," H rolled his eyes and looked at Tony. "You got your game on?"

"Yeah," Tony said. He liked this one. He had a scratchy, growly voice and sapphires for eyes. Probably contacts. There was a good feeling basking about the man. And he liked the way H2 seemed to whine around him.

"You sure?"

"Yeah."

"'Kay," H said, nodding. He glanced towards the washrooms. "Frank's on his way back. Luck, man," he aimed at Tony.

Incredibly, or at least a high grade freaky, Frank turned the corner the instant H stopped talking. That was some cool handling in Tony's book. Frank passed H and shook his head in disdain, as if he did not like his trooper fraternizing with the opposing team. H dipped his head at Tony's table and followed Frank back to theirs.

Debby appeared with a pitcher and a crystal goblet containing a strawberry daiquiri.

"You going, Tony?" Lucy asked him as he took his drink.

"Yeah," Tony replied and shuffled his ass out from behind their table to stand up. He sipped as he did so. "By the way," he said as he stood and pointed at H2. "He's gay."

H2's face went slack then, and Debby giggled as she placed the pitcher down. Tony left the table, not waiting to hear H2's riposte. He got the fucker good that time. He would like to see H2 talk his way out of that one, but time was pressing. And *time was a human measure.*

He took in the music. Felt the chill of the daiquiri in his head and belly. Took in the cosy décor of Paradise's alcoves. Wondered if it was night outside now and guessed it was. Then, he was in front of Frank and H's alcove, before their table with his half-drained strawberry daiquiri in hand. Frank and H waited, their hands on the table's worn surface like old gamblers showing their honesty. Mugs of beer stood before them. Another full pitcher rested in the middle of the table and reminded Tony of a glowing lantern. That led to an image of a wintry cabin deep in a forest frozen in January.

"Can I sit down?" Tony asked.

"Sure you can sit down. Have a seat," but his words did not sound friendly. They sounded tolerant. Frank rolled his eyes over to H, who was staring at Tony as if he were a ninth inning relief pitcher brought in to save the World Series. Tony slid in behind the table on H's side, placing his drink down. Frank frowned at the cocktail.

"I guess I'll stay and watch, then," H commented, seeing as he was pinned in.

Frank ignored him. "You look surprised," he said to Tony.

"I am."

"Did you think I would've said 'fuck off' instead?"

Maybe, but Tony didn't say that. Instead, he sipped on his drink. He looked around the table, at the seats, at the ceiling.

"Yup." Frank said. "Same as the one you came from. So, start talking."

Tony gulped back another portion of his drink. There wasn't much left now. It had taken him two hours to get to this point with the help of the beer, and he hoped mixing at this point would not make him sick. Frank waited, setting both elbows on the table, and watched him over his folded hands. Tony wasn't sure what to say, only that he was supposed to say something. He knew what Frank did, and he knew what Frank *wasn't* doing, and he knew that maybe he had a shot at getting the man back to doing what he did best. Tony crunched up his face. Death was across from him *drinking* for Jesus' sake! There were people out there suffering at this very moment, waiting for Death—probably even wishing for him—and here he was, sans scythe or sickle or whatever the hell it was he used, drinking beer! Beer! Like Death could actually drink beer in Paradise! What in the sweet fucking hereafter could Tony say to this man so leisurely enjoying his alcoholic beverage while millions were in agony? What could he say? What *would* he say to this piece of shit that refused to see his mother and end her suffering or the hundred or so like her in Halifax who were also dying by the hour of cancer. To be denied the simple pleasure of enjoying a meal because his mother's disease had eaten away at her. What could he could say to this cocksucker?

Tony looked Death squarely in the eye.

"You," he jabbed a finger at the man for emphasis, "are a fucking asshole."

Frank's expression went slack. It clearly was not the lead in he was expecting. He was probably expecting Tony to beg him to start working again. *Oh, please, for the sake of my mom, PLEASE go back to what it is you do!*

Instead, he got another "You are a fucking asshole."

Frank leaned back, his hand lying flat on the table's surface. H leaned back from Tony, looking at the Mundane with absolute shock and thinking a mental white sheet. Neither of them had expected this.

But Tony had only opened with a pop. He was just warming up with all of the confidence the beer and the strawberry daiquiri supplied him.

"YOU are a FUCKING ASSHOLE!! You MOTHERFUCKING BUNGLICKER! COCKSUCKER! WHAT the SWEET FFFFFFFFUCK," spittle flew from Tony's purpling face, "ARE YOU doing HERE and telling ME to start TALKING! I mean sweet CHRIST on a telephone pole! You have the *biggest* set of balls on you! PIG'S BALLS! You ever see a set of pig's balls, Mr. fucking Grim Reaper? They're like this!" Tony's hands came up and measured a size roughly the same as a football. "LIKE THIS! And they are fucking DANGLING from you, man. You ARROGANT, CHEAP PRICK! YOU SHITBUBBLE! You MISFIRED SPERM! You bastard! BASTARD! You hear me? BASSSSSSSSSSSTARD!"

An unimpressed Frank nodded at H. "Any other time, I'd have to spend money to get sworn at like this."

H was inclined to agree. He wasn't sure if Tony had thought over what he was going to say to Frank or not, but he was certain that *this* wasn't the approach he would have used.

"You fucking asshole!" Tony blared at Frank only a few decibels lower than before. The bar staff was looking in their direction. H wondered if Paradise employed bouncers.

"Thought I was a bastard a moment ago," Frank said.

"The boy's confused," H noted dourly. "Or baked."

"So, why?" Tony demanded in a hoarse voice. "Why are you doing this?"

"Doing what?" Frank wanted to know.

"This?" Tony grated in red-faced outrage, fanning his hands over the table as if trying to magic it away. "Dick all! You have a job to do. You should be fuckin' workin', man! Fuckin' *workin'!*"

Frank leaned forward. "Why should I be working?"

"Yeah? Why?" H added. He figured it couldn't hurt to appear unbiased.

Tony's shoulders heaved as if it were the dumbest question he had heard in all of his existence. "*Because!*" he wailed as if the word explained everything.

But it was there he ran out of steam. Tony drained the last of his cocktail. He looked at H and then back at Death, like a swimmer that has just realized he has gone past the halfway point, that it was continue all the way to the other side now, or just drown.

Frank took the opportunity to light up a smoke. "Because?" he asked quietly, inhaling as he did. Smoke fired out of both his nostrils and Death squinted through at Tony through it all. "I'm waitin' here."

Tony fixed him with the killer look he saved for his difficult assignments. The "*I could kill you right here without blinking*" look. It did not seem to work on Frank. Then, through the haze of the beer and the daiquiri, Tony remembered just who it was he was trying to intimidate. He gave up. He decided he was still mighty pissed at the man, and resumed the look anew. "You should be killin' people."

"I should, huh?" Frank's fingers played with his cigarette. The tip glowed in the smoke and dim light.

"Yeah, you should. People are, like, needin' you, man! And you're here! You're not doing your job."

"I'm not, eh?" Frank repeated just as quietly and gave a sideways glance at H, who was pinching the bridge of his nose.

Tony noticed this, and suddenly, he was not so sure of himself. "No, you . . . ain't," he said.

It probably was right there when Frank decided to unleash his own salvo. He had listened to this whiny prick of a Mundane enough.

"What the fuck do you know about it?" Frank lasered at Tony, daring him to say otherwise.

"I know lots."

"You know *dick* about my job, sonny," Frank shot at him, again, and leaned close with an ugly snarl. "You just informed me as much with that drunken rant you just went on. Or did you forget who you are talking to? Punk. You *think* you know. What did you do? Fight in a war? Huh? You a doctor? Hm? You see me all the time? How do you *know* about my job? Hm? My work? When I know that YOU," a single finger that might have been able to punch through steel stabbed in Tony's direction, "know absolutely nothing about what I do. I do know about you, Mr. *I'll kick the shit outta anyone if you pay me.* Mr. *I'll be back tomorrow and you better have the money or you'll be pissing and shitin' blood for a week.*"

It was Tony's turn for his mouth to drop open.

Frank feigned shock. "Oh, you thought I didn't know about you? You and your kind are all alike. Morons. Fence posts waiting for the nail. This is why I quit man, see what I'm sayin'?"

H nodded that he understood, his sapphire eyes pinning Tony.

There was quiet at the table for the moment, but Frank could see the defeat in Tony's face.

Tony was cut to the core. Death was right. Who was he, with his history of beating the shit out of gamblers and junkies and just about anyone for cash, to try and convince anyone that people should not be suffering? Despite the large amount of booze in his system, Tony never felt so sober in his entire miserable existence. He simply wanted to get out of there, crawl back to his car, and gas himself.

But then Frank sighed, and stabbed out his cigarette. "Y'know, maybe I should talk about this. Get the goddamn monkey off my chest. Maybe even you can spread the word," he took a pull of his beer, "so I don't have to feel so goddamn guilty when I go on vacation."

This made Tony squint at Frank sitting across from him. "You're . . . you're on vacation?"

"No man, I'm on strike," Frank said. "I'm sick of this job."

"Why?" Tony exclaimed, pulling himself back into the conversation

"Why?" Frank repeated, the disbelief in his voice made Tony feel stupid. "Why? Have you ever worked in, say, customer service?"

"No."

"Have you ever counselled people?"

"You mean like a shrink?"

"No, not like a–" Frank wildly fanned his hand about, as if clearing the air of a rank fart. "Have you ever stopped a suicide?"

"Stopped a suicide?" Tony repeated, feeling even more stupid now. What was Death getting at? He wanted to stop people from dying?

"How about comforted people? Huh? You ever do any of that?"

"No."

"Not even your mom?" Frank asked.

The words froze Tony in his place. "A little."

"Yeah, a little," Frank said in a hard tone. "I know all about you and your mother. I know goddamn well what's going on with her and you. Let's be honest—what do you think about when you think about your mom?"

Tony's fingers touched the edge of his glass. "I hope she gets better."

"Bullshit."

"What?"

"I said 'bullshit.'"

Anger rushed into Tony's face. "What are you sayin'?"

"I'm sayin' you want it over. You want her dead."

Tony's mouth went dry right then, and every ounce of beer or hard booze in Paradise would not moisten it up. "You take that back," he told Death, squinting at the man.

"You know what she goes through, Tony. And you know her kind of cancer is the slowest. The worst, most painful kind. Right up to the end. The woman can't eat. Hell, she should have passed on ages ago, right? I mean, fuck, how do you think you found me? Huh? How do you think you got here? Just following your nose? I'm connected to people like that. Your mom is suffering with every breath, and the painkiller she's hooked up to is only barely keeping her pain away. You want her to last as long as possible? The same mother that saved up her government checks so that you could have a bike? The same mom that convinced your dad to take you to see your first movie? The same . . ."

Tony leaned in. "*Fuck* you," he said with quiet savagery.

"There you go," Frank backed off with a smile. "You dig deep enough you'll hit water, every time."

A rush of images went through Tony's mind then, all of his mother, and he floundered for something to say, but the anger he felt at Frank made him just sit there and tremble. The wind flared out of his nostrils, and when he reached for his drink, he found that his hands were trembling. Then, he realized his drink was long gone. All of those things his mom had done for him, and now she was in a hospital waiting to die.

Only she couldn't.

Because the prick sitting across the table from him was on strike.

"You're a piece of shit," Tony whispered, his eyes branding Frank with their intensity. "A real piece of shit."

"Why?"

"You know why," was all Tony could manage.

"Yeah, but this is where it gets painful Tony, my son. This is where the truth really stings. Why am I a piece of shit?"

Tony would not answer him.

"You better say it or this conversation is over," Frank warned him with a finger.

"If it is I'll rip you a new asshole."

"I think you'll try," Frank said with a glance at H. H's eyes sparkled as if he held a killer poker hand.

"I think you'll try," Frank repeated, "but you won't. So, say it."

"You won't let her die," Tony whispered.

"Thank you," Frank breathed. "And you're partially right. Except I don't *let* anyone die. I never did. And I'm not doing anything for anyone until things are cleared up around here. Not until things change. I'm sick of the way things are. I want job clarification."

"What?" Tony croaked and blinked. He was caught trying to control his anger and the emotion he felt for his mom.

It was Frank's turn to lean in. "For the record, I don't *kill* people. People kill people. Nature kills people. *Time* kills people . . . but I don't. I have nothing to do with . . . *killing*." He spat out the word as if it were raw sashimi served up bad.

Tony almost laughed at him. "Oh, yeah? So, what do you do then?"

Frank looked him straight in the eye. "I *rescue*."

CHAPTER 37

The lock clicked, and Sarah let out a sigh of contentment. Work was over for another day, and she made it home without incident. Her car was pulling to the left, so that might be a trip to the service centre tomorrow. Sarah breathed again, feeling her lungs expand, just as she came into her apartment. She was medium height, and had shoulder-length, brown hair, highlighted sparsely with red—nothing too fancy to cause an uproar at work. She was a teller at the Royal Bank, and they gave her dirty looks whenever she wanted to go to the bathroom. It was an unknown statistic that tellers suffered the most from bladder infections and other urinary tract problems because of the bank's work shifts.

But she liked handling money. She liked counting.

She rubbed at her eyes and checked her face in the mirror. She had a screen-door scattering of freckles that most guys thought as cute as her figure. She wasn't certain of that. She thought her ass was fat.

Slipping off her sneakers (she always left her heels at work), she wandered into the kitchen, unfastening the long sleeves of her black blouse and rolling them up to the elbow. There wasn't any mail to check, so that was one less thing to do. All that remained was dinner, and then she could engage in her favourite pastime.

She headed into the bedroom, and since the heat was on in the apartment, changed from dark slacks to short plaid shorts. She ran her hand over her legs and thought it might be a good idea to shave them. She then tossed off her blouse and slipped into a comfy t-shirt with twenty five suggestions on "how to deal with stress" on its front. She didn't know how anyone could let stress ruin their lives. It didn't ruin hers. Sara didn't do stress. She worked out, being a firm believer in taking out any negative energy on weights and turning it into something positive.

Sarah thought about calling up some friends and maybe heading out for a beer, but decided against it. Her original plan was best. This was to be her night and, glancing at her forearms and legs, tonight would be delicious. She could only treat herself so often and tonight, after almost three weeks of skin packs and practically swimming in aloe vera, she could do her hobby again. The only thing that truly made her feel alive

But first, dinner.

The fridge contained the remains of a vegetarian lasagne, and it was shoved into the microwave. Sarah got herself a steak knife, a fork, and a glass of milk. She knew there was a tub of cookies 'n cream ice cream in her freezer, and she suspected she would get into that later on tonight—fat ass be damned. She'd go for a thirty-minute walk tomorrow. She watched over her warming food, waiting for the *ding* and caressing her arms. The nuker announced that her food was ready, and she gathered everything up and moved to the living room. She watched the evening news, noting how lucky a pair of kids had been to have survived a head-on car crash, and a lady who had managed to get pulled out of her burning house.

Finishing her meal, Sarah relaxed and simply lay back on her sofa, pushing the dirty dishes on the wooden coffee table. Her grandmother always told her about cleaning up immediately after eating, saying she didn't understand what all of the fuss was about, anyway. Cleaning the dishes took only five minutes at least, and then, when they were done, they were *done*. Why some people had a problem with that or whined about cleaning them in the first place was beyond her. This evening though, Sarah would be bad. She would do the dishes later.

But then, Sarah sighed at the memory of her grandmother and relented. She got up from the sofa, and six minutes later, the dishes were on the rack, drip drying. She returned to the living room and kicked away the little brown rug lying on the floor between the sofa and coffee table. Tomorrow would be a cleaning day, and her one bedroom apartment took about a morning to sparkle.

But that was tomorrow.

Sarah got up again and toddled into the kitchen, picking out another steak knife—an exceptionally sharp one. She then went into the bathroom and retrieved her curling iron and three thick red towels. She again returned to the living room, and placed them on the coffee table.

She kicked the rug again, repeatedly, until it was well away from her. In its spot, she plopped down the three cherry bright towels, and arranged them one upon the other. She pulled out an extension cord from behind the sofa and plugged in her curling iron. Then, with a little grunt, she lowered herself down on the towels until she sat cross-legged. Sarah flicked through the channels with her remote control and tuned into a repeat of *Friends*. She smiled in some places, chuckled in others, while letting her fingertips explore her exposed flesh.

She eventually picked up the steak knife and, still watching the program, slashed the inside of her left forearm. The cut was barely an inch in length, but it buzzed and tingled with pain. Blood dribbled to the towels.

Then, it was commercial time.

She inspected her self-made cut with great interest, like a doctor inspecting fresh stitches. She had cut well, right next to the scars of previous sitcoms and other maddening movies. It usually took a good two weeks before she could start cutting again, and she attributed that to a healthy diet. However, recently she was beginning to think that her skin was losing its resiliency from too many self-inflicted wounds. She carefully placed the tip of the blade along the new wound, moving up towards the valley of her elbow joint. She angled her arm so that the blood plopped freely unto the towels and cut again.

And shivered.

She ground her teeth against the pain. The exquisite pain. The only true thing that ever made her feel alive.

She sliced again.

And again.

Until her arm began to look like the gills of a choking fish.

Then commercial time was over. *Friends* was back on.

By the time of the next commercial break, she had finished slicing her left arm and decided it was a good idea to start on the right. She was a little light headed, but nothing she hadn't felt before. She took great care in her cuts. Nothing too deep and nothing close to a major blood artery or vein. The flesh of her right arm was in harder shape that her left, mostly because of her awkwardness in handling her blade with her left hand. It took a little more effort, and the cuts were usually a little longer. A little deeper. The pain sparkled like a bottle of very fine champagne. She swooned with the electric buzz and dropped her knife. That happened sometimes. Rivulets of blood ended in darker stains in the red towels. She placed a finger into one of the stains and brought the inky tip to her face. Tasted it with one dart of her tongue. The sparkles she experienced were like sun rays reflecting off fresh snow. It was better than booze or dope. It was better than screwing. It was a natural high for her, and the best there ever had been.

Sarah sat for a moment, worshipping the ecstasy of her cuts and enjoying the blurry whine of the TV in the background. Her cuts would scab over by morning. She had cut herself too deeply in the past and had to stitch herself up, relishing the prick and punch of the needle. But tonight was fine. And tomorrow, she would wear a long-sleeved shirt or sweater to work. No one would see or suspect anything.

Still dizzy from her blood loss but only beginning, she felt a shock to her system would bring her back to clarity. The curling iron on the coffee table was ready now, and she picked it up by the handle. She would never injure her hands if she could help it. Her hands were too important. As were her face and feet. Almost everything else—anything that could be concealed—was fair game.

She brought the hot iron in close to the inside of her right thigh, perhaps three fingers up from her knee, feeling the heat of it. She eyed the burn scars already there. They would never heal back to true flesh. She didn't care. She moved the iron closer, felt her skin tingle, burn, and then, ever so slightly, she pressed the iron into her flesh. The hurt exploded in her nerve endings and head like windows being blown off an old house. Her head swung to the left and right, bobbed up and down. She bit her lip—made it bleed. She moaned and dropped the instrument, collapsing against her sofa, somehow still having the sense to keep her bleeding arms over her towels—she didn't want any of it on the sofa's upholstery.

When the pain subsided, Sarah picked up the iron where it fell, like a junkie eager for another hit. She ignored the smell of burnt flesh. She did this over and over again, lighting up her synapses just as they were dimming, suppressing her little girl squeals. Blood dripped from her bottom lip, and only then did she realize she had gnashed it. She continued burning herself, bringing herself to bright highs of agony, like multiple orgasms, until she could take no more. She would dearly love to go further, but she was no lover of death. She did not want to die. She only wanted . . . pain. At some point in time, in the future, she planned to do some travelling, and she envisioned herself doing things to her arms, legs, breasts, and even her belly on some exotic beach before a bare moon.

But that was a far time away.

For now, her beach would be her bathtub. Her moon would not exist, but the star tips of her surrounding candles would light up the darkness. Still giddy from her administrations, she got up and went to the bathroom. There, she would drift in and out of consciousness while filling the tub with near boiling water—the hottest she could take without seriously harming her skin—light her candles and get in. She intended to stay there until she fell asleep, travelling to the very edge of life and death and listening to the drums of her heart and pulse.

She so loved times like these.

In her pain-induced daze, she bumped-walked to the bathroom. She could hear the water gushing into the tub, and tried to remember turning on the faucet. She couldn't recall doing it, but she must have. Who else would do it for her? The door was locked, and she was always alone.

She entered the bathroom, wounds still dripping and staggering, and leaned against the doorframe for support. There was a man at the tub. A big man. He was *huge* like a pro wrestler. What was even more interesting was that he was naked, hard bodied and scarred, and smiling. He was in his forties, perhaps, with a shaven head. He must have been from somewhere tropical because he had a dark, all-over tan which Sarah found incredibly arousing. She thought his eyes were black, and his smile was beautiful—crisp and pure.

"Baby, *baby*," the man said in a seductive purr. He held out a hand. His eyes gleamed like black marbles. Sarah felt a longing stir within her, and she stumbled towards him.

"You . . ." the man's smile got wider, "are *my* kind of girl."

CHAPTER 38

"See?" Frank spoke to H. "He's smiling. Thinks I'm crazy. That's what sucks. I need a massive PR campaign man, I'm tellin' ya."

"You're fucked in the head," Tony told him.

"Oh? Am I? Look at it this way. See if I can't convince you. I should be everyone's best buddy, yet in all the movies, all the books, the news, and in all the conversations, I'm the one people hate and, dare I say it, loathe. I'm the ultimate in evil. Incarnate. Realized. To quote Ali, I'm so bad I make medicine sick."

"But you are," Tony said.

"This coming from the guy that wants his mother's suffering to be over," Frank shook his head in disdain. "I've never *killed* anyone. Something else did. Something came along and did enough damage or set something off or smashed it into something, and I get the call to come in and get there *fast*. Be*cause* when I get there, I can save the person from all the pain and suffering someone will otherwise experience. I'm not the enemy, man. I'm your firefighter. Your cop. Your first responder. Shit. I figure Lucy would have already told you all this by now."

Tony ignored that last bit. "Yeah, well, you're doing a pretty fucked-up job."

"I do what I can with what I got."

"That's fucked up."

"Really?" Frank said dubiously, regarding Tony with unfriendly eyes.

"Yeah, cuz you . . . you hold off on people! Why do some people die straight away and others take longer? Like my mom?"

"Resistance," Frank said simply. "The will to live, to survive. I don't fight with that. A lot of people cling to life instead of letting go. Some instances, the shock of coming over to the other side is strong enough that people let go right away. Like being in an explosion or being shot. In those cases, people usually give up and come with me."

"What?" Tony asked. "That doesn't make sense. How do you do that? You can't do that. It's not possible."

"It's not about what is possible or impossible. It's about what is. You can try and use logic or science as much as you want. Go ahead and give me the giggles. It's in your nature to analyse and rationalize. But in the end, when it's a person's time, they get to meet me, and I give them the choice. Accept what is and come along. Or resist. Some choose life and go on as best as they can. I don't know why. It's not my place to ask really. The ones that agree to go, they come with me, and I take them to the other side."

"The other side?"

Frank smirked. "C'mon, now. You know all about that."

"You mean . . ." Tony lead in, waiting for Frank to fill in the blank. Only Frank didn't. Tony waved his hands, urging the other to respond. Frank did not. He sipped his drink instead.

"The other side," Tony finally said.

"Yes, the goddamn other side," Frank snapped, suddenly pissy. "You having another?"

"Huh? Oh. Yeah," he looked at his empty glass.

"You're not gay are you?" Frank asked him.

"What?" this jolted Tony. "No! What? Just because I drink daiquiris?"

"Strawberry ones," H added. Frank's eyebrows went up in *yeah really!* as he waved for a waitress.

"So, I like strawberry daiquiris," Tony said petulantly. "Ain't nothing wrong with that."

The two men were silent.

"There's *not*."

H drained his mug. Frank looked away, trying to spy the waitress.

"Fuck you both, then," Tony grumped.

"Another pitcher," Frank said to the waitress that appeared. "And another daiquiri for the princess here."

The waitress smiled and left. Tony felt a little annoyed at both of them.

"Never thought Death was an alchy," he said.

"Yeah, well?" Frank fixed him with a knowing stare. "What do you do for a living?"

Point, Tony conceded. He should be living out of a bottle.

"Hey, what's your real name anyway?" Tony asked him.

"You want me to write it down for you? It's a helluva lot better than Death, I can tell you that. Christ, what were you cocksmokers thinking. The Muslims call me *Malak al-Maut*. Ancient Greece referred to me as Thanatos. *Thanatos.* That's some cool shit."

"Hey, I didn't name you," Tony defended himself. "So, don't get pissy with me. What's his name?"

"He's H," Frank told him.

"Just H?"

H smiled. "It's a game we sometimes play. You use the names all the time, so we like to see folks guess our names. Our nicknames."

"So, you all have nicknames and real names?"

"Mhm," Frank acknowledged.

"And you chose 'Frank'?"

"What's wrong with 'Frank'?" Death asked.

"Nothin'," Tony said. "Fits fine if you ask me. Death is Frank."

"Better than Dick."

That drew a chuckle from H.

"Yeah," Tony agreed. "Stick with Frank. Dick could be a little, what's the word, confrontational. You'd be hunting for people then."

"I don't do that."

"Oh, no?" Tony was interested. "So, if you heard on the news an announcer say, oh for example, 'Twelve people were dicked last night in a highway collision', you wouldn't be pissed off?"

Frank screwed up his face in annoyance. The waitress returned with their orders before he could retort. She sat the drinks down before them and retreated with a smile. H grinned a thank you at her.

"Fuck you," Frank shot at Tony.

Tony sipped on his fresh daiquiri. It was plenty tangy and good. "Yeah, thought so."

"How's your drink, dear?" Frank asked.

"Great. Yours, Dickie?"

H began to choke on his beer, enough to turn his face red. Frank let him.

"Ain't you gonna help him?" Tony asked Death, taking another relaxed sip.

"Why? Not like he's going to choke."

"To Dick," Tony corrected him, and grinned.

Frank was not amused.

"But you aren't bothered by that," Tony pressed on.

"Alright, 'Death' is fine," Death finally conceded.

"I think I'll call you Death from now on," Tony said, his head abuzz with the amount of booze he had consumed in the last few hours. Maybe some of that funky time travel or distance warping or whatever the hell it was had something to do with it, too.

"Unless you think it sounds suspicious or something. You don't listen to Speed Metal, do you?"

"I listen to Ministry," Death admitted. "And old country songs. From the 70's. Not the 90's shit. And the Carpenters."

"That's all good," Tony said, inspecting his drink. They made this one strong. The mule had some kick. He could not recall who the Carpenters were, however.

"It is all good," H added, over his coughing fit. He was beginning to like this Mundane.

"He listens to boy groups, too," H said, indicating Death across the table.

Tony pointed at his drink. "And I'm a princess for this?"

"And he sings karaoke," H went on, "He's not bad, either."

Frank was beginning to feel a little betrayed by his long-time companion. "Anything else you want to share with the audience, Toolboy?"

But H kept smiling. Perhaps the beer was affecting him, as well, but Tony realized more and more that H was an ally, and that made him feel much better. Then, something went off in his head, and he pointed a finger at H.

"I know who you are—or what you are—you're Hope!"

H's grin spread even wider, but he acknowledged nothing.

"Yeah, you're Hope," Tony saw it all clearly now. "And you're still an asshole," he flung at Death.

"You sure have a strange way of convincing folks to get back to work," Death said, shaking his head at the balls on this man.

"And fuck if I know what I'm doin'," Tony slurred. "All I know is I'm supposed to convince you to get back."

"Yeah?"

"Yeah."

"Yeah, well, I'll give you a hint," Death went on. "Calling me an asshole or any of that other shit from earlier ain't gonna do it."

"What do you want, then? You're on strike, and you're talking about . . . what? PR shit. What is it you want? Exactly?"

Death took a long pull on his beer. He thought about it.

"What I want, you can't deliver," he finally said.

That was probably true. "But maybe I can pass on the request?"

Death smiled tightly. "I can guess who *that* will be."

"Yeah, well, what is it then? C'mon, let's hear it. People are waiting for you, man. C'mon back to the stage and get the show moving again. Rock star! People are sufferin'."

"No one suffers cuz of me. I told you that. People suffer because of something else. And then, when I come along, they resist. They fight me when I'm trying to save them. They cling on. Only the nastiest go with."

"So, people should just give up and die?"

"No," Death said sardonically. "Look, that's the problem right there. You fuckers just don't know when to stop whining. In all my travels I've never come across any one race so damned self-centred. It's all me, me, me!"

Tony blinked. *Any one race?*

"People are scared of me. They fight me. People curse me when all I'm doing is my job. Which is to simply end their suffering and bring them across to the other side. To ensure a safe . . ." Death stifled a beer burp, "a safe transition. I'm not there to hurt them; I'm there to make sure they get to where they're going. I . . ." Death's shoulders slumped. "I don't want to be feared, or . . . hated anymore."

Tony felt kicked in the gut. "That's what you want. Only that?"

"Yeah," Death stared at him. "You get it all?"

Tony cocked his eyebrow and considered his drink. How the hell was he going to be able to accomplish what Death wanted? "Yeah, I got it all. But I'm sure going off and playing golf isn't going to help your case."

"No?" This time Death's expression posed a question. "It got yours, didn't it? It got someone else's attention, too. Soon enough, others will tune in, *millions*. And then, we'll see."

This information silenced them all. Tony had heard this already from Lucy.

Death fixed his attention on Tony. "Still think you can help me out?"

"Fuck, yeah!" Tony blurted. "Sure thing, man . . ." and trailed off with an expression of anything but confidence.

It was okay by Death. He'd seen that look before on many of the faces of his passengers: The look of futility. There was no way this side of the Purge that a Mundane could help his situation. No way in Hell, either. The thought made him pause and look into the gold that was his beer. Not since the Ages had he felt this way, so utterly fed up with the entire show, as H would sometimes refer to it. And he remembered what happened then. He remembered what the others did to get him out of his funk. This was different, trying to get a Mundane to get him back on track. Death smiled to himself then. He and H2 would sometimes play chess together. H2 was a prick, but he played a mean game of chess. *When in doubt, move a pawn*, he would sometimes say.

When in doubt, move a pawn.

Death regarded the Mundane across from him. A mortal mind trying to decipher how to set things right. Maybe even strike a bargain of sorts. It would be amusing to see what he came up with. That was something Death both admired and despised in them, their undeniable creativity.

And their spunk.

Across from him, Tony downed the strawberry goodness that was his daiquiri.

"Next one's on me," H said, looking at Tony fondly.

"Thanks," Tony said, and went back to thinking about the impossible.

"Time for a pish," Death announced. He suddenly had enough of the merriment.

"You pish like a horse," H observed.

"Yish," Death smiled and got up. "Get another pitcher for us, bitch."

H frowned at him. He didn't like to be bossed around in front of Mundanes.

Death walked unsteadily towards the washrooms, saying something to the bartenders in his wake and making two of them grin. Then, he was gone around the corner.

"He really has a problem with his plumbing?" Tony asked aloud. He wondered if Death ever had trouble with his prostate. Seriously, how old was the guy?

"I'll let you in on something, but don't tell him," H said, his eyes darting in the direction Death went. "He caught something from a woman he picked up in a bar once. Chlamydia."

"What's that?"

"STD that goes after your urinary tract. He couldn't stop pissing. He was like a running faucet all the time.

"He . . . caught an STD?"

H nodded. "Fucked up, ain't it? Don't know who you are sleeping with these days."

"So, what happened?"

H caught the attention of the waitress and motioned for another pitcher. And another daiquiri. "Saw a doctor and got treated."

"*Death* saw a *doctor?*" Tony repeated.

"Yeah."

"This is too goddamn weird for me. He's just like one of us, for Christ's sakes!"

"At times, he is," H agreed. "He feels that, by being one of you, he can help you better when the time comes. Empathy, y'know? And he understands where you guys are coming from. Just that, well, say job satisfaction for him is at an all-time low."

Tony was speechless.

"You're doing well, by the way," H informed him.

"I am?"

"Oh, yeah."

"Don't feel like it," Tony admitted.

"Just talk about normal shit, okay?" H told him. "Talk about—I dunno—titties for example."

Death appeared in front of their table.

"What about titties?" he demanded. "Goddammit, I said what about *titties!*"

"Just referring to the lovely waitress coming to us with our beer," H said.

Death looked. The woman was new, curvy, and unsmiling at the way Death was sizing her up. She placed the pitcher and the daiquiri on the table, took H's money and retreated, ignoring Death.

"Christ," he muttered, watching her go. "Some right big titties on her," he exhaled and sat down. "Getting horny here, H. Drunk and horny."

"Dangerous combination," H said. Tony was filling their glasses, and H nodded his thanks at him. Death watched the Mundane with a drunk's intensity. He just couldn't decide what to make of the young fucker.

"Hitting on a waitress," H said with disdain. "You know they get hit on every night of the week. Every *hour* of the night on Fridays and Saturdays. Why do you even bother?"

Death fixed the man with a curious look. "Cuz I'm horny. Didn't I just explain that?"

He drained his glass. H drained his. When they placed their mugs on the table, Tony filled them almost immediately. H nodded at him with appreciation. Death merely frowned.

"Starting to like you," he sighed and raised his drink. "And when are you two gonna come over?" he yelled out. "Jesus Christ! You need a special invite or something?"

A second later, Lucy and H2 appeared. H2 carried half a pitcher of beer. "Like gold," he said with drunken affection.

"Took you long enough," H told them.

"We were talking," Lucy said, her eyes just a little heavy lidded. Was she drunk, too? Tony couldn't believe it. In the short time he'd known her, it seemed so un-Lucy-like to be smashed. She also looked gorgeous.

"About what?" Death asked.

"Guys with big penises," Lucy said, without blinking.

Her words made Tony's jaw drop. The others did not seem to notice.

"What do you mean?" H asked, squinting at her.

"Freaks of nature," Lucy explained. "Athletes, whatever. Some guys are just naturally freaks of nature. I mean really, really big. Really. I can't get over it sometimes how large some of these boys are, you know. Like, how big can they get? Really? Know what I'm talking about?"

The table was silent.

After a very unsettling moment, Lucy decided to go hunting. "How about you, Frankie. You ever see any freaks of nature?"

Death thought about it. "You mean chicks with big dicks?"

And the table went up. Uproarious laughter escaped from them all except Lucy, who merely smiled sweetly and shook her head.

"Forget about it," she said, waving her hand before her face.

"No, really," Death persisted. "I *really* want to talk about this now, especially in front of our Mundane Tony here. Don't worry," he said to him. "She always talks filth after a few beers. A real hypocrite our Lucy is. '*Oh I don't swear.*' '*Oh I hate it when you say that.*' But after a few pitchers, she gets really nasty."

H leaned in. "The other day, I even heard her say," he paused and glanced furtively around, "*fudge.*"

"Sweet pickles," Death threw in.

"I like that one, actually," H2 grinned. Lucy elbowed him hard.

And Tony simply sat and watched and listened. He was at the borderline separating pissed and shitfaced, and from his warped point of inebriation, he couldn't care less about anything except for the looming words in his head '*Lucy said penis!*' There was something oddly erotic about it, and he felt himself stirring. Only for a moment, as his bladder quickly reminded him. Booze. He had to slow down. He had to pace himself with these people. People! They were like people! Real, honest-to-God people, and that confused Tony. Weren't they, for lack of a better word at the moment, like *entities* or something? How could they have personalities? How could they get pissed off at work, or have sex, or get drunk, or talk about male appendages or female fun bags, or even have *time* to do all that?

How could they just sit around a table and get plastered? They were like kids, for Chrissakes!

He abruptly nudged H to move over, indicating that he had to get to the washroom, and H complied. Tony stood up, swayed, and shuffled off towards the washroom. The shuffle quickly became a run. He had to get away from them. Had to get to a toilet. He felt his stomach contract and his throat lurch, and he knew he had to make best speed to avoid voiding right in the middle of the bar.

They watched him disappear around the corner.

"Now you did it," H muttered. "You've made him sick. I hate having folks around with puke breath."

"I supposed *that's* my goddamn fault, too," Death grumped. "So, fucking shoot me."

H2 made a finger gun and slowly levelled it at Death. Lucy swatted him across the back of the head for even thinking it. She then looked at Death with very serious, pleading eyes.

"Why don't you just go back, Frankie? You know how bad it's getting out there. Exponentially."

But Death did not acknowledge her. He kept his silence, studying how the tiny bubbles in his beer rose to the foamy surface of his mug. His party mood was dying out faster than he wanted. He was no longer horny. He searched the faces of those sitting around him and saw their anxious expressions. There was a balance to be kept, and his friends were trying really hard to persuade him to go back to his trade.

And this Tony wasn't such a bad guy . . .

"I'll think about it," he granted them all.

Given the circumstances and the time and knowing him personally, it was a step in the right direction. They gave a collective sigh at Death's swaying in the right direction.

"I think," Death suddenly announced, "that a test is in order. Yeah. A test. That'll do it."

"A . . . test?" Lucy asked uncertainly. "Why the hell do you have to have a test?"

"Hey," Death pointed at her, "if leprechauns can demand a person to guess their names, I sure as hell can ask for a test. Let's get that straight right fucking now. I don't exactly take the garbage out once a day, you might remember."

Tony returned, swaying as he went. Death felt the ring of his own bladder again and indicated that he wanted out from the table. Lucy and H2 both moved.

"Again?" H asked him as he went.

"Yes, again, goddammit," Death snapped. "Not my goddamn fault I piss every five minutes. It's either there or all over you, so I guess there won't be an argument?"

Both of H2's hands went up, "Go piss."

"Thank you, I will."

The Mundane and Entity eyed each other, one arriving and one leaving. Death winked at the man, and Tony instinctively nodded back. It wasn't until he sat down he realized that Death had just winked at him.

That was fucked up.

Paradise was fucked up.

He sat down heavily next to H. "How am I doing?" he asked.

There was a long pause from them all. It was H that finally spoke. "At least you ain't swearing at him anymore."

CHAPTER 39

Death stopped in front of the wall-length mirror opposite the stalls and urinals. There was a big guy standing by the condom dispenser. Over his shoulder, Death could read the words "Works! Got laid!" scratched on the wall above the dispenser. He went to the urinal and began his business. He wrinkled up his nose at the pissy smell in the air. Death heard a flush from nearby and immediately forgot about it. He was in another world, thinking about people, Tony, and the lay of the land.

And the right big tits on that last bar wench.

The stall door opened and a Mundane stepped out. Except it wasn't a Mundane. In the reflection of the glass, the man's eyes were black. At the same moment, the big guy inspecting the condoms swivelled and placed himself in front of the washroom door, barring any exit. The Mundane coming out of the stall wore a huge pair of heavy winter gloves; the industrial, deep cold kind that scientists probably wore in the North or South poles or on the surface of the moon. He adjusted them as he came closer to Death.

The trap was sprung, Death thought, and smiled.

"Toilets are overflowing, I see," Death said to them.

"You're coming with us," said the man with the gloves. He had an exceptionally dark complexion as if he had been trapped in a tanning bed for too long. The big one blocking the door merely stared. If Death had been closer, he might've heard the growl. Regardless, he was feeling cocky at the moment. He realized who these "men" were. It had been a long time since he had to deliver any of their ilk to the other side, and when he did, they struggled tooth and nail. But they died all the same, just like anyone else, and instilled no fear in Death.

"And what if I don't?"

The man with the gloves gently placed his hands on Death's person, turned them into fists as he clenched cloth and leather and, without a change in his expression, lifted Death off his feet. Death's expression went from drunken defiance to surprise. He had forgotten how strong they could be. And this was the little one.

Peters brought Death in close, smiling as if he had just bagged the prize of the millennium. "We burn it."

Death screwed up his face. He could tell a prick when he heard one.

Peters waited for a smart-ass remark. He might just torch Paradise anyway. It would be an easy thing to do this close to Armageddon. Nothing fancy for this place. Just a plain old firebomb to herald in the Burning Ages. The more he thought about it, the more it appealed to him. Why wait the week? Why not just fucking start right *now*?

But Death only sighed, as if tired of it all. "Okay," he muttered. "Let's go."

Peters' smile faltered, and Death struggled to keep from smiling himself. Like handling old dynamite, these Minions, but he would manage until he did not want to anymore.

Peters set him down on the floor.

"But no hitting me as we're heading out," Death warned both of them with a finger. "I don't go for that shit. Understood?"

Peters and Bull Wash exchanged evil looks of amusement.

"Old man," Peters breathed, "you'll go out in a fucking *shoebox* if I say so."

Yes, this one was a prick. Death sighed. Captured by pricks. He had sunk low this day. It was a good thing he was drunk. Old man, his ass. He *specifically* made sure he looked late thirties.

Bull Wash moved aside and opened the door. He stepped out first. Peters motioned Death to follow. "Do anything I don't like, and I'll send this place up like a fireball."

Death did as he was told, half because he was drunk and half because of the novelty of it all.

Peters did not like the way the Boatman was stalling, so he shoved him from behind.

"Listen," Death said mildly, his eyes downcast, "I'm telling you again. Keep ... your goddamn hands off me ... Okay?"

The thing in a man's skin smiled, showing fearsome teeth. "Get going," it said and shoved Death towards the door again.

Death didn't like to be manhandled, and slowly shook his head with drunken contempt.

They just didn't know who they were fucking with.

CHAPTER 40

"So, y'see," H2 summed up with an authoritative air, "women are herbivores, 'kay? Men are carnivores. And gays . . . are also herbivores."

"That include dykes?" H asked, his brow crunched in the kind of puzzlement only huge amounts of alcohol could bring on.

"No, they're carnivores." H2 declared in a controlled voice, though pretty wasted himself.

"Lesbians are carnivores?" Lucy asked. She, too, was smashed.

"Yeah, see, cuz . . . ," H2 wanted to put this as lightly as possible, "they'll eat out herbivores."

Lucy looked at him. "Don't you mean '*eat*' herbivores?"

H2 waved a *whatever* hand in her direction.

But Lucy did not stop. "What about bisexuals?" she asked.

"They're *omnivores*. Those guys will eat anything. Don't trust them cocksuckers, whatever you do," H2 warned Lucy.

"Jesus Christ," Tony ejected, also pretty drunk, "I can't believe the shit you people talk about."

They ignored him.

"Transexuals?" H decided to ask.

H2 thought about it for a moment. "Good point," he admitted. "I'll get back to you on that one. Never thought about them before."

There was a growing need in Tony to empty his bladder. It felt as if he were about to spring a leak out his asshole, and he didn't think he could last long. And didn't he just get back from the can? He considered the drink in front of him with piss-hole eyes, and felt that all too familiar roll of his tongue and palate, suggesting *if* he finished that drink, he just might throw up. He thought about his bladder again and wondered how it was possible to fill up so damn fast.

Maybe he should see a urologist. The high given to him by the booze sloshed up and over his senses like flood waters breaching sandbags, and he decided the walk would do him good. The thought Death had been gone for almost fifteen minutes did not enter his mind.

"Where you going?" H asked as Tony got to his feet and struggled out from behind the table.

"Again?" Lucy blurted out. "You pish just like Frankie!" She looked lovely to him. Her cheeks looked darker than before, perhaps brought on by the flush of the beer. Or the light. Or both. *Bladder*, Tony abruptly thought. *Must. Void.*

"No more than two shakes," H2 warned him. "Any more than that and you're tuggin' on it, and there's barely enough toilet paper in there anyway."

"Is that what you use?" Lucy chortled, happy at getting one in. She slapped H2 on the shoulder, startling the man.

"I," H2 informed her with great dignity, "use towels."

Lucy screwed her face up at that.

"Much more absorbency," H2 stated, taking the joke one notch further. "I'm all for saving the trees."

H started to giggle. The thought of H2 saving anything was hilarious.

Tony left them and made his way to the can. Their merriment became drowned out by a loud rock tune pulsating throughout the bar. He arrived at the washroom and pushed the door open. He staggered to a urinal, unzipped himself and placed one arm against the wall for support. In his condition, a good wind would have been enough to blow him over. He definitely had to lay off the daiquiris for the next little while.

"Hey, Frankie, you in here?" Tony suddenly yelled out. Death must be in the stall, he figured. "Frankie! *Frankieeeeeeeeee!*" he wailed in his best marine voice.

But Frankie did not answer.

"Aw, c'mon," Tony grated, "You aren't pissed at me, are you? I thought we were done that! I'm done that! Really! Let's talk, *mon a me.*"

Still nothing. Tony stood there, quietly peeing, listening to the dull crashing beat of the music and the sound of his urine splashing against porcelain. Death might not even be in here, it occurred to him. Probably got by him somehow. Figuring that was the case, Tony finished and zipped up. He ran his hands quickly under the water and flick-dried them as he headed out the door.

He made his way past the bar and the gathering people. Paradise was starting to fill up it seemed. There were at least a dozen people in here now, mostly beer drinkers. He walked by them, trying hard not to appear drunk, and looked ahead. He saw their table in the distance. Death was not there.

Tony stopped and blinked. Paradise was not that big. There was nowhere for Death to hide. He glanced around. No Death. He blinked and looked again, this time concentrating with all of his inebriated might. Death was not among the patrons. Tony backed up and turned to the backroom of the bar where there were more tables and a few well-used dart boards hanging under off lights. The backroom was empty. He retraced his steps to the bar and looked in the direction of the modest dance floor. Empty again. There wasn't even a DJ in the booth.

A growing unease began to form in Tony's mind. The washroom. He headed for the toilets, walking faster, and pushed the door open a little too hard. It bounced off the wall with a crash. Tony didn't give a shit. He went to the stalls and started pushing in the doors. There were three. All opened to empty, clean looking toilets.

What the hell was going on? The thought glowed in the fog of his mind. Had Death decided to leave Paradise without telling anyone? What was up with that? Tony yanked the washroom door open and heard it slam against the wall again. A bartender warned him with a shout. Tony barely heard the man. Instead, he banked to his right and headed out into the night.

The air was cool, refreshing, and smacked him in the face. He found himself fighting the booze's effects and his rising anxiety. Tony couldn't think. Where the fuck was Frankie? Where would he go? *Why* would he go? Tony stood in the middle of a road, facing a parking lot with less than a dozen cars all arranged neatly under bright street lights. There was no movement on the lot. There was no one at all.

Just then, on impulse, he turned his head to the right. At the end of the street, slowing at the intersection, was a car. A black Ford Taurus, its taillights red. It was heading away from Paradise.

And it was full of people.

"Hey!" Tony yelled and began running after the car. "*Hey!*"

The car did not stop. It pulled out into the main road and increased speed. A face in the driver's side flashed in Tony's direction, and then was gone as the car pulled away.

Tony broke into a run. He bounded over the far sidewalk and the greenish yellow lawn beyond, picking up speed as he aimed towards the main road. He stumbled and nearly fell, but his flailing arms somehow got into sync with his feet, and he righted himself on the run. He reached the road and watched the car's taillights wink out of sight around a dark curve. There was no way for him to catch it.

Just then a taxi approached, heading in the same direction.

Tony's arm flashed up and he ran at the cab. The car stopped, the driver's face annoyed at this approaching drunk. Tony thought if the dude decided to drive on, he would jump onto the hood as it passed by. As Christ was his witness he would.

But instead, the cabbie allowed him to get in. Tony slammed the door shut.

"Hey—" the driver began.

"Follow that car!" Tony barked.

The driver was a middle-aged man in his forties, dark hair streaked with silver and bushy eyebrows that jumped up high on his forehead. He stared at Tony.

"What the fuck you waiting for?" Tony barked again. His arm shot forth, pointing. "Drive, goddammit!"

"You can get out if—" the driver began.

Tony grabbed the man.

Perhaps it was the booze. Perhaps it was the situation. It was probably both. Tony grabbed the cabbie's shoulders and shook him. The driver was not a big man. He grabbed onto Tony's wrists and screamed. Tony screamed back. The driver screamed louder. Tony shouted at him to shut the fuck up or he would be thrown out of the cab. The driver dove forward, reaching for something.

Tony snapped. He did not have time for this shit.

With all his strength, he yanked the driver back and through the gap between the front seats. The man wore a seat belt. Tony swore and clamped his arm around the man's neck, while his other hand went for the seatbelt release button. He found the button and undid it without a problem. The driver screamed and clawed and moved to bite. Tony felt the enamel against his earlobe and instinctively smashed the side of his skull into the driver's face.

"You fucker!" the driver screamed at him, one hand still on Tony's arm, while the other went for his jaw. Tony didn't care. He just wanted the guy to drive. Was that so fucking hard to do? Couldn't he see that he was in a goddamn *hurry?* Jesus H. Christ!

Tony hauled the driver's ass between the front seats and into the back. He somehow opened the rear door and shoved the cabbie out. He held on to the door. Cursing, Tony climbed out and kicked the hand off. He slammed the door and pointed a warning finger at the cabbie on the pavement, who backed away from the crazy stealing his car.

Tony didn't give a shit. He was on a mission from God, or at least Lucy, to find Death. He had found the fucker, and God damn him if he was about to let some shithead taxi driver fuck up his pursuit. Tony jumped in behind the wheel and slammed the door.

"You bastard!" he heard from outside. "You bastard! Fucking bastard!"

Tony put the car into drive and stomped on the accelerator. He threw the seat belt back and swore at it. The headlights showed the road ahead and the curve. He gunned the engine, ignoring any pedestrians and hoping to Lord above they had the good sense to stay out of his way. Then again, if someone did get in his way and he accidentally ran someone down, they weren't going to die anyway.

The thought made him speed up.

Red taillights ahead of him. Tony was sure it was the Taurus. He gunned his car, getting it up to a hundred and closing the distance quickly. When he got close enough, he flicked on his high beams. He was close enough to see three heads in the back seat. One of the heads turned about.

It was Frank.

Death.

And he was smiling.

The head next to Death also turned and squinted.

Target acquired, Tony thought, and brought his car in closer to the Taurus.

CHAPTER 41

"Who the fuck is this guy?" Peters asked no one in particular.

The interior of the car was lit up from the car behind them. The two Hansons were up front, driver and navigator. The driving Hanson swore, reached up and turned the rearview mirror down to get rid of the glare. He hated tailgaters that hung onto his ass.

Death continued to smile.

Peters, sitting on Death's right while Bull Wash was on his left, zeroed in on the smile. He came close to Death's ear.

"You know who he is?" Peters demanded.

Death winced. The Minion's breath reeked.

"He's my boy," Death announced, and distantly thought he should not have revealed that information. Not to these head lice. Then he reconsidered, and thought, *fuckit*. "My amigo. My aide. Probably saw you abducting me."

"Your buddy is he?"

"He's not my . . ." Death shook his head in annoyance. That was a slip. The Mundane wasn't his friend.

"Well, then," Peters smiled, "drive on."

"He's up our ass," the driving Hanson complained. "I can't drive like this."

Peters looked back again. "Wait 'til we're out of town. Then, we'll do something."

Death did not like the sound of that. "What?"

"You just keep your fucking mouth shut," Peters warned him and suddenly smiled. "Please."

Death grimaced. The Minion's breath stank of decaying shit.

"Fucking manshit," Peters swore, frowning at the way the car's interior was lit up. No wonder he wanted to burn this world down.

* * *

Tony realized they were heading out of town. That would not do. It was time to get a little more proactive in his pursuit. Baring teeth, he floored the accelerator and pulled out from behind the Taurus. He overtook and passed the car, hazarding a long look to see who was inside. Death was there, looking stoned. There were four others as well, looking tons pissed off.

Well, Tony thought, they sure as hell won't like this.

He brought the car in front of the Taurus and immediately slammed on the brakes, red taillights blazing in the darkness. The driving Hanson swore aloud as he reciprocated. The Taurus shrieked to a halt. He and his brother lunged forward and cracked their faces on the dash and windshield. In the rear, the men crashed into the backs of the fronts seats with grunts of surprise. No one had thought to wear a seat belt.

Tony got out of his car and marched towards the halted Taurus. He focused on the rear door, ignoring the slumped over figures in the front of the car. One of the rear doors swung open. That was good. He would not have to smash open a window to get to Death.

A figure got out. He straightened up, shaking off the daze of the sudden stop. It was a big man. The size of a pro wrestler. Perhaps he was. Tony didn't give a shit. He shook his hands loose at his sides. If the monster wanted to get busy, he was up for it. The man looked down at Tony, black eyes shining with anger. Tony brought his hands up; it looked like there was going to be some action after all. The rising of his blood shoved aside the effect of the alcohol in his system. His body went into machine mode, and he looked to get some hurting done. Tony closed the distance and swung first, straight from the shoulder, his fist snapping out with bone-shattering force.

His foe brought up his forearms and absorbed the punch.

Tony snarled, and in the next second, threw a jabbing left, aiming for the midsection of the giant. He hit it and felt hard flesh. He hit it again and again in rapid succession, and sidestepped, throwing another punch towards the big man's face. The monster blocked it. Tony roared, feeling a fighter's rage now, an urge to inflict pain, and punched the man in his kidneys, twisting his fist for greater force. It landed hard. He threw another body-jarring punch into his target's right side, then unloaded a salvo of battleship shells square into his foe's mid-section, roaring as he did so.

Then, without warning, his world exploded.

He came to, lying on cold asphalt, staring up into a starless night sky. He was on his back, splayed out, and it slowly occurred to him that he had been hit. What was worse, he had been knocked out. He tried to move something, but all of his limbs were offline. He tried to lift his head, but his neck would have none of it. His jaw ached as if it were impaled on a tuna hook. His awareness suddenly switched viewpoints on him to gaze down on his prone form in the road. Then, he was looking at the sky again, forcing himself to stay awake.

He felt someone grip the front of his shirt. He was lifted up, like a weightlifter curling an easy warm-up rep. Tony's toes tiptoed on the asphalt, and instinct fed him no bullshit as to how serious his situation was. He opened his eyes and rolled his head to stare into eyes so black he thought they were burnt-out sockets. His vision focused a little more, and he saw the icy flecks of life within them.

Bull Wash smiled at the man thing. He let Tony's feet touch the ground and held him upright with one hand clamped iron-tight around his throat. Wash's other fist, the size of a meteor, came in and gently touched Tony's nose. Bull Wash pulled his fist back. Tony saw the cocked fist, reached up weakly with both hands, seeking the thumb of the hand that held him so that he could try a joint lock and escape. He groped at fingers of steel. Bull Wash let him, wondering for a moment what the little man was trying to do.

Then, the fist smashed into his face, and Tony's consciousness imploded into the blackness of his skull.

"What are you doing?" Peters stuck his head out the window and yelled

Wash held his victim up with one arm. He punched Tony's body and face again and again, methodically, like a chef tenderizing a meaty, but still-bloody steak.

"Better kill him," Bull Wash replied, loading up to punch his victim again.

"You *can't* kill him, you fucking moron," Peters wailed.

Bull Wash turned about, his features darkening. In answer, Peters gestured to the man sitting inside the car. The giant's head went back in understanding. "Ooooh, yeah. That's right."

"Besides, you wail on him anymore, you might bring the *other* one on." Peters warned him. "And we don't need that right now."

Bull Wash ceased punishing his man-shaped punching bag. "We leave him, then?"

Peters thought it over for a moment. "Put him in the back seat." He regarded Death smugly. "Your amigo is gonna wake up in 'fucked up' land."

"You guys are fucking tits you know that," Death said. He could see the beating Tony was taking through the windshield. It bothered him to see it. It shouldn't have, considering it was the Mundanes that drove him to this in the first place. This whole situation was beginning to bring down an otherwise great buzz. Death started to question the wisdom in allowing himself to be abducted. "Stupid pricks."

He had Peters' attention.

"Didn't they tell you about me? Who I am?" Death flung at the Minion.

Peters scowled at the man beside him. He didn't like this asshole's attitude. Maia had said to take precautions, but, thus far, Peters could not fathom why. Death struck him as being a drunken wuss. Then, on impulse, he rammed his forehead into Death's face. The Boatman's eyes rolled up and shut, and he slumped forward in the car. Peters let him. So much for that experiment.

Death fell from conscious thought then, but in his descent, he heard a receding voice.

"I know who you are," the voice said.

Then, oblivion.

CHAPTER 42

The snow was still coming down as forensic pathologist Jordy Garlich arrived at the Bellevue City Hospital, New York. He was bundled up in a black trench coat with several layers of cotton sweaters underneath. He was of average height, wore round John Lennon glasses, and was in a bad mood. It was night time, and he hated being called in at night, especially in the winter. Once he retired, in another fifteen years, he was hauling up the family and heading to Florida. He looked forward to adopting an alligator.

He pulled his hat off as he strode towards the hospital mortuary, revealing a head of light brown hair only getting lighter as time went on. Garlich briskly made his way to the front desk, identified himself to the nurse stationed there and asked for directions to the morgue. Garlich thought she wasn't in a particularly cheerful mood. He thanked her and headed for the stairs. The mortuary was two levels down in the basement.

He entered the stairwell and descended, not really paying attention to the bright light and the cement all around him. Garlich had the day off tomorrow, a nice thing, and he should be home with his wife, in bed, his front to her back and a handful of soft breast. But, as he faced the door to the mortuary, this wasn't to be. At least not right away. He knocked on the door before entering.

The room was lit up brightly, despite what one would see in a vampire or zombie movie, and a wall of steel freezers shone. Gurneys were pushed off to the one side in a non-designated gurney parking lot, and the rest of the room was filled with tables containing sheet covered bodies. The air was cold down here and smelled of chemicals. Two men in white examiner's coats were behind a single desk with a computer. One man was standing, the other sitting. Both looked in his direction when he entered.

"Jordy!" One man greeted anxiously and came forward. "Sorry about this. I wouldn't have called you if I didn't think it was really important. Extremely important."

He had sandy hair and a bad complexion, as if he had fallen asleep in a chicken coop and the hens had pecked him without remorse. But the man's smile was warm and bright. He shook Garlich's hand, pumped it twice, and indicated the man sitting behind the desk.

"This is—"

There was a groan in the room then, a low sound of air escaping lungs but ending in a tired note of pain. Garlich looked to Aaron Roeder, the man greeting him, and Aaron merely cocked his head uneasily before nodding that, yes, he heard it too, and, no, Garlich wasn't imagining things.

It came from a huge examination table, where a mass of something was covered by a dark grey sheet. Another table was set up beside it. An assortment of instruments lay on the table: shiny scalpels, bone saws, rib cutters—the heavy shears used to cut through rib cages—and hammers with specially fitted hooks to remove the tops of skulls.

The man behind the desk slowly got to his feet and made meaningless motions with his hands as if he didn't quite know what to do with them.

"What the hell was that?" Garlich asked in a quiet voice.

Roeder's smile disappeared. "That's the reason why I called you here tonight. Seems we have—" he gestured to the other man, "something of a puzzle, I guess you could say."

"Someone presumed dead woke up?" Garlich asked in all seriousness. It happened once, back in the '90s. A young skateboarder who had been electrocuted suddenly came to life on the medical examiner's table.

Roeder didn't respond right away. He forced a smile. "Something like that. This is Ted Myer. He's the Medical Examiner on duty here tonight."

Garlich shook the man's hand. He then faced Roeder. "So, why are you here?"

"Ted called me in, just after the, uh, *deceased* started making noises."

It was usual for bodies to sigh or make "last breaths" as organs released pent up oxygen. Garlich focused on Roeder. The man was a senior, experienced doctor that knew all about what a body usually did or didn't do after death. Garlich usually called *him* up to ask for advice if he had something different or just to confirm a hunch. Not the other way around.

Garlich was not a person to assume much of anything. "Like what we just heard?"

Both men nodded. They looked like shit. Myer had the nervous ticks of a person in bad need of nicotine. Roeder didn't smoke, or drink as far as Garlich knew, but he looked as if he needed a shot of something.

"What have you got?" Garlich asked.

Roeder and a quiet, nervous looking Myer led him to the table on the other side of the room. Roeder switched on the overhead examiner's light while Myer took a hold of the grey sheet and pulled it back.

Garlich blinked. A heavy sigh escaped him, and he dearly wished Roeder had called someone else. There was no way he was going to sleep *this* night. It was the worse death he had seen in a while, and he saw the remains were actually on two examiner's tables pushed together. Given the condition of the corpse, it was easy to see why.

It was a woman. An older woman, that much Garlich could tell. Her body and skull had been crushed by some god-awful weight. Myer unravelled the sheet back, all the way to the corpse's toes. Her body mass had been flattened out as if she had been aged cookie dough mashed by an uneven rolling pin.

Garlich pursed his lips together. He straightened up as he beheld the sight before him. "When was she brought in?"

Myer spoke. "Two days ago. Early morning. I wasn't here and there was a backlog. I came on today."

Garlich gave no reaction. He leaned in close to the corpse. The woman had been crushed to a bloody pulp. Shards of bone stretched black skin up towards the light, and in some cases, raw bone splinters had punched through tissue. The smell of blood and gut was not so strong. The Diener had done a good job in cleaning her up. Garlich inspected the carnage of the body. There were sections that had been crushed, but flesh and tissue matter had risen to create grooves. He was reminded of Saturday morning cartoons his kid watched, where the character that gets squished by an anvil walks away with the shape of the anvil in its body. The cause of death was obvious. Someone had run her down, and kept on running her over.

"Cause of death looks to be homicide in nature," Garlich declared. This wasn't a hit and run. This was a hit and mash. He touched the woman's ruined ribcage. "What tests have you—"

The corpse groaned again. Garlich froze. The hair on the back of his neck pricked up like needles, and his testicles drew up. He took one step back from the woman on the table and stared in fascination at her destroyed face. Half a red jaw had pierced her cheek. White jelly from destroyed eyes surrounded it. The other half of the jaw was missing, probably pulverized.

Garlich stood and stared, listening. When no other sounds came from the body, he started to breathe again.

"What was that?" he calmly asked the men present.

Roeder had long come to respect the steel of Garlich. In his time, he had witnessed a few forensic people lose their lunch or nerve when examining bodies. Not Garlich. The man was Mr. Spock.

"That," Roeder informed him, looking him in the eye, "is the reason why I called you down here. She's not . . . quite dead."

Garlich thought he was crazy. But he did not say so, and he would not say so in front of Myer anyway. He did not know Myer. But Garlich knew Roeder. He was a professional to be respected and listened to.

But, and Garlich's eyes swept over the body before him, *Jesus Christ*.

Myer was running his hands over his face now. He was sweating freely, and his skin had lost all color. He was still with them, although he dearly wanted to be somewhere, anywhere else.

"How . . . are you defining this?" Garlich quietly asked Roeder.

Roeder smiled weakly. "Well, that's my question to you. How would you define this? Besides being something unnatural."

Across the table, Myer giggled. Both Garlich and Roeder looked questioningly at him. Myer stifled it.

Another groan, the softest of sighs, left the area where the mouth would have been if the body had been whole. The sound brought the three men to attention.

"She's been here for two days," Garlich stated.

Myer nodded with enthusiasm. Garlich studied the way the woman's right hand had been rolled to a pulp. It looked like a purple-black oven mitten made of flesh and bone fragments.

"Is this . . ." *a joke* Garlich was about to say, but the expression on Roeder's face was the honest to Christ truth. "This is . . ." he gestured with a hand, as if performing a feat of magic. He could not finish his sentence.

"There are brain waves," Roeder informed him. "We've determined that much. No pulse. No heartbeat. No breath. No other regular determiners that signify life."

"Autopsy?"

"We were in the process of performing an autopsy when she started . . . making noise," Roeder told him, shrugging his shoulders as he did so. He pointed to a place in the woman's dull, black torso, "This is where Myer made his first incision, and when she first cried out. We tried again, in the same spot, and the same reaction. That's when we did what tests we could without . . . causing her much discomfort."

Myer's hand found his throat. He pulled up a small silver crucifix hanging from a chain and began rubbing it between his fingers. Garlich caught the gesture and chose to ignore it. He built his career on knowing facts. He wasn't ready to start thinking about the undead just yet. He sighed inwardly. He shouldn't even be thinking the thought, but he was no fool . . . and he had seen enough zombie movies to know what was up.

The three men stood silently then, regarding the animated non-corpse on the examination table. Myers continued to rub his crucifix. Somewhere, coming from the stainless steel sinks, a single drop of water *plucked* against metal.

"What do you suggest?" Roeder asked, more than willing to follow Garlich's lead.

Garlich thought about it. "First, morphine," he said quietly. Then he nodded towards the examiner's table. "For her, too . . ."

CHAPTER 43

At the same time Roeder was fixing a painkiller drip for the crushed woman in the morgue, other things were developing across the globe. A Jordanian man, accused and convicted of strangling his three children, was led to the prison gallows in the brightness of early morning. Prayers were said, as well as curses, for the soul of Habis Akbar as he was led up the steps, positioned over a metal trapdoor and blindfolded with a black cloth bag. He felt the rope going around his neck, felt it tighten, and waited for death, whispering to himself that the afterlife would not be as miserable as the events that drove him to take the lives of his children.

When the lever was thrown and the trapdoor flew open, Habis fell the regulation six feet into emptiness, the rope and his own body weight snapping his neck with little effort. He spun clockwise, and the officials watching noted how the man's legs kicked once, twice, and then were still. The execution was quick. Habis's neck broke. His spinal cord severed. They let him hang for several minutes, and in that time, he was deprived of oxygen. His jugular veins and carotid arteries, unable to circulate blood, caused cerebral oedema. Under his mask, Habis's eyes bulged and his tongue plunged out. Little blood marks from burst capillaries slowly appeared on his face and eyes. His bladder released, his bowels let loose and the sweet, strong stink of shit flowered the air.

When the prison official lowered him to the ground and released the rope, they removed the mask to see a purple-faced Habis, stretched neck and all, blinking frantically. From his mouth came the growing gush of a soundless scream. The prison officials, taken aback by the blunder, nevertheless were professionals. They quickly masked the criminal, replaced the rope and, rather than carrying the man up the step to the platform once again, simply used a mechanical winch to haul his carcass up until it dangled again, motionlessly, a good foot from the ground.

They hung him for ten minutes this time.

When they removed the mask a second time, the strangulation marks around his neck were ghastly, but not near as frightening as Habis's eyes, bug-eyed and bloodshot from burst capillaries. He blinked at the world and tried very, very hard to scream.

One shaken official did not want to hear that scream. He drew his service revolver and shot Habis at point blank range in the chest.

Habis continued to blink.

The officer shot three more rounds into Habis's chest, exploding it.

Habis made low grunting noises when he should not have.

Sweating now and fully aware that the others were swearing aloud and calling for holy intervention, the officer steeled himself, took careful aim and blew out the back of Habis's head with one shot. Right between the eyes.

He felt his knees tremble when the grunting continued.

Most men fled the room then. The shooting officer and two others remained and gathered around. Composing themselves as best as they could, they removed Habis's ruined body to his final resting place, covering his head so that they did not have to stare at his destroyed face. They buried him in the late afternoon in a desert graveyard for criminals, hurrying away quickly before they could hear the soft grunts of the still-not-dead Habis escaping from the earth—little, pathetic, God-frightening noises that continued on even as they were throwing the dirt on him.

The aftereffects of the sloppy execution were quick. All the men were immediately counselled for the disturbing events of the morning. One man, however, the officer who had shot Habis five times, quietly returned home. He locked himself away in his apartment with his own firearm, and sat before a window overlooking the great city of Amman. It was evening, and the sky was becoming orange at the edges. He lit himself a cigarette, placed his loaded revolver on the table nearby. He thought about his career and life and the gun on the table. He thought about the grunting Habis, and how they buried a man that should have been dead. He thought about that for a long time. And as the sun dropped below the cityscape line, and the day became black, he took longer draws on his cigarette. When he finished it, he lit a new one.

Finally, in the darkness of his room and the glow of the moon, he eyed his weapon on the table. Eventually, with fingers trembling, he touched the gun metal, caressed it.

And took it into his hand.

CHAPTER 44

In the blackness of unconsciousness, Tony heard voices speak once in a while, loud and clear. They said nothing important to him, and he would not be able to recall exactly what it was they were talking about, but he heard them, like a child setting his ear to a thick door and listening to big words spoken on the other side. He would hear them twice, and then no more.

Then, he woke up.

It was cold. That was the first sensation he felt. With his chin resting on his chest, he kept his eyes closed as he came to his senses. He sat there, in between two warm bodies of people he did not know, in the rear seat of the car he had once pursued. He did a damage check on himself and noted with satisfaction that nothing else hurt except his head. It felt like there was a nail in his skull, and it was gouging out a message on the inside of his brainpan. Tony cringed and felt the sticky, moistureless, gummy feeling that came with the morning after a night of heavy drinking. He smacked his lips groggily and wished for water.

Then, he realized his mistake.

"Think he's coming around," said a voice to his left.

"Mhm," agreed a voice on his right, quick like a PC stereo check.

"I think he's playing now."

Tony felt someone shift beside him. A stinging backhand slapped across his face. His eyes went open in reflex, and he raised his fist to protect himself.

He felt something cold at his throat and froze.

"That's right, dicksuck," the voice on the left purred. "That's right."

The Minion named Peters turned and stared Tony in the eye. Tony cringed, both from the nail in his head and the steel at his throat. He couldn't remember ever having a knife this close to him. Peters studied him quietly, seeing what he was about. Tony saw the back of Death's head between Peters and the giant that had subdued him. The big man was now driving. From what Tony could remember, before being laid out cold on the highway, they weren't in the front seat in the beginning. Why had they changed positions? Why would anyone change positions while driving? To give the lead driver a break?

Jesus and Mary, Tony thought, where were they?

"You just sit there and be good." Peters winked at the Hanson holding the knife, and Tony felt the blade drop away. "There's no need for rough shit. We can get that anytime we want. Anytime we want."

"He's awake?" Death asked, interested.

Peters altered his gaze just a bit so he could stare at the side of Death's head. He did not speak right away but merely stared like a carpenter, instinctively focusing on where to hammer in the next nail.

"Now what makes you so goddamn concerned?"

"Just askin', is all."

Peters continued to stare at Death's profile. He stared at the contours of the man's ear, inhaled and smelled the budding sweet odour of a body gone for a long time without a shower.

"Funny shit," Peters said then. "You askin' seems to me like you're worried about this piece of shit. And why would that be? I mean, you're here, aren't cha? If you gave a good goddamn in the first place, you wouldn't even fuckin' be here. I'd still be back at the station, waitin' for the call. But now, I'm here, *we're* here, driving, and you're right here with us." Peters smirked then, showing yellow teeth. "You are a fucked up piece of work."

"Only asked if he was awake," Death muttered back. "No need for a fucking speech."

The grin disappeared off Peters' face, and Tony felt the temperature in the car, as cold as it was, drop even more. He had a sense for things like this, and he sensed that right here and now, this man talking to Death from the passenger side was about to kill him.

But Tony was wrong.

Instead Peters reached up and gripped Death's chin. He leaned in close to his ear and opened his mouth and hissed. It was a hiss of pleasure, just before the bite that would release a blast of blood. Tony cringed for a moment. He thought the man was going to bite Death's ear right off.

"Here's a speech for you, old man," Peters said in a low voice.

Tony knew Death would not like the *old man* reference.

"You just sit there and keep your tongue inside your head, and when we get to where we're going, you'll be just alright. You'll see. But if you keep asking stupid questions or just keep on shootin' the shit—which would bewilder the fuck outta me—I'll make a mental list of it and remind you later of every stupid thing you said. When I'm peeling the skin off you, and putting' fire to what's exposed."

For a moment, Death did not say anything, and Tony was both relieved and surprised. He was surprised Death did not say anything back. In the short time Tony had known Frank, he always seemed to have the last word. But this time...

"*Fuck you*," Death said clearly.

Peters' expression slackened in surprise.

"What did you just say to me?" Peters said in a menacing tone.

"You heard me," Death replied, and cocked his head away from his interrogator.

"I don't think I did,"

"Then, you're fuckin' *deaf*, as well," Death said in a voice that was filling up with a sad, sad anger at the other's repeated failure to recognize just *who* in fact he was addressing.

Peters did not feel the same way. He leaned in close. Death pulled away. Peters grabbed Death's skull and pulled it towards him.

"Fuckin' stupid, too," Death said.

In the rear view mirror, Tony caught the brow of the big man driving arch upwards in surprise, his attention diverted.

Peters pulled Death's ear and touched it to the angry gash of his mouth. "You listen to me now, old man, and you listen good. We still got a ways to go, but when we get to where we're going, the first fucking thing I do is tie you down and shoot you up."

"Just like I said, fuckin' stupid. What do you think torture is gonna do, hm?" Death countered.

"I'll ask the questions, shitbird."

"You wanna bring *him* into this? Hm? Go ahead and torture me or try and fuck me up. You'll bring him along faster than shit through a sick bitch of a goose."

Peters bared his teeth. "That's where you're wrong, fucker. Think we were driving you all the way up here without any toys to play with? Think we would miss out on the motherfucking, almighty ending? We *asked* for this shit, motherfucker. We asked for it. When the time comes down, we're going to be inflicting pain on your ass like you've only just begun to imagine. And fuck if'n I'll make a vow right here to hear you sing out. I'll make you sing, you old cowfucker. I'll make you. And there'll be no need to wait. I got something special back in the trunk. That was my plan all along, see. Some of that spinal shit they inject into women just before birth. Right into your spine. You won't feel a thing." Peters was smiling now. "You won't feel shit when we start taking turns cutting pieces off you and cooking them right in front of you. That's right, you righteous old fuck, we're heading out for a midnight barbeque, and you is the main steak. You won't feel a fucking thing. At least, I don't figure you'll be able to feel anything. All you'll be able to do is watch us cut and cook. We'll start with your balls first. Do us up some honest to gawd prairie oysters."

That drew chuckles from all around, except Tony. He had no idea what prairie oysters were, but the fate these maniacs had planned for Death made him panic. They had to get out of here.

"And the nice thing about the cook up," Peters went on, "is that you'll be able to talk or curse all you want. I might even feed some of you to you. How's that sound?"

"Fucked up," Death admitted.

Peters grinned at his own wickedness.

"In all my existence," Death went on quietly, "I've met Minions before. And as a fucking rule, Minions are the stupidest goddamn motherfuckers ever to grow out of fly shit."

Peters blinked and released his grip on Death's head.

Death went on. "I mean, I've met and carried over Minions that without a doubt have done shit, the stupidest shit, just like the shit you're talking now, and think 'this is the smartest shit—the smartest shit I've evah, *evah* done'. And it's simply too goddamn annoying for me to listen to anymore. I'm so fucking bored and fed up listening to stupid fucks like you. The truly *special* kind of stupid. You know that level of stupid? Of course, you don't—because you're a fuckin' *dolt*. Why am I even asking you such a question? I know the answer. And you, you know who I am? I mean, do you honest to fuck *realize* just who you got here? Beside you? Huh? You know who you got here, you dipfuck? Who you're conversing with?"

Peters' face was crimson, "No one talks to me that way."

"No, I can see that you don't," Death went on, ignoring the Minion at his ear. "And that just proves my fucking point. There has never *ever* been a Minion of any fucking goddamn worth, and there never will be. You're all just too fucking stupid. And you, in particular, are a fucking moron. All of you. A tit has more intelligence. No, wait, a tit is a fucking *genius* compared to you. The Mundane I can forgive because he doesn't know what's what, but you should. Who gives a flying squirrel shit about you little chicken fucks? And you *still* don't know who I am? I can see that you don't."

Then, Tony saw it, clear as the day beyond the windshield. The man listening to Death went silent and his eyes narrowed with caution . . . and fear. He suddenly *knew* who he had caught and he drew back, sensing with growing dread something he forgot. A vulnerability he only now realized. Tony knew who he had, too, just as clear as he was sensing something very bad about to happen.

And then Death, for this was *Death* in all of its frankness, made it so.

"Listen up, Tony," he said.

Death looked ahead at the narrow highway, flanked on either side by snow-capped wilderness. Then he gazed into the rear-view mirror, and Tony met his dangerous stare there.

"It's time to introduce myself."

Tony's eyes damn near bulged out of his head. He had been warned so many times now, so many times, that even as Death finished his warning, Tony knew he should have *known* this was going to happen.

The Minions had left Tony's hands free for whatever reason, and he clamped them over his ears and shut his eyes. His palms were practically in his ear canals, and for the needed second, he heard nothing, but expected something very bad to happen. Then, he felt a vibe ripple through the air like spent lightening, and wet warmth washed over him and made him open his eyes. The short time he had his eyes open, then closed, and then open again, was like a mad animator flipping one page of a very short but horrific cartoon. What had once been a clean and intact interior was now madness. The four men—now four headless torsos—fountained blood into the cold air like sputtering fire hydrants clearing their pipe system. The two bodies on either side of Tony were spasming like bodies being fried by an electrical current. Reaching and clinching hands waved in front of and around Tony's face, striking him harmlessly, searching for *anything* to grab onto for reality's sake. Tony was covered in blood, bone, and brain matter. The car seats were covered in more blood, bone, and brain matter. The windshield was covered in a thick blood stew.

And that thought smashed through Tony's mind.

They couldn't see where they were going.

No sooner had he realized their situation when the car veered to the right and off the highway. It sailed over a drop. Tony felt weightless for a split *"oh fuck me"* second. The car hit the ground hard, and Tony felt his teeth mash together. His head slammed against the ceiling. Bodies crashed into and landed on him. Hands of the headless grabbed and released him. He slapped the hands away. More blood blinded his vision. Death was yelling, "fuckohfuckohfuckohfuck*OHFU*—"

And then the car was rolling.

Tony heard an explosion.

And for the second time in as many days, a first for Tony, he was unconscious again.

CHAPTER 45

When Tony woke up, the first thing he realized was the amount of blood covering his face and in his eyes. Through his clogged vision, he blinked and squinted and saw the headless bodies of his captors slumped over at interesting angles. He moved an arm and wiped their gore out of his eyes as best as he could. He wanted a rag. He studied himself and groaned. He was covered in blood. He felt dizzy then, and closed his eyes, breathing through his mouth. He tasted more blood, winced, and spat it out. For a moment, Tony simply lay there underneath the bodies and limbs of the two men in the back seat with him. He realized being in the back seat had saved him. He had wound up on the floor, wedged in firmly between the seats. Feeling better, he opened his eyes again and moved his arms. Everything worked for him, and he untangled himself from the limbs and corpses, grunting in loud disgust. Fuck, there was *so much* blood. How many litres were there in a human body? Eleven? It did not occur to him just how much eleven litres was until it was all over the place. Then multiply it by *four*. His clothes were saturated with it, dripping and sticky. He wiped his face again, leaving wide raspberry smears across his cheeks. A panic was building up inside of him, and he arched his back. He saw how the roof of the car had been splashed-sprayed with blood. Tony heaved bodies off himself. He reached over one and felt for the door handle. It would not budge. He studied the shattered window, noting the shards of glass lining the bottom where the pane rose and fell as needed. Tony put his elbow over the thick glass and wormed his way out of the car. He flopped his upper body onto the snowy ground and pulled his legs out behind him, landing on his chest and rolling over onto his back. The snow was deep and thick, and felt absolutely wonderful. The cold drove the fog of the crash out of Tony's brain He just lay there, gulping in mouthfuls of clean northern air. He drew it down through his nose, becoming instantly high from its purity. Or perhaps it was just the relief of being free of the car and the dead meat within. Whatever it was, Tony did not care. He laid there, closed his eyes and wished that when he died, he could be buried in a snow drift.

The cold began to work into his bones, until the blood coating him became thick. He opened his eyes and got to his elbows. He looked at the wreck of the car. Getting to his feet with loud grunts and curses, he staggered to the window. Tony peered inside and set his jaw against the sight and smells of the corpses inside. The four headless corpses.

Where was Frank?

Tony noticed the windshield. It was shattered, blown outward by something leaving the car. He stood up and took in the huge tree that the car had wrapped its right side around, crunching its front and engine block with quiet indifference.

"Oh, shit," Tony murmured to himself. He staggered through the deep snow, pushing through thick spruce boughs covered in white, and headed behind the tree and beyond.

He spotted Death sprawled out and motionless at the base of a tree. Tony went to him, swearing all the way. He could see the man's right leg twisted out at a ninety-degree angle and figured it for broken. Frank's face was also cut up and bruised, his flesh whipped by stiff boughs as he had flown through them. Blood seeped from a deep cut in his scalp.

"Holy shit," Tony muttered, standing over the still form. Death looked banged up pretty bad but, seeing as he went through a windshield, Tony supposed it could have been a lot worse. Death had flown from the car to come to rest some twenty feet away. Tony dropped to his knees and patted Death's cheek. No response. He felt for a pulse. There was none, but what did *that* mean? Was Death really alive anyway? He slapped him again, harder this time. No, Death was mortal, Tony thought. He pissed out enough beer to prove it.

Then, Death's eyelids fluttered, and black eyes calmly looked up at Tony. The Mundane sighed.

Death screamed.

The sound froze Tony to the spot. Death screamed out again, ending in a deep throat sound of agony. He bared white teeth and hissed out steam on the winter air.

"*Jesus Christ!*" Death barked and looked down at his leg. What he saw made him roll his head on his shoulders in exasperated agony. "Christ on a monkey stick! My leg! My legs!" He reached for them and stopped just before making contact. Setting his jaw, he grabbed Tony instead and hauled his face in close.

"*Knock me out!*" Death commanded.

"Wha—?" Tony sputtered, confusion slackening his features.

"I said *knock me out!!* Oh, JESUS H. CHRIST!" Death released him and fell back on the snow. He bared his teeth at the pain he was experiencing. This was not part of his plan.

"*Listen to me,*" Death hissed through a set jaw. "If you don't knock me out right now, the meanest goddamnedest bastard in all of existence is going to–" Death winced. The pain he felt took his breath away. He crunched his eyes together and got his breath under control. "he'll come *right here.*"

"Wha—?" Tony could only say stupidly.

Death looked him straight in the eye. "*Do it.*"

Not understanding why, Tony made a fist and, shaking his head, sent it across the side of Death's head.

It did not knock him out.

"SWEET FUCK ALMIGHTY!" Death wailed in Tony's face. "I said knock me out!"

Blinking, Tony reared back and struck again, rocking Death's head to the side.

Death's face rolled back to face him.

"You fucking *moron!*"

Tony's brow knotted up in annoyance. He hit him again. Harder.

Death only grunted, still conscious, and gave him a glassy-eyed glare, "Y'punch like a gay leprechaun. No fucking wonder your Ma is in the hospital! Now hi—"

At the mention of his mother Tony fired his fist out, twisting it for extra force, and slammed it square on Death's chin. The sudden force snapped Death's head back, his spinal cord cracking like a whip, and he went limp.

Silence enveloped Tony. He stared down at the unconscious mess that was Death, and gauzy snowflakes began to fall.

CHAPTER 46

In another part of the country, on a straight strip of the 401 of the TCH, the force known as Pain tensed up, hunched over and put both of his hands on the dashboard as if bracing for impact. His eyes narrowed to slits as if he had heard something, but wasn't quite sure. He cocked his head, straining to get a whiff of the vibe that had totally and unexpectedly caught his attention. It was a very special vibe, one that Pain had not felt in ages. Like an ancient, evil spider hanging in a web that spanned places even it had forgotten about, it waited for that one gossamer strand to vibrate again, to tell it exactly where its stricken prey lay.

But it did not. Pain grunted like a Cro-Magnon brute, his brow furrowing as he willed for that single delicious tingle he felt so abruptly. He bared his teeth, impressive incisors flashing, as hope began to give way to bestial anger. Fingers began digging into the dashboard of the car, actually cracking it, displaying a strength the Stickman did not want to believe possible. The man had already freaked him out as, at times, he could swear Pain *flickered* in his peripheral vision, as if for the briefest time, just a blink, he was no longer there.

Instead, seeing an opportunity and recognizing it as such, he decided right then to rid himself of a passenger he had come to hate and fear.

Swinging with every ounce of might he could muster, Stickman swung his fist right into the exposed nose of Pain.

The nose exploded in a flash of blood and cartilage. Stickman felt the pebble-like grind of shattered bone and gristle under his fist. He could not bring his hand away fast enough as Pain's blood gushed over his fist. Stickman felt a very real chill electrify his spine and senses. Pain's blood was as *black* and crude as raw viscous oil. The sight of Pain's blood spraying from the wreck of his nose paralyzed the Stickman.

But only for a second.

"Bludova*bitch!*" Stickman swore and ploughed the edge of his fist into Pain's face, again. And again. He grabbed Pain's head and rammed it forward, bouncing it off the dashboard. Stickman pressed his advantage. He kept his left hand on the wheel and reached with his right across Pain's body. He grabbed for the door release. The car swerved, and Stickman had to jerk the wheel to keep himself on his side of the road. His eyes flicked from the road to the door handle to the road, again.

Pain grabbed his wrist.

Screaming, Stickman yanked back. The door popped opened a fraction. Pain was regaining his senses, his eyes focused on Stickman. Pain smiled, showing teeth smeared in foamy black.

Stickman freaked.

His right fist flew into Pain's face again and again. He got his right leg up and drove it into the hip of Pain, shoving the thing—for this was no true man—up against the door and forcing it open. Pain grabbed for the head rest of his seat, eyes glazed from the force of Stickman's attack.

Then, Stick slammed on the breaks.

The result was not as spectacular as hoped. The car was speeding along at roughly ninety kilometres an hour on a deserted highway. When Stickman hit the brakes, the car spun around twice before coming to a halt. Stickman held onto the wheel with both hands, his upper body wedged between the dash and the windshield. Pain crashed up against the door and dash. His shoulder pressed into the hard plastic to a point where any second Stickman expected to hear something crack. But he wasn't going to wait for that. Adrenalin shooting through him and his foot-eye coordination coming together as only months of hard training could develop, Stickman contorted himself in the driver's seat until both feet were aimed at Pain's torso. Then, he pistoned his legs out.

Pain flew from the car like a heavy bag of unwanted pig flesh. He landed hard on his side and rolled onto his stomach, a trail of black blood marking his passage. Stickman couldn't give a rat's ass if the dude was dead or alive. He frantically reached across and groped for the door. He slammed it hard enough to make the car shake on its chassis. He crashed back into the driver's seat, put the car in gear, and stomped on the accelerator. The tires screeched and the car shot forward like an out-of-shape missile. Stickman drove the vehicle at arm's length like a stock-car racer making up for lost time. He grinned wickedly. He had tossed the motherfucker out the door! Out on his ass! Stickman howled and glanced into the rearview mirror as if expecting to see a rising shadow on the receding horizon.

Then, his smile faltered.

Stick realized he was driving in the wrong direction, back towards Nova Scotia.

"Well, *fuck* me!" the Stickman swore as he quickly dropped his speed and did a two-move turn around, working the gears of the car like a professional about to head into a killer turn. The scene ahead of him was grey and overcast, with snow heaped on the sides of the black strip of road. It looked like a wet spine running up between two huge, white shoulders, towards a place where a head should be, but wasn't.

And on the right side of the road, just getting to his knees, was the Stickman's fucking bane.

Baring his teeth, Stickman pushed down on the gas. The car sped up, heading straight for the figure now standing up. Stickman hissed an oath. The fucker wasn't moving anywhere, wasn't even attempting to get out of the way. The car shot forward, and for the briefest of seconds, the Stickman knew what the bastard was going to *try* to do, and could not believe it.

Pain saw the car come straight at him. Fury and agony buzzed through his person, making him feel more alive than any million people escaping certain death. A four-wheeled dumpster of a car rushed at him. Pain could see the Mundane behind the steering wheel of the Sunbird, hunched over and bracing for the impact that was to come. Pain hunched over and spread his hands, palms up, his knees bent. He smiled, blackness dripping.

The Stickman saw the man tense up. He could not believe that he was actually going to attempt to jump the car.

Then, Stickman remembered who his former passenger was.

At the last possible moment, Stickman cut the steering wheel to the left, clipping the killer pedestrian with the side of his car and sending him over the hood. A hand slapped down on the windshield, but the man kept on flying, failing to secure a grip. Stickman's Sunbird did a fishtail, and he struggled to contain it. He hit the brakes and spun around, looping again on the highway. He expected any minute for the car to go off the road.

But it didn't.

Instead, he came to a halt, realized he was pointed in the direction he wanted to go, and urgently looked in his rearview mirror and then over his shoulder.

Pain was down again, a black lump on a shoulder of white.

Even though he wanted nothing better than to turn back and drive over the form to ensure the man was road kill, the Stickman did perhaps one of the smartest things he would ever do in his life.

He drove on, leaving the prone figure behind and watching it wink out of existence. He fought down his fear and began to relax after a few moments, realizing that he was free of the *thing*, and he had left him in the middle of God knows where, in the death throes of a contrary winter. The thought put a satisfied smirk on his face. *And fuck Jazz, too*, for whatever unknown reasons the oath popped into his head. Now, it was on with his mission.

A kilometre behind the Stickman and still lying on his back, Pain petulantly pursed his lips and gazed up at the overcast sky. The Sunbird's receding roar grew distant and disappeared. All was quiet around him except for the dreary wails of a dying winter.

Pain sighed.

That didn't go *quite* the way he wanted.

CHAPTER 47

In another part of the country, a black Toyota Celica hummed along Highway 401, heading west. From the air, it looked like a glistening, hard-shell bug zipping along a frosted strip of grey. It looked peaceful.

It was anything *but* inside the vehicle.

Sitting like a king in the passenger seat, Fear stared ahead at the snow covered morning and swore. This was taking forever. He should have called Time a while back, but he was enjoying doing what he did best with the two cattle with him. Idly, he fished out his cell and dialled a number, not paying any heed to the two terrified Mundanes.

It took Danny everything he could to maintain control of the car with both hands on the wheel when Fear reached in his coat and brought out the phone. That simple movement alone almost made the legendary bouncer defecate himself in pure panic. He did not know who this man was, or what he wanted, except that his orders were brief after both Crew and he had been subdued.

"Get in the car," and "Drive."

Those five words had carried such a wave of fear that both the bouncer and the hit man were reduced to almost senselessness. Danny did not look in the rear-view mirror. He did not want to. He focused on the road ahead. He knew Crew was back there, curled up as if someone had smashed his testicles. Helpless and silent, with both eyes closed and hoping beyond hope that the fear within him would soon pass.

Crew had been like that for nearly three hours.

How much fear could a sane mind take before deep psychological damage was inflicted? Danny did not have the capacity to think about it. He felt his heart banging in his ears. He felt the rush of blood in his temples. The swell of desperate energy in his chest. He fought to contain the adrenalin coursing through his system, surging through his legs and just begging him to bolt. Just drive the car off the road, flip the fucker and fucking *jet* to higher ground. He breathed in deeply, trying desperately to control his fear and just barely hanging on.

"It's me," the man on his left said into the phone. Those words made Danny flinch as if he were about to be hit. In the back seat, Crew drew himself in even further, like a human armadillo.

Fear noticed the jerk of his driver's head and gave him such a look of menace that the Mundane actually whimpered and hunkered down over the steering wheel.

"How are you doing?" Time asked on the other end of the connection.

"We're on our way," Fear informed him with a scowl. He had no patience with Time's pleasantries. The Entity acted as if he were in an amusement park with free access to all the rides. His brightness made Fear want to tell him off. They were at *war* here.

"I need a boost," Fear said curtly.

"Now?"

Fear sighed heavily.

Sensing the denseness of his remark, Time quickly sought to correct himself. "Yes, yes, of course. Right now. Get them ready. You know where you're going?"

Fear hung up. Of course, he fucking knew where he was going. After this was all over, he and Time and the bitch called Lucy were going to have a not too pleasant sit down. He stewed in annoyance at the thought of her letting Tony the Tool actually eject him from what he still considered to be his ride. Although, all things aside, and flicking a quick glance at the sleek interior of the Celica, this was much better.

Still, it was the *principle* of the matter.

She made him lose control of a Mundane. He absolutely hated anyone who did that.

He sat and chewed on thoughts of revenge. Then, he remembered Time's words regarding the zombies in the car with him. To *get them ready*.

Fear's head tilted to the side. It was bad day to be a Mundane. If these pusheads were of any worth at all, they would make it. If not, well, Fate would be another bitch Fear was going to have a chat with. All considered, there were going to be a couple of Entities walking around with some pretty sore tits after he was through with them.

Fear stabbed his cell phone back into his coat. He yanked his seatbelt down and over his shoulder, wishing it was someone's tongue.

Fuck the Mundanes.

With a silent word, the command was given.

And without any warning at all, Danny and Crew went into warp-speed hell.

CHAPTER 48

Giant wet gobs of snow fell and gathered on the shoulders of a quiet Tony Levin as he sat and studied the unconscious form of Death lying before him. He wore nothing heavier than his black winter trench coat, the one he got compliments on just about everywhere he went back in Halifax. If he waited with his ass freezing to the ground he sat on, the heavy material of the coat would be covered in white and Tony would simply become one with the landscape. He felt numb all over and wondered if the crash had anything to do with that. Or perhaps being covered in blood had something to do with it? Or was it that he just knocked out the man known as Death? Did he do the right thing? Death had commanded him to do it, so how could he be at fault? And then there was the shit that Frank screamed at him about being found by someone. That made Tony think. Whoever it was, it might have been an idea to let him find them, just so they could use his car or truck or whatever and get the hell out of the country. Tony looked up then. The sky was grey, overcast, and freezer-cold looking. He'd have to start moving soon and drag Frank's unconscious ass with him. That was something he really looked forward to. He took a deep breath and considered the time. How long before dark? And where were they anyway? There was no sun above, and Tony's sense of direction was totally unreliable. He looked back to the wreck of the car and the highway beyond. It wasn't even a highway. It was a two lane road.

A two lane road.

The thought stuck in Tony's head. He got to his feet and stretched, testing his limbs. Everything seemed to work fine, but he could smell the blood on his person. Tony made a face as he took himself in. He was a mess. Completely covered in the life juice of four very dead men.

That thought made him pause.

He looked back at the car.

Jesus Christ.

Those guys were *dead*.

What was up with that? Tony's right hand came up to rub his jaw as he stared at the car and the corpses within. Did Frank lose his power or something? Did it have something to do with his knocking Frank out? Was Frank really out? Tony gazed down at the still form of the man, an angry grimace on his face. Even while unconscious, Death still managed to look pissed off. Wondering if he was faking it, Tony kicked him in the ribs, shaking off the snow that had gathered.

Death did not move.

His grimace was still there.

Tony kicked the man again. Harder.

Nothing.

"You suck on donkey cocks," Tony shot off. There was no reaction at all. He was convinced. Death was done. For the time being, anyway. But it still did not solve why their abductors were currently deceased. Muttering oaths under his breath, Tony supposed it was no big deal. Right now he had a bigger problem on his hands, namely the carcass of one dead to the world Death.

Tony made his way back to the car, not really wanting to, but he felt drawn to the gruesome display within. Four men with their heads blown up and off. Tony shook his head in amazement. That was *power*. He supposed that was all right since Frank was Death and all, and should have some sort of special power to go along with the job but *fuck!* Say your name and *whoomf!* Lay out all within hearing range. Un-fucking-believable.

Tony studied the bloody remains inside the car. He knew what he had to do, and set about going through the coats of the headless dead and pulling out everything he could find. He found a cell phone in the chest pocket of the driver's shirt, which was good as he could not find the one Tim had given him not so long ago. His relief at finding the phone did not last—the thing would not work. Tony opened it, held it up to the sky as if it might improve the chances of it working, but it remained dead. It looked like Death had power over inanimate objects, as well.

Making a face, he tossed the phone and rummaged through the four bodies in the car. He pulled out wallets and gathered out a collection of three hundred and forty six dollars, which he stuffed into his own pockets with a hateful thought of *fuck 'em*. One of the bodies had a mean looking knife with the word *Beretta* stamped on the side of the short, three-inch blade. It came in a belt sheath, which Tony removed from the owner and attached to his own. There was a long military boot knife, complete with sheath, on another body, and he pocketed it, as well. He found a cheap palm-sized flashlight in the glove compartment, the kind that did not need batteries but generated its own light by squeezing its sides. He stuffed that into his coat, too. There was a lighter which he pocketed. He found maps and McDonalds' coupons, which he also took. When he got out of this mess, a couple of discounted cheeseburgers would go down just fine.

There was nothing else in the car.

On impulse he reached in under the front seats. He felt the butt of something. He stretched, wrapped his hand about it and withdrew a worn but still venerable baseball bat. Tony bared his teeth and stood with the bat before him, samurai style. With the knives and the bat, he was ready for a small war. He took a swing and grimaced almost instantly. There were parts of him, all in his back it felt, that did not want him to be exerting energy just yet. He placed the bat to one side and got down on his hands and knees, and stuck his head under the legs of a body, peering up under the front seats to see if there were any other surprises.

There were not.

Tony got to his feet, and then remembered the trunk.

He reached back into the car, baring his teeth again at the destruction Death had wrought amongst his captors and retrieved the blood and goo sticky keys from the ignition. One of them would open the trunk. A part of Tony hoped to God above there wasn't a body in there. He didn't think there would be, but it was one of those weeks, so he hoped just in case. He walked around to the trunk, slogging through the gathered snow, and held the keys up to his face. There were three, on a bloody rabbit's foot keychain. He stood in front of the trunk and inserted a key. Tony paused for a moment, hoping to God above that maybe, just maybe, there would be something of some good use in there. He looked to the road and swore softly. Which way was which? North? South? Which way were they headed? Where were they now? Tony sighed heavily.

And turned the key.

The trunk popped and opened. Tony lifted the lid and hoped again to God that there wasn't a body. There wasn't. Instead, there were a number of things of interest. There was a five-litre, red plastic container containing gasoline. There was a small black briefcase which caught his attention, and a forty-ounce bottle of Jack Daniels, still in a decorative box, with ol' Jack himself showing a rather distinguished profile. Tony smiled at the bottle, picked it up and held it at arm's length. Of all the weird shit that was happening in his life at the moment, of all the chaos, this one bottle of sour-mash whiskey put a grounding smile on his face. Tony sighed deeply, patted the bottle, and deposited it into one of the deep pockets of his coat. The pocket wasn't quite big enough, but he didn't care. Ol' Jack was going with him, and he patted the bottle again, happy with its comforting weight.

There was a set of booster cables in the car, which was of no use. As was the car jack. There was an old blanket, which he took and draped over his shoulder. Then, he held up the briefcase. He turned it over, inspecting it in the grey gloom of the afternoon, and plopped it back into the trunk. He fumbled with its latches but finally popped it and threw back the lid. He blinked at the contents.

Staring back at him was the biggest syringe he had ever set his eyes upon in his life. What was it that the leader had said to Death just before he had introduced himself? Something about painkiller? Tony picked up the syringe. The needle was a good four inches long and as serious looking as any of the knives he removed from Death's victims. It was packaged in plastic and had wording that read "*Spinal Needle—spinal needle Quincke type point.*" There was a little black and white picture beside the name, showing a needle that was hollow and making Tony think of a gigantic, mutant proboscis. A small fifteen-millilitre bottle of a clear liquid called bupivacaine lay in the case. He placed the syringe back beside the bottle and picked up another item. It was a black holster of sorts, but it contained six black plastic tubes with writing. Tony extracted one. It read "*Zyomet Autoinjector.*"

What the fuck was a Zyomet Autoinjector?

He looked at the writing beneath the big words, muttering "Morphine injection" and squinting at what he had. He didn't know what he had at all, but he wondered if it were anything that Frank might be interested in after he woke up. He hoped it would be. He inserted the injector back into the holster beside its brothers and dropped it back into the case. On second thought, he grabbed it all up, and stuffed everything into his pocket opposite ol' Jack. His coat felt heavy, but he wasn't worried about anything tearing under the weight.

That was it for the treasures of the trunk.

Not even anything to eat.

Tony shook his head. Were those guys actually serious about the barbeque? They had the right choice of booze for it. But only the one bottle. Tony sighed. Weren't the bad guys supposed to be boozers or crack-heads or something like that? Why did he have to get the equivalent of pissed off Mormons? Pissed off Mormons that walked around with what looked to be combat knives. And Zyomet Autoinjectors of morphine. Something which Tony had a hard time pronouncing and hoped to Lord above it didn't bring on the shits.

Then, something he thought of made him pause.

Mormons.

Mormons liked to stick together.

Shit.

Tony looked back to the road. Where were they going? He broke into a lumbering run, the snow rising up and over his ankles. He reached the side of the highway, and looked to the left and right. He had no clue as to which way was back to civilization. He saw no road signs, only a long road that twisted off into a white, snow-covered forest. Snow, large fluffs of it, floated on the air. Grey clouds hung low in the sky, pressing down on mountaintops in the distance and obscuring the sun. Where could they be? Panic started to swirl up inside Tony then, and he growled with effort to control it. He had to think. He would stick to the road. Listen for cars. Maybe if he could see the driver or drivers, he could wave one of them down for a ride. He could not stay here. Here was where people might come looking; the buddies of the four dead douche bags of the Apocalypse. And if no one did come by, they would not make it anyway. The cold would do them in. He remembered something about staying active, that people could live for a long time in cold temperatures if they just kept moving. It was when they stopped it was dangerous. The thought occurred to him of dying in BC due to exposure, and it made him snort with morbid humour. Then he realized that he could not die. But the dudes in the car had died easily enough. What would happen then? He straightened and decided he did not want to find out. He did not want to think about *not dying* as weird as that sounded. He would follow the road and simply get to where it led, and he would take care with approaching cars. Just in case.

Checking his gathered items and patting the bottle of Jack Daniels for luck, Tony chose a direction, stomped his feet clean of snow on the pavement, and started walking.

He stopped not three steps away, turned, and looked back in the direction of the crashed car.

"Well, *fuck*," he cursed.

He had damned near forgotten about unconscious Death.

CHAPTER 49

Something was wrong. Something was really wrong. Peters had not contacted Maia in a very long time. The last time they called, they had an unconscious Death in their clutches along with a somehow important Mundane. They were heading north, as far away from civilization as possible, to a little cabin Maia knew of and maintained especially for times like these. That was where they were going.

And that had been roughly three hours ago.

A feeling of wrongness wormed around in Maia's guts, trying to get into his brain. Could something have gone wrong? What could have gone wrong? The thought made him curse. They were transporting *Death* for Christ's sakes. *Everything* could have gone wrong! Maia had explicitly told Peter to take precautions when handling the Boatman. Had that infernal weasel somehow escaped?

Maia stomped around his office like he was searching for flesh to smash. Not finding anything to his liking, he threw back his head and growled in absolute disgust. There was a knock on his office door. Maia whirled on it and glared enough heat to laser a hole through the metal surface.

"Get in here!" Maia commanded.

Marvin entered. He looked nervous in the presence of a very agitated fire chief. Maia focused his stare of hellfire at the Minion and rooted him to the spot. He pursed up his mouth and debated whether he should kill Marvin just out of rage. He had the feeling he had sent four of his best into battle, and all of them had fallen. The thought put enough colour into his face that Marvin thought it could potentially burst under pressure.

When he spoke, Marvin was listening.

"Peters and Wash didn't make it," Maia informed him, feeling the truth behind his words even though he had no way of knowing. Marvin's mouth dropped open with shock.

"Gather up the rest of the boys," Maia went on. "We're heading to the cabin."

CHAPTER 50

A dry-looking TCH lay before the Stickman. Mounds of snow were on either side of the strip of highway, suffocating trees whose tips could just barely be seen. It was an overcast sky, and beneath it was a grey strip of highway splitting craggy mounds of white. The emptiness of the land around him did nothing to dampen Stickman's disposition. He was jubilant to be free of the thing that had taken him captive. He hoped it was minus fifty out there, so the creature's ass would freeze to the asphalt, and hold him there long enough for a transport trailer to run over it.

The Stickman felt great. Just great. He didn't even feel the ache of his face or any of his bruises and wounds from the battle with Boomer. He was so happy that he actually had fond thoughts of Levin. Perhaps he would let the man live, but only after Stickman did a dance on the man's legs. What he did to Badger could not be completely forgotten. Then again, thinking further on it, perhaps Levin was the type of person that would try and exact revenge on the Stickman for breaking his legs. Maybe Levin would even go as far as hiring someone or calling in a favour to deal with the Stickman to even the score. The idea had merit, and it made Stickman chew on the inside of his cheek in thought. He finally decided it was safest just to dispose of Levin. Stickman was glad to have thought the whole thing through. Badger would have been proud of him.

He continued driving and considered putting on some music. He glanced at the empty road ahead, looked down at the radio and reached for it. When he looked up to watch the road again, he saw that there was a hitchhiker ahead, standing with his arm outstretched and holding onto his head. A head that was topped off with a yellow and black toque.

Just like a bee.

* * *

Lucy saw the approaching car and stuck out her thumb. It was freezing on the roadside, and she didn't know why she had to be exactly here anyway, except *this* is where ol' Father Time wanted her to be. Maybe it was punishment for something? Who knew? The faster she got picked up, the faster she could get on with her task. And that was getting back to Tony. Right now, she figured Tony and Frank were getting on just swell. It was a gamble they were taking, a big gamble, and not even Lucy was certain of where or how it was all going to play out. When it came to the Mundanes alone, she could influence it. When it came to the Entities, she had no more influence than a flea in a dog's decision of which way it wanted to turn.

The car approaching her was a Sunbird, but she didn't know the year. It slowed down, and Lucy did a little appreciative hop. Her ass was freezing in this weather. The car pulled up alongside of her and stopped, its exhaust fumes shooting out from behind and blowing about her. The passenger window was frosted over. She could not see inside, and when she tried to open the door, she discovered it was locked. That was strange, Lucy thought.

"You gonna let me in or not?" Lucy said over the loud rumble of the engine.

There was a pause.

Lucy then saw a hand distorted by the ice unlock the door. Lucy opened it immediately, and a gasp of foul air went by her. She bent over at the waist to look inside at the driver. The driver regarded her with a face that looked as if it had been bashed in with a baseball bat. A black eye, a huge cut on his forehead that had scabbed over with black blood, two cheeks that probably were a hair away from being shattered, and a mouth rimmed with a fighter's fat lips. Lucy hesitated, staring at the face before her, before smiling sweetly and glancing down.

"Sorry," she said. "I didn't mean to stare. You're like the first person I've seen out here all day, and here I am staring at you. Very sorry about that. Anyway, can you give me a lift?"

"Where's ye goin'?" asked the driver. His teeth were small, but looked undamaged.

"West," Lucy answered.

"Get in."

Lucy did so, thankful to get out of the cold. She did not see the driver sizing up her legs as she did so. "Thanks. Lucky me you came along when you did. I was freezing!"

The Stickman's head lilted to one side as he put the car into drive.

"Lucky I," he said with a greasy smile.

CHAPTER 51

Walk, Tony told himself. *March.*

He looked up at the long, open throat of a road, grey and wintry, stretching out and eclipsed between two forest-covered hills with dark mountains all around them, mountains whose girth was hidden by a low, overcast sky and the constant falling of great, lazy snowflakes. It all looked and felt cold to Tony, who walked the white road, one foot moving stiffly after the other. He shrugged his shoulder, feeling the weight of Death's unconscious form slung over it. He felt the weight of Mr. Jack in his coat pocket, and all of the other things he had taken from the car. He felt dirty from the freezing blood on his person. He kept the baseball bat in his left fist, which was also draped over Death's legs. March, he told himself again.

Or die.

The thought brought a stiff grin to his face. It made Tony realize how damn cold it was. But he would not die. He could not die. He had Death over his shoulder like a great sack of potatoes. How could he die? It would not be from exposure. He was moving along fast enough to prevent that. But he was getting so tired. Everything was so heavy. And the snow covering the edges of the road, the same snow that quickly became huge banks of whiteness that looked so soft to him, so incredibly soft, tempted him to just drop his load, just dump Death into the fluffy bank.

And join him.

They could sit and wait for the first car or truck to happen along. Maybe even have a nap while they were waiting. That would be so nice. Just sit and . . . sleep. A huge sigh left Tony. Old Frankie boy was heavy. Bastard had eaten too many fucking chicken fingers. Tony was getting a workout, however. He noted how he was taking big strides when he left the car wreck, heading where he thought was north. He realized, as time moved on, that his strides had become more like shuffles. He looked up again at the distant road. It was unwavering and simply ceased to exist over the approaching hill. Tony thought it would be too lucky to find a town just over the rise, and it seemed that he just did not have that sort of luck, not since Lucy, anyway.

At one point, Tony stopped and exhaled a mighty gust of breath. His breath was no longer visible on the air. His legs ached. His shoulders ached. He wanted a short breather. He lowered Death to the side of the road, easing him into a snow drift. Tony plopped right down beside him. The snow was high enough that he was in a reclining pose with a pleasant brace of cold snow at his neck. It felt wonderful. Tony wiggled a bit and regarded his legs stuck straight out onto the highway. He wondered how that would look to oncoming traffic, a pair of dark legs sticking out of a drift. He closed his eyes. Tony hoped, dreamily, that whoever did find them didn't sound their horn. That would be just too damn noisy. He breathed in and felt the icy air fill his lungs. He would catch a nap. Just a little nap. And then, he would get up and continue on. Honest to God he would.

Snowballs.

He dreamt of snowballs.

"Snowballs," a voice to his right said.

Tony's eyes cracked open.

"Hey . . . snowballs. Wake the fuck up before I bitch slap you!"

With a jolt, Tony looked at the face of Death. He was grimacing.

"Listen, you have to knock me out again, ok?" Frank said, clearly in pain.

Tony was stunned. His mouth opened, but Frank waved him off.

"You have to. I have to stay unconscious. I can't feel any pain, ok?"

"I think I have morphine," Tony blurted out. "Or some kind of painkiller."

"Morphine?"

"Yeah, right here," Tony struggled to get to his feet.

"I can't wait. *We* can't wait." Frank looked at Tony with eyes that were beginning to flood with increasing agony. "Knock me out!"

Tony stood over the man, his arms limp at his sides. "What in the hell is going on here, Frank?"

Death waved him off savagely. "Will you JUST FUCKING—"

Tony didn't let him finish the sentence. He punched Death square on the chin, knocking his head back and causing the man's eyes to flutter in his head like an out of whack slot machine. He was out. Again.

"Well, fuck me!" Tony bellowed at the low grey sky. "How the fuck is *this* supposed to help anything!"

A great roar of frustration left him then. Snow continued to fall, and after the sound of his voice had ceased, the even greater sound of absolute silence filled his ears. Tony stood and stared pleadingly at the clouds in the sky. Willowy flakes fell into his eyes and face and he blinked. He felt the need to bolt in one direction. Just leave Death where he lay for whoever happened along the road. This was not Tony's problem. Leave him for the others to find. Tony found him, easily, so it would be just as easy for someone else. But he wouldn't. Even as he thought he could, he knew he wouldn't. And goddamn it, it was only going to get harder if he stayed. He held his head with both hands and took in the unconscious form of Death.

He had to think. What was the shit he took from the car? He fumbled for it in his pockets, yanking out the syringe and the bottle of bupivacaine. He studied them for a moment. What was it that one guy back in the car said about this shit? Painkiller? *Spinal* painkiller? So that Frank wouldn't feel a thing when they were cutting and cooking him up? He held up the syringe before his eyes. It was a big needle, centimetres long, and they were going to stick this thing into Frank. The gears of Tony's mind rolled over. Frank did not want to feel any pain, and Tony had the means to grant him that. But sticking this weapon into his spine? Could he do that? He glanced down at Death in the snow, looking as if he had just gone to sleep in a plush white chair.

Then it struck him.

What was the absolute worse that could happen? Frank couldn't die. Or could he?

Grunting, Tony pulled Death out of the snow and landed him on his stomach, on the freezing white of the road. He gripped at his coat and hauled it up. He yanked up the shirts underneath until he came to white flesh just above a black belt line. Frank's back was hairless, and looked exceptionally human to Tony. He pushed the clothes back up, so the lower part of Death's back was exposed. Tony looked at his spine, and he felt fear creep into his heart. Perhaps, it wasn't such a good idea. But before he allowed himself to think on it any further, he prepped the injection as best as he could, taking the lid off the little bottle of bupivacaine and sticking the needle in. He drew the fluid up like blood in a proboscis. He held it up when it was filled, not knowing why but thinking it was something doctors did. Then, he placed the tip of the needle to the bare skin covering Death's spine.

Tony paused.

There was bone there.

A voice screamed *no shit* in his head, and he wondered how the hell he was supposed to inject it through bone. But what if he got it into the space between the discs? Could he do that?

He reached around Death's waist and pulled him up so that his ass was sticking into the air. But that position did not bend him over like Tony wanted, where the discs in his back could be potentially parted. He looked around. There was nothing except the snow drift. Cursing, Tony got to his feet and left Frank on the road with his butt pointed skyward, ready for a bicycle to be parked. Tony fell to the edge of the road and started piling up snow. He packed it hard so that he had a good-sized lump to bend Frank over.

Then, he moved Death into position.

When it was done, Tony thought it would do. Death was lying in the snow face down with his bent and exposed mid-back facing Tony. Tony knelt beside him and placed the loaded syringe where the spine was located. He hoped it would go in. He hoped he would be able to inject the painkiller.

He hoped he would not fuck up.

Tony took a breath, placed pressure on the syringe, and, taking yet another breath, injected the load. There was resistance. Tony didn't know if it was bone or something else, but he pressed harder. The fluid entered Death's spine. Or, at least his body, Tony figured. It felt strange, as if he was penetrating a strip of hardened rubber. He watched the fluid leave the syringe, and once it was gone, he pulled it out.

Death did not move.

Tony sat down beside him, listening to the hush of falling snow and the absence of wind. For all he knew, he might have just killed the man. He did not think so, but the operation was enough for him. He pulled out the bottle of Jack Daniels, opened it, and took a shot. He shuddered at the taste of the sour mash whiskey, feeling the warmth rush down to his core. He stared at the label for a few moments, waiting for the burn in his mouth to subside. When it did, he took another shot. He put the bottle back into his pocket and looked to the empty road and the wilderness surrounding them. It was hard to believe that in such a short time so much had happened. So much. He thought of Lucy, thought of her face, and hoped she was okay.

"Tony?"

Tony blinked at the sound of Death's voice. He looked around, realizing that he did not tuck in Frank's shirt after the injection.

"Yeah?" Tony responded.

Death did not move his head. "Did you just fuck me in the ass?"

Tony winced. "No, man, I gave you an injection. That shit those guys were talking about. That spinal shit."

"Spinal shit?"

"Yeah. I injected it into your spine."

Death was quiet. "Is that ... why I can't feel anything ... below my waist?"

A big fluff of snow drifted in Tony's eyes, causing him to blink. "I hope so."

"I hope so too," Frank agreed. "Cuz I was certain you just fucked me."

"I didn't fuck you, man," Tony said wearily.

"Ok, ok," Frank said. "Just checking. I really can't feel anything. I can't even move my legs. I'm trying but nothing. Can't even feel my balls."

"I can't feel my balls, either, man" Tony said to Death beside him. "Too cold."

There was a pause. "You have balls?" Death said.

They were both silent then for a moment: Death, unmoving and on his belly, and Tony, quietly watching it snow. It was a moment they both needed, but it could not go on for long. Death eventually broke the silence.

"We gotta go," he said simply.

It sounded fine to Tony. "Where to?"

Death tried to push himself up in the snow drift. Apparently his arms worked fine. The snow was soft around him, though, and Tony helped him to a sitting position. Death did not thank him. He looked right and left, and then made a sour face.

"Fucked up," Death muttered. "Fuuucked up."

"What is?"

"All of this," Death said with a wave of his hand. "Hard to say which way to go. You have a cell phone?"

Tony shook his head.

"Well," Death declared. "Let's head that way," he pointed to the right. "You gonna carry me?"

Tony made a sour face at that.

"Just asking," Death said. He did not say that he thought Tony did a good job injecting whatever it was into him. His pain was nil right now. There was nothing below his waist to suggest there were broken bones down there. Tony had probably saved them both a very rude visitor. Death also realized he would have to explain it all to Tony. In time.

"Let's go then." Death said. Tony hauled him up and threw him over his shoulder.

"How long will it last? What you injected me with?" Death asked Tony as he started walking.

"Don't know man. Why?"

"Just wondering," Death replied uneasily.

He did not say any more.

They kept marching for what seemed to Tony like hours, yet the day did not get any darker. Nor did the sun manage to penetrate that grim greyness hanging overhead. The air did become colder, and Tony huffed with the ever growing weight of his passenger.

"Now," Death said from behind Tony's back, "I know what it was like to travel in a chuckwagon."

"Figured you would have done that already," Tony said. "You being Death and all."

"You're right. I have done it before."

"I have a question," Tony said between huffs. He would have to stop for a break soon.

Death groaned. "I ain't saying nothin' about what's on the other side."

This took Tony back. "What?"

"You were going to ask me what's on the other side. After Death."

"No, I wasn't."

"You were. You all do."

"No, man, I was going to ask about those four guys back there."

"Those idiots weren't *men*. They were . . ." Death trailed off. "What were you going to ask?"

"What were you going to say?"

"About what?"

"Those guys. You were about to say what those guys really were."

"They were dicks."

Tony knew a lie when he heard it. "You weren't going to say that."

"Not a lie. They were fucking dicks. In fact, to call them dicks is an insult to fucking dicks."

Tony gave up. "Whatever. My question, if you'll let me finish, is how come they died?"

"I sent them over," Death said.

This caused Tony to stop in his tracks. He half turned to speak to Death when he realized he was speaking to his ass. Same thing, he supposed. "You what?"

"I sent them over."

"Over where?"

"Where do you think?"

"You mean death?"

"Death isn't a place, moron, it's a gateway."

"Hey," Tony warned him, "you think about who you're calling moron, or I'll let your ass crawl to wherever we're going here."

"Oh, shit," Death said, "that would be a loss of comfort, now wouldn't it?"

Tony started walking, again. The road was becoming slippery. There was ice underneath the feathery snow that had fallen.

"When did you do that?" Tony wanted to know. He waited for his answer, but none came. "When did you do that?" he repeated.

"Huh?" came Death's voice.

Tony stopped again. "Quit fucking around. I asked you a goddamn question."

"I sent them, I said," Death repeated.

"Yeah, and I asked when!"

"When I went through the windshield."

"Whaaa?" Tony was stunned. He turned again to speak to Death's ass. "How could you do that?"

"Listen," Death began, "I can be extremely busy at times. So, I have to be fast. In fact, I was created to be fast. Fast enough that I can carry over millions of dying people if need be. You have no idea how fast that is, do ya? Well, when I went through the windshield, I was flying. I had about five seconds of flight there, see? In those five seconds, I rolled over twice in the air before hitting the tree. Probably would've gone farther if it wasn't for the tree, but, anyway, I had enough time to realize that Minions without any heads are just as bad as cockroaches without any heads. So, I sent them over. Take a second and chop it up into in thousand pieces. I used just one sliver of that second to do that. That's how long it took. Smart thing to do, too. Even without their heads, they would have found you, probably me, and fucked us up."

"You killed them?" Tony asked.

"I didn't *kill* them. They would've gone right on living. I took them, forcefully in this case, because they're Minions."

"You made their heads explode!" Tony argued. "That's killing to me."

"Yeah, well that's cuz you think in a box. And you're a moron."

"So, you took them cuz they wouldn't die on their own?"

"That's right. I'm the ferryman," Death confided.

"Fucked up."

"Can't get your head around it, can ya?" there was a smile around Death's words. "Anyway, I suggest that right now you start walking and get us over that hill, ASAP."

"Huh? Why?" Tony started walking all the same.

Death was quiet again for a moment. "Because Tony, you knocked me out. Twice. There's another part of my job I didn't tell you about. One of . . . guarding."

"Yeah? What?" Tony asked. He was impressed that Death actually called him by name that time.

Death sighed. There wasn't any other way to hide the truth from the Mundane this time. He would find out sooner or later. And Death was under no constraints to hide this particular issue from him. In fact, a part of him looked forward to it.

"Yeah, well, when I bring Mundanes across, some don't want to go. Not many, but some. And they fight. I bring 'em across, of course, but they still fight. And when they are on the other side, they try to come back, to cross over, again.

So, I have to keep watch and put them *back* where they belong. It's not hard to do, and I have the time to do it in between the other tasks I have, but sometimes, if I let my guard down, or I'm distracted, or I'm, say—" Death cleared his throat uncomfortably, "knocked unconscious..."

Tony stopped walking. "Oh, Jesus." His mouth dropped open in disbelief.

"They can cross *back* over." Death finished.

"You mean escape?"

Death paused. "Yeah," he eventually said in a quiet voice.

"People can cross over."

Another pause. "Yes... People... And other things..."

CHAPTER 52

The snowdrift trembled once, disturbing the white blanket of silence. Nothing moved for a moment, but then the snow shook for a second time. The forest remained quiet for a few moments more. Crows, overhead in treetops, eyed the white mound. They could feel the ripple of dark energy in the air.

Something was waking up.

Something that should have stayed dead.

Bone ripped its way clear of the snow bank, clawing and swiping its way free of the weight that covered it. Worn claws of about fourteen centimetres in length pushed down on the snow and then heaved upwards. The snowdrift shook again and a huge shape, half dissolved by the elements, emerged from its cold cocoon. At its shoulders, it stood a thick five feet high. A half rotten snout, as big as a man's thigh, sniffed the air out of instinct. The teeth, exposed in places where the lips had completely rotted away, were shards. Black eye sockets, half filled with white snow, looked ahead. A maw opened wide and tried to scream. Nothing came out.

And even though there were trees and forest debris all around it, the grizzly looked straight ahead, as if it were looking directly at the Boatman, who was just a little less than one kilometre away.

Making very little noise in the falling snow, the bear began sniffing at the earth and shambled forward, willing decayed muscle tissue to work.

It moved in a straight line.

Towards Death.

CHAPTER 53

Tony was pissed off.

"What do you mean other things, man? Why are you being so fucking—what's the word I want here?"

"Vague? Ambiguous?"

"Yeah, yeah both of those! Just tell me what these things are, why don't you?"

"Don't want you to go crazy, is all." Death said from behind.

"Crazy?" Tony started walking again. He wanted to scream. "I'm carrying fucking Death on my shoulder just after witnessing four dudes' heads explode! And you're suddenly worried about my goddamn sanity?"

The thought made Tony sputter in annoyance. He punched Death.

"You feel that?"

"No," Death said guardedly. "What did you do?"

"I just punched you in the balls, man."

Death's eyes went wide. "You did not."

"Did too."

"Wow," Death breathed as he stared at the bouncing road below him. "That's some good shit. Can't feel a thing."

"Yeah well, it'll probably wear off sometime and when it does, I won't want to be you. Broken legs and smashed testicles, you'll be crying for me to kill ya."

"Alright, alright," Death spat out. "I'll stop being like that. Just don't punch me in the balls, again."

"I ain't promising you anything," Tony said with heat in his face. "Goddamn secretive fucker," he added as an afterthought.

"Alright," Death began, "These things are basically the recently dead. Or not so recent. If they have no body, that ain't so bad. If they have a body and decide to return to it, well, that's the easy thing to do. So, they do that."

"They go back to their bodies?" Tony asked as he placed one foot in front of another. "After they're dead? That can't be pretty."

"No, that can be pretty goddamn ugly," Death said.

"And what do these things do when they're up?"

"Well, what's the first thing you do after a long sleep?"

Tony made a disgusted face. "They shit?"

Death stared at the bobbing ground for a moment before barking his reply. "No, they don't shit, you fucking moron!? Okay, what *other* thing do you do in the morning?"

Tony's mouth hung open. It came to him at once. "Eat."

The answer was dead on. It made Death smirk.

Oh, shit! Tony thought. They eat. *Jesus and Mary.*

Tony began to walk faster on the icy road, looking this way and that. His increase in speed did not go unnoticed. Death smiled from where he hung, his arms flopping. If he had known that information would make the Mundane walk faster, he would have imparted it earlier. One of their oldest fears, spanning the ages in fact, was the fear of being consumed; being eaten, dead or alive, by something magical or simply savage. Mundanes were *terrified* by the prospect of being devoured. They might scoff, joke or say otherwise in conversation, but when faced with the reality . . .

They all pissed themselves.

They found the new road just over the rise in the highway. Just next to it, a single white post rose up from the snowdrifts, but the sign was missing. The road itself was covered in drifts of snow. The trees rose up and formed an icy arch overhead. It looked like a collapsed snow tunnel to Tony, but it was a road and that interested him. Roads led to places.

"Could be a cabin in there," Tony grunted to Death's butt.

"Turn to the side," Death told him. "I can't see."

Tony did so, and Death studied the new road for a moment.

"Probably goes nowhere," Death said.

"Listen," Tony began, " I have no idea what time it is or who's on this road—if anyone is—but one thing is for sure: it's gonna get dark soon. I feel better holing up in a cabin somewhere for the night than staying out here and freezing, man."

Death mulled it over. "I don't think it's cold," he said.

"Man, you can't feel your own nuts right now."

Death supposed that was true. "Alright," he spoke after a moment. "You're going to walk in there anyway. Not much I can say about it."

"You have a say in this," Tony informed him.

"No, I don't," Death retorted.

"Sure, you do."

"Alright, I think we should stick to the road."

"Fuck that," Tony said and started walking onto the new road. "If we're lucky, there'll be a cabin nearby and you, me, and ol' Jack can have a party."

"Who's ol' Jack?"

"There was a bottle of Jack Daniels in the trunk of the car."

"You have a bottle of Jack on you?"

"In my pocket," Tony informed him. Instantly, he felt Death's hands pawing at him. "Fuck off!" Tony barked. "Save it for later when we find someplace to stay."

"That's a forty ouncer!" Death was excited.

"And I found it, and it's mine, and fuck you if you think you're getting any," Tony fired at him. "Gay leprechaun, my ass."

From where he bounced along on Tony's back, Death shook his head in sullen silence. "I fuckin' hate you guys," he declared to Tony's posterior.

Tony had nothing to say that. He was marching along a deserted road which quite possibly led to nowhere. It was winter. He was freezing. The undead were potentially stalking him. He had Death slung over his shoulder.

And Death hated him.

Hunching over a bit more and ignoring the growing pain in his shoulder and legs, Tony slogged onwards through the snow. He did not say another word.

Neither did Death.

They marched for about an hour, and Frank kept his mouth shut for the entire time. He was in a pissy mood. He wished he were back in Paradise. There were women there. Hot women. There were no women in the wilds of British Columbia. There was only Tony. And Tony was getting tired. They would have to find a place soon, if not, Tony would freeze. He'd freeze, too, he supposed. But he wasn't ready to go back just yet. He didn't *want* to go back just yet. Not just yet.

"Hey, I see a house!" came Tony's excited voice. "I see a fuckin' house!"

"What?" Death turned his head to the side. All he could see were trees and a roadside draped in white. "Where?"

In answer, Tony pivoted his hips to the right and swung Death's dead weight with it, allowing him to see.

"Oh, wow!" Death said.

There, in a small clearing that seemed to be crowned by white tree lines on either side of the road, were two cabins. Except, they were a little more than simply cabins to Tony. They were the size of regular houses where he came from. The house on the left was two storeys high and peaked with a steep church-like roof. The other house was perhaps twenty metres further up the road and on the right. It had only one floor, but had a long summer deck before its front door. Both houses were deep in snow. If there were owners around, they had not been here in a while. And if the snow kept up, the houses would eventually disappear.

Tony made his way for the first house on the left, swinging Death back and ignoring his curses. He plodded his way through knee-deep snow, over what he figured was a front lawn in the summertime. He stepped up to the front door, leaned to the right to peer into a dark looking window. It was curtained from the inside.

"Well?" Death inquired.

Tony tried the door. "Locked."

"Well, of course it's locked. Kick it in."

A heavy breath left Tony. It had to be done. He eased Death down and leaned him against the side of the house. He took a step back and then kicked out his right leg. It connected hard with the door but did not break it.

Tony kicked again.

The door did not budge.

"What the fu—" Tony muttered in disgust.

Death merely sat and watched, not saying a word. His gaze went from the door to Tony and back to the door, again. On the third kick, Tony realized what was wrong. The door opened outwards. Creatively cursing to himself, Tony bunched his fist up into his coat sleeve and put it through the checked window. He cleared the lower right square of glass and reached in. A moment later, he had the door open, and a chagrined Tony stood looking inside with arms hanging at his sides.

"Say a fucking word, and you can drag your ass in there," Tony warned Death.

Death did not.

Tony stood in the doorway, examining the frame and the damage his kicks had done. There were some cracks but nothing too severe. He would have been kicking for a while before anything was going to give. It was a strong door. He peered inside and noted a comfortable looking interior. A cosy living room with what looked to be a full kitchen in back and a set of stairs heading up to an open loft area and hallway.

"Holy shit," Tony breathed. "This is some person's cabin?"

"Why?" Death was curious. "What's in there?"

"Place is better than my apartment."

Death leaned over, appearing in the doorframe at Tony's knees. He gauged the living room and creature comforts. A plush L-shaped sofa facing a wide screen TV. A fireplace. A decent looking kitchen. Table back there, too. Cosy. Death smiled. He approved.

"Some luck after all," he said. Tony looked down at the man, frowned, and picked him up with great effort. He wasn't sure how far or how long he had carried him, but he was near exhaustion. He carried Death over the threshold like a limp bride and deposited him on one end of the sofa. Tony then closed and locked the door from the inside, and then went to the other end of the sofa. He groaned when he sank down into it. Heaven had to have sofas. Tony closed his eyes and let his arm hang over the edge. He took a breath and savoured the deep chill in his lungs.

"Hey," came Death's voice.

Tony squeezed his eyes shut tight. He willed for silence.

"Hey. Get up."

"I'm taking a break here, okay? I think I've earned it."

"Oh, really? Well, then sleep away. Fuck if I care."

Tony's eyes cracked opened. "What do you want?"

Death wasn't even looking at him. He was staring at the thick wooden beams in the ceiling. It reminded him of old churches. "Better not sleep for too long."

"Why not?"

"Something's coming."

"What?"

"Something not dead. And plenty pissed."

Tony slapped his hands to his forehead and face and slowly dragged them down, stretching his flesh. He groaned. He wanted the day to end. He wanted all of this to end. And he wanted to sleep.

"Can't you do anything about that?" Tony whined. "You *are* Death."

"What's that got to do with scum-sucking undead creatures of the night?"

Then, before Death could set off a further thought on the subject, something landed against the side of the cabin. Something massive enough to make the heavy wooden frame shake all the way down to its foundations, something frightening enough to make Tony sit up straight and attempt to look everywhere at once. The sound came from the north wall, and it moved towards the shut door. It dragged itself along like something gunshot, leaning heavily on the wall for support. Timbers creaked. In the silence of the smothering snow, each groaning fibre made Tony feel as if his spine were being plied apart by a crowbar. With each long, heavy drag, the thing moved closer to the door, and the temperature inside the cabin dropped lower. Tony's eyes were bulging. His quickening breath was easily seen.

"What the fuck is that?" he whispered harshly.

From where he lay on his side of the couch, Death merely crossed his arms on his chest, mummy like, and stared at the ceiling.

Tony would spare no more attention on the Boatman. The thing and its sound were drawing closer to the door. Wood squealed as the unseen weight pressed itself up hard against the cabin. Tony listened as if his senses were able to discern ghosts. His eyes darted from the wall to the door. What could he do? His heart was thumping in his chest, and his breathing accelerated. He took a breath and slipped off the couch, making a fist around the baseball bat he still carried.

"Hey," Death whispered.

Tony looked in his direction.

"Give me the booze," Death said, his fingers snapping in the air.

The thing hit the wall again, hard. Tony heard timbers crack. Without a thought he pulled the whiskey from his pocket and shoved it into Death's hands. It brought a fond smile to Death's lips. "Together again, my friend."

"Shhh," Tony hushed. The thing outside was perhaps no more than five feet away from the door. The sound of something scraping along the wood, gouging it, perked the dead air, and Tony felt a lump of dread forming up in his chest. What the hell was that thing?

"Hey," Death said.

Tony's head nearly came off his neck it snapped around so fast. "*What?*"

Death had the tip of the Jack Daniel's bottle resting against his cheek. He was watching the man carefully. "Remember. It can't kill you."

That did not make Tony feel any better.

"And you can send it back."

"How?"

"Smash in the head."

"And that'll stop it?" Tony demanded.

"That shit—" *will stop just about anything* Death was going to say when the thing outside crashed against the door, stealing the words and their mutual attention. Tony's eyes bugged wide. He could see a greyish-white ridge of something pressing up against the wood through the broken window he had made. The rest of the window was curtained, but Tony had seen enough to know that whatever the thing was, it was big. It slammed its weight against the door again and the frame puffed inwards. Tony could see multiple places where the wooden frame shook and weakened. It struck the door, again, making it bulge. Tony realized if the door was hit a third time, it would split.

It made Tony scream.

The scream startled an otherwise relaxed Death.

Breathing wildly and bat in hand, Tony charged the door only to turn at the staircase. He pounded upwards, out of sight. Reaching the second floor, Tony saw there was a short hallway with four opened doorways. Behind him, gloomy daylight came through a kite window. The fear had a hold of Tony now, but it was not the paralyzing fear that had crippled him around Freddie. This was a fear that was igniting into something else. It was fear that was beginning to burn, and rage was replacing it.

Baring his teeth, Tony charged the window.

CHAPTER 54

With a roar, Tony crashed through the glass and thin wood like a man escaping a fire. He flew through the air, legs drawn up and bat held over his head. He glimpsed the thing below him, in front of the cabin door. If he had waited inside and done nothing but wait, the terror surely would have frozen him as solid as a cheap TV dinner. But fear was his friend now.

And rage was a tank of gasoline with a lit wick.

Tony landed in a snow drift just beyond the mass of bone and decaying flesh. He yanked his feet free and charged the beast, seeing that it was the rotting remains of a huge bear, almost two metres high at its bare-boned shoulder. Black flesh and rotten fur hung off its skeleton, and it raised its half-decayed head still armed with teeth in Tony's direction. Empty eye sockets regarded its attacker, and its maw opened in a tongueless hiss.

But the man was faster.

The bat crashed into the bear's head, crushing the skull with the sound of breaking clay. The impact froze the beast to the spot. Roaring, Tony swung again, smashing the skull to the right. Bone and teeth fell to the snow. He landed another heavy blow to the bear's head, and a chunk of black bone matter and tissue flew and smacked against the cabin's wall. The strike paralyzed it. Tony reared the bat up high and brought it down with whatever strength he could generate, smashing through the remaining brainpan, and removing what was left of the head.

The abomination stood still for a moment, almost as if considering what to do in this unexpected predicament, then collapsed. Its legs dropped its dead-again frame to the deep, white freeze of the surrounding snow, and the rest of its body sunk into itself as whatever energy sustaining it left in a deflating gush.

"Fucked your hibernatin' ass," Tony quietly snarled at the corpse.

The wind rose up in reply and chilled his face.

When Tony was certain it was no longer alive, he went to work bashing and breaking every intact bone he could find, releasing his remaining fear like a bad meal being regurgitated. He smashed the legs, the paws, the back, and the ribs until the frame of the great bear was nothing more than a lumpy mass of shards and splinters. In the end, he kicked snow over its carcass to cover the thing from the light of day.

Having done that, Tony fell backwards on his ass in a snow drift.

Great breaths left his frame, and he stared at the newly buried corpse before him, believing and yet not believing that he had just kicked the shit out of a zombie bear. The realization eventually brought a weak smile to his face. He was good at this. He had just faced evil and kicked its ass—with a bat, no less. He regarded the weapon still clinched in his hand, and his smile widened almost breaking into a laugh.

"*Youuuuuuuuu.*"

The voice made Tony clamber to his feet. He whirled about to face the road, standing with his bat at guard. If there was another *thing* around, he discovered he still had enough energy to have at it.

There was.

The wind continued to pick up, driving the snow up in ghostly cauls of white and flinging it about. Standing just far enough away that Tony could not make out its features was a single figure that did not appear to have feet. It stood dark against the veil of snow that swirled around it. Its arms hung limply at it sides, and it made no movement, but it was looking straight at Tony. He felt it. A new freezing cold went through his frame, and he knew that it wasn't because of the weather.

"*You, fuck off!*" Tony screamed at the wraith, brandishing the bat like a crusader's sword.

The form did not move.

"*Youuu,*" the voice came again right next to Tony's ears, it seemed. He flinched at the sound and spun about in the snow, making sure the cabin was at his back. Seeing that he was indeed alone, he faced the dark shape once again.

"Give him. To. Ussssss."

Tony bared his teeth.

"And you. Live."

"Come any closer, and *I'll fuck you up!*" Tony hollered back. He took two threatening steps to emphasize his intent and cocked the bat to his ear as if the thing were going to launch a fastball at him. Instead, the shape merely stood on legs that did not seem to have any feet, in a snowstorm that was intensifying. It did not flinch. It did nothing in response to Tony's advances. Tony stopped after taking another step. Something kept him back. He did not want to see the thing's face. He knew if he did, it would probably haunt his nights for a long, long time. The snow was falling and blowing harder now, coming up to his shins. The thing was further up the road than Tony wanted to go and for a split moment, he suspected the ghost *wanted* him to come a little closer. It wanted him away from the cabin. It was attempting to *lure* him away. His fear rising, Tony glanced over his shoulder.

The cabin was still there, still close by. The door was still closed.

When he looked back, the thing in the snow was gone.

Baring his teeth, Tony ran back to the door in great leaps, flicking up snow in his wake. He reached through the broken window and unlocked the door from the inside, his fingers scrambling over the doorknob like a crab on slick ice. Once opened, he shoved his body through the doorway and slammed it shut behind him. He crouched and peered back out the window at the growing storm, searching for pursuers. There were none. He quickly locked the door from the inside, thought of the curtains, and almost tore them down in closing them. The hole was still there. Tony would have to do something about that. Perhaps there was a hammer around.

"What's up?" Death asked innocently from the couch.

Tony glared at him. "What do you mean, 'What's up'? Didn't you hear that thing?"

"What thing?" Death asked, clueless.

"That fucking thing, man!" Tony nearly shrieked, jabbing his bat at the door. "It wants you!"

"I thought you got it," Death said mildly "I heard you smacking something around out there."

"I did, but there was another thing! A man thing!"

Death's features slackened. "Oh," he said.

"And it wants you!" Tony thrust his bat in Frank's direction. "Said if I give you up, I can live."

Death snorted. "Yeah, right."

"You think I'm lyin'?" Tony snapped and took two steps over to where Death lay on the sofa. The bat rose up.

But Death remained cool. He met Tony's fury with the calmest of expressions. "What I meant was if you were to give me up, of course, you would live. You'd live for a very long time. At least, until the War."

"What war?" Tony demanded. His hands were shaking now; Death could see that. The man was controlling, or rather, *had* controlled his fear up until now, but he was slipping.

In response, Death offered up the forty ouncer of Jack Daniels.

Tony stared at the bottle for a moment and then snatched it away. He stalked to the other end of the L-shaped sofa and fell onto it. Breathing hard, he took off the bottle cap and sipped at its contents. He made a face, coughed, and sipped again. When he lowered the bottle to his lap, he arched his head back and stared at the ceiling.

"Why does . . . it want you, Frank?" Tony asked quietly, opting to use the more human name of his charge. He was gaining more control with each passing second. Ol' Jack was a quick doctor.

Death shrugged. Outside the wind's howling rose and dropped. "They hate me. Just as much when they're dead as when they're alive. Maybe more."

Tony looked across the way at him. "Who?"

"You. People. The dead." Death looked very tired. "Like I said earlier, man, it's my job. It's just my job. But I get it from all sides. I get accused of everything. People die, I get blamed. The dead can't get back, I get blamed. I'm just the middle man. The transporter between here and there. I end the suffering. For that, I'm hated, when I should be appreciated."

"Animals, too?"

"I take care of *everything* that has to cross over," Death confided. "Animals are just as scared as the people, but they don't fight as much. Usually."

"That bear was looking for you," Tony informed him.

Death's brow shrugged.

The wind lashed the house and made it creak. In the silence, it sounded loud and haunting, but neither Tony nor Death made any move. They simply lay still and were quiet, content to just listen for a while.

"Why are you afraid of me?" Death finally asked.

Tony blinked. "What?"

"You. Mortals. Mundanes. You're all scared of me. Why?"

The absurdity of the question made Tony smile. He leaned over and handed Death the bottle of Jack. Tony watched him sip.

"Because, man," Tony said after a while, "you're the fucking Grim Reaper."

The words brought a smile to Death's face. "Always liked that one."

"It is cool," Tony agreed.

"I like 'Angel of Death', too."

"That's you?"

Death nodded slowly. "Yep."

Tony supposed it was. He never gave it any thought before. He thought some more. "You hurt us."

"That's not me though," Death raised a finger. "That's another guy. I end the hurt. I end the suffering. I step in like a referee when a fighter has had enough. When the fight is over. That's when I come in."

"So, who is the other guy?"

"He's an asshole."

"What's his name? Agony? Suffering?" Tony threw out, trying to remember the names of the Riders of the Apocalypse. Or was that Horsemen?

"Close," Death studied the whiskey in the bottle. "Pain."

"So, Pain is the asshole?"

"What do you think?" Death said simply, looking Tony in the eye.

"Yeah, so what's your point? That you're a cold-hearted bastard that'll let people suffer on their way out?"

"I get *blamed* for Pain's work!" Death spat out, his hands going up. "*I get blamed for the pain!* I don't hurt people. It's *not* my job. I *end* the hurt. But I *always* get the fucking blame for the suffering. I'm sick of it! Just so goddamn sick of it! It's not me who speeds on icy highways after a quart of Crown Royal. It's not me who decides to stick their dick in an industrial vacuum. And it's not me who does Russian Roulette with an automatic. None of it is me. I don't starve kids in Africa. I don't drown thousands in tsunamis. I don't initiate genocides. I don't make you grow old. But I end it all! Any and all suffering. And I always hear the same shit! 'Why did they have to die? Why did Death take them? They were so young. There's too *much* Death in the world. I *hate* Death!' I mean, Jesus Christ, if it were up to me, I'd take everyone in their sleep when it was time."

"Then, why don't you?"

"Because . . ." Death rolled his head in frustration. "I didn't design the system."

Tony's brow crunched up "System?" Tony knew the man—Death—had said something he wasn't supposed to.

"Nothin'. Forget about that," Death said.

"I wanna hear about that."

"No."

"Alright then answer me this . . ." Tony paused for effect. "Why do we have to die?"

Death leaned forward as much as he could. "Alright, alright, you wanna know why you die? Why you have to die? You wanna know why anyone dies? It's a lesson to those who are still alive. That's why you die. Why anyone dies. Every passing is a lesson, and when you finally cross over, there'll be someone waiting to ask *you* a question."

This sounded serious to Tony. "What?"

"What have you learned?" Death informed him.

The look of confusion on Tony's face made Death frown. "Look. There are things that your science will never accept. Never explain. Life and Death are two of your biggest questions. Why are you here? The answer is there ... Some people find it. Some have to wait until they cross over. You *all* cross over. *You* will cross over. I'm just pissed off about taking the blame for something I don't do. I don't make people suffer as they cross over. People live; eventually, they'll experience pain blinding enough to summon me to take them to the other side. When that happens, I take them. And that's *all* I do. People should fucking *love* me."

In that moment, Death took another swig of whiskey. It was a deep drink, one from the movies where the actor is usually chugging tea. But this wasn't tea.

"You ask a thousand people how they want to go, what do you think they'd say?" Death quietly began again, his lips glistening with residual booze. He didn't wait for Tony to answer. "They'd say 'in their sleep' or 'quick' or 'without pain'. There are people praying for me to end their suffering. People praying to end *others'* suffering. They say, 'they should just die. Why don't they die? They should'. But ... you know about that, don't you."

Tony did not say a word. He reached for the bottle, and Death passed it to him. Tony took a long, burning drink and stopped only when this throat and guts choked him to submission. When he lowered the bottle, he was looking at the floor and the old rug covering it. He thought of his mother.

"Don't you?" Death repeated, quiet but firm.

"Yeah," Tony answered.

"Yeah, thought so," Death said, he held his hand out for the bottle. Instead, Tony took another drink and coughed when he was finished. The grimace on the man's face made Death smile.

"I can see Ol' Jack doesn't like you."

"I like him," Tony winced and handed it over. Outside the wind battered the cabin and sang through the broken window. "Why do you take so long then?"

Death took a deep breath and studied the bottle of Jack Daniels. "There's a long line up. And everyone does their best to survive. It's instinct. You're programmed to survive at any cost. Some can go against the programming. Most fight. Hope. Pray. And ..." Death never took his eyes from the bottle. "I can be a bastard. When they are ready to go ... I'm supposed to take them. If they fight, I let them wait. Just like a parent with contrary kids—a parent that knows better but decides that the kids need to be taught a lesson. I'll let them suffer longer. Even when they ... they've had enough. Even after they're more than ready to go. To cross over. Just for spite."

"You let them suffer longer. On purpose," Tony charged him in a low tone.

Death took a moment before answering. "Yeah. Sometimes."

"Maybe it's time for a career change man," Tony reflected.

"Yeah," Death agreed, thinking for a moment. "Maybe."

* * *

Outside the snow continued to fall, and the wind blew harder. Daylight faded. And if either Death or Tony had taken the time to look out the window, they would have seen the snow thickening in blustery chunks, reducing their visibility. Just beyond that, where the snow became a grey sheet hiding everything, dark forms gathered.

And began to mass.

CHAPTER 55

Stickman drove the grey Sunbird with a growing sense of direction, as if he were hooked through the front grill and something incredibly powerful were pulling him in. And there was perhaps one of the most beautiful passengers in Lucy sitting beside him. Every now and again, his eyes would stray to her legs covered in tight black jeans. He wished it wasn't winter. He could check out what was upstairs if she weren't wearing her leather coat. And she had removed her toque to reveal her black hair with a ribbon of white just to the side. The woman was hands-down sexy. And she was friendly, too. He thought they had gone through the usual Q and A quite well. She laughed at his jokes, and she said that his accent was cute.

The Stickman liked.

He had turned on the radio for some driving music. The news had eventually come on, and when it did, she went quiet. It was beginning to bother the Stick. He found that, after being exposed to that sunny smile of hers—and her smile was so gorgeous—he wanted more. He wanted to make her smile.

"Anyting wrong, me love?" Stickman asked her.

Lucy shook her head.

"Y'can tell I. We's come so far, ye and I. No secrets, now."

"Well," Lucy began, "it's just that . . . there's so much going on in the world today. So much pain and suffering. It's a little depressing."

Behind the wheel, Stickman smiled gently. "Ye can only do what ye can wit what ye got."

"I guess but . . ." Lucy frowned then, and Stickman took his eyes off the road to see it. He was glad he did. "But, well, sometimes I wish I could just do something. Don't you?"

Snow flew at the windshield, and Stickman turned on his wipers. It was an interesting question. "Yeah," he answered after a while, "I do."

"Do you have anyone special, Stickman?" Lucy asked him, gazing at his profile.

The man hunched over the steering wheel. He cocked his head to one side. "Not anymore."

"But there was someone, right?"

Stickman glanced at Lucy, looking her in the eyes for as long as he dared while driving.

"Whazzit to ye, Lucy me love?"

"Where is she?" Lucy persisted.

There was something about this woman that made the Stickman feel good. Made him feel better about himself, especially after doing the terrible things he had done. Things a person should not do to another human being. He remembered reading in the Halifax Herald about refugees from some African country where the women would be raped first before they had their breasts cut off and left to bleed to death. He remembered thinking about just what kind of man, or animal, would do such a thing just for pleasure alone. And then, he remembered having done the same kind of things. Not cutting, but cruel things to rival drug pushers. They had still been men. Still people. Badger had been all talk then. He talked a good fight when he wanted to get back at a couple of punks trying to move in on his corner, but when they actually abducted the men at gunpoint, it became obvious to the Stick that Badger wasn't about to do anything except swear at his captives. Badger was a lot of things, but he was not a killer.

So, the Stickman stepped up.

He did it fast. He did it by hand. He placed one man in what the MMA fighters would call a guillotine and choked him to death. Then, he did the other one. The other one screamed for a short time too, but then Stickman had his neck and was squeezing the life from the man as surely as one might have coaxed toothpaste from the middle of the tube. He would think about it sometimes. He would remember the doughy texture of each man's throat as he slowly took their life.

It changed him.

Badge knew it did, too.

Stickman snorted. It was good for his street reputation. And he swore he would never do such a thing, again.

But he had. Mr. Tigh and Boomer.

Stickman stared at the road ahead, over both hands on the steering wheel.

"I'se . . ." Stickman smiled, again, and Lucy felt the sadness emanate from him. "Lucy, me love," he sighed.

"What was her name?"

Silence. Then, "Beverly."

"Where is she now? Would you like to find her?"

That brought a dark chuckle from the Stickman. "Sure. Y'gonna help I, are ye?"

"I can."

There was something in her voice and looking at her face. Stickman could see she was serious. *So pretty*, the Newfoundlander thought.

"Can ye?" he asked, hypnotized.

"I can," Lucy solemnly replied and meant it.

Stickman dragged his eyes back to the dark road. Dusk was coming on, and the chill it brought could slowly kill.

"Alright, me love," the Stickman said.

Lucy nodded. "But there is something I want you to do for me . . ."

CHAPTER 56

It was early morning, Thursday, when Ted Myer opened the door to his downtown apartment in New York, located six blocks away from the hospital. Ted immediately closed the door behind him with a bang and proceeded to twist, throw, and slide the six various locking devices. Then, with eyes wide and red looking from sleep deprivation and too much coffee, he reached inside the nearby closet and hauled out the two metre length of two-by-four wood. There was a knob of wood in the floor which Ted had nailed there himself, and against this he placed one end of the thick board. The other end went against the door itself. The brace was thick enough, Ted figured, to stop anyone from coming through. The only concern he had was if someone used an axe or, even better, explosives to force entry. Then, all of Ted's attempts at securing his castle went down the fucking toilet.

But the drawbridge was up for the moment, and Ted flittered about the entryway, kicking off his boots and throwing off his thick coat. He was an overweight man with a lot of money invested in his paunch. His hair was reddish and thinning, but still had its curls. He had huge teeth that were accentuated by his overbite. Ted had to make a conscious effort to keep his mouth closed at all times, for if he didn't, it looked as if he were about to gnaw on something good and hard. He had been the Medical Examiner at Bellevue for four years, and in that amount of time, had witnessed a lot of freaky things.

But this past night was just simply incredible.

Ted went to his kitchen and broke out the bottle of Jack Daniels. Even though he could afford the more expensive stuff, he just liked the nostalgia Ol' Jack brought him from his years in medical school. He didn't go for a glass. *Fuck* the glass. With the bottle of booze, he went into his cosy-looking living room. He cracked the little toe of his right foot on the edge of the heavy sofa and let out a huge, throaty yelp of pain. Ted cursed and swore and even made to kick the sofa, but in the end, he resisted with a whimper and sat his large posterior on its cushy goodness. He placed the bottle of sour mash on the coffee table in front of him and with his free hand, snatched up the remote control. A huge Samsung flat-screen TV, complete with a surround sound system came to life, and Ted began to channel surf. He got the news channel, clicked past it too fast, screamed *"fuck!"* and went back. Once he had the news station, he just sat there for a moment. It was the 8:00 a.m. news, and Ted's eyes went wide, searching.

He watched.

And he was rewarded.

A family of four had been shot and left for dead in their home in the northeast part of New York. They were discovered by their neighbours a day later. The family sustained shotgun blasts to their faces and torsos, and yet were miraculously still alive.

A transport truck driver on one of the turnpikes fell asleep at the wheel and ploughed his vehicle through a family's living room, running over three kids watching cartoons. They all lived, even the driver, who sustained heavy injuries to his head and chest.

Another driver speeding on the New Jersey Turnpike lost control of his car and rammed into a new length of guard rail being installed. The rail stabbed through the windshield and impaled the man through the upper chest, almost severing his right arm completely at the shoulder. The victim was in an intensive care unit of Saint Ann's Hospital.

Ted took a shot of whiskey and kept on channel surfing, seeking out the morning news from everywhere. Even in the war zones, where death seemed as casual as a yawn, there were no reports of anyone actually dying. There were reports on bombings and shootings, yet all concerned survived.

Earlier in the morning and nearing the end of his shift, Ted got permission from Aaron Roeder to have a smoke, and left him and Garlich to the prize on the examination table. Ted badly needed a cigarette, and halfway through, decided on an impulse to head up to the ER ward to see what was happening there. There had been some disturbing cases. Some druggie had injected himself (herself?) with bleach and was holding on, much to the dismay of the doctor attending the victim. An attempted suicide had opened up her wrists and her throat, and lost damn near all the blood in her body, yet she held on for four hours before someone found her in her apartment and rushed her to the hospital. She was still breathing. This prompted Ted to make a quick call to Steve Leeds up at General to see if there were any people refusing to die up there. There were lots, in fact, according to Steve. The staff on duty were either shaking their heads in wonder or celebrating with the number of close calls that could have claimed many lives. *Should* have, even.

Sitting there in his living room, staring wide-eyed at his wide-screen, Ted had a thought. A lot of people weren't dying. A lot of people that *should* have died weren't dying. In fact, all news broadcasts reported there were plenty of survivors, but *no* deaths. What did this mean? Was Ted the only one to have noticed such a thing?

"It's fucked up," he muttered aloud. He couldn't wrap his mind around the idea, the *concept*, that if *he* decided to do himself in right now, there was a very good possibility he would not die.

He sat and drank and thought. He kept on scanning news reports for something. Anything.

The drinking continued until noon. Ted should have been in bed long ago, but instead, he was pleasantly shitfaced. The redness in his ruddy cheeks was a deep hue, and yet his eyes hardly strayed from the TV. He absorbed every news broadcast there was. Information. He craved information.

His telephone rang around 2:00 and again around 4:00. Ted did not bother to answer. His answering machine clicked on, and voices were recorded. He ignored them. His cell phone rang twice, but he had left that on the counter in the kitchen. He sat and watched practically all day with the exception of going to the bathroom. And as the day moved on, it became obvious to an inebriated Ted, all alone in his apartment, that there were some serious things not happening in the world.

"Nobody," he burped out at one point. "Nobody at all. Fucked up, man. Fucked *up*."

The sun dropped out of sight, and Ted marked the absence of light by mechanically switching on a nearby lamp. His phone rang several more times in the evening, and at last, perhaps around 8:00, he got up, marched around his apartment and ripped both landlines out of the wall. He baseball pitched his cell phone into the toilet. The phones were a distraction. With three-quarters of a very large bottle of booze flooding his system and senses, Ted did not need anyone to distract him. He would not report to work later. What he had discovered was more important than work. It was far more important than anything.

It was *awesome*.

But Ted wanted to beat the boys in the basement to the punch. He wanted to be the one to announce to the world that, in case you haven't noticed, not one person in the whole world had died. Not one. What do you think about that, Dave?

A smashed smile spread across Ted's face. To be interviewed by Dave Letterman would be *awesome*. He could call the studios in an hour, already forgetting how he had disposed of his means of communication. Ted returned to the sofa and sat down with the weight of a drunken ogre. He spied the TV and decided to keep it on CNN for the rest of the night. Just a little more proof was all he needed to confirm his suspicions.

Just a little more proof.

Then, it hit him. Like a comet blazing a path straight through the space between his eyes. The ultimate in proof. What better way to prove you couldn't die anymore than by shooting yourself on TV! That was the cat's ass in Ted's liquored up mind. He mulled over it. Oh there would be a few non-believers in the audience who would think it were all special effects, but Dave would sure as hell be impressed!

He sat on his sofa with CNN on, scratching his upper lip with his lower teeth.

"Better have a test run," Ted declared aloud. He staggered to his feet, threw out his arms for balance and staggered towards the kitchen. He had something there. Just the thing. His father's snub nose .38, already loaded and ready.

Ted got the gun from the kitchen cabinet over the fridge. He checked the rounds and smiled tightly. Holding the gun in his right fist, with sense enough to point it away from himself, he got back to the sofa and planted himself once again. He placed the gun on the coffee table before him and stared at it.

Gun black. Snub nosed. An ugly name for an ugly piece of metal.

"Jesus," Ted muttered to himself. Was he really going to fucking *shoot* himself? The idea was great in the beginning, but now that the gun was out and right before him, not even the confidence bestowed upon him by the old magician Jacky D. could stop the sudden shrinkage of his scrotum. Ted stared at the gun for a long time. It was one thing to think about doing it, but it was another to actually have the balls to do it.

And what if he was wrong?

Ted swayed on the couch.

Where would he shoot himself that would cause minimal damage if he was wrong about his assumption? He drank on that thought. And he drank more when he could not come up with somewhere to shoot himself that would potentially kill him if he didn't suspect he couldn't die. If he shot himself in the head, he ran the risk of brain damage. Anywhere in the chest could produce similar grave after effects—if he lived to tell. Ted snorted. Of course, he would live! The proof was on TV and in the morgues and ER wards of New York!

He picked up the gun, hefted it, and placed it at an angle underneath his chin. A rush of fear went through him. If he pulled the trigger now, the dice would be rolled and there would be no going back. No reset button. Christ, he thought darkly, how did the suicides of the world do it? To be driven to a place where taking their own lives was the final solution to their problems. It struck him to be something of a paradox. The courage they found to do themselves in was a monstrous thing, and yet it wasn't enough to carry on living, to face the fears that drove them to the edge in the first place.

But what did Ted really know about it?

Looking ahead at the wide-screen TV, he adjusted his grip on the pistol and took a breath. His finger tensed on the trigger.

He would find out.

CHAPTER 57

The light was fading outside, and Tony was feeling good about it. It only took him a moment to realize that Ol' Jack was doing his rounds. That made him smile. One could count on Mr. Daniels. He sat off to one side on the same L-shaped couch as an equally pickled Death. The forty ouncer of sour mash whiskey had slowly disappeared between the two of them in the final hour of daylight. Death did not talk anymore about being pissed off with people, and Tony did not debate the matter with him. How could he? It made sense, what he was saying. The last thing most everyone ever felt before dying was pain, and Death was the firefighter to the rescue. Now that the firefighter had decided to stop working, it was clear to Tony just how important that individual's role was. He remembered watching the news in the hotel room with Lucy not so long ago, and he recalled his slow uptake on what was happening. Nobody dying. Anywhere. How long would it take for someone to figure it out? How long would it take for the crazies to take advantage of it? How long did they have *left*?

But what could Tony say to convince the man next to him to return to work?

"Hey."

Tony glanced to the still paralyzed and now smashed Death on the couch.

"You got shit to do," Death informed him.

"I do?"

"Yeah," Death wiggled a finger at the door. "They'll be coming soon. They'll try to get through that door."

"More of those things?"

"Yeah."

"Sweet Jesus," Tony grumped, pulling himself up off the couch. "Why can't you just go back?"

"What?" Death smiled wickedly. "And miss the fights? I got a ringside seat here, buddy!"

"Asshole," Tony muttered under his breath. He made his way to the door and bent over to look out through the broken window. The darkness was deepening. "Looks dark out there."

"They'll be coming sooner, then," Death said picking at the label on the whiskey bottle.

"How do you know?"

"They usually do," Death informed him. "It's a dead thing. Same with them eating the flesh of the living. Romero got that part right. Why couldn't you be him? The conversation would've been a lot brighter, methinks."

Tony straightened up. He placed a hand on the door and held his bat in the other.

"Why am I going outside, again?"

"Look around," Death told him. "Find a hammer and some wood. I'd barricade the house up real good if I were you."

"I won't have time for all that."

"You should've thought of that before you started drinking with me," Death scolded.

Shaking his head in annoyance, Tony yanked open the door and plunged out into the night.

"Bring back something t'eat, eh?" Death hollered after him.

Tony grabbed his crotch and gave it a quick, meaningful squeeze. Death could eat that, he thought darkly. He slammed the door behind him and looked about. Tony ignored the place where the bear had fallen. He peered out into the greying dark and the swirling snow. Dead things gathering. Just his dumb luck. He should have never taken this insane job in the first place. It was going to leave a scar. He could feel it. The snow went into his eyes, and he squinted against it. He kept one hand on his bat and the other against the wall of the cabin as he trudged around to the back. It was darker behind the cabin, but Death was right. There was a shed back here. Small, padlocked, and practically knee deep in the fallen snow

Cursing, Tony stomped his way to the shed and dropped to his knees. He began to dig, clawing at the base of the door and heaving snow. He had it cleared within moments. He stood and studied the small padlock on the door's latch. It was a simple thing. Perhaps, there was a key back in the house somewhere. It would take time to find it.

Snarling, Tony stepped back and smashed at the lock with his bat. He struck it hard, but the lock held. He smashed it, again, grunting. Still it held. Swearing, he went to war on the padlock, swinging and striking and smashing it with all of his desperate strength. The lock and wood surrounding it eventually surrendered to his blows, and the padlock dropped into the snow.

I'll look for it in the spring, Tony thought angrily and yanked open the shed's door.

He was in luck.

Whoever the owner of the cabin and shed was, he was something of a carpenter. It was cold and shadowy inside. The air smelled sweet of sawdust, and for a moment, Tony just stood and breathed in that wonderful scent. It brought him back to reality, grounding him against the forces that were massing beyond the snow and gloom. All manner of tools hung on walls or lay on shelves. A modern Black and Decker Workmate stood in a corner of the shed, opposite an old but still serviceable wooden bench. Old fashioned buck saws, axes, and hammers hung here and there, and on the wooden bench was a bare tin can, dull in the fading light and full of two and three-inch nails. There were shelves full of the tools any skilled woodsman would have at his disposal, but Tony could not name them all. He quickly scanned for what he needed. He snatched up a hammer and nails, jamming them into his deep pockets, and then gathered up planks of heavy wood from one corner of the shed. Grunting and swearing, he struggled with the materials, carrying it all back to the cabin where Death lay waiting with his whiskey. Or what was left of it.

Death came awake with a fright when Tony banged opened the door and dropped everything in the entry way. He stood there for a moment, slap-wiping his hands and gazing at Death with a disgusted look.

"Sorry to disturb your rest, your highness."

"Suck on my royal knob," Death retorted. "Found some stuff, did ya?" His words were slurred and unsteady.

But Tony was gone, again. Death grumbled to himself about respecting elders in his day, even when the elders were pissed out of their gourds. Not with Mundanes, though. Oh, no. They were just too goddamn special to wait around and listen.

But then, Tony was back, again, with another load of wooden planks.

Death blinked at him. "Father Time must be fucking around here somewhere, the old cocksucker."

"What?" Tony gasped, not listening. He was feeling his arms with the second load of wood, and this time he brought along a mean looking hatchet.

"Nothing," Death muttered. "What cha brings us?"

Tony held up the short axe with a grim smile.

"Nice," Death nodded.

"There was a chainsaw out there, too," Tony said closing the door behind him and shoving a thick piece of wood up underneath the doorknob. Selecting some long nails, he began pounding them into the wood, bracing the door. "And a bunch of other sharp looking things. I think fuckin' ninjas live up here in the summer."

"Why didn't you bring the chainsaw?" Death wanted to know.

"No gas for it. I looked."

"No gas?" Death regarded his almost empty bottle. "Jesus. Christ. Almighty."

He watched as Tony moved from the main door to the one window next to it. He hoisted up a broad looking wooden board and positioned it across the window frame. In moments, he was hammering away, nailing it into place.

"Industrious little bastard, ain't cha?" Death remarked, watching the man work through piss-hole eyes.

"You just lie there," Tony said as he quickly worked. "And don't move."

Death gave him a drunken salute.

"Damned if a bunch of snow zombies is going to take you away from me," Tony muttered under his breath. "Fuck that."

"Did ya see any out there?"

"No," Tony said, and that was the truth, but on the second trip, the hair on the back of his neck was standing up. His spine chilled, too. No, he did not see them, but he sensed them sure enough. And sensing them was probably just as potent. His legs felt weak, and he was certain it wasn't merely the cold. There was a growing fear there, as unwanted as a cancer, and it was moving north. Already he could feel his scrotum tighten and his stomach knot up. He stopped for a moment, feeling the weakness in his legs transform into energy for fleeing. He began hammering at the wood harder, putting his shoulder into each swing. Sometimes he connected with only an edge of the nail head and sparks flew. He began to miss the nails more and more, and still he hammered away at the wooden beams. The energy in his legs flowed into his arms, and he harnessed it, pounding away at the wood.

"Tony," Death called to him.

He whirled about, hammer at the ready, wide eyed, and sweating rivers.

There, on the couch, watching him with perhaps the first genuine smile Tony had ever see on his features, was Death himself. His breath hitched in his throat.

"Tony," Death said in a voice that did not betray anything about the amount of booze he had consumed, "slow down. Slow down, man. You're doing more harm than good."

"They'll get you," Tony blurted out. "They'll get us."

"They won't," Death said calmly.

"Why won't they?"

"Because I have a few tricks."

Perhaps it was Death's relaxed form on the couch that did it. Perhaps it was the calmness in his voice. Whatever it was, Tony got a hold of his fear.

"You got something? Like in the car?"

Death nodded. "Like the car, but not quite."

"What is it?"

This brought a frown. "I ain't telling you, man! But I will tell you this. When they come, they'll be surprised. And there won't be a damn thing they'll be able to do about it."

"So, I can relax?" Tony asked.

"Fuck, no, you can't relax," Death blurted out. "But you can hold up on trying to put the hammer through the wall. Okay?"

Tony's shoulders heaved upwards with the deep breath he drew. He felt the heat flow into his cheeks now. He was afraid, and Death called him on it. When was the last time he had actually lost it in front of someone? With the exception of fuckhead Freddie, he could not recall.

"Sorry," he apologized and meant it.

"No need for that," Death assured him, "but don't stop hammering, either."

Tony nodded. He got back to fortifying their position. He thought about all the people he had seen on the news in accidents or disasters. He thought of his mother back in Halifax.

"They ain't getting you," Tony vowed under his breath.

And swung his hammer.

CHAPTER 58

"The snow's getting thicker," Marvin muttered, hunched over the steering wheel of the fire truck. Thick gobs of white mashed into the windshield almost as fast as the wipers could clear it, and it was hard to manage the big rig on the slippery roads. His brow creased with the strain of driving. He wore his firefighter's gear as if it was armor, and he was going into battle. He did not dare glance over at Maia. The fire chief was staring straight ahead with a look that could challenge the sun. He held his Halligan bar across his lap like a battle axe. The Halligan was a tool for prying open doors. It was a length of steel with a tapered spike and blade at one end, and a short claw at the other. Marvin had seen Maia use the tool on locked doors before. He wondered what it would be like to use such an instrument on a human skull or any available orifices. That thought made him suppress an evil smile. It wasn't wise to be smiling around Maia when he was in one of his moods.

There were only five of them in the pump truck, all dressed in their regular gear, and searching for their fallen comrades. Maia knew that Death had somehow gotten the best of them. Now, it was his responsibility to unfuck the mess. He made it a point to stay away from any washrooms mirrors before he rallied his troops. He did not need any messages or threats to know what was at stake. He knew.

Maia knew big time.

He decided in taking out the pump truck, a massive red machine with all of the traditional equipment firefighters needed for a wide range of fire fighting and rescue tasks. He took this over the other because of the fire monitor—a deck gun capable of blasting out fifteen litres of water per second or up to thirty bars of pressure. That was enough to tear up cobble stone streets under a sustained onslaught. It was certainly enough to break bones. Maia once witnessed an industrial water jet cutter cut through twenty centimetres of rock, and while he would have loved to have gotten the city to purchase such a device, there was no real means to justify it. The images of what such a device could do to bare flesh entertained his mind for weeks. But he had the water cannon on the roof of his truck, and that would suffice if they needed it. The truck carried a full tank of two thousand litres of water. It would be enough to stun even Death, if Maia saw the chance to use it.

Squinting, Marvin took his foot off the gas and gently applied the brake.

"What the fuck do you think you're doing?" Maia asked in a calm but dangerous voice. It frightened the shit out of Marvin. He put his foot back down on the accelerator, and the pump truck picked up speed in the growing blizzard and darkness. For a single terrifying instant, he had a vision of his chief burying the pick end of his Halligan into one of his eye sockets. Saunders, Edwards, and Northman, sitting quietly in the back and thankful to be behind the chief, *remained* quiet.

Maia went back to looking out at the road. They were heading north off the main highway now, heading into the great wilderness of Northern British Columbia. It was just the place where if someone wanted to get lost, it could easily be achieved. Maia wondered how many had lost their lives in the surroundings timberlands and mountains in years gone past. He wondered how the coming War would change the landscape. It would be changed. He would be right there with a napalm rack on his back and a flashing nozzle in his hands. That thought calmed him, so he kept right on thinking it.

The red machine sliced through the white arcs of snow that had collected on the highway. There was no traffic on the stretch of road, and the snow piled up. The fire truck had no real trouble going through, but it was the black ice that was proving to be tricky. Marvin hoped there would not be any sudden stops anytime soon. If there was, he would be at the wheel of a very large piece of machinery sliding out of control.

Onwards they drove, moving through the death of the day and not impressed with the coming of the dark. It would be difficult to hunt in the dark. The fire truck's lights flicked on, and the snow began to flash into both the headlights and windshield like chunky comets.

"Slow down." Maia ordered after a while. He was leaning to his left. His arm came up pointing. "What's that on your side?"

His crew looked. Although the snow had covered up the tracks and partially filled the gap in the snow bank, when the car left the road, it left behind the wake of a rocket. When Marvin realized what it was he was looking at, he stopped the machine. The Minions peered through the gloom and saw the path the car made before the tree stopped its flight. Even in the gloom of the falling night, it was an impressive wreck.

"You stay on the wheel," Maia ordered Marvin. The chief then glanced back at the other three. "You all come with me. Keep your eyes open."

Maia briefly met the impassive gaze of Grey Northman. The man had said nothing since the fire station, and for that, Maia was both relieved and suspicious. He did not trust the grey one. There was something about the Minion he just did not like. He did not want to be any more careful around his Minions than he routinely had to be. They were pyromaniacs after all, but his gut cautioned him about Northman.

Doors popped open, and the Minions disembarked their pumper, dressed in their heavy Nomex fire coats marked in bright stripes of battle yellow. They carried axes. No one wore their helmets, wearing black ski masks instead. They fell in behind Maia, wary of their chief's Halligan. Silently moving through the snow in their heavy boots, slogging ahead as the snow came up to their knees.

The snow covered most of the blood around the car, and the cold stifled the smell like one great outdoor freezer keeping meat. The interior of the car was still a mess despite snow having blown in through the broken windows, covering the four headless corpses. Maia stood back for a moment and simply took in the scene. The other three Minions gathered around the demolished vehicle with their axes at the ready. After a moment, Maia stepped forward and stuck his head in through the passenger side window. He could tell Peters and Bull from their body sizes and clothes. He gazed up at the gore coating the ceiling of the car. Behind his ski mask, his mouth cut into a grimace of disgust. All dead. *Without even a fight*, he guessed. It made him sick.

Maia straightened up and beheld the car once more. "Fuckin' Angel of Death," he muttered clear enough for his Minions to hear. "I told you stupid bastards to be careful. Should've chiselled the words into your goddamn foreheads."

The Minions surrounding the car could see what had been done to their companions. A sense of dread, awe and perverse excitement rippled through them. They had been afraid of missing out on the fun of torturing Death while they waited for the End to arrive. They had been extremely resentful of not being selected to take care of Death, dangerously jealous of not being in Maia's finer graces to have been assigned the task of finding the Boatman and whisking him away. Now, it would seem they would have their chance after all. And the reality of their brethren's demise was just as freezing as the temperatures of the great north. Whatever resentment they might have felt had evaporated.

This was *Death* they were hunting.

The fucking *Grim Reaper* himself.

He would not go lightly.

And there would be casualties.

Maia broke the cold silence surrounding them.

"Alright then, motherfucker," he quietly swore at the headless foursome in the car wreck. Maia had fucked with the best in the past and won. He would do so again. "Alright."

He turned and locked gazes with the ski-masked Grey Northman standing on the other side of the car.

"What?" Maia demanded of the Minion. Northman did not reply. He merely stood with the snow coating his Nomex coat, slowly coloring him white. He held his axe two handed across his pelvis.

"You got something to say, fucker, you say it now!" Maia roared at the figure. Saunders and Edwards glanced uneasily at each other. They had heard this tone from their chief before. It was usually before he did something incredibly violent. They had long sensed their leader's dislike for the newcomer, and perhaps now was the just the ignition needed for the chief to do something about that dislike.

"Or you just going to stand there in the fuckin' snow?"

Northman kept right on staring at the fire chief.

Livid, Maia brought his Halligan up like a spear, and moved to circle the car.

At the same time, Marvin sounded the horn on the fire pumper.

The sudden blare of the red beast froze Maia in the snow. Edwards and Saunders both whirled about in the direction of the horn. Northman kept his attention on the Minion fire chief. The three Minions that were looking could see what Marvin could see in his rearview mirrors.

There was a car approaching.

CHAPTER 59

Stickman took long and deep breaths, trying to fight the wave of nausea threatening to empty the contents of his stomach. Lucy explained what she was going to do, and he listened with a smile. Hell, he even nodded his understanding when she asked for it. And then, she went and did exactly what she said she was going to do.

Stickman's Sunbird went into warp speed.

There was no other way to describe it, and yet, wasn't there supposed to be like G-forces or something like that? He didn't feel any sensation of being pushed back into his seat although the streaking lights outside of the moving car did bring on the stomach sickness. Day faded rapidly. He felt he was going to barf at any time, and his throat started to hitch.

"Oh, no," he heard Lucy say, and then the car was slowing down.

There was a fire truck in the middle of the road.

Stickman slammed on the brakes. The car slid. He kept his hands on the wheel, and somehow the tires found purchase. It would stop long before it kissed the ass of the red behemoth taking up the road and filling up the Stickman's windshield. In truth, it didn't bother the Stickman much, colliding with a fire truck. If one had to slam into a vehicle, it might as well be a first responder unit. The Sunbird slowed to a stop not two metres from the rear bumper of the fire truck.

The Stickman opened the door on his side, dropped out onto the cold pavement on his hands and knees, and vomited. Repeatedly.

And on the final retch, the one where his stomach felt as if it should throw out his kidneys, liver, and any other organ handy, Stickman moaned and let his forehead touch the black snow-covered asphalt. His only concern in the world right then was not lying down in his own pool of puke.

"Oh, Jeezus Christ," the Stickman moaned into the frigid wind and was thankful for it. "Oh, Joseph and Mary . . . Lord tunderin Jeezus . . . Murphy."

He felt hands on his shoulders and knew instinctively it was his angel Lucy. God bless her heart. He wanted to say exactly that, but instead, pushed himself away from the contents of his stomach on the highway. He rolled over onto his back, blinked, and saw the concern on Lucy's face above him. That caused him to smile.

But only for a moment.

"Is he okay?" a man's voice asked, and Lucy's smile disappeared. It was replaced by a look of distrust and even loathing. It was enough for even the Stickman's smile to frost over. He arched his head to see.

He saw heavy steel-toed boots. He saw the greenish protective pants worn by professional firefighters. He saw that this particular firefighter was also carrying a red axe. This puzzled the Stickman. Why would Lucy have cause for alarm with ordinary firefighters?

"I asked if he was okay, lady," the voice repeated, and the question hung in the air.

Then, another voice cut in. This one was mean and angry sounding. Stickman cringed. It sounded like Burr from long ago, the same Burr that had raped him in the showers. It sounded so much like Burr that Stickman felt that his back and balls had just frozen solid to the highway.

"Jesus Christ, you idiot," the voice snarled. "Can't you see who *she* is?"

Lucy backed up as a black, ski-masked firefighter pushed his way past the first axe-wielding firefighter and stood before her. She could just distinguish the blackness of the cotton mask from the obsidian gleam of the Minion's eyes. The realization of who they had almost run into made her want to scream.

Maia stepped forward, actually plodding into Stickman's steaming pool of vomit and not caring in the least. He hoisted up his Halligan and jabbed it in her direction. "Picked the wrong fuckin' road, didn't cha, bitch?"

Lucy did not reply. Terrified, she backed up and bumped into the open driver's door of the Sunbird.

Maia paused and regarded the helpless form of the Stickman in the road. He bent over, and slowly with one hand, finger by finger, clasped the front of the Stickman's coat. He lifted the Stickman up as an adult might pick up a child's doll. He brought the Mundane in close, inspected him briefly, and snorted his disgust into Stickman's rolling face.

"Cur," Maia scoffed and tossed the helpless Stickman a full five metres across the road. He landed out of sight in the snow. The fire chief forgot about him. He was only a Mundane. A speck of fly shit. But the woman was a different case. It wasn't often Maia got to see one of the Entities, but the glow was unmistakable.

She was one. He didn't know which one, but it did not matter. The Entities were all the same to the Minions. They all looked down upon them, forever favouring the human cattle and forsaking the Minions. Many were the times Maia wished and prayed he could exact revenge on just one of their kind, but they were crafty, the Entities, and hard to locate when they took on their suits of flesh. But this one, for whatever reasons Maia did not think or care about, just happened to appear right at a time when Maia wanted to lay a hurt on *something*. It made the fire chief smile.

"Lucky, lucky me," he purred, baring teeth.

And then, just like so many times before, because it was Lucy's nature to have such luck, the absolute luckiest thing that could happen at the moment of danger happened. Headlights blazed through the darkness of the highway, back from where both fire truck and Sunbird had come. The vehicle raced towards them, not slowing in the least. Maia turned in the direction of the approaching vehicle, swearing. "Who the fuck—"

Those were three of the last five words he would ever speak.

CHAPTER 60

Behind the wheel of the Celica, Danny gritted his teeth, tried very hard to contain his fear. Sweat popped out on his forehead, armpits, and chest; and still, he could not turn away. He tried so very hard to turn the wheel, but his master—for Fear was both Danny's and Crew's master now—merely snorted at the feeble gesture and did not even bother turning his head to acknowledge the attempt.

Fear focused on the road ahead. He knew who the firefighters were. *What* they were. He knew who it was they had pinned up against the piece-of-shit Sunbird. And while Fear wanted nothing more than to get pay back for the rubbing he had sustained at Tony's hands thanks to Lucy, he despised Minions even more.

"Ram them," Fear ordered Danny quietly, his voice full of hatred.

Grinding his teeth, Danny stomped on the accelerator.

CHAPTER 61

"Is that?" Maia's scowl vanished as the black Celica showed no signs of slowing. Even as he realized what was about to happen, the car's engine sang out with the sudden burst of power Danny delivered to it. The Celica fired forward with a roar, hitting all three of the Minions in its path and sending them up and over the low-riding car's hood and roof. They fell behind the car in ragged broken heaps. Maia landed squarely on his face, crushing his nose, and sending bone and cartilage fragments into his sensitive nasal cavity like a ball of needles. He shattered both arms, along with his rib cage and one unlucky leg. Saunders and Edwards were just as unfortunate. Edwards also landed on his face, smashing all of his front teeth on his fire axe and snapping both his arms to compliment his already broken legs. Saunders landed on his hands and knees. His femurs splintered, the bone ends puncturing muscle tissue and skin to make tiny tents underneath his Nomex pants. His wrists snapped as clean as icicles when he kissed the asphalt.

The car missed Lucy by a fat centimetre.

The Celica's brakes clamped down, and the car fish tailed off into the darkness. Rear lights burned like something evil in the distant dark. From where he sat, Marvin watched the car bring itself to a stop, and he looked into his rear mirror to see what had happened. He heard the approaching car, but his attention was distracted by someone, one of the Minions, running back into the forest.

Then there were the sounds of impact, and the car sailed on by.

He stared at the car ahead. It was still in the blackness of the winter night. He looked in his side mirror and saw the crumpled forms of three of his comrades lying in the road.

"Holy shit," Marvin spat out, as he reached for the light switch.

Then his door was yanked open, and he was grabbed.

Danny hauled the man from behind the wheel of the fire truck and threw him to the ground. Marvin landed on his side. He grunted loudly and regained his feet as nimble as a cat. He shook his head clear and zeroed in on his attacker. His lips pulled back, and in the second before the sound left his throat, Crew's fist cracked across his chin, dropping the Minion to the ice-slick asphalt. The firefighter shook his head, again, and struggled to his knees. Crew kicked him hard in the face, breaking teeth, nose, and part of a cheek. The firefighter toppled over onto his back, his legs twisting at the knees. He gargled on blood and slivers of enamel. Dazed as he was, Marvin decided that he would just rest for a while.

"Finish him off," Fear commanded as he strode up to Crew. Danny stood just behind the man, looking down at the hit man's handiwork. Crew studied the man at his feet and shook his head. Both men felt sick to their stomachs.

"Finish him," Fear ordered, again, looking at Crew's profile.

"No," Crew whispered in a strained voice, fighting back his nausea. As sorry as it sounded, he had rules. He was a contract killer. He didn't kill without a contract. He felt the push from Fear, but the force was less than before. Crew resisted.

Fear knew why, even if Crew didn't. "Fine, then," he said. He stepped past Crew and did not waste any more of his essence on the Mundane. There were bigger beasts in the woods now, and part of him would enjoy putting this particular one down. His eyes met those of Lucy's as he passed her. She said nothing to him. She knew what the four men were on the road. She knew what they weren't.

Fear picked up the Halligan tool where it had fallen on the roadside. He inspected the instrument's tapered pick before walking back to where Marvin lay. Almost casually, Fear thrust the steel pick into Marvin's skull and left it there. Lucy gasped. The Minion's back arched, like an impaled spider, and then went limp. Blackness spilled from the hole just above Marvin's still open eyes, but there wasn't as much as either Danny or Crew would have thought. Then, they realized that whatever was coming out of the hole wasn't blood at all. It smelled like rotting meat.

"Jesus," Danny whispered, coming very close to vomiting. He could not take his eyes off of the impaled man on the road and the dark pool forming around his head.

Then, he heard the others.

The others he had run over. They were all moaning in agony.

Fear heard them, too. He looked to Lucy. She held his gaze.

"We have to get out of here," she said to him.

Looking uneasy, Fear nodded, mentally vowing that there would be another time to confront the bitch. "Get back to the car," he commanded Danny and

Crew. He sent a wave of pure fear in their direction. Even with Lucy's presence, the force struck them hard enough to make their hearts suddenly palpitate. Both men staggered backwards, clutching at their chests and moving in the direction of the Celica.

"I need one of them," Lucy said urgently.

Fear scowled at her. She pointed to the edge of the road. "He's over there. We can't leave him. We'll need him."

Fear looked to where the Stickman had fallen. He regarded Lucy and snorted in disdain. "Help her," Fear ordered Danny, stopping him cold in his tracks.

Danny did not hesitate. As much as he wanted to, he could not do anything in the presence of the man he had rode with for what seemed like an eternity. Ignoring the churning of his innards, which was lessening now, he moved to help.

"He's over there," Lucy pointed.

Snow swirled past Fear and Lucy, and the wind howled around them. They both felt the vibration in the air. There was no mistaking it. A train of such terrible power was coming that neither of them had any control over it. And it was coming fast, like some prehistoric shark catching a scent of spilled blood across miles of ocean. Fear had no problem whatsoever with the situation. He fixed Lucy with the coldest of stares.

And ran for the waiting Celica.

Lucy watched him go with a swelling sense of terror inside. She knew that Fear was playing with her now, but she could do nothing to stop it. This time, fear was a motivator.

"Hurry," she called out to Danny. She opened the back door for the men before slipping in behind the wheel of the Sunbird. The feeling of approaching doom was intensifying. She was breathing faster now. Something very bad was going to happen soon. "Please *hurry!*"

Danny almost swore. The man he was fumbling for was deep in the snow. He grasped the edges of a coat and pulled. There, in the twilight of the fire pumper's headlights, he saw the Stickman's face. He had found the bastard that had placed his friends in the hospital. The Stickman was unconscious and in his grip.

Danny's hands sought his throat.

"Hurry UP!" wailed Lucy from the driver's seat. Her voice made him look back. She was clawing at the air, gesturing for him to return to the car. There was something frightening about it.

"Come ON!" She shrieked, looking around wildly.

Then, Danny noticed it.

The wind had stopped for some reason.

"*Come on!*" Lucy screamed hoarsely.

From where he lay on the road, broken, ruined, bleeding, and still not dead, Maia's eye's flicked in the direction of the scream. The lady knew how to scream, Maia thought through his blizzard of pain. He had never experienced such agony while in human form. He supposed it was a taste of what would come once he returned to whence he came. That brought a chortle from his crushed ribcage, a pitiful rattle of a sound that caused the Minion's black blood to ooze from the corners of his mouth.

"*Now!*" Lucy continued to shriek.

Danny wanted nothing to do with this human sack of shit in his hands. He wanted to kill the fucker right now. He bared his teeth and held onto the Stickman's neck, thinking it would be so easy to squeeze, just squeeze with all of his might and see what would happen to the killer in his grasp.

Then, the car was behind him.

"*Get in!*" Lucy screamed at him, her eyes wild. "*Get in before it's too* fucking *late!*"

Danny looked at the wild woman behind the wheel of the car. She had backed the thing up almost on top on him.

And he did something that he would not understand later. He listened.

He released the Stickman's throat and hauled on his shoulders. He hoisted the little wall of a man out of the snow and practically threw him into the back seat of the car. He placed both of his hands on the roof.

"Oh shit," he heard the woman say weakly.

The words made him pause. And look. Back in the direction of East.

There. A man. A big man.

Danny's face slackened.

He was naked from the waist up and as heavily muscled as any bodybuilder in their prime. He seemed to take shape out of the deep blackness of the highway night, and he walked up to the first firefighter lying on the road. The newcomer wore heavy workman boots. The kind with steel toes.

When he got close enough to the first firefighter, he kicked the unmoving man's face in. Danny heard the crunch of metal on bone.

"Jesus Christ!" Danny blurted, holding onto the roof.

"*Get in!*" Lucy begged him with red, wet eyes.

The firefighter on the ground moaned in agony. He could not get away. The bare-chested behemoth stomped on gloved fingers. The scream that it produced did not impress Pain in the least. He wanted more. This plaything was almost spent it seemed, but nowhere near dying. Nowhere near at all.

"Please," Lucy begged in a hoarse pitying voice.

It was enough. Danny jumped aboard the car and pulled the door shut. He landed on top of Stickman coming back to his senses. There was recognition in his eyes, but he still did not have the strength to protect himself. A second later, he was slammed against the back seat as Lucy gave the Sunbird a heavy shot of gas. She could not remember ever being so close to physical danger. In fact, she knew it was only the pain of the near-dead Minions on the highway that had saved her, distracting the monstrosity's attention long enough so that she could make her escape. She cursed Fear. He knew. Weeping over the steering wheel, she promised she would have a stern talk with that one.

The Sunbird sped away from the fire truck and the scene that was unfolding.

Maia heard the car speeding away. They had escaped. He fucking knew it. They had escaped, yet again. The Entities had a fortune about them that was enraging. He slowly blinked, hearing the sudden wail of Edwards. Then, it was Saunders, closer now. Maia tried to breath, tried to take a calming breath, but he could not. His rib cage felt like a shattered egg shell, kept only together by pink flesh and tissue.

Then, he felt the presence nearing him.

Maia sighed. It was not supposed to end this way. There was supposed to be War. There was supposed to be Hell on Earth. He was supposed to witness it all. It was not supposed to end this way. He attempted a snarl at the cruelness of it all, but it hurt too goddamn much.

Then, the shadow was over him.

Maia's eyes watered.

And the thing known as Pain smiled upon him.

From the cover of the forest, holding his axe before him like a holy symbol, Grey Northman watched impassively. He watched as the bare-chested giant of a man pulled the fire chief apart with his bare hands. First, the thing pulled both arms out of Maia's shrieking body, then the legs, twisting them this way and that, working them against the joint until they tore free like dead pieces of chicken. Then, the man went to work on Maia's crotch.

Grey Northman watched it all, unflinchingly. He recorded his brethren's suffering in his mind. He listened to their cries and moans of pain. It would motivate him later, those sounds and images. He was told that Maia could potentially fail. His Master had foreseen this happening. Maia suspected that Northman had coveted leadership in his little coven of hell raisers. Nothing could have been further from the truth. Northman had been sent to ensure that the War would still happen. Northman had been sent in case of Maia's failure.

Grey Northman was Plan B.

Northman eyed the fire truck. He could probably steal the red beast while the thing was still feasting on the agony of his brethren. If he was quiet, he might still survive. Northman corrected himself. Of course, he would survive. He was not like Maia. He would be careful. He was the last of Maia's group now. He *had* to be careful. He had to survive.

To ensure the death of a world.

CHAPTER 62

Somewhere in the night, Tony came awake and was instantly alert. He had finished boarding up the five windows on the bottom floor of the cabin (he considered it lucky that there were only five) and sat down on the couch. Only for a moment, he told himself, only for a moment. But then, he was waking up. He had been seduced by the softness of the couch, and Death had let him. He glanced over at the other end.

Death was snoring like a rusty buzz saw, the near-empty bottle of Jack Daniels cradled in his arms. If it were any other time, Tony might have laughed.

But there was a bumping at the door.

It was low, as if whatever it was had just fallen. Or maybe it was just a little zombie. A dwarf zombie. Then, it started to rise upwards towards the glass of the window. Something heavy hit the side of the door, and made Tony sit up straight. He stared wide-eyed at the darkness. He blinked and swore and remembered he had a flashlight. He went for his pockets and hauled out the palm sized self-generating flashlight. He began squeezing and releasing the grip of the light where a sizeable button stuck out. The light only flickered, and the short brazen bursts of light panicked Tony. Then, he saw there was a switch on the flashlight. He thumbed it, and the light remained. He got to his feet in a hurry, waving the ghostly beam around the cabin as if he were trying to attract the attention of any low flying aircraft. He pinpointed the beam on the door.

On cue, something big struck the door, *hard*. Glass broke, but the wood inside held. Tony gasped loudly and went into a combat ready crouch. He felt his pockets, again. He had the two knives he took from the corpses. The bat was on the couch. The hatchet, the mean looking one that looked more suitable for hacking up flesh instead of wood, was on the floor next to the bat. How did it get there? Tony lunged for it and snatched it up with his right hand. He whirled about and lit up the door. His heart was going wild now, and he could see his breath in the silver light.

Something hit the planks, again, and the wood bulged inwards.

Tony's breath hitched in his throat. It was like that movie where the kids got caught out in a haunted forest. Except, these woods weren't haunted. They were fucking *zombiefied*. Another punch thrown at the planks covering the window made the wood tremble. Then, another. Then, there was a storm of pounding on the entire house. It seemed as if someone had set up a line of pitching machines and decided to let go right then and there. But that wasn't the worse of it.

The worse of it was the moaning.

Whoever they were outside, wherever they had come from, they moaned and sighed and groaned a terrible harmony that almost made Tony shit himself. Already he was covered in sweat and trying to see everywhere at once. They were surrounded. Tony wondered wildly if any had managed to climb to the second level. There was a broken window up there, and he hadn't barricaded it. A gut-paralyzing lump of fear swelled up in him then. What if they were climbing up there right now? Tony waved his light at the staircase and cringed at the sounds of the dead. He brought the hatchet to his ear, cocking it for a strike. The boards on the door shuddered. He went to it and wanted so badly to put his back against it. There was nothing else to brace it with, so he stood there and watched the wood pulse with every connection from the outside. And still, they cried out from beyond the door, a howling that would turn a man's hair pure white. Tony gasped for breath again. He needed to get away. No! He needed to stay here. He needed to be ready. He needed—

"Tony."

Tony spun about and there was Death, still lying on the couch, watching him with eyes that gleamed in the flashlight's glow. Black eyes with bright flecks of silver that reminded Tony of old vampire movies where, if you had a cross and believed in God above, you were just fine.

"I'm almost out of booze here," Death said, looking at his bottle. "Goddamn shame, too. You think the Lord drinks, Tone? Well, he does. The old man can fuckin' drink. Don't let some priest shout out blasphemy to change the subject. They know what's up. He loves nachos, too. God, that is. Never would have figured that, would ya? The Lord has a hankerin' for Mexican food. Big time. He can't get enough. 'Specially round the hockey playoffs. Chews with his mouth open, too. Fuck, I hate that."

Tony slouched, staring at the man on the couch. "Are you fucking high?"

Death shrugged and half smiled at him, then pointed at the door.

There were four fingers worming their way underneath one of the planks. Four fingers covered in black rotting flesh, the fingernails either broken or missing.

Shrieking, Tony lopped them off with the hatchet. Voices howled in agony. There were no more, so he looked back to Death.

"You're trying to take my mind off this."

"Course, I am, y'fuckin' retard."

The pounding at the door intensified, distracting Tony. Another hand sought to slip in underneath the boards. Tony hacked it half off. The hand hung limp under the planks, dark bone and rotten flesh exposed in the light. Tony felt himself gag.

"Hey!"

Tony regarded Death on the couch with sick eyes.

"Don't you do it!" Death warned him with a finger. "Don't you puke in here. You push through that shit, Tony!"

"Where are these things comin' from?" Tony moaned.

"Triad human trafficking. Whole shipping containers of people trying to get into the country. Sometimes, a few of the containers get forgotten and people die. The Triad dump the corpses near here. Mass unmarked graves."

Tony winced.

Death pointed at the other window. Tony hit the spot with his light. Another hand had inserted itself underneath the wood covering the window, and dark fingers with their tips tapering off into grey bone were seeking purchase. With one swipe, Tony removed two of the digits. A second chop and the other two dropped to the floor. The pounding on the house became louder as if the two men were trapped inside a drum. The walls of the cabin, thick and solid, would hold for however long it needed to. That was evident to Tony. The only weak spots were the windows. There were five of them on the ground floor including the small narrow one in the bathroom. Tony didn't know how many were upstairs. But if they got up there, it would not matter, anyway.

"Here!" Tony screamed and quickly passed the flashlight to Death. "Shine it where I can see!"

Death directed the light at the window over the kitchen sink. The fingers of the dead come back were trying to wedge themselves up under the wooden barriers. The slow squeal of nails being forced cut through the air and frightened Tony badly, energizing him. He rushed to the window where a maggots' nest of fingers were trying to find a grip and began hacking furiously at them.

Then, he split one plank with an overzealous swipe.

"Shit!" Tony screeched.

The wood cracked from the force of the hatchet and Tony's arm. It was all that was needed. With the pressure building up behind it, the wood split apart a second later, and three arms snaked their way into the cabin. Upper torsos followed. One owner turned its half flesh, half skeletal face towards the gap, pressing its cheek and lower face into the shoulder of another zombie. The jaw of the creature mashed against the bone of its companion, and Tony watched as it came unhinged and cracked, hissing all the while. Tony backed away from the gap, his eyes rooted to the breach, his mouth hanging open in terror.

"TONY!" Death roared. "*Move* your fucking ass!"

Tony moved. He stepped into striking distance of the nearest arm, angled away so it could not grab him. Tony brought the hatchet down and took the limb half off. He could feel the blade crunch through rotten bone like crusty wood exposed too long to the elements. He swung the hatchet again and took the arm off. The stump tried to pull back. The second arm flailed at him. He knocked it aside with his forearm and brought the hatchet down, removing it. The hideous face remained, glaring at Tony and hissing its grave-rotten breath. The smell caused Tony to stop in his tracks. His knees buckled. In that instant, another arm burst through the gap and grabbed him by the collar of his trench coat. It pulled him towards the hole. He looked up in time to see a hissing zombie trying to force its broken jaw apart so that it could bite into his forehead. Adrenalin fired and energized his limbs. He grabbed the hand holding him and bent it backward. It snapped with a dry crack. The fingers let go. Tony hacked into the arm with the hatchet, laying the flesh of the limb open. It retreated. Tony repeatedly swung the axe into the skull of the hissing zombie, shattering teeth and bone until the zombie seemed to fall away.

Only to be replaced by another.

Tony cracked the axe into the new zombie, right into its coal black face, and cried out when an eyeball popped out.

The screams got louder.

Then, Tony was fighting in the darkness.

Death swung the light to the windows near the door. Arms that moved like dark spider's legs managed to worm themselves into the cabin, using leverage to slowly work the planks apart. Wood and nails squealed at the invasion. Tony got there in time to hack off three of the arms in a savage flurry.

"It's like fucking Tetris, man!" Death roared with laughter from the couch.

"Do something!" Tony screamed as something black and thick and totally vile splashed on his face and upper body. The contact of the substance on his skin made him want to claw it off.

"I'm fuckin' paralyzed over here!" Death pealed, the flashlight beam going wild as he laughed.

Then the light was back on him and the battle.

Tony grunted and roared and chopped another arm off at the elbow. Blackness spewed from the end, and the zombie owning the limb actually tried to aim the blood at Tony's face. Tony freaked. He shoved the arm back and planted the hatchet deep into the shoulder of the spouting appendage. There were two more arms breaching the barricade, and Tony hacked away at them all with an energy he did not know he had. But now there was the carrion smell of rotting blood and meat on the floor of the cabin and on Tony himself. The stench was potentially gut heaving.

The beam from the flashlight flicked away.

At that same time, Tony heard the frightening sound of wood splintering, succumbing to the supernatural forces that had gathered beyond.

"Goddamnit!" Tony screamed out in frustration. "Fuckin' fight *fair!*"

Fingers clawed at Tony's hair, grazing his scalp.

The light came back, and he saw a zombie trying to force its upper torso through a widening crack of the window. Its lipless grin was black and barren of teeth.

The sound of more wood splitting apart cracked in the air. The pounding on the walls went on as if there were hundreds more out there trying to get in. Tony twisted and tore away from the claws of the undead, swinging the hatchet back and forth, striking coal-black flesh wherever possible.

Then, the light went away again.

"We're losing it here, Tony!" Death updated him. "There are two trying to climb in through the kitchen window!"

"Shit!" Tony spat. He struck at the smiling zombie coming in through the window before him, cleaving the undead's skull in two. The creature's advance ceased almost immediately, dropping and hanging in the hole. Blackness splashed onto the cabin's floor.

But Tony killed one.

The thought gave him hope. Enough hope to fight back his fear.

He checked where Death was aiming the light and saw what he said was truth. Zombies were slipping into the kitchen through the window over the sink. Tony bolted past Death on the couch and bounded into the kitchen area. He drove the hatchet blade deep into the skull of the nearest. The thing collapsed into the sink, its lower half still outside.

But another zombie grabbed Tony's wrist.

Even through his coat, the feel of dead flesh on his arm was almost enough to drive Tony over the edge of sanity. He yanked the hatchet out of the first zombie and smashed it into the side of the second zombie's head. The thing did not release him. Tony hit it, again and again, killing the thing on the second blow and smashing it to one side of the sink with the third and fourth.

The bodies in the kitchen window momentarily blocked it.

"Where?" Tony yelled out, cocking his hatchet arm and looking to crush something dead.

Death swung the light back to the front of the cabin just as a plank popped off a window. Two bodies oozed into the room, reaching for the floor. Tony made to run for them, but something landed on his back, something that smelled like the deep earth. He twisted and saw the three zombies latching onto him. The sight of those undead grins froze him to the spot. They piled onto the man, forcing him to the ground. Tony felt skeletal fingers brush against his chest and bare throat. He tried to get up, but both arms were pinned. The flashlight beam whipped overhead, allowing Tony a glimpse of the horror slowly descending for his throat. The zombie's jaws hissed open wide, a burst of rancid breath making his stomach heave.

"Tony!" Death blared out. "*Tony!*"

Somewhere, Tony heard more wood shrieking as they were pulled or ripped from their nails. More thumps. That was it. The citadel had been breached. The natives were inside the barricades. *But how*, he thought madly and knew the answer immediately. The window in the toilet! Tony gnashed his teeth.

They were fucked.

Death was shouting something, but Tony did not hear. He only saw the rotten shards of teeth descending, going for his throat in cinematic slow motion. He couldn't believe how slow the thing was moving. He had to do something, so Tony squirmed like he had never squirmed before.

Then, he lost it and just screamed.

CHAPTER 63

In the back seat of the Sunbird, where the only light was red from a lit-up dashboard, Danny kept his eyes on a grimacing but fully conscious Stickman. The Stickman could feel the anger emanating from the giant man opposite him, but he had not fully recovered all of his strength to deal with the situation. When he did, he would deal with Danny Boy, the other half of the Beacon bouncers. Stickman knew why the man was here. He was here for *him*, and the Stickman didn't blame him in the least. He had, after all, fucked up his boss and co-worker. That was reason enough for revenge in his book. After all, the Stickman was on the same mission himself. But he was not about to let him slow or stop him in getting his hands on Levin first. When Levin was done, Danny Boy would get his dance, for better or for worse.

"You boys know where we're heading?" Lucy asked as she drove. They did not answer her, and Lucy glanced into the rearview mirror. Both men were coiled up back there like two rare but dangerous snakes eyeing each other. There wasn't much room for men of their size, but there was a space between both that was being kept. Lucy did not know what would happen if one of them infringed upon that space.

She looked ahead, seeing the red-eyed taillights of the car leading them. Fear's car. It was no mistake that he had gotten here.

"Oh, c'mon, guys . . ." Lucy trailed off, and then the red eyes of the car ahead seemed to charge her. Lucy slammed on her brakes and thumped her forehead off the steering wheel. She felt her seat push ahead as Danny's mass ploughed into her from behind. Then, they were still, just breathing while the wind outside whispered and dared them to come out and play. Gripping the steering wheel, Lucy righted herself and gazed ahead. The headlights lit up the Celica's rear. It had stopped in what she could see was a wall of snow. Fear and his man had driven right into it. What was worse, none of them were driving any further on this old road. The gathered snow made it impossible. Sighing heavily, Lucy watched as Fear and the man she did not know got out of the car. She felt the latch of her own door and pulled it.

It was freezing outside, and the rising wind made it worse. Wind chill, Lucy's mind whispered, conscious of the immediate shivering all over her body.

Fear walked over to her.

"Didn't see that, did you?" Lucy asked him. His dark, almond eyes studied her, but he said nothing. That was one of the reasons Lucy disliked Fear. He only paid attention to you when he had to.

"We'll walk on," Fear said, snow blowing by his face. He planted his hands deeply into the pockets of his heavy winter coat.

By this time, Crew had joined them. Danny and Stickman stood behind Lucy, eyeing each other warily. Crew's head came up like a hound that had caught the scent of something when he spied Stickman. Fear did not miss the man's interest. He did not miss the guarded positioning of the three Mundanes. He would not have any of it.

"You do as I say," he spoke to them. "Understood?"

Tendrils of fear grabbed their attention. This time, Lucy allowed it. Whatever thoughts of revenge they might have had fled.

"You could have just asked them," Lucy commented. She pulled her toque down as much as possible over her freezing ears.

"Asked them?" Fear hoarked and spat. "That's what I think about that."

Lucy scowled. She *really* disliked this one.

"So, what do we do?" she asked, allowing him to take the lead before he just took it.

"We march." Fear said.

"In this?" Lucy asked in dismay. Snow swirled in and around the headlights of the Sunbird. The Celica's lights were under a bank of snow. "How far?"

Fear smirked. "As far as we have to go." *Bitch*, he mentally projected.

He turned to the three Mundanes. "Which one of you has a flashlight?"

Stickman slowly raised his hand.

"Get it," Fear commanded.

The Stickman jumped to it.

"You're an asshole," Lucy said with loathing.

Fear ignored her. She could walk with them or stay right here and take her chances. Then, Stickman was back and handing Fear a long security flashlight, the kind that could club a seal to death. Fear did not take it.

"Get on ahead," he ordered the Stickman. "Shout when you see a side road."

The Stickman trotted away, the flashlight beam coming to life and zigzagging in the deep night. He wanted to run but fought down the urge. Lucy was back there. He didn't want to leave her. He climbed the bank of snow and disappeared over its peak.

Fear fell into step but ten strides behind Stickman. On a mental note, he tugged both Crew and Danny into following else their hearts explode. Fear did not care in the least. He did not need or require any of these cattle, and he sent forth a single pulsating thought to clear the way to his objective. Fear was on the way. *He* was the cavalry. *He* was the light brigade. He was the fucking *fist* of God.

Lucy watched the four figures and quickly fell into step behind them. She did not want to be left behind out here. Not with the monster on the loose.

And somewhere behind her.

CHAPTER 64

"Get up you stupid bastard. Get up!"

The sound pierced the darkness of Tony's mind, and he slowly opened his eyes. It was black inside the cabin. It was cold. A wind blew, coming from the wrecked barricades. Tony breathed deeply of that fine, freezing air. He was still amongst the living and was thankful for it. But where were the walking dead?

He slowly contracted his abdomen and rose like a vampire rising from its coffin, groaning as he did so.

"There you are," Death's voice said, relieved. "Thought some zombie bit your dick off."

The thought made Tony wince. "What happened?"

"Hell if I know. This place was swarming with them undead cocksuckers, and then, they all just up and left. Like they got wind of something. You sure as fuck didn't have anything to do with it. Christ almighty. You moved around the place like your ball sack was nailed to one place."

Tony struggled to his feet. He teetered for balance and made his way to the couch. Death was still there, shining the flashlight at the ceiling. Tony crashed down onto its softness with a groan and the sound of straining wire springs. The relief he felt was second only to the joy of being alive.

"They were on me," Tony muttered.

"Who was on you?" Death said. He studied the man from his side of the couch. He looked terrible, but considering how he *could* have looked, Death was thankful.

"Those things," Tony said, sighing and letting his head drop to his chest. "Got in through the bathroom window and sneaked up on me. They were on me. Gonna bite me. My throat."

His hand found his neck and gave it a reassuring rub. It was almost too much for his nerves to handle.

"Hey."

Tony glanced up and saw the Jack Daniels bottle being offered to him. There wasn't much left, but he took it, anyway.

"Thanks," he said and took a brutal sip. He made a face when he lowered the bottle, but he kept it close.

"You did well," Death informed him. "Just too many. We were overrun."

"Yeah," Tony agreed. He was thinking otherwise. He wanted the whole episode replayed, like a reloaded computer game on a difficult level. The ending would be different. He swore it would be.

"I know what I'm talking about," Death said quietly. "I've seen it before."

"Yeah? Where?"

Death chuckled. "Pick a war."

The words made Tony regard the figure on the couch in a new bewildering light. He was Death after all. He had already accepted that. But he had to really concentrate to even begin to comprehend the magnitude of his last words. *Pick a war.* He had been in every conflict there had ever been, from armies against armies, mass crushing mass, to individual duels between gentlemen or savages. This man on the couch had been there.

Death was ageless.

Death had been around for it *all*.

Time is a human measure.

"Oh, man," Tony breathed under his breath.

"Oh, yeah," Death grinned. "Been there, done that. Did *all* of that, my boy. And more. That's just one part of my job. Want details?"

Tony thought about that. The wind blew softly through the cabin, and he felt himself shiver. He took another stiff sip of the whiskey and saw that there was only a swallow or two left. Then ol' Jack would be leaving them. "No," he said after a quiet moment. "I just want to take a breather."

Death regarded the man. Then, he considered the flashlight with its beam focused on the ceiling. He turned off the light to conserve power. The pair of them sat on opposite sides of the couch in the cold dark and respected the silence. And the silence stretched on.

"Did you?" Tony asked suddenly, a spectral voice in the dark. "Did you . . . meet anyone important?"

"Met them all," Death acknowledged with a solemn nod.

"Really?"

Tony could not see Death nod. "Yes," the missing boatman eventually stated. "I met them all."

"Like who?"

"Pick someone."

"Michael Jackson."

Death cocked an eyebrow. "Met him."

"What was he like?"

Death thought for a moment. "Scared."

"Really?"

"Most of them are. Were. Whatever. Despite their faith or beliefs, religious or not."

"Of what?"

"The other side," Death answered. "Of what was over there."

"What is?"

A smile in the darkness. "That's tellin'. Can't do that."

"Bastard," Tony let slip before he could check himself. "Sorry. Didn't mean that."

"'S'okay," Death said. "I'm used to it."

"I guess you are."

"I am," Death said. "Why do you think I drink? Or abuse any other substance I can get my hands on?"

Thoughts ran through Tony's head. Then, a question formed in his mind. He cleared his throat. "You know my mom?"

A moment passed before Death answered. "I'm aware of her."

"Why haven't you taken her over yet?"

"Told you before. Some folks resist. Scared of crossing over. Scared of what's beyond."

"She's ready now."

"You *think* she is," Death stated. "You think. Did she tell you she's ready?"

"Not in so many words."

"Hm," Death grunted.

Outside the wind sighed, and somehow, a snow flake found its way to Tony's eye. He blinked. He looked over at the dark lump bundled up on the couch. "What do you want me to do?"

"To do?"

"For you to take her. You know. End her suffering. For a long time Death did not answer. Tony grew impatient, irritable. "Well?"

"I don't do deals. That's someone else."

"You fucking prick," Tony swore quietly. "You fucking, self-righteous prick. Who are you to decide who goes, and when and how much they're supposed to suffer. How many people have you fucking taken that didn't deserve to go over? Huh? Went over too soon. Went over without even being born? Went over too late? I don't think you realize what you're doing, do you? Oh, you *think* you do, but you don't, and the sorry thing is you see it every day all over the fucking globe! You don't know what it's like to be human. You might look like it, but you're not. You don't know."

"You got that right," Death commented dryly.

"No, you don't have the faintest goddamn clue. All you know is how we whine. How we piss you off cuz we groan or cry or refuse to go with you when it's time. How we all want to die in our sleep. Or, okay, we blame you for shit that you don't decide on or aren't responsible for. Well, I got news for you. Let me give you an idea of the life of your regular Mundane. We're born into a life of shit, of uncertainty, with the only certainty *being* death. So, okay, we whine; we bitch and resist. With some of the shit we put up with, I think we're okay to do a little of that. You don't know anything about life. Not a goddamn thing. You said to me yourself you're just the delivery man, and you've been hearin' the same thing over and over. Well, we're only here for a fuckin' short time, and to make matters worse, we get old. You say we're asked what we've learned. Well, shit, we only have a short time to learn anything, and those that learn it all don't have the time to pass on what they know cuz you fuckin' take 'em. We hurt. We go blind. Go deaf. Lose body parts. We can't eat what we want, and when we do, we put on fucking weight or start feeling shitty! We got diseases that rot us out, eat us up, and give us the shits. Diseases that turn our kids into old men and women, and smart people into idiots. We shoot each other, torture each other. Some never see the light of the day cuz their existence is in a hospital. Some shit in a plastic bag all their lives. Some have a life of misery and win the fuckin' lottery and find out that their friends and family are nothing more that greedy bitches and bastards who want their cut and threaten them if they don't get it. Some of us would fucking make war on the entire human race if we could get away with it. We got neighbours that would make better leaders than the ones we got, and we got leaders that we would fuckin' shoot dead if we had them as neighbours. Our loved ones *die*. That's right up there man. Watching someone you care for fuckin' croak. We got it fucking *tough* if you ask me, man. Just think about that for a minute, will ya? Just think. We got it piss pot *poor*. What's that shit about the candles burning bright or long or the brightest gets smoked out or some shit? It fuckin' sucks donkey cocks to be us, man. It really *sucks!* We got tons of shit against us, and when you decide that you're pissed at us and had enough just cuz we complain too damn much, well, see, that just makes our existence all the *more* miserable cuz then it'll never end. It'll *never* end. You see what I'm saying?"

"So, what then?" Death asked, his voice edging on annoyance. "You saying you don't appreciate life or what?"

"I . . ." Tony hands clawed at empty air. "No . . . I . . . I don't know. Look, I'm just a regular guy. I made mistakes. But other people don't. They do what they can with what they got. It works out for some more than others. But even then, there are problems. Some people got it really fuckin' good, and then, they die. All that goodness, whether they deserved it or not, gets taken away. And some people deserve it all. Everything good, they deserve it. Life can be great, I know, but . . ."

"You're ranting here, man."

"Sorry, but, well, it's like this," Tony directed at the dark lump on the couch. "Life can be good and bad for us. Good shit happens as well as the bad. Fair and unfair. I guess what I'm saying is . . . you are the only certainty in life. We need you. At the end of it all. Yes, we can be bitches and bastards, but given our daily routine . . . can you blame us? Can't you give us a break, man? Sure, we shit the bed and get upset when you take someone who we think isn't ready to go, isn't ready to die, or shouldn't have died. But we still need you. Live forever? Fuck that. Without you . . . facing what we have to face, life would be hell."

Silence. The wind blew into the room, and Tony shivered. Out of the corner of his eye, he thought he saw moving shadows in the room.

"Even if you were rich, could never grow old, and were surrounded by hot women all the time?"

An interesting thought. "Well," Tony supposed and smiled in the darkness. "Even that could grow old."

Across the room, Death tsked. "Fool."

"Maybe," Tony said quietly, thinking of Lucy. "Maybe." Then, he collected himself. "Did I give a good argument there? Cuz it's all true, man. All of it."

But Death did not answer.

He merely lay in the cold darkness and thought.

CHAPTER 65

In Barcelona, Spain, a madman's plot to poison a day care centre's children with a deadly homemade concoction succeeded. Paramedics arrived on the scene to witness the staff in hysterics while thirty-three children squirmed in their own pools of blood that seeped from every bodily orifice and tried to cry out from throats where the vocal chords were eaten away.

In Iraq, in the southern district of Baghdad, a car bomb went off blowing apart fifteen women, children, and men. Limbs, torsos and an immeasurable amount of blood cascaded down in the aftermath, covering the living and the streets. The fifteen caught in the blast were still conscious, moaning miserably, and begging for assistance. Those people not affected by the blast shock screamed just as loud as the should-be-dead upon seeing shredded remains of people wriggle in the bloody street like gutted fish.

Off the coast of Sao Paulo, a group of seniors were swept overboard by a rogue wave. The wave flipped their twenty-person private yacht and spun it underneath the water as if it were in spin cycle. Some seniors underwater spiralled with it, quickly disoriented by the motion and trying desperately to swim to the surface. Any and all air pockets filled within seconds. The bobbing vessel became a piece of deadwood in the water. Unable to hold their breath any longer, the last of the seniors gagged and inhaled sea water, filling their lungs as their limbs and brain convulsed.

But they did not die.

Instead, they drowned, again and again, eventually screaming out for release of their lives. The submerged yacht grazed some of the undying, raking the flesh from their bones and filling the water with blood.

And still they would not die.

Not even when the rogue wave released them, their deathless forms bobbing to the surface with their limbs and sanity twitching.

Not even when the sharks appeared to feed.

In New York, sitting in a room illuminated by a wide-screen TV and the white noise of an off-the-air channel, an utterly smashed Ted Myer held his father's snub nosed .38 to his temple and took a breath. As the night dragged on, and Ted's senses became more and more blasted by booze, he had placed the gun to other parts of his body, only to lower the weapon and grimace. He could not do it. What if he were *wrong*? He'd be committing suicide. *Suicide.* Wasn't that bad? He had a good job! Great benefits and occasionally got laid by nurses. Why should he gamble all that away?

Because, a voice said in Ted's head, it was the *truth*.

He could not die.

Yet damn if he could bring himself to squeeze that trigger.

He took a deep, deep breath and looked about the darkness of his living room. It would be dawn soon. He would probably lose his job if he didn't have a good excuse. What was better than this? This *experiment*. Maybe he should do it at the hospital? That would be smart, Ted conceded. He looked about himself. He was a mess. He couldn't go to work like *this*. Hitching up one corner of his mouth, he decided against it. He would do the deed here. He would do it *now*.

Ted brought the gun up again and tucked it underneath his chin for maybe the fifth time. Under his chin seemed the best choice out of all the other places he had considered earlier. In his drunken state, thoughts of his condition after he had pulled the trigger had been forgotten somewhere during the night.

This was it though, Ted knew it.

He cocked the hammer and increased the pressure on the trigger.

He waited for the bang.

After a few seconds, he started to weep. Again. Then, grimacing, he lowered the gun and cursed himself.

And he thought Med school was difficult.

CHAPTER 66

They walked along the highway, heading into a wind that felt like it was branding their exposed flesh and deep freezing their cores. Snow smacked into their faces and eyes. It coated them in crystalline beads. White drifts as perfect as the rolls of an ocean came up to and beyond their knees. The flashlight beam illuminated their path ahead, and when they finally came to the side road, it was Fear that took charge.

"Turn here," he called out, raising his voice above the wind.

The three men did as they were told.

With her arms folded tightly across her chest and her hands deep in her pits, Lucy made a face and followed. *Cold.* She believed her tear ducts had frozen shut. She could spit flecks of ice if she wanted to open her mouth. Her limbs, especially her legs, felt like something carved from arctic ice. Why did Death have to come to Canada? Why couldn't he have taken time off in Mexico? Cancun? Someplace tropical? She was not made for such cold weather. Cold? No, the word did not do. Freezing? Closer. A deep space freezing cold that would root her to one place if she stopped moving for longer than five seconds.

"How much further?" Lucy shouted to Fear.

But he ignored her.

She was really starting to dislike Freak Boy.

CHAPTER 67

They sat in the darkness, sometimes quiet, sometimes not. Tony eventually became aware of the cold in the cabin, so he went upstairs to the bedrooms. He found several heavy cotton blankets and stripped them from the beds. On the way back down, he went to the window he had dived out from earlier and squinted outside. There was nothing to see, so he returned to Death.

"Here," he said, dumping three thick blankets on Death's paralyzed form. "Don't ask me to tuck you in."

Death gazed up at the black shadow before him. He did not switch on the flashlight. "Well, how else am I going to get these things on me if you don't. I'm paralyzed here."

Tony supposed that was true. "Fuckin' Death," he swore as he dropped two blankets he had for himself on the floor. He then made quick work of covering Death from his toes to his chin, tucking the ends in where he could.

"Feel better?" Tony asked him when had finished.

"I'm fuckin' *paralyzed* here man," Death grated. "I don't feel shit below my waist."

"But you're okay above your waist?"

"Well, I did down the bottle of Jack."

"Goddamn alchie," Tony grumbled with a smile. He went back to his side of the couch. He sat and wrapped the blankets around himself. He was cold, but the blankets protected him from freezing. But then, he didn't have to worry about freezing to death. Or so he was led to believe. He still *felt* cold though.

"You know what it's like to freeze to death?" Tony asked.

"You ain't gonna freeze to death. You ain't gonna die unless I say so."

"What about frostbite? Don't they amputate shit that's been badly frostbitten?"

"Only the genitals." Death remarked and smirked at the sudden silence of his companion. "Not like you've been using it lately."

"I get plenty of opportunities," Tony said.

"Yeah? Lucky guys."

"Fuck off. I almost got a blowjob from someone we both know."

"Yeah? Who?" Death asked. "Lucy?"

"Mhm," Tony said and regretted it. Though it wasn't entirely true, he supposed it was as good as any other almost. A little exaggeration wouldn't hurt.

"You *almost* got one, right? Doesn't surprise me," Death commented. "You ain't *that* lucky. She's a popsicle tease if there ever were one. Ever see her work an ice cream cone?"

"Well, no . . ."

"A thing of beauty. She'd make eunuchs take out loans for dick and nut transplants."

That she would, Tony thought. *That she would.* But he took offence at Death's comments. He didn't like Death talking about her that way. He wanted to change the subject.

"Anyone you ever regret taking?"

Silence.

"Frank?"

"Yeah?"

"Anyone—"

"I heard you."

For a moment Tony thought he might have said something wrong. He felt that vibe of wrongness when someone says something they shouldn't.

"Lots," Death said, reflecting on the faces he escorted across on the last day before he decided to go on sabbatical. How many did he save from Pain? In just that one day? How many places had he travelled in the world answering the call when it came? How many did he deliver to the other side when it was their time?

He didn't bother counting anymore.

"Why do you think I drink?" Death asked him.

"Thought you enjoyed it," Tony answered.

"I do, I do. Too much maybe," Death confided. "It relaxes me."

"Don't think I could drink enough to get over what you do," Tony said. "Not ever."

"Well, then," Death gave him a nod, "that's a first step in realizing what I go through. I won't go into details. If you watch the news, you understand what I mean. Some of the shit I see. The craziest shit. It's a wonder I don't do heavier drugs."

"Yeah," Tony admitted thoughtfully, "I guess so." Then he thought of something.

"Company's coming," Death announced quietly. "Well, well, well."

This got Tony's attention. "Who?"

"You'll see."

"Oh, don't do that man. Tell me. I only just fuckin' fought off a mess of dead-heads!"

That caused Death to reconsider. "Well, let's just say, I know why they retreated when they had us."

"Why?"

Though it was still dark in the cabin, Death levelled a look of annoyance in Tony's direction. "Nag, nag, nag."

The storm seemed to intensify, and soon Lucy found herself stumbling along the winter road, the snow now up to her knees and getting deeper. Somewhere along the way, Danny had stopped in his tracks until she reached him. Then, without a word, he lifted her up out of the snow. He hunched his shoulders and focused on the thin beam of light that lit the narrow road.

"I can walk," Lucy managed to get out through chattering teeth.

But Danny did not respond. He fell in behind the others with his bare head bowed against the wind. The wind shrieked and blew ice and snow into their faces, stinging them. Crew swore over and over that if he didn't die of exposure, he was moving permanently to Costa Rica. The Stickman merely peeped up every now and again, wondering how the hell the funny looking guy managed to know where they were all going. The man had taken the flashlight away from the Newfoundlander just minutes ago, causing him to jump in fright. There was no word of warning, the flashlight was simply snatched away. There was something terrifying about him. But so far, he had not led them astray, so that was fine by Stick. And as bad as the weather was, Stickman knew they were sheltered a little by the tall black evergreens on either side of them. If the trees weren't there, the wind would slash them all to frozen strips of meat.

But none of them spoke a word to Fear.

They were scared to.

They marched on for a spell of time that none of the men were able to gauge. They wore watches, but the time seemed to be slowed by the cold just as their limbs had been.

Then, the walls of trees on either side of them fell away, and the ground became more open. The wind howled in their faces, no longer held back by the wilderness. Out of the gloom and half buried in snow came a two-storey log cabin.

Stickman smiled weakly, feeling how cold his face had become. Then, his eyes squinted up in numb puzzlement.

The snow surrounding the cabin was stomped down. Stickman could make out tracks coming from all directions and converging on the cabin. It was starting to fill in, again, but it was flattened enough to make Stickman think of a concert crowd mobbing the stage. Then, he saw what looked to be the huge rotting carcass of the biggest bear he had had ever laid eyes on. It was trampled flat, like a rug, but there was no mistaking the shape.

"What da fuck?" he muttered to himself.

Fear was the first to reach the door. He pounded on its surface. "Open the fuck up!"

There was no sound from within, and the Stickman, standing still as he was, slowly gained a greater appreciation as to how cold it was. When he was moving, there wasn't any problem, but now, the air crept inside his coat and clothes and numbed his flesh like bare ice. He remembered a book he had read, *"Death on the Ice"*, which told the true story of a crew of Newfoundland seal hunters who lost their lives on an Atlantic ice patch. Separated from their vessels during a snow storm and caught on the open ice with no shelter, seventy-eight men had frozen to death during the night. The Stickman could not remember all the details of the tragedy, but he remembered the author's descriptions of men sitting upright on the ice, frozen in place in the morning light. He thought he was beginning to understand how such a thing could happen. His limbs, face, and especially his balls, all felt frost gnawed.

The door opened a crack, and Tony Levin stuck his head out. The flashlight lit up his features in a ghoulish way, and he shied away from its brightness. "Fuck off with the light," he swore, his hands going up.

The Stickman held his breath. This was the man he had hunted for. His mind screamed at him to do something, and yet, he knew his current companions would not allow him his revenge. Taking a breath, the Stickman gave a little contented smile, and imprinted Tony's face in his mind. His time would come. Badger would have his pound of owed flesh.

Fear spoke, "You gonna let us in, dickhead?"

Tony's hands dropped. He studied Fear for a moment and grinned.

"Hey, Frank," Tony abruptly called out. "Fuckhead Freddy just showed up on our doorstep!"

"Tony!" Lucy cried out, clutching herself against the cold and beaming at him. Tony blinked in shock. Lucy was the last person he had expected. The sight of her lifted his spirits like only love could.

"Lucy," Tony answered, suddenly breathless. "Wow."

Fear rolled his eyes. "Outta my way, fuck nuts," he growled, pushing his way past the Halifax man.

He had no time for budding romances.

It turned his guts.

CHAPTER 68

Far beyond the circle of light supplied by the flashlight, and hidden by the gusting winds and sheets of snow, Grey Northman stood and watched the group he had followed through the freezing night. He was coated in frost, red-eyed, grimacing at the numbness in his limbs and the hatred for his quarry. The wind lashed around him, but he did not waver. He was a rock in its fury. He watched them all enter the dwelling. The door closed. The castle had been sealed. The defenders were within.

"How many of you are there?" Northman hissed, eyes unblinking as the water in them had long since frozen.

From the darkness, a figure shuffled near. The cold air lessened the stink of dead flesh, but there was still enough for Northman to notice. He did not turn to address the creature. There was no need. He had sensed them and sought them out as soon as he had arrived. He knew what they were. And he knew how to control them.

"*Many,*" came the same voice that had bartered with Tony earlier.

That was good. Northman would need every last one of them for the battle to come. "Why do you wait?" he wanted to know.

The Speaker for the Dead took its time in answering. "*We . . . feared . . .*"

This made sense to Grey Northman. The creature talked about the Entities.

"I will take care of that," Northman promised. He had been granted powers to combat such fear.

There was a pause from the Speaker for the Dead. "*You?*"

"Yes," Grey Northman hissed, and allowed the dead to feel a surge of the power that his Lord had given him. The corpse stiffened with the energy. If it could draw breath, the Speaker for the Dead would have choked in shock and awe. In that moment, the undead knew its place. It knew the Northman was its new master. It's general.

"Gather your host 'round," Northman commanded, the snow swirling about both of them and the winds as loud as horns.

"Do as I say . . ." the Minion bared his teeth in the storm's fury. "And I will give you your revenge."

CHAPTER 69

They quickly barricaded the door as best as they could with the wood and nails that remained. It was cold inside, but at least they were out of the freezing wind. They crowded in the space that was the living room, with the exception of Lucy and Tony, who moved around the sofa that separated the living room from the open kitchen. The new arrivals were quick to size up the interior of the cabin, and Death lounging on the L-shaped sofa. The Stickman broke the silence when, upon seeing the sprawled out form with an empty bottle of Jack Daniels, stated in a voice still frosty from the cold, "Oo dafuck's ee?"

That earned him looks from both Danny and Crew.

Fear ignored the man. He zeroed in on Death. Lucy, standing next to Tony in the open kitchen, placed both hands on the back of the sofa and gazed down at the missing sailor.

"What happened?" she asked in a dismayed voice. "What happened to you?"

Death waved his hand in the air. "Minions. Fuckin' cockroaches. Jumped me in Paradise. They piled us both into a car and drove us here, except I got pissed off and wasted them."

Fear listened to Death and studied him with his dark, almond-shaped eyes.

"There were more," Lucy said. "We ran into some back on the highway. It's a whole nest."

"I knew about them," Death said in a low voice. "There's one more. He's outside now. Marshalling the troops. Looks like there's going to be a war. Right here." He considered Fear. "Took you long enough."

"See what I'm working with?" came the disgusted reply.

"What's this about the troops?" Tony threw in. "You mean they're coming back?"

"Who's coming back?" Lucy wanted to know.

"The dead." Tony breathed, and Lucy's expression gave way to astonishment.

"How did that happen?" she asked. Death rolled his head on his shoulders. It was all he needed to have Lucy pissed off at him. He knew her dark side.

"I was unconscious, see," he explained to both Fear and Lucy, "When I took out the Minions, we were in a moving car at the time."

"We saw the car," Lucy replied.

"Yeah, well, I went through the windshield and royally fucked up my legs. Had to get Tone to knock me out before you-know-who arrived. The pricks who took us had this spinal anaesthetic. Tone shot me up with the shit, and here I am. Under siege by a bunch of goddamn corpses. They almost had me, too, except they fucked off when you guys got close." Death gave Fear a sly nod. "Mr. Magic here."

If Fear was responsible for the mass retreat, he gave no indication. He merely kept on listening.

"So, you can't feel a thing now?" Lucy said.

"Nah," Death answered her. "'Cept the sting of the cuts and bruises. But I have booze here to dull that pain, so I'm good."

"How long does this painkiller last?"

"Probably not much longer. I'd say I'll be feeling everything there is by morning. Broke both legs, you know. Fuck knows what else down there."

"How did you get here?" Tony interrupted.

"By car," Lucy answered.

Hope blossomed in Tony face. "Where is it? How far from here?"

"Nobody's getting to the car," Fear told him cryptically. "Not with the snow falling and those things outside. Snow's probably buried it anyway."

"We can dig it out, man!" Tony almost screamed. "You brought the three amigos here! We can dig it out in no time!"

They did not answer him. Instead, they stood looking dismally at Death's broken legs under the blanket. They were on a timer, and they knew it.

"We wouldn't make it," Fear stated.

"He's right," Lucy said. "And there's more out there now than just the undead. Pain is here."

"Pain?" Tony's browed scrunched up in puzzlement.

"I knows ee," Stickman said quietly. Danny flicked a dirty look at him. The Stickman stood in a corner of the living room, facing Danny and the other man he did not know. He had a good guess as to why he was here.

"Pain," Tony repeated dully. "Who's he?"

"He's the reason I had you knock me out," Death said from the couch. "He's the one that wants me to stay as I am so he can enjoy his playtime . . . which is making Mundanes suffer."

"Why?" Tony asked trying hard to understand.

"No reason," Death shrugged. "He's got no reason at all. It's just his nature. His existence. He exists to make you—all of you—suffer all the way to the end. And he's got free reign now. He can fuck up people as he pleases. Whoever and whenever someone gets hurt."

"Even you?" Tony asked, looking down on the figure on the couch.

"Yeah," Death grumbled. "Especially me. If I feel enough, he'll be drawn to it, and he'll do a dance on me just cuz of who I am."

"Why?" Tony needed to know.

"Because I'm the one that ends his fun all the time. When I take people away, whatever pleasure he gets from making them suffer, ends. I'm the party pooper. I shit in his bed. And he hates my guts for it far more than these two," he nodded at Lucy and Fear.

From where they stood blocking the door, Crew and Danny exchanged curious looks. What had they walked into here? Danny held up his hand.

"Excuse me," he said in a deep voice "but, what are you talk—"

"None of your goddamn business," Fear said and sent enough fright through Danny to silence him. But instead of falling to the floor as Fear had expected, the big man merely flinched.

"Will you stop that!" Lucy yelled. She had blocked Fear again. "Can't you see we're going to need them?"

Fear's face contorted into disgusted realization. "Well, shit."

"Why, oh shit?" Tony demanded. "I mean I found him, right? Why can't we call Time now? Huh? Why do you need us?"

"To cover my getaway," Death muttered. "Look," Death said directly to Tony, "the vacation's over. I would've done it anyway. I've done it before."

"Done what?" Tony asked in growing horror.

"Commit suicide."

"*What?*"

"That's how I get back, man," Death said plainly. "That's how I leave this place. I do myself. Course, I can't do myself now, seeing as I'm the most fucked up I've *evah* been. The car crash would've done the trick, but I wasn't ready to leave then."

"Why not?" Tony demanded.

"I just wasn't ready."

"And now?"

"Pain is too close." Death explained. "He knows I'm around here. Too many of us *special folk* in the area. You can bet that cocksucker is just waiting for the next vibe of agony, so he can zero in and kick the living shit out of me. And it'll happen when this spinal shit wears off. Fuck that. Time to go. I had my days in the sun."

Death looked Tony straight in the eye. "Give me the morphine."

The request made Tony hesitate. "Morphine?"

"Yeah, the morphine you got. You think I forgot or something?"

Again Tony hesitated. Then, he reached into his pocket and felt the injectors he had retrieved from the car trunk so long ago. There were six of them. He pulled them out and slowly handed them over. Death took them one by one. He gave Tony an approving nod. He plucked the plastic tops off of the autoinjectors and studied the needles. Nodding to himself, Death wasted no time in placing one to his neck. He placed a thumb on the end, ready to deliver the load, and then took a breath.

"Wait," Tony said.

Death looked up at him.

"I mean, that's it?" Tony grated. "I travel warp speed across the country to backwater BC to find you—which I do—and then get to watch you shoot up?"

Death made a face. "You wanted me to go back, right? I'm convinced. If Pain gets his hands on me, he won't let me die. He'll just keep right on torturing me for all fucking eternity. And if I'm in fucking limbo, where does that put the human race? All the bad parts of the Bible. And probably worse." He regarded them all. "Well, that's it then. It's been real people, and it's been fun, but it hasn't been real fun."

With that, he jammed the autoinjector into his jugular.

He grimaced for a moment and held the injector in place while the load of morphine was delivered. When it was done, he dropped it to the floor and readied the second one. "What?" Death fired at them. "Never seen someone overdose before?"

"Not on purpose," Crew commented quietly.

Death injected number two, and held it there for a moment. He sighed and smiled. "Well, you're in for a treat, buddy. You're going to see a lot more before I'm done here."

Then, the cabin shook in fury.

It was a loud collective slap, as if four separate waves had clapped the walls of the dwelling at once, and it was frightful enough to make all within jump, with the exception of Fear. The weathered planks covering the breaches made by the attack earlier began to buckle inwards. Wood splintered loudly. Sounds of the dead permeated the interior. The Stickman pressed himself in a corner, eyes wide with fright. Danny and Crew fell back towards the kitchen to where Tony and Lucy stood. All of them looked to the door. Something was pressing very hard up against it.

"Keep those fuckers outta here!" Death wailed at them.

"Keep them out!" Tony screamed at the men. They all looked at him with eyes flooded with terror. Hands, black hands of the dead, seeped in underneath the wood nailed over the doors and windows. They turned like huge seeking worms, looking for purchase, clawing into the wood's surface.

A frantic Tony reached into his coat and withdrew the knives he had. He gathered up his hatchet and bat. He gave the seven centimetre Beretta knife to Danny, who took it but merely gazed at the horrors trying to enter the cabin. Tony gave Crew the military boot knife with the ten centimetre blade. He moved and shoved the baseball bat into the Stickman's hands. "Stay in the middle!" Tony shouted at Lucy. Her beautiful face looked petrified. Tony mentally vowed to let nothing happen to her while he drew breath.

He flew at the door and hacked away a hand with one chop of his hatchet. He placed his shoulder against the bulging wood and heaved back. Another hand sought to grab his shoulder. Tony twisted away and chopped. Fingers fell to the floor. Another hand burst through the wood in an explosion of shards and splinters, and clawed for his face. He caught the wrist and cut through it with one swipe of the hatchet.

Then, he looked back.

The others were frozen.

"*Fucking move!*" Tony screamed at them. But he could see they could not. Their fear was too great. The Stickman had wormed himself as far into his corner as he could, bat clutched before him. Danny and Crew crouched, looking everywhere at once, and doing nothing. They were rooted in place by the sudden ferocity of the undead's attack. Over their shoulders, Tony saw the wood covering the window in the kitchen burst apart, and a dark writhing mass of bodies began to ooze through. At the door, he felt the planks crack and bulge from the pressure building outside. An icy blast of wind blew through the house.

And Fear stepped up.

Tony saw him—saw fuckhead Freddie—take a quick look around at the situation and then focused on the men in the room. Almost instantly, Tony saw their expressions of fright melt away. Incredibly, he felt the same way, and he quickly looked upon Fear with an expression of wonder and understanding. Perhaps that was why Time insisted Fear come along in the first place. For so long, Tony thought of the thing called Freddy as something evil, but now he saw Time's wisdom in including him in the hunt for Death. Only now did Tony understand when it was most important and needed.

For not only could Fear *inflict* his nature with but a thought...

He could also *take it away*.

Whatever terror, dread or panic the men felt suddenly disappeared and left them blinking, wondering pointedly *what just happened?*

It was Crew who moved first. He bolted for the breach in the kitchen, grabbing a zombie halfway through the window by its rotting head and twisting it clear off its shoulders. The corpse shuddered, and its upper torso fell into the sink while its lower half remained outside. But Crew did not stop there. He grabbed limbs where they snaked in and broke them with such savagery that Tony could only stare at the man's single-handed butchery of the dead.

"Holy fuck," he breathed as he watched Crew halt the dead from coming into the kitchen.

Danny also moved. The big man rushed to the windows in the front of the cabin and began stabbing and slashing at the limbs attempting to break through.

The Stickman bounded past him, bat raised and crying out at a stunned Tony "'Old on, me son, 'old on!" He smashed in the face and skull of one zombie just above Tony's head. He fought with the fury of a man without a drop of fear. Tony's own adrenalin rushed in then, and he lifted his hatchet to swing.

And the battle for the cabin began in earnest.

Injecting morphine shot number four, Death watched it all go down with a spaced-out smile on his features. Everything seemed to move in super slow motion. What was it they called it in *The Matrix?* He remembered then. *Bullet time.*

In the kitchen, Crew fought with a terrible energy that actually pushed the tide of zombies back. He felt no fear whatsoever, and what remained was an overwhelming desire to kill the should-be-dead. He was a rock in a river, and any corpse that sought to pass had their limbs twisted and broken, or, much to Crew's surprise, simply ripped free. He removed the heads of five of the dead, the heads falling to the kitchen floor like stringy black coconuts. He punched when he could and used the military knife in an underhanded fashion. He slashed the fingers off one seeking arm, and when it did not retreat, he drove the blade through the rotten skull of the owner.

That seemed to be the last.

When he was done, he stepped back and surveyed the area. *Hell's kitchen,* he thought with dark humour, witnessing the mass of ownerless limbs, black blood, and fingers splashed all over.

At the front of the cabin, Tony, Danny, and the Stickman fought with a calmness that could only be matched by the best locally-grown pot. They placed their shoulders to the splitting timbers, and as limbs came through, they held and cut, dropping the limbs in seconds. They held the attack back before Tony jerked his head up and looked over the Stickman's grimacing face.

"Danny, get to the washroom!"

"Why?"

"They can get in there!"

"Shit," the giant hissed. He broke away from the door and window, and headed for the john.

"Just ye and I now, me son," the Stickman smiled at Tony.

He did not smile back.

Two powerful frostbitten arms smashed through the planks and grabbed a hold of the wood before either man could react. Black fingers gouged wood, making it squeal. The arms pulled backwards, and a huge hole cracked open in the front window. Dark bodies pushed forward, moaning as they came on. Tony chopped with his hatchet, taking one zombie between its unseeing eyes and splitting open its skull. The thing fell back to be replaced by two more. The Stickman threw down his bat. He grabbed and broke three of the arms in a matter of seconds while Tony dealt with more clutching hands. They fought side by side, fuelled by adrenalin, and in perfect timing with each other. When one man stepped back, the other stepped in and held the line. If a stray hand sought to grab the man standing before the breach, the other would disable it by breaking it, severing it, or simply ripping the hand off its rotting wrist.

"How many are there?" Tony heard Lucy ask from somewhere behind.

The front door exploded inwards with a loud snap and groan of wood. Zombies fell into the living room with tidal force. Lucy and Fear stepped back, placing the sofa between them and the rush of undead coming into the cabin. The dead pushed past Tony and the Stickman who were still holding the front windows, and staggered and pawed their way towards the form of Death on the couch. Death watched them shamble at him. He had just finished injecting the fifth shot of morphine into his system. He smiled.

And flipped them the finger.

One tall undead reached for him, its lipless mouth opened in a feral hiss. The thing still had eyeballs in a head that had been grotesquely half caved in. Death could no longer smell the thing because of the morphine, but he winced all the same at the horror. The thing was about to touch his ankles.

"Ugly fucker ain't—"

A baseball bat whipped through the air and removed the head from the zombie's shoulders. Danny stepped up then and swung at a second head, shattering it with a sound of breaking clay. But the river of bodies did not falter, and they pushed the big man back before he could swing a third time. Zombies grabbed his bat, his arms, and his shoulders. A zombie right in front of him leaned over the bat being held by a half dozen undead hands and opened its mouth wide to bite. Danny watched it coming.

There was a crack and wet crunch as Crew buried his knife to the hilt in the skull of the creature. He left it there. Then, he was moving forward, placing himself between a very stoned Death and an amazed Danny. The hit man had not carried a weapon into Halifax when he arrived, and now Danny understood why.

Crew was the fucking *terminator*.

He assaulted the zombie tide from the side and tore into them with a fury and speed that either destroyed or crippled everything he touched. Anything that laid its hands on him was struck down immediately by fist, spinning elbows, or devastating knees and kicks. Crew shattered kneecaps, snapped arms, popped elbows, and plied back wrists. He flipped undead over his back and stomped on them when they hit the ground. In a blur, he punched and grabbed when he could, hooked thumbs into eye sockets, and twisted necks from their shoulders. In one instance where four zombies piled on and seemed to have him, two of them suddenly crumpled to the floor with their knees broken and the remaining two were dispatched by fist and open hand.

Even Death was impressed.

The counter-charge of Crew was fierce enough to clear the room of attacking corpses in less than a minute. Danny plodded behind the man at a distance, smashing in the heads of any fallen foes still moving. Then Crew was at the door and, with a vicious front kick, drove the remaining zombies back out into the night. He paused and looked back at the others.

"Go fuck 'em up!" Death roared from the couch.

Crew smiled briefly. Danny handed him his knife and the two men exchanged a moment. The Stickman and Tony realized there was nothing outside the windows anymore and the sky was actually beginning to turn early dawn grey.

"That can't be right," Tony said, finding it hard to believe the night had passed so quickly. But the darkness was fading, and the wind had also dropped. No snow fell. Peering outside, dark shapes formed up against the white gloom of the snow.

Crew had no trouble seeing them. "Only a few left. We take 'em?"

"Hell, yeah," Danny growled at his side. The Stickman moved to the door as well with Tony right behind him.

"Be careful out there," Lucy cried after them.

Three of the men piled outside, but Tony hesitated. He turned to look at Lucy standing next to Fear. Fright and panic filled her face. To Tony, it was her most beautiful expression yet. "Don't worry," he breathed.

And then he was gone.

Death dropped the last spent autoinjector on the floor. He exhaled mightily and smacked his lips. "Got any more of that shit?"

"You took it all?" a surprised Fear asked him.

"Yup," Death replied.

"You're not dead," Lucy almost shouted out.

"Nope," Death agreed, popping the 'p' again. "Not even close. Wasn't enough shit. Fuckin' shit . . . shit," he ended, studying himself seriously.

He regarded the open door of the cabin. Saw the snow that lay beyond. "You better get one of those guys back here."

CHAPTER 70

As dawn approached, the snow began to take on the dark blue of morning. The storm had all but vanished. The wind subsided to a light breeze. Grey Northman watched impassively as the last of the undead horde was torn apart by the men emerging from the cabin's wrecked husk. He still wore his black ski mask, his face protected against the cold. He stood knee deep in the snow, his Nomex protective gear coated in frost. He shook his head in distaste. There were greater powers afoot here than he. The men were not being taken by the undead as they should have been, and now they were attacking? Where were the terror-stricken cattle Grey Northman had expected? These Mundanes were fearless. Even worse, they were inspired. The game had somehow been raised a level without Northman's knowing it.

"You've failed," he hissed to the Speaker for the Dead. The corpse at his side chose to remain silent. It gazed across the snowy field to where the last few zombies were being destroyed.

"*Revengeeee,*" it finally managed, heedless of both Grey Northman and the destruction of its brethren. A terrifying sound came from the ruins of its throat.

The Minion watched as the four men dispatched the last zombie in their midst. It took only a moment before they spotted them, standing across the road made non-existent by the snow.

"Yes," Grey Northman agreed, his face wincing in the diminishing night. "Go, then."

The Speaker for the Dead moaned a frightening sound in what Northman alone understood as a battle cry, and then it lurched ahead to meet the four men coming towards them. In the early morning, the rags hanging off the dark corpse did not move, but its fingers flexed in bloody anticipation.

"You will give me a little time at least," Northman said as he watched with dispassionate eyes. He was Plan B. He would not fail his master. Not when they were so close. Not even if it meant his own destruction. All of his time on this plane of existence had come to this. It was no surprise to him.

"A little time," Grey Northman whispered, holding his fire axe two handed across his pelvis.

His fingers flexed on his weapon.

The Speaker for the Dead closed with the first man. Crew looked back to Danny and gestured for the bat. Danny tossed it to him. Catching it, Crew quickly went into a batter's stance and spread his legs wide for balance.

The Speaker for the Dead did not falter. Its fingers, rotted to bare, black bone tips, came up like pointed hooks. It meant to plunge all ten into the flesh of the man before it. It did not pay attention to the warrior's stance. Its white marble eyes widened, its battle moan reached a peak.

The bat took its head off as neatly as an axe.

It landed in a plume of snow and disappeared from sight. The Speaker's body stood upright for a moment, its claws flicked open and close on air.

Then, it dropped quietly to its knees.

Crew landed the second swing of the bat into its torso, bending the corpse backwards on its legs and flattening it in drifts of snow.

The four men gathered around the last of the dead, studying its grey-black flesh and saying nothing in the gloom of the growing morning. They became distinctly aware then of how quiet it had become, of how the wind had disappeared. And how quickly the night was fading.

"This must be Time," Tony spoke aloud.

"'Oo?" The Stickman grunted.

"Time," Tony said. He looked up to the sky. "You never met him."

"We didn't?" Danny asked. There was too much shit going on for him to try and disbelieve all of it. It was better to just accept all and go along for the ride. That's what Boomer said whenever he went on a bad mushroom trip.

"One more over there," Crew nodded.

"Ee got an axe, too," the Stickman observed.

"For all the good it'll do him," Tony commented. He looked up and studied the last of their attackers. This one had held back for some reason. Perhaps he was the brains. Then, Tony recognized the figure's gear. "A fuckin' fireman?"

Danny shook his head. "That ain't no fireman, Tony," he said quietly. "Don't know what the fuck it is, but we met up with a few of its partners back on the highway. It ain't no fireman."

"No fireman," Crew said. He tossed the bat back to Danny as he went forward, "I'll finish this." He produced his knife.

"TONY!!"

The cry of his name caused Tony to look back to the cabin. Crew paused only for a moment to recognize that it was the woman calling out, and that Tony could probably take care of whatever it was she wanted. He continued onwards.

"What is it?" Tony shouted back.

"Come here!" Lucy called to him. "We need you!"

"More dead things?" Tony asked.

"No, no!" Lucy said. "It's Frank! He wants you!"

Nodding, Tony looked to the Stickman and Danny. "Make sure that fire prick over there doesn't get away. And keep a lookout."

Both men nodded. When Tony moved in the direction of the cabin, they calmly regarded each other. The Stickman stood unflinching not one metre away from the Legend of the Beacon. He was torn between staying and following Tony back to the cabin. But Danny was watching him. Danny studied the man with the same sleepy intensity that made him a force to be feared. In his hands, he held a black-stained bat. The Stickman eyed it. Then, Danny did something that surprised the Stickman. He reached into his pocket and held out the short Beretta blade.

"Think you can use this?" he asked.

"I tink so," Stickman said taking it.

Danny nodded and studied him grimly. "Just so afterwards, when I shove this bat up your ass, you don't go whining you didn't have a fair chance."

To that, the Stickman just smiled.

Trudging through the knee-high snow, Crew closed the distance between him and the last of the firefighters. He drew to within two metres and brought up his knife. He watched the black ski mask. He readied himself for a swing of the fire axe. But the firefighter did not move.

"You waiting for something here?" Crew asked. "An invitation?"

Grey Northman scowled behind his mask. He disliked having to converse with such shit-low forms.

"Well?"

The sky had lightened considerably in the time it took the Mundane to get to him. Grey Northman estimated that it would only be another few minutes, and the sun would crack the mountain line and frame it all in red. He did not care for the sun. He decided then and there that he was a thing born in darkness.

And so he would perish in it, as well.

Grey Northman flexed his fingers on the shaft of his fire axe. The game was not finished yet. He had one last card to play. In one nimble move, he dropped a leg back for balance and raised his axe to strike, bringing it up like a sword.

Crew buried his knife in Northman's throat.

The pain exploded in the Minion's neck just above his Adam's apple. He could feel the wrongness of the impalement and welcomed the blissful agony that rushed through his senses, firing up his nerves like lit fuses. The pain was mind paralyzing, but Northman willed himself to perform one thing, even as he fell to his knees, dropping his axe.

His fingers found the hilt of the knife.

Crew watched the firefighter without emotion. He had watched men die before. It was nothing new to him.

But then, while on his knees, with blackness spraying out over his protective coat and staining the snow, the firefighter gripped the knife and *twisted* it. He gargled something, but then the life seemingly left him, and he fell over on his side.

The action caused Crew to draw back. That shit was fucked up.

He stepped in, crouching, only half thinking about retrieving his knife.

A shadow fell across him.

Crew had just enough time to glance up when the fist caught him square underneath the jaw. Several of Crew's front teeth were shattered. He flew backwards to land flat on his back in a cushion of snow, his limbs sticking up and outwards as if he had just been shot and left in a dumpster.

It was the brazen sound of flesh striking flesh that caused Danny and the Stickman to turn their heads. Danny did not know who he was looking at. The Stickman knew, and froze in his tracks, wondering if he ran, what his chances would be.

For standing over the twitching form of Grey Northman was the tall, half-naked form of the thing known only as Pain.

Gazing from the window of the wrecked cabin, Fear's mouth dropped open just as Tony crossed the threshold of the cabin's wrecked entrance.

"Well, shit," Fear muttered.

"'Sup, frightful?" Death quipped from the couch, pleasantly high.

"You'll never guess who just showed up."

Tony turned around in the doorway. Lucy ran to the window beside Fear and peered out.

"Pain?" Death asked, his senses barely returning to orbit around his planet.

"Yeah."

"Shit," Tony cursed and headed back out.

Fuck, Death mouthed soundlessly and laid his head back on his pillows.

"Do what you do, man," Death called out to Fear. One arm shot up from the couch like a missile being primed for launch. "*Cry Havoc!*"

Fear's brow crunched up in concentration as he focused on the Mundanes.

He would do just that.

CHAPTER 71

In the pre-dawn light, Pain grinned at the fallen Crew and flexed the fist that had put the man down. Dark skinned and head shaved, his face was worn and weather beaten, but not old. He drew himself up to his full height, perhaps a centimetre or two above Danny and that much wider. Pain studied the two men watching him. They stayed in place for a few seconds, and then they slowly approached. The Entity nodded and grunted loudly. That was good. He hated it when he had to chase his victims.

He produced a short, harsh chuckle. He flexed his upper torso and everything rippled with muscular power. He beat a fist against his hairless chest and roared at the stalled men. His fists clenched open and closed, and a thin line of saliva trailed from his lips. His biceps bulged as if he were trying to curl an invisible weight. Pain took one step forward, fully expecting the now three men to turn and bolt for the hills.

When they did not, his sharp smile widened all the more.

"Who the fuck are you?" Danny whispered.

Only the Stickman heard. "I ditched dis fucker a ways back on de 'ighway."

"Yeah?" Danny gripped his bat tighter, looking at the giant of a man who now wore nothing but faded blue jeans and a smile. He wasn't even sure if he wore boots or not.

"You guys need help?" Tony said as he appeared on the Stickman's left. Both men glanced his way before looking back at the fearsome sight before them. None of them felt a flick of fear.

"Alright then," Tony said, holding his hatchet. He stepped forward.

Danny and the Stickman were a second behind him.

"*Yeah!*" Pain roared and clubbed his chest again, the sound briefly echoed through the morning air. Pain exhaled mightily, white breath like that of a dragon. "Bring it *here*, man! *Bring it!*" His head flicked this way and that as if he were clearing his ears of rocks.

"It's too cold in the morning for this half-naked shit," Danny observed, holding his bat samurai style before him.

Tony held up his hand. "Listen, dude, we don't want any part of you. Okay? We just want to get out of here with our friends in one piece, okay? Just stay out of our way, and we'll keep our peace."

A short laugh cut through the air. Pain took a step towards them. "I thought I was the stupid one," he growled, lathing his white teeth with a black tongue. "Listen. What I want is in yon cabin there. I can *smell* him. Can't tell you how fucking *long* I've been waiting for a chance like this. I'll let you get out if you stand aside. Just cuz I feel so good. Howzat sound?"

The Stickman looked questioningly at Tony.

"Fuck. You," Tony said, meaning both syllables. Danny nodded, grimacing against the chill of the morning. The Stickman wasn't exactly sure what was happening, but he knew he did not like the tanned wrestler. There was something big going down here. Something beyond the Stickman's current grasp on reality. But he was a hands-on sort of guy, and this was one skin-headed bully that had ruled the schoolyard for too long. The Stickman could tell that this half-naked savage needed his ass handed to him good and proper. Just on the principle of it. "Don't need a car to kick yer ass," he said as he held out his knife.

Tony felt charged for what was about to happen. He felt righteous. He felt no fear. He supposed he had Fear to thank for that. And if he survived what was coming, he promised himself he would do just that.

Pain barked a short savage laugh. His eyes were black and shark-like. "More's the pity," he hissed.

And charged.

The big man took two steps in the snow and fell flat with an "OOPH!"

Crew disengaged his legs from Pain's and got to his feet, he spat blood into the snow. Pain raised his head, and Crew kicked it, breaking teeth and flipping the man on his back. Crew then performed something from the movies. He leapt into the air, arms spread wide, and brought both knees down on Pain's midsection. The air gushed out of his lungs. Crew planted both knees on the man's shoulders and lined up his face. He pistoned a fist into Pain's nose, smashing bone and cartilage. Black blood spurted. Pain's eyes squinted against the crackling agony he felt, and he groped with his huge arms. Crew would have none of it. He smashed another fist downwards, followed by another and another. Pain's arms dropped to his sides, suddenly lifeless. The other three men gathered around the pair like kids on a playground watching a brawl. Crew punched and punched again, shattering teeth, breaking cheeks, splitting skin, and purpling eyes. Pain's face began to take on a grotesque yellowish-purple hue from the beating, and Crew *continued* to wail away on the man pinned beneath him, until his own battle-toughened knuckles began to ache with the contact on Pain's skull. It was perhaps the only part of his head that had not caved in.

"Jesus," Tony breathed, watching with growing horror. With each punch, Pain's legs would spasm briefly. It was enough for Tony to almost dry heave, for in truth, he had nothing in his stomach to come up. "Jesus, he's done man. He's done."

"I think so too," Danny said quietly over the smacking sound of fist into face.

"Lord Tunderin almighty," the Stickman swore, "Ye've kicked the livin' shite outta 'im. Lay off already."

Running out of breath and his arms feeling like lead, Crew stopped swinging at the unmoving face underneath his knees and simply knelt there. He breathed in heavily, saturating his muscles with much needed oxygen. He lost count of the number of punches he had put into the man underneath him, but he exacted his revenge for the shot earlier. Cold air smacked him in the face and he welcomed the freshness of it. He regarded the others standing around him. "Well," he panted, "he ain't getting up anytime soon."

That made Tony chuckle aloud and Danny smile. Even the Stickman shook his head at the dark humour.

But in a second, Pain shifted in the snow, his arms came up, very much alive, and easily grabbed the shoulders of a stunned Crew. Pain flung the man through the air, where he landed flat on his back perhaps three metres away.

Pain got to his knees.

The baseball bat crashed into Pain's purple and black face, right across the bridge of his nose. With a bestial grunt, he went down again, landing on his hands and knees. His back was exposed to the three men standing. Danny wasted no time as he slammed the bat flat across the man's flesh. Danny struck him again, getting a grunt from the man at his feet. Then the Stickman delivered a crushing boot to Pain's ribs.

Tony did not join Danny and the Stickman in the pounding on their foe. It was clear to him that the fight was almost over. Pain's head was slumped down low between two massive shoulders, and Tony could see blackness pouring onto the snow. Crew regained his feet and watched the beating with dark approval.

The two men stopped to catch their breaths.

Pain immediately straightened up in the snow and faced his attackers. His face was a horror show of broken bone, punctured skin, and black blood.

Two eyes, barely seen through the massive swelling of his broken cheekbones, appeared as empty slits of blood-stained white. The face was frightening enough to stop anyone in their attacks, but the men were not afraid. They did not feel any fear at all. They stopped because of sheer amazement, staggering back from the abomination.

Expelling a mighty breath, Pain threw his arms wide.

And grinned.

"Jesus H. Christ," Tony swore breathlessly, stepping back with his hatchet still in hand. Both Danny and the Stickman backed up as well, their faces filled with shock and awe at the destruction they had collectively caused the man, and yet how he still functioned.

Pain backed away from the men towards the cabin behind him on the other side of the hidden road. His arms were at guard. He took only three steps when he bared his ruined teeth at the men. "C'mon. Over here. *Bring it!*"

Back in the cabin, Death looked up from the sofa, and asked, "Is it over?"

Fear's mouth screwed up in distaste. He didn't bother answering.

Pain beckoned with huge paws that passed as hands. Tony found it incredible that the man was able to breathe let alone talk after the brutal beating. Pain's head was a dark, discoloured medicine ball with the stuffing hanging out of it. The Stickman could see wide dripping wounds in the man's shaved skull. They looked like long lipless mouths that drooled incessantly.

Pain roared at them and Danny's testicles drew up an inch. It was the sound of extraordinary rage. He had come across some very drunk, very violent people in his time at the Beacon. The booze sometimes ignited a deep rooted anger in a very rare few, like a perfect storm, and they would be a handful to control. Boomer would call it "priming themselves to explode" and more often than not, Boomer had called it right. Except this time, the thing that was goading them had already primed itself.

As far as Danny figured, it had already detonated.

"Guys," Tony said, "listen up. I know things have been really fuckin' weird for you these last few minutes. Maybe even hours. But I shit you not. What was said about all the bad things in the Bible happenin' here is true. We ain't fightin' each other now, got that? We can't. We're fightin' *that*," Tony pointed his hatchet at Pain. "And *that* wants the guy inside on the couch. We have to put him down long enough for Frank to kill himself and get out of here. That's all."

Another roar cut the morning air. The clouds had raced away somewhere and left a dark diamond blue sky blazing red at the lower edges. Pain poised himself as if to charge.

It was not lost on any of the men.

"Angry bastard, ain't he?" Danny commented.

"He's angry, all right," Tony commented, but the Stickman did not buy it.

"Angry, me arse," the Newfoundlander observed with a harsh eye. "Ee's likin' dis."

The words made the rest of them pause. Crew knew the words the Stickman had spoken were true. Cold horror sunk into him and the others as they realized the same. Pain was enjoying himself. His screams were the excited screams of kids strapped into the most terrifying rollercoaster.

Crew felt a huge stone of doubt sink in his guts.

"TONY, PLEASE!"

His head whipped around. It was Lucy, coming out of the cabin. All the men turned to see her standing outside of the cabin.

Even Pain.

"Oh, *baby*," he growled through a mouthful of teeth shards.

Tony's attention flicked back from Lucy to Pain and from Pain to Lucy, again. Feelings of rage erupted within him as he pointed his hatchet at Pain. "You can fuck off right now, man, and maybe we'll let you live."

A hoarse bark of laughter came from Pain, and he eyed Lucy as best as he could. It was enough for her to back up towards the open door of the cabin.

"Tony, we need you!" Lucy cried out again. "Now!"

He nodded. "Guys," Tony said.

"Go, man," Danny said, keeping an eye on Pain. "We got you here."

"Keep him busy!" Tony told the three.

In answer, Crew was already moving to Pain's left. The Stickman summoned up his invisible shields just like Sensei Bill had taught him. He only wished Sensei Bill were with him for this fight. The Stickman did not wish for Badger to be with him.

Badger was shitty at fighting.

Taking a last look at the three men, Tony turned and hoofed it back. Pain watched him go and his smile faltered just a bit.

"We're still here, man," Danny informed him, raising his bat. "It's okay. We're just gonna talk this out, okay?" The Stickman was on his left now, and Crew was on his right. Danny was in the middle looking at a man he realized was bigger than him.

"You with me, Crew?" Danny asked of his recent partner.

"Sure am," Crew answered. His eyes zeroed in on Pain.

Danny had no doubt there. "Stickman?"

"I'se 'ere."

"You ain't gonna fuck us up now?"

The Stickman regarded the man with such an insulted look that made Danny almost regret posing the question. Almost.

"Alright, then," Danny said loud enough for all to hear. "Let's get this *last man standing shit* on the road."

Pain watched the three advancing on him with blood stained eyes, and bared the remains of bloody teeth.

"Yeah," Crew said. "Well. Fuck you, too."

Under a dark blue sky just about to burst at the edges with sun, the bouncer, the hit man, and the ex-prisoner raised their weapons and closed the distance between themselves and their foe.

CHAPTER 72

The men were just about to engage the monster when Tony once again crossed over the threshold of the cabin's wrecked entrance and marched over to Death lying on the couch. His mouth hung open, and Tony thought he didn't look well at all. The man—or whatever he was—had come a long way from the deserted golf course where they had first met.

"Fuck you lookin' at?" Death quipped at him.

Tony's mouth dropped open. "What the fuck? Are you *high?*"

"I am . . ." Death paused for effect. "*The* black sun of the universe. The black matter of existence. The last stuff you'll ever see. Thanatos, himself. The Omega man. And yes, I am stoned as all fuck."

Tony looked to Lucy. She shrugged.

"Aren't you supposed to kill yourself?" Tony demanded.

"Couldn't do it," Death snapped back. "Too goddamn full of life!"

The confusion on Tony's face was as clear as the rising sun outside.

"He tried, Tony," Lucy spoke up, "but the morphine wasn't enough for him. It just got him stoned. He couldn't die from it. You have to do it."

Tony blinked in horror.

"Kill me!" Death burst out. "Take me out. Fuck me over. No . . . wait on that last one . . ."

"I can't *kill* him!" Tony insisted.

"You were hacking up people a while ago!" Death pointed out.

"Lucy!" Tony pleaded.

"Look, I'd do it for you," Death said quietly in a suddenly sincere voice. The switch made Tony stare at him in confusion.

"Tony, look here," Death said, sincerity dispensed with, "listen, you are the *only* one here that I trust with the job. The only one. Freddie over there can't do it. He's balless. And Lucy is Lucy. You, now, you're special. I see that now. Took a while, but I do. You convinced me to go back with that rant of yours. Just take that axe and plant it right here," he tapped his forehead with a finger. "And I mean really *fucking* clap me with it. You have to. Anything less, and *he'll* be here to *really* fuck me over. And you have to do it now."

"Lucy," Tony said, "I can't do this."

"You're the only one," Lucy explained. "The others are fighting Pain. He can't be allowed to get to Frank. If he does, he'll *never* let him die and this world will be plunged into a deathless existence. "

"And other shit, too," Death threw in, eyes glassy.

The thought did nothing to motivate Tony. He looked down at the defenceless and quite stoned Death, and shook his head.

"Why couldn't you just die back at the car wreck, then?" Tony persisted. "If this was the way things had to be, why didn't you just go then?"

"Couldn't. Wouldn't," Death said simply. "Wasn't enough of a flight for that. Didn't quite do the job. Bottom line, I'm ready now. Ready to go back to work. You have to send me over. I can't cross over in this suit," Death touched his chest. "Doesn't work that way. You're the one to kill me. What are you worried about? Your soul or something? A fear of God? Listen, who do you think I work for? It's o-*kay*, goddammit! Just do it! And do it before that asshole out there gets a hold of me."

"The guys will take care of him," Tony muttered.

That caused Death to cock an eyebrow. Even from the window, Fear half turned around upon hearing the words.

Death looked Tony straight in the eye. "Nobody takes care of Pain, Tony." Death did not blink, and the morphine suddenly had no hold on him. "Not when it's that strong. You can't *kill* it. You can only *suppress* it. *Endure* it. Until *I* take you."

On cue, the screams from outside sounded distinctly human.

CHAPTER 73

Pain charged.

Crew leaped and snapped out a solid boot that crunched into the creature's head. The blow stopped him in his tracks. The American whirled and a back fist knocked more of Pain's teeth into the snow. Crew threw a combination of punches, jabs, and martial arts strikes that the Stickman recognized and Danny had only seen in the movies. Each connection hit with the blunt sound of bone on flesh. Each connection drove Pain backwards, towards the second cabin across the way, opposite Death's. Black blood sprayed. Crew started throwing kicks when the big man did nothing to defend himself. A roundhouse kick damn near broke Pain's neck. A side kick shattered more of the man's ribs and caused a great cough of blood. Another side kick smashed in the other side. Then, it was the axe kick from hell. Crew's right leg went straight up, while he pushed off with his left. With whatever power he had left in him, plus the weight of his body, the axe kick came down and landed square on Pain's upper chest.

The big man flew backwards, arms wind-milling, through the front door of the cabin. The men heard the wood snap. The lock and the frame of the door shattered. The door itself sprang back in place and then swung slowly inwards with a whine. Of Pain, there was no sight.

Danny did not expect the man to come out. As far as he was concerned, the thing was dead.

"Chirst *awmighty*, me son," Stickman grinned in awe of Crew. "Dat 'ad to be the wickedest ting I've ever seen. Y'killed 'im."

In the growing glow of morning, Crew stood breathing hard, regaining his strength. It was hard to kick in snow. He was exhausted.

Danny studied him with an amused look. "I can see why you never brought anything with you."

Crew did not say anything to that. He merely sucked in cold morning air.

The Stickman made his way to the cabin. "I'll check on 'im."

"If he ain't dead, stick your knife in him," Crew advised. "Stick it in his eye."

The Stickman bounded up to the cabin and pushed open the doorway. He immediately saw something that took his speech away.

There, standing just out of sight and hunkered over so he could fit into the narrow hallway, stood a fully *healed* Pain.

And he was smiling.

"'Eyyy," the Stickman said in stunned awe, "dat ain't fuckin—"

Fair, he never got the chance to finish.

Pain's boot connected with him squarely in his stomach. The impact sent the Stickman flying backwards some three metres, past the surprised faces of Danny and Crew, to land in a twisted heap in the snow. When the Newfoundlander hit, he did not get up. He did not make a sound. He lay there in the freezing cold, limp and seemingly dead as if shot through the skull.

Standing in the snow with their mouths hanging open, Danny's and Crew's minds were just as paralyzed.

The cabin's door flew off its hinges and a reconstructed Pain stepped back out into the world. He was still covered in blood, but the bruises and cuts were gone and every broken bone, including his battered skull, had mended. Bloodshot eyes fixed on the two men with such a feral intensity that Fear himself, looking on from the cabin window across the road, had to concentrate fast and hard to remove the explosion of pure terror within the pair. Fear bared his teeth with the effort, placing both of his hands flat against the edges of the window.

He fucking *hated* Pain.

"How . . . did . . ." Danny started as he retreated a step.

An advancing Pain grinned at him and *shushed*. "You don't worry about that now."

Both Danny and Crew stepped away from each other as they backed up. They were no longer fighting a man. They were fighting a *thing*.

"C'mere," Pain smiled cruelly at them. Black blood laced his now perfect smile. "You ever wonder what it's like to have your head twisted off? I'll show you."

Danny rushed Pain and swung the bat. It broke across Pain's upraised forearm. Danny swore and jumped back three feet in the snow, tossing the splintered end away. He got his hands up in time before Pain lunged at him, arms spread wide like some deep-sea net. Danny set his feet and slipped an arm underneath Pain's right arm, flipping him onto his back. The big man landed with a loud grunt and giggle. Crunching his stomach, Pain pulled himself up into a sitting position.

Danny began punching the man in the face. Fearsome combinations heralded by locomotive bursts of breath. He put his body weight behind each punch and snapped his wrists for extra power. He knew how to throw a punch, and he was sending in missiles. Pain's head rocked to and fro like a character in a cartoon.

But he did not go down. Instead, he got to his knees.

Crew slipped around the back of the creature while Danny remoulded Pain's face with his fists. Crew slipped both arms around Pain's sizeable neck and began to squeeze. Danny could see the destruction he wrought on Pain's person when Crew locked in the choke hold. Pain gasped, and blood and snot blew out of his nostrils, but he smiled his bloody smile. Crew increased the pressure, baring his own teeth.

He held on for seconds. Long seconds.

Pain's smile grew. He grabbed onto both of Crew's arms and *stood* up.

Crew's eyes went wide in amazement. How many people had he placed to sleep with the same technique? How many people had he killed?

Pain swung the man clinging onto his back around, *hard*. Crew managed to wrap both of his legs around the thing's waist for support. Instead of slinging his baggage away, Pain realized that it had clamped onto him even harder. Roaring, Danny moved in and unloaded fist after fist into its chiselled midsection. The muscle there was as hard as armoured plate, and Danny broke the skin on his knuckles. But he punched away at the body before him, driving punishing fists into his foe.

Pain absorbed them all.

Then, inevitably, Danny became aware of the growing ache in his shoulders, the heaviness in his lungs, and the slowing of his reflexes. He backed away.

A bloody-looking Pain regarded the man with a slow reproachful smile. "Tired?"

He swung.

The first punch took Danny across the face, and he felt his nose break. The second punch broke three ribs. Danny dropped into the snow.

"Now you, princess," Pain said to Crew, who still held onto the monster's neck. Pain grabbed Crew's arms again. He did not try to swing the man. This time, he made sure Crew was in place and began running backwards.

Towards the cabin wall.

Crew summoned up every last remaining bit of strength he possessed. He did not want to put Pain to sleep. He wanted to snap his neck. The wall, the hard frozen wall of the log cabin was back there. Crew increased the pressure even more. Any moment his back was going to be broken on the exterior of the cabin. With a roar, Crew squeezed every last bit of pressure he had into his grip and snapped the neck of Pain. He felt bone and vertebrae buckle, and Crew's breath let go in a grateful huff.

Then, he crashed into the wall.

The impact broke his hold on Pain, and Crew crumbled into the snow gathered at the base of the structure. Crew blacked out for a split second, but he rolled to his hands and knees. He looked in the direction of Pain, seeing two of them. His vision swayed and blurred. It was difficult to focus. He willed it, and it faded back. He saw the towering, half-naked frame of Pain reach up and take his head in both hands from where it hung limply on his shoulders. Pain raised his head up, and Crew could hear the mending of whatever he had broken. His vision blurred. When it came back, he could hear Pain grunting. The Entity made his way over to where Danny was lying.

"Sleepy?" Pain said to the man. Danny saw him coming. He got to his knees.

Pain's fist struck him like a meteor. It flattened him on his back. Pain stooped and grabbed Danny's limp hand. The contact brought the man back to earth, and he resisted, but Pain yanked the arm towards him, straightening it out.

"Yer gonna hate this part," Pain said, and plied back one of Danny's fingers, breaking the bone clean.

Danny yelped and instinctively tried to free his arm. Pain held on. Worse, Pain kicked him hard in his ribs again, taking the fight out of the big man. Danny went limp, but Pain shook his head. He did not want his playmate to go into shock. Not when it was his turn for fun. He twisted Danny's wrist in its joint, snapping it like a thick icicle. Danny grunted and bared his teeth.

"Hurt?" Pain asked evilly.

He heard the steps coming towards him.

Pain dropped the ruined arm and, with one hand, turned to catch a charging Crew by the throat. The stiff armed tackle stopped the American in his steps. Pain held him at arm's length for a moment, studying the man's frightening expression, and applied pressure.

Crew's eyes went wide. Both of his hands came up to try and free himself from the grip. He tried to apply thumb locks. He tried to kick out Pain's knees. He clawed.

Pain absorbed it all with a grin.

Crew's face became crimson, a whine escaped his lips and his vision began to darken.

"Hurts, doesn't it?" Pain asked with a savage grin.

Then, the Stickman stabbed the monster through the crotch.

CHAPTER 74

The screams from outside distracted Tony for a moment, but Death did not let him focus on it. He grabbed the front of Tony's coat and pulled him close. "Listen to me. They only have so long. He's playing with them. But you can save them if you kill me with that axe!"

Tony stared into Death's eyes, his mouth was open but no sound came out.

"Ever wonder *why* they choose you? *Them*?" Death almost yelled.

Tony could only stare. "Because I don't hurt as much as others."

"That's what she told you," Death paused for a moment. "The *real* reason you were chosen and why you found me so easy is because you're going to cross over, Tony. *You're going to die*. Soon. Everyone looking for me eventually finds me. The Cancer, Tony. Your mom isn't the only one who has it."

Tony set his jaw. He was speechless.

"Yes!" Death nodded vigorously. "*If you seek Death you shall find him!* But not *now*. Not with me like this. Pain's just gonna make people suffer everywhere. And he's gonna love every fucking second! But I can save them!"

Tony stared into Death's eyes. They could both hear the war going on outside. Tony heard the candy crack of bone. Roars of anger and agony. At the window, Fear looked on grimly and shook his head at the raw carnage being wrought.

"I can't kill you, man," Tony whispered. "It's not in me."

"Not even for your mother? For yourself?"

Tony stared at the man beneath him, horror and revulsion in his face.

"It ain't easy, is it?" Death asked with a cruel smile. "To take a life? Is it? Living with the guilt is hell in itself. And all I get is the negative press. Y'know they made fucking movies of me being the bad guy? Now you know why I drink! *Why* I went on strike. It all got to me."

"I can't," Tony whimpered. "Jesus, I can't."

Death stared back and saw defeat in the man's eyes. He had hoped that being reminded of his mother would galvanize Tony into doing what had to be done. But for all of Tony's tough talk, Death could see that he was no killer. The thought was a sad one. He needed a killer *now*. His features hardened, and he nodded. He had begged and failed. He had tried being nice. In bringing up Tony's mother, he had tried for hate. It was time for extreme measures now.

"Lucy," Death said.

Tony's brow crunched up in sudden, furious puzzlement. "You leave her outta this!"

"Oh, Tony." Lucy's exasperated voice.

The sound of it diffused his anger in a second. He looked up. She was standing on the threshold of the ruined doorway. Dawn was almost breaking, and the nearness of it allowed Tony to see her face.

"Do it," Lucy said to him.

And ran into the growing light.

CHAPTER 75

If only Sensei Bill could see him now, the Stickman thought. He came to with a bunch of broken ribs to see the tall, glass-of-dipshit Pain holding Crew at arm's length and smiling. Stickman did not like cocky smiles. Burr had a cocky smile. Amazingly, Stickman realized he had managed to keep a hold of the combat knife. All right. *Proper ting!*

The Stickman got to his feet and ran as lightly as he could through the snow. He wanted to cut the man's throat at first, but this was personal now. The fucker had some sort of regenerative power which he thought was *totally* unfair in the fight. No, Stickman thought as he closed the distance. The monster was completely absorbed with strangling the one called Crew. *No*, Stickman thought again, *not the throat*. The fucker's neck was too high for him to stab anyway.

The Stickman decided to stab him through the balls.

The sharp intake of breath was rewarding, and Pain dropped Crew in the snow. He grabbed at his jeans and the torrent of blackness exploding there. Blood soaked through denim, turning it dark. Pain stood shaking as if he were caught in some sort of paralyzing fit.

The Stickman was more than pleased with himself, and stabbed him in the balls, again.

And again.

Pain's elbow smashed him just behind the ear. The Stickman dropped to the snow in a daze, but not out. For a brief moment in time, he felt glad.

The fucker wasn't smiling anymore.

Holding his bloody crotch, Pain squeaked. He grimaced and bared his teeth, black eyes wide in absolute torture. He turned on Stickman. He drove his boot into the Stickman's face, feeling bone break. The blow flipped the Newfoundlander onto his back. Pain reached down and grabbed the man by the testicles and crushed them in one fist. The shock that went through the Newfoundlander was mind ripping. He dry-heaved, his stomach spewing out gastric juice onto the snow, and then he went foetal. Pain towered over him. He meant to rip his ears off, but sensed movement from behind.

The Entity turned and saw both Crew and Danny on their feet. He lunged at Danny, who was closest. Pain swept him up off his feet in a bear hug, his massive arms going underneath Danny's arms. Baring teeth, the monster squeezed with a primal roar. Danny felt his ribs and back break. Bone shards pierced lungs and blood spouted from his mouth. The breath went out of him, and his arms fell lifelessly to his sides. Pain continued to squeeze, feeling bone shift inside his prey like marbles inside a cloth sack, and then savagely threw the man to the ground.

He whirled on Crew.

Crew threw a combination of strikes at Pain's face. Pain's head whipped to and fro, and after the first couple of hits, the cocky smile reappeared. "Hit me!" Pain screamed at the American, presenting his battered face. "Hit me!"

Screaming, Crew did just that.

During his martial training in both MMA and Kung Fu, Crew had been introduced to the finger board. The finger board was a piece of wood perhaps a centimetre thick. His instructor had told him it was for strengthening his fingers. At the time, Crew had only nodded, just to satisfy his master. But then the man had showed him. He drove two fingers, Crew *thought* it had been two fingers, through the wood of the finger board, shattering it. The display stunned Crew. His master told him that such a feat could be achieved by Crew if he practiced often, every day, by resting his hand on a piece of similar wood and forcefully tapping the surface with each digit on one hand, repeatedly. Over and over.

Until it broke.

When it did break, after almost a year, Crew presented the broken finger board to his master, thinking to impress the man.

His master only directed him to the plastic pans filled with pebbles. Now it was time to toughen the rest of the hand.

Crew's hands were the only weapons he ever used to kill people, to kill his targets.

And with whatever strength he had left, with whatever *chi*, he plunged his spike-tough fingers into both black eyes of his foe, knuckles deep.

Pain's head whipped back, and he howled, disengaging himself from Crew and throwing himself back into the snow. There, the big man thrashed about, his legs almost doing a sprint in the air. Horrifying shrieks cut the morning air. Crew watched him cautiously, sparing quick glances at the fallen wrecks of Danny and the Stickman, lying still in the red snow.

But then, Pain's legs stopped kicking.

Crew's breath came out in a disappointed sigh. If the thing got up, that was it. He had nothing left.

Pain got up. Both of his eyes were back. Whatever Crew had clawed out of his head had somehow repaired themselves. Crew shook his head in exhausted disgust. He did not even bother bringing his arms up to guard. The fight was too rigged for it to matter. "Well, fuck you," Crew stated in quiet, exhausted defiance.

Pain broke Crew's jaw with one punch. He dropped to the ground. Pain fell on top of him. He planted one knee at the base of Crew's lower back and reached under Crew's chin, clasping his thick fingers there. Then, as soon as his grip was secure, Pain hauled backwards, bringing Crew up, bending him backwards and snapping his spine. Pain pulled the man's upper body back far enough to pause at his ear.

"You think that hurts?" Pain whispered and smiled. He caressed the man's throat, feeling the stubble there, and then clamped down on Crew's windpipe with his fingers. Thick fingers sunk into his flesh until a crackling noise could be heard.

"*Hey!*" a voice cried out.

Pain looked up. He let Crew go, who collapsed back into the snow on his belly. Things had suddenly gotten very interesting in his world. Smiling, Pain climbed to his feet. He stomped on one of Crew's knees, breaking it just because it was there. Then, he dusted the snow off his frame and ran his hands over his shaven skull.

He knew this one. He could smell her.

With water in her eyes, Lucy ran to the thing known as Pain.

CHAPTER 76

"Where are you going?" Tony shouted after her. He tried to pull away from Death on the couch, but he grabbed him by his coat and held on. Tony pried his hands away and started to run after Lucy. Death grabbed him by the back of the coat, costing him seconds in his pursuit.

"You fucker!" Tony cursed and struck Death across the face. Death released him. Fear turned at the commotion, a frown on his unique features, but he made no effort to intervene. It was smart on his part. Tony could not bring himself to kill, but he sure as hell would waste no time kicking the living shit out of anyone who got in his way at that precise moment.

Swearing as he ran, Tony lunged towards the door and flew into the new day.

Back in the cabin, Fear looked at Death.

It was Death who spoke first. "You can see why I hate 'em now," as he rubbed his jaw. "Shit."

Fear turned back to the window. "Not much time left."

"You know it," Death muttered, staring at the cabin's ceiling. He grimaced. "Spinal shit is starting to wear off."

Tony froze in his tracks as if he had just been caught by a blast of liquid nitrogen. His mouth hung open, his arms wide. He still had his hatchet in hand, but for the moment, did not know what he could do with it. Standing not twenty feet away from him was the thing known as Pain. And Pain had Lucy by her hair. The bee's bottom toque was on the ground, and Pain had Lucy hauled up to her full height with one arm. Lucy was holding onto his big hands. Behind both of them, in the light of the dawn, Tony could see the fallen forms of the three men. He did not think they were dead, but considering the amount of blood on the snow, it was perhaps better if they were. Lucy looked to Tony. He could see that she was terrified. Fear wasn't doing his thing with her, not like he did it for Tony and the others. Maybe it was revenge for her getting him kicked out of the beast. He would talk to Fear later. Now, he had a bigger problem.

Pain shook Lucy by her hair, which produced a little grunt from the woman, but she did not scream. *Good girl,* Tony thought.

"Let her go man," Tony warned.

That brought a dark chuckle from Pain.

With that, he lifted one large leg, the one next to Lucy's own, and drove it into her knee with enough force to shatter it. Lucy screamed a shriek of agony that pierced Tony's core. Her leg was at an angle it was not supposed to be, kept only together by her jeans. Tony looked to charge the monster, but Pain hoisted Lucy back up by her hair, dangling her like a rabbit held up by the ears.

Pain grinned.

"Look," Tony said, struggling to control his voice. "Just let her go. I won't ... hurt you."

For a moment Pain blinked, as if he had just heard the stupidest thing ever. Then, he barked a cruel laugh. He shook Lucy like a rattle and produced the sounds he wanted. "And they call me stupid."

He twisted one of Lucy's arms up behind her back. She shrieked. She shrieked louder when it popped out of her shoulder joint with one brutal shove.

The sounds of torture coming from Lucy had Tony almost on the brink of losing it. "Listen! You can have me instead, okay? Just let her go, okay?"

Pain considered the offer. "Nah," and swung Lucy around so that he could punch her full in the face with his other fist. The sound of the connection made Tony take three steps forward, but Pain again hauled her up by the hair, causing Tony to freeze in his tracks. Lucy bled through the nose and mouth. She looked in shock.

Pain warned Tony. "You come any closer, and I guarantee I'll break something really important."

Tony's grip on his hatchet tightened. If he could get closer he would bury the full blade in that shaved skull. Instead he stood right where he was and kept his eyes on the bloodstained but healed again form of Pain.

"Now," Pain said, "ask me what I want."

Angry enough to chew lead and spit bullets, Tony narrowed his eyes. "What do you want?" he asked through clenched teeth.

Pain smiled. "What do I want ... ?" he said, wondering aloud, puzzlement filling his features. "What could it be?" He pulled Lucy towards him, hugging her to his chest. Both of his massive arms embraced her lower back.

"Ah ... I know," he said sweetly.

And squeezed.

The sudden grunt of agony escaping Lucy made Tony break into another charge of three steps. Pain's eyes flashed and halted him.

"You must hate this lady," Pain said through clenched teeth, smiling over Lucy's head. "The closer you get to me, man, the more I'm gonna love her. You got that? You *got* that?"

"Okay," Tony barely got out. He backed up three steps. "This good?"

"That's good," Pain agreed. He twisted the good arm of Lucy up behind her back, placing stress on the joint. She moaned, placing her forehead against Pain's massive chest.

"*Wait!*" Tony roared, holding out his hands. "Just wait!"

"You tellin' me to wait while you got that axe in your hand?" Pain countered.

Tony regarded the axe. "You let her go if I drop the axe?"

Pain looked amused. "Sure. Why not?"

The glib response woke Tony up. It was as Death said. Pain was just amusing himself. With Lucy. With them all. He was just playing with Tony, having a good old time. He had no intention of letting Lucy go. Not until he extracted from her every excruciating drop of suffering he could get. Then, he would move on. To Tony. To Death. Tony shook his head. There was only one way to put Pain down. There was only one way to stop the madness. He realized it now, only when the woman he had feelings for had sacrificed herself to make him realize it.

One could not bargain with Pain. One could not reason with it.

One could only . . . *suppress* it. *Endure* it. Until *he* took you.

His throat constricting, Tony took a step backwards. "Lucy," he called out.

Her head turned ever so slightly. The movement made Pain glance down.

"Lucy, I'm sorry," Tony said in a begging voice.

"Tony," Lucy called back weakly. "*Go!*"

Tony grunted, and ran *back* towards the cabin.

"Hey!" Pain shouted after him. "*HEY!* I'll . . ." he glanced at Lucy again.

The bitch was smiling.

With a roar Pain crushed her back and rib cage in one quick bear-killing hug. Lucy gasped and went limp. Pain threw her aside like broken wood. He knew what the game was. He knew the stakes. He also knew he had been a fool. *Stupid!*

He charged, screaming for blood.

Tony heard the battle cry. He ran as fast as he could through the snow. He could hear the monster pounding after him. If the big man caught him, it was all over. Tony was five feet away from the cabin door.

Behind him, Pain saw the Mundane running straight back for the cabin. Simultaneously, he felt that same sweet vibe in the air that he had only just recently begun to sense, but had lost before he could fix on the exact location. He fixed on it now. Pain bared his fully restored teeth in a feral grin. The man did not have a chance. Pain could move at the *speed* of pain, like a guided missile. As long as he had the direction. And he was headed in the direction of Death right now.

Snarling, Pain *warped*. He aimed to be waiting for the man just as he entered the cabin. That would truly freak the Mundane out. Pain would then gloat for a few moments before ripping the little bastard's head from his shoulders. Then he realized something suddenly was terribly wrong.

The warp had *stopped* just as soon as it had begun.

He saw Tony pass through the doorway of the cabin.

Pain's eyes went wide. Froth began to form at the corners of his mouth. He realized then what had happened even as he brought all of his incredible strength to bear, even as he strained to move his powerful limbs and frame faster than they presently were. But he was moving no faster than glacial ice. Rage exploded within him.

His *warp* had not failed him.

His warp had been *slowed!*

Pain roared in fury. He then realized with even greater chagrin that even his own *voice* had been slowed.

TIME!

Tony passed into the living room and immediately moved to the waiting form of Death on the couch. He lay there, looking relieved and relaxed, with his empty bottle of Jack Daniels in his lap. He had drawn the blanket up to his chest for greater comfort. When Tony came into the room, Death gave a little satisfied smile.

"You believe me now?" Death asked.

"Yeah," Tony answered.

With tears in his eyes, he crossed the space between them and buried the hatchet deep into Death's skull.

CHAPTER 77

Like a water balloon bursting after being filled beyond capacity, all across the world, people began to die again.

In England, in an extensive burn unit located in a York hospital, fifty-four survivors that were more melted slabs of flesh than human, expired at the exact same time. The sudden death of all the ferry disaster survivors in the English Channel would later spark a savage investigation of the hospital staff, and a ferocious debate over euthanasia would flood the media for weeks. In the end however, no one person would be held accountable for the deaths.

In Barcelona, Spain, twenty-two of the children poisoned at a day-care centre finally went to sleep and did not wake up. The remainder of the victims would live on without the ability to speak.

In a hospital in the southern district of Baghdad, the still living, writhing flesh of fifteen bomb victims consisting of women, children and men ceased moaning and perished.

In New York, Doctors Garlich and Roeder as well as about a dozen medical assistants, exhausted from their endless hours in the morgue studying a total of six individuals that simply refused to die, straightened up and stared. The room that was filled with moans of pain only seconds ago had become eerily silent.

In his apartment, frustrated with his lack of courage and only just coming out of the massive drunk of the night before, Ted Myer, sitting on his couch in his undergarments, picked up his snub nosed .38 and angled it at his right temple. There was nothing to fear. He was not going to die. Why did he waste so much time over nothing?

"Ah fuck—" *it* Ted wanted to say as he pulled the trigger.

And got the surprise of his death.

CHAPTER 78

When Tony came to, he discovered he had lost consciousness and collapsed on the rug. He gazed up at the ceiling, blinking slowly, and for a brief moment, wondered where he was. Then, he remembered everything. He remembered Time and Freddy visiting him long ago. He remembered leaving his mother and driving across the country in hours. He remembered Paradise, and the first time he met pain-in-the-ass Death.

He remembered a smiling Lucy and her dark Asian eyes.

A great sigh left him, and he blinked. He was cold, he realized, and sat up.

There, watching him from the couch with his black, unfriendly glare was Fear.

The man brought a grimace to Tony's face. He noticed then for the first time in a while that he was still wearing a coat covered in a lot of blood. The Minions back at the car. He never did clean his coat off. Or any other part. He felt sticky all over. He looked back to Fear sitting patiently on the couch.

"Where's Death?"

Fear took a moment before answering him. "Gone back."

"He went back?" Tony asked.

"That's what I just said."

Asshole, Tony thought.

"But . . . you'll be seeing him, again," Fear rumbled. "But not from the Cancer. He took that out of you. As a gift."

What was it Death said to him? Tony remembered. *"How do you think you found me? Huh? How do you think you got here? Just following your nose?"*

"What about Lucy?" Hope surged within Tony.

"She went back, too."

Tony felt a rush of misery. "You mean she's dead?"

Fear looked at him. "I *mean*, she went back."

That brought a heavy feeling of sadness. He wanted to see Lucy, again. He wanted to . . . hope that she could have stayed with him. "Why did you stay?" Tony asked. Of all the people, why Freddie?

"I'm special," Fear said with a little sarcastic smile. That did nothing to improve the sense of loss flooding Tony's heart and mind. Recognizing unhappiness when Fear allowed himself to, he decided to let Tony have his moment of grief. He allowed him exactly ten seconds before speaking again.

"Hey," he said. Fear only had a short time, too, and damned if he was going to spend it watching a Mundane remembering sad songs. "Everything's okay now."

Tony blinked. "What?"

"Everything's okay now. It's all good again."

"It is?"

Fear did not repeat himself.

"My mom?"

After a moment's hesitation, Fear nodded solemnly. There were things that even he did not violate.

"Was it . . . was it . . . ?" Tony could not finish his question.

"Painless," Fear stated quietly, and looked towards the sun. "Think of it . . . as another gift."

The rush of tears to his eyes surprised Tony, and for several seconds, he did nothing to stop them. Then, he remembered who he was speaking to. He wiped his eyes with his palms, giving a quiet word of thanks for the passing of his mother.

"You say things are okay now, right? But for how long?" he asked.

Jesus, Fear thought. The scrapper wasn't satisfied. Fear couldn't hang around here for long, it was turning his guts. Sensitivity was *not* his job. "That depends on you now, doesn't it? You got a word to spread, right?"

Fear stood up. When he did, Tony saw the empty bottle of Jack Daniels lying on the couch. He was momentarily fascinated with the bottle as Fear walked casually to the door and paused. "I've been told to inform you that there is a fire truck on the main road. That's your best bet for you and the others to get back."

The others? Tony thought.

"There are cars, but they're probably snowed in. And the money that's owed you is in your apartment. Those cars, though, damned if I know if they'll start. But then who knows, maybe Lady Luck's still with you," Fear grumped. He lingered in the doorway, resplendent in the new sun.

"Who?" Tony managed to get out.

In response, Fear pulled on his black toque, pulling it down over that strangely shaped head of his. He flipped up the collar of his winter trench coat.

Half his mouth hitched up in what he thought passed as a smile, and he presented it to Tony. Then, he nodded in the direction of the great outdoors.

Before Tony could ask another word, Fear stepped outside.

Clambering to his feet, Tony rushed to the open doorway. The air was cold and crisp, and Fear was nowhere to be seen. The snow was marred from the battle fought between the two cabins on the country road, but Tony saw three figures lying still. There was no sign of the thing called Pain. There was no sign of Lucy. No sign of Lady Luck. Goddess of Fortune. Tony remembered the cars. That was one trick suddenly clear to him. *Lucy*.

It made him smile just a little.

The sun was just over a range of treetops and a dark outline of mountains. Sunlight beamed down on three broken bodies lying in the snow. Tony walked to them. The *others* were lying in white, beaten down drifts stained with great gobs of blood.

The *others* were seriously fucked up.

Tony walked and dropped to his knees at Danny's side. Danny was the only one he knew. Tony inspected the mess of him. He wanted to shake the man, but he was afraid Danny's head might come loose and simply roll off his shoulders. And of the three, Danny appeared to be in the best condition. They *couldn't* be alive.

"Jesus H." Tony whispered and was unable to finish.

From where Danny lay in the snow, a single eye cracked open, squinting at the sun.

"Tony?" the big man asked, in a strained, pain-filled voice.

"Oh, *shit*," Tony whispered "Danny?"

"That you?" Danny asked weakly.

"Yeah, it's me."

"Tony?"

"Yeah, man?"

Danny collected his strength.

"Get me the *fuck* to a hospital."

CHAPTER 79

In the following days, the world would remember the strange happenings as freak occurrences and nothing more. The awareness of the populace's immortality for a week was never realized for what it was, much to the grief of a certain few. There were stories of shock and horror, of people suffering terribly yet clinging courageously to life, only to succumb in the end. And if the stories reached high enough ears, they would be smiled at, and perhaps there would be a chance debate on two of the greatest mysteries known as Life and Death. In time, the events that took place during Death's absence would be scoffed at, discredited as bad science fiction, even though a strange, eerie coincidence still remained . . .

The number of people suffering from various life threatening maladies or in critical conditions, who had all expired at exactly the same time on the same morning, across multiple time zones.

Almost as if Death himself had suddenly remembered them.

Eventually, that particular week in time would be reminisced by the first responders, the ambulance drivers, and the people working the graveyard shifts in public mortuaries and hospitals. A tale told to the newcomers, just to see how gullible they were. Strange things happened around dead folks and the nearly dead. Strange things happened all the time. And when they did, it was best to just deal with whatever was happening, note it and quietly move on. After all, miracles of people escaping death did indeed happen. All the time.

Three of them were delivered to a hospital in Surrey, British Columbia, by a single man driving a fire truck. The man refused to give his name or any other information to the medical staff. He quickly unloaded the three men, evaded any attempt to keep him at the hospital and drove off. The police were contacted, and a deserted fire truck would be found later, north of Surrey, along with two abandoned cars that were discovered as belonging to two of the newly admitted patients.

Months later, after numerous life-saving and reconstructive surgeries, steel plates, rods, implants, and finally physical therapy, in addition to the swiftest recovery time any of the medical staff had ever witnessed, the three miracles were strong enough to be released back into the world.

One of the men returned to the States. He went back to the place he called home, decided he had enough of his line of work, and eventually disappeared.

To someplace tropical.

The two other miracles were of a different mind. They had past issues unresolved—anyone could see that in their rehabilitation. It was in the way they spoke to each other, civil yet wary. One therapist even remarked that she heard the soft spoken gentleman from Nova Scotia saying that things were "still done" and that "it wasn't over."

Regarding whatever "it" was, the constantly smiling gentleman from Newfoundland with the thick accent seemed only too agreeable on the matter.

But all agreed that it was heartening to see both men actually encouraging the other to get stronger. They seemed to draw mutual strength from each other's miraculous recovery.

Then, as all recovered patients do, they were discharged from the hospital. It was a bright day in late August, and the humidity factor was high. As healed as they were ever going to be, they drove away in their respective cars.

Both men drove north.

Sometimes one took the lead over the other, passing on the straighter strips of highway.

They arrived at the two cabins on a Sunday. Both men got out of their cars, parked in the middle of the country dirt road. The air was warm and moist and full of the smell of trees. It was a lush contrast to when they had first come here. They could see that the owners of the cabins had never returned during the summer, thus the damage done in the winter remained. They gazed around the front of the second cabin, and remembered their battle with Pain. In the grey of the crushed stone road, neither Stickman nor Danny could see any evidence of the war they had fought.

"Well," the Stickman said. "'Twas wintertime."

Danny nodded. Then, he walked away from the car, to the rich front lawn before the cabin where the siege had taken place. The Stickman followed. The day was hot, and the sun shone down from directly overhead.

Danny went to the far side of the lawn. There, he took off his shirt and tossed it to one side. At the other end, a smiling Stickman did the same. Both men regarded each other in silence, noting the scars on each other's bodies. It was indeed a miracle they healed so fast.

"Ye ready, me son?" the Stickman asked. He thought briefly of Beverly. If fate was on his side, if it was meant to be, he would be searching for her shortly.

"I'm ready," Danny had replied. He had his own plans. One concerned a woman and the other centered on turning the Beacon into a regular bar.

"Alright, den," the Stickman declared with a nod.

They both realized they could have been friends, especially after going through therapy together. In the beginning, it had been hard. Danny saw the Stickman only as unfinished business. He was the man that killed his two best friends. They talked about it, and Danny agreed that Stickman was seeking revenge for his best friend Badger. It was all a big mistake, seeing as through their conversations together they figured out that Pain was responsible for Badger anyway. But the Stickman did what, Danny had to admit, he would have only done himself if the roles had been reversed. It was fucked up. Gary and Boomer should have talked. The Stickman should have listened. What was done was done. Mistakes had been made. And blood was spilled. But Danny could not allow the punishment and death of his friends to go unanswered. Understanding where the big man was coming from and losing his own friend, the Stickman offered Danny a solution. When they were both able to leave the hospital under their own power, they both agreed on one way to remedy the past. Perhaps it was stupid, but neither one of them thought so.

Both men stood opposite each other, stretching and flexing in the warm sun. Both men knew the other was strong from their time in therapy. Both knew each other's reputation from back East. Both men remembered their friends.

Smiling, Stickman slipped into his fighting stance. He drew up his invisible shields and asked for Sensei Bill to watch over him. He was about to fight the twin of the tower that had almost killed him.

Danny raised his hands. He was a legend in the Halifax bar circuit. He was a peacemaker. He was about to fight the killer of his two best friends.

"What'll be den?" the Stickman asked, shadow boxing and eternally jovial. "To de end?"

Danny smiled grimly at the crazy Newfoundlander. "To the end," he said wondering if it would go that far. He then wondered if they would be watched.

The Stickman wondered the same. "To de end, den," he repeated, bringing his arms up to guard. "Come at me, me son."

There, on the front lawn of the log cabin, the two men closed the distance and began circling each other. They moved closer together. Danny was all serious. The Stickman wore his grin.

And both swung at the same time.

ABOUT THE AUTHOR

Keith C. Blackmore is the author of the Mountain Man, 131 Days, and Breeds series, among other horror, heroic fantasy, and crime novels. He lives in on the island of Newfoundland in Canada. Visit his website at www.keithcblackmore.com.

DISCOVER
STORIES UNBOUND

PodiumAudio.com